UNDER THE SOUTHERN
CROSS

A TALE OF THE
NEW WORLD

DEBORAH ALCOCK

UNDER THE SOUTHERN
CROSS

A TALE OF THE
NEW WORLD

cántaro
publications

www.cantaroinstitute.org

Under the Southern Cross, Deborah Alcock

Published by Cántaro Publications, a publishing imprint of Cántaro Institute, Jordan Station, ON. L0R 1S0, Canada

Book Design: Steven R. Martins

Library & Archives Canada
ISBN 978-1-990771-27-9

Table of Contents

I

Fray Fernando's Mission

"Cœlum, non animum mutant,
qui trans mare currunt."

ON A BURNING AUTUMN AFTERNOON,—in the
Sixteenth Century, which had then passed its
meridian by rather more than ten years,—Don
Fray Tomas de San Martin, the stately prior of

the great Franciscan monastery of Ciudad de los Reyes, now called Lima, was sitting alone in his private apartment. Meaner and idler men were dozing the sultry hours away; but it was not in the nature of Fray Tomas to seek repose while the duties of his calling, the interests of his Order, or the concerns of any of his numerous friends required his attention. In spite of physical languor and exhaustion, an expression of satisfaction lit up his countenance as he finished his second careful perusal of a letter he held in his hand. Then he laid the document on the table before him, pausing, however, to glance, with a slight smile, at the pompous armorial bearings inscribed on the seals with which the floss silk that bound it had been secured. The prior was not a man given to soliloquy; but if we might translate his unspoken thoughts, they would run somewhat after this fashion: "Sixteen quarterings for honest Marcio Serra de Leguisano, the tailor's son I Where, in heaven's name, have they all come from I Truly saith the Preacher in the Book of Ecclesiastes, I have seen servants riding upon horses.' He might have added,—and there be none such headlong riders. *Pues*, every man to his taste. These little weaknesses of Marcio Serra's may well be borne with, after all. For amongst the conquistadors there is many a worse man, and not one better. Would that all, like him, broke off their sins by righteousness, and their iniquities by showing mercy to the poor. Certainly, it behooves us to aid him to the utmost of our power."—And, stretching out his hand, he rang a little silver bell that lay near him on the table.

But the attendant, whose duty it was to answer it, was lying on a mat in the ante-chamber, fast asleep,—and not until the prior had more than once raised his voice and called loudly, "Antonio!" did he make his appearance.

"Send me hither Fray Fernando immediately, and then go finish thy siesta," said the prior, cutting short his apologies with contemptuous good-nature.

Fray Fernando, who was not asleep, came in a few moments; and having made the accustomed reverence, stood silently before the chair of his superior.

Fray Tomas was an able man and a good ruler. Both within the walls of his monastery and beyond them he was thoroughly respected. Yet few could have looked on the two who now stood face to face without the thought that they ought to have changed places,—that Fray Fernando ought to have commanded and Fray Tomas to have obeyed. Everything about the younger monk, from the broad white forehead to the nervous taper fingers, bespoke the refinement and sensitiveness of high breeding. Yet he did not look like a man of the schools and the cloister. Power and determination gleamed from his dark, deep-set eye, and showed themselves in every movement of his vigorous though attenuated frame. You would have said that he ought to have worn the plumed casque instead of the tonsure, and have shouted, "St. Jago for Spain!" instead of telling Ave Marias on the rosary that hung from his belt.

The prior addressed him with great urbanity. "We do justice, brother," he said, "to that singular zeal for our holy Faith which animates your breast."

Fray Fernando bowed, but a look of pain passed over his face.

The prior blandly continued: "Therefore it is that, an opportunity being afforded to some brother of our honorable Order to undertake a work of peculiar toil and self-sacrifice for the glory of God and the salvation of souls, our thoughts turn to thee, as to one who will cheerfully, nay joyfully, embrace such a mission."

"I am ready to go whithersoever my lord the prior shall command," said Fray Fernando.

The prior laid his hand on the letter. "This have I just received from the most noble knight and conquistador, Don Marcio Serra de Leguisano. Doubtless he is known to you by reputation?"

"My lord remembers I am a comparative stranger here."

The prior had too much good sense to retail idle stories: such as that the good knight's parentage was said to be of the humblest; that on the division of the spoils of Cuzco the massive golden sun of the great temple had fallen to his share; and that, with the recklessness of a *parvenu,* he had gambled most of it away at primero in a single night, complaining pathetically, the next morning, that he had "lost a good piece of the sun." He merely explained: "Don Marcio Serra hath received, in *encomienda* from our lord the king, a noble estate, rich in gold and silver, as well as in the ordinary productions of the soil.

It embraces a very fertile valley, called Nasca; and stretches upwards, even to the land of mist and snow, where the mighty Andes raise their giant heads. High up, in that rarely-trodden region, at the summit of a bleak mountain, called Cerro Blanco, gold was discovered a few years since. A shaft was sunk, and the mine was worked, as usual, by the forced labor of the Indians. But these unhappy people died so quickly, that at last Don Marcio, having the fear of God before his eyes, and being mindful of his soul's salvation, began to take thought of their miserable case. Possibly he was the more disposed to compassionate them, because he hath taken to wife an Indian princess, one of the Children of the Sun, as they call them, after their vain heathenish fashion. Therefore he hath purchased a sufficient band of Black slaves, both men and women, which he hath been at great charges to transport from the coast to the heights of Cerro Blanco. And there he hath set them to work under competent Spanish overseers."

Both the churchmen accepted this substitution of black laborers for copper-colored ones as an effort of the most sincere and enlightened philanthropy. Nor were they, perhaps, as much mistaken as might be supposed.

"But," continued Fray Tomas, "as the good knight's piety is fully equal to his humanity, he is now desirous to extend to these benighted savages the inestimable blessings of our holy Faith. He therefore entreats me to send him some brother of our Order, who may be found willing, for the love of God and the good of souls, to banish himself to a dreary inhospitable region, where the frozen earth brings forth little more than a few blades of stunted grass; and where, from one year's end to the other, scarce a face will greet the exile's eyes save those of the black slaves."

Had the picture he was limning been intended for any other eye than that of Fray Fernando, Fray Tomas might have softened its lines, and have interspersed here and there a few lighter touches. But now he did just the contrary; because he had taken the measurement of the man he was addressing. When he ceased speaking, there was a moment's silence; then Fray Fernando said quietly, "I willingly undertake the mission."

"May God and our Lady recompense thy zeal and piety!" was the prior's benign reply. He then proceeded, with equal affability and good sense, to discuss the details of the lengthened journey which it would be necessary for Fray Fernando to undertake.

The younger monk seemed not only willing, but actually eager to occupy the post assigned to him. Not during his whole novitiate (which had but recently terminated) had he appeared so cheerful, not to say so animated. It was currently reported that nothing gave Fray Fernando pleasure except self-mortifications and austerities; which he carried to a greater length than any monk who had been in the monastery since its foundation.

"I have found the very man for your Excellency's affair," wrote the prior that evening to Don Marcio. "He is a brother of our house; exceeding pious; and so consumed with zeal for the Faith, that he desires nothing so much as martyrdom. The more difficult and painful an enterprise, the less of worldly honor or profit it is like to bring, the more attractions it hath in the eyes of our holy Fray Fernando."

Such were the reflections of good Fray Tomas de San Martin; who was as much, and as little, able to penetrate the mystery that veils every human soul as any other shrewd man who fondly imagines that he can read the hearts of his neighbors at a glance.

II

Cerro Blanco

"I mete and dole
Unequal laws unto a savage race,
Who feed, and hoard, and sleep,
and know not me."
~ TENNYSON

FRAY FERNANDO HAS BEEN NEARLY a year in his
new home. But it seems a mockery to call it by
that sacred name: since not to any living thing

was Cerro Blanco a home in the true sense of the word. Yet between forty and fifty miners, with their families, ate, drank, and slept in the cluster of cabins that nestled, almost literally, in a cleft of the rock, for protection against the stormy winds of the Andes. These cabins were built of adobes, or mud-bricks dried in the sun; and were thatched, very neatly and carefully, with the strong grass called *ychu*. All this work had been done, before the arrival of the Black people, by the Indians of the valley, as part of the labor required from them by way of tribute to their lord. They were also obliged to provide the little colony with the necessaries of life. At stated intervals they might be seen treading the steep and winding mountain-paths in long procession, bearing on their heads or their shoulders large baskets of maize, of potatoes, or of quinoa—the rice of the country—as food for the Black people. Nor would they fail to bring also a couple of alpacas, and a good supply of chica, or native beer, to suit the more luxurious tastes of the Spanish intendant of the mine, and his servants. For in that elevated situation few things would grow (at least, without very careful cultivation), except stunted grass and little mountain-flowers, mostly blue and yellow.

Still higher than the village—indeed, on the very summit of the mountain—was the mine, which was worked in rude and primitive fashion. The ore extracted from the earth by the labor of the Black people was smelted, after the manner of the Indians, in a large oven made of clay, and placed in such a situation that the strong mountain-winds seldom failed effectually to fan the furnace. The gold thus obtained was transmitted twice a year to the intendant of Nasca, who accounted for it to his lord, Don Marcio Serra de Leguisano.

Some strong motive was certainly necessary to make a lengthened residence in such a spot tolerable to a free man, who could go elsewhere if he would. The intendant, Diego Rascar, his four Spanish and two Creole servants, were bound to their post by the strong cords of avarice. But Fray Fernando had no such tie. His life was very empty; there was neither the love of gold, nor, to speak truth, the love of souls, to fill it. He did his duty, so far as he understood it, to his dusky flock. He baptized the infants; he married the young men and maidens; he buried the dead. He even tried to repress gross crimes amongst the black people, and to prevent gross cruelties on the part of the Spaniards: he sought to keep the latter from lapsing into utter heathenism, and he taught the former to hasten to the little chapel at the sound of the bell, and to fall on their knees at the elevation of the host. It did not occur to him that he ought to teach them anything more, or that it would be possible to do so. The Negro slaves were savages, but one grade removed from the lowest type; a type differing very greatly and very sadly from the imaginary picture of the "noble and virtuous savage" which a sickly and sentimental civilization has amused itself by delineating.

With these degraded beings—whom, in his pride, he accounted scarcely human—Fray Fernando had nothing in common; and he felt nothing towards them save contempt and disgust, sometimes mingled with pity, stirred by their sufferings. How could it have been otherwise? With deep truth has it been said, "There is but one Mediator between man and man, as well as between God and man—the man Christ Jesus." But Fray Fernando knew the man Christ Jesus not at all as Mediator; he only knew him as Judge. He could not therefore say, with the noble Las Casas, "I have left in the Indies Jesus Christ our Lord, suffering stripes and afflictions and crucifixions, not once, but thousands of times, at the hands of the Spaniards."

The love that embraces all men for the sake of Him who took man's nature upon Him, and delighted to call Himself the Son of man, was as far above Fray Fernando's comprehension as the brilliant stars of the Southern Cross were above his head. And thus it was that in that barren lonely place no love, human or divine, came to soothe and soften his heart, and to efface the deep, jagged characters graven there by the iron pen of pain.

Could the beauties of Nature have taken the place of human interests, Fray Fernando need not have felt forlorn, even on the summit of Cerro Blanco. He had but to ascend the height where the miners' shaft had been sunk, to command a view sublime and glorious as the imagination could conceive. Far above, the magnificent snow-clad peaks of the Andes pierced the cloudless sky; while as far beneath, the rich and cultivated vale of Nasca wound like a variegated thread from the mountain's base through the sandy desert to the distant ocean. It is true that often, while the mountain-peaks glistened in sunshine, a thick veil of mist obscured all that lay beneath; yet even then the scene had a wild, weird grandeur of its own.

Will it be believed that Fray Fernando's steps but seldom led him to the spot that commanded such a prospect? Not that he was unimpressed by its sublimity; rather otherwise,—he felt it too keenly. The everlasting hills shadowed and oppressed his spirit with the sense of a Power and Presence too awful and too near for his peace. "Surely God is in this place!" was the language of his heart; and, unhappily, God was a terror to him. He desired nothing so much as to forget Him; or, if that had been possible, to hide himself in secret places where He could not see him.

From part of the pathway between the mine and the galpón, or square—as tilt miners' village was called—might be seen the mountain-pass by which travelers sometimes made their way from the valleys of the coast into the interior of the country. Such travelers, if Spaniards, were usually glad to accept shelter and hospitality from the little mining colony; and it need not be said that the intelligence they brought with them from the civilized world was considered ample payment by the exiles. But if the wayfarers were of Indian race, their fleet footsteps only grew all the fleeter until the lair of the hated and dreaded Spaniards was well out of sight.

It became a habit with Fray Fernando to walk to the spot whence the pass could be seen. Why he did this it is not easy to say. Perhaps, in spite of himself, he clung to the shadow of the social life now shut out from him; or perhaps he dreaded visitors rather than hoped for them. However this may have been, a restless impulse seemed to drive him thither two or three times in the day, and sometimes even late at night.

But this might have been because he slept little.

One bright, cold, moonlight night he was taking this walk as usual, when the sound of a wild, peculiar chant, somewhat mellowed by distance, broke upon his ear. Startled, but not greatly surprised, he paused and listened. "Yes," thought he," it must be so!—Those five civilized Spaniards, who are lords and masters here, and bound to show these black people an example of Christian living, have made themselves drunk with new chica,—and the most active and daring of the slaves have managed to elude their vigilance, and to steal out of their quarters for the purpose of enacting some forbidden and detestable heathen rite."

Guided by his ear, Fray Fernando bent his steps towards the spot whence the sounds proceeded. On a little grassy plateau amongst the rocks, some dozen Black people were engaged in performing a wild mystic dance. Hand in hand they moved; now keeping time to some barbarous tune led by one of their number—now setting time and tune at defiance, and leaping, shouting, screaming like hideous maniacs. But the unexpected appearance of the monk's gray cowl and mantle brought the weird ceremony to a hasty close.

"Shame, shame on you!" he cried, as the dusky group scattered in all directions. "Shame on you!" he repeated once again, advancing to the center, and raising his arm in a threatening attitude. "You— Christian men, *neofitos, reducidos! —you* to return to these vile heathen abominations—to worship the devil!—you who have been taught to know the one living and true God, who made heaven and earth, and all that in them is! Are you not afraid lest He strike you dead, and cast you into the fire that burneth forever and ever?"

The Black people were far from comprehending every word in this address, yet they well understood its general import, and were duly impressed by the solemn tone and threatening gestures of the speaker. They were thoroughly cognizant also of the fact that the Spaniards were the masters and they the slaves. They fled in all directions with the activity of fear; some clambering up the rocks, some running down them, and others hiding in their crevices. Few stayed to hear the cogent and thoroughly intelligible peroration with which the friar concluded his harangue:—

"If there be a man among you not found within his quarters ere the moon has passed from beneath yonder cloud, Señor Diego shall reckon with him in the morning."

One only of the Black people—a stalwart ebony giant, recently brought from the wilds of Africa, where he had been a petty chieftain—stood his ground fearlessly, and looked Fray Fernando boldly in the face.

"*You,* Pepe!" said the monk. "I expected better things from you."

The African threw out his great bare arms with a gesture of despairing sorrow.

"What would you?" said he, in broken Spanish.—"If we worship the Zombi, the Spaniards scourge us, and we die;—if we worship not the Zombi, he sends the small-pox, and we die. —Either way, we die."

"Not so, Pepe," the monk answered more gently. "The Zombi is an evil spirit, a devil: he cannot harm you if you trust in God, for God is stronger than he. Put your confidence in God and in our Lady, and no evil can befall you."

"Look, padre," said the negro: "I said to our Lady the prayer you taught me; yet all the same, Señor Diego—"

But, not waiting to finish his sentence, he turned quickly, first his head, then his whole body—and bounding or scrambling over whatever rocky impediments lay before him, he began a headlong career down the hill towards the pass that wound beneath it. His senses, sharpened by the exigencies of his previous savage life, told him correctly that a party of travelers halted there, and were calling for guidance or help of some kind, aware that the mining village was at hand. He knew well that his services in bringing them safely thither would be rewarded with a holiday, plenty of sora, or spirits, and certain other indulgences which he highly valued.

Soon as Fray Fernando understood the matter, he too hastened to the nearest point whence the pass could be seen. In the struggling moonlight he discerned a little band of Spaniards on horseback, with glittering calques, and a long file of attendant Indians with burdens on their shoulders. He saw the leader engaged in an earnest parley with Pepe; and soon became aware that the party had put themselves under his guidance, and would reach the galpón in a few minutes.

Rather ashamed of the state of things they

were likely to find there, the monk quickened his steps, that he might give warning of their approach. Diego and his servants were aroused, with difficulty, from their heavy slumbers, and soon every soul in the galpón was astir. Fortunately, food was plentiful,—the Indians of the valley having brought their tribute recently. The flesh of the alpaca was prepared as speedily as possible by the Negro women, and set before the Spaniards with cakes of maize and skins of chica. Nor were the Indians forgotten. Fray Fernando pitied these poor people, who seemed exhausted with fatigue, and benumbed by the cold of the mountains, to which they were unaccustomed. He gave them maize and chica, and found room for them to sleep in the huts of the Black people. While busied in these kindly duties, he noticed amongst them, with awakened feelings of warmer compassion, a boy about ten years old, beautiful in form and feature, and distinguished from the rest by his peculiar costume. Unlike these, whose clothing was coarse and scanty, this child wore a pretty tunic of fine white cotton, fastened on each shoulder by some precious stone. He was bound to one of his adult companions, as a prisoner whose safe keeping was considered an object of importance. Fray Fernando gave him some fruit, which the boy took with a look half shy, half confiding, in his dark eyes, large and soft as those of the mountain antelope. But almost immediately the little hands dropped their burden, and the weary child sank down at the feet of his companion in a profound sleep.

After he had seen the Indians comfortably accommodated, Fray Fernando repaired to Diego's "house" (so called by way of eminence), to sup with the Spaniards, and to hear the news from the civilized world. But they had none. Their leader, calling himself Don Ramon de Virves, was on his return from an expedition along the coast, undertaken to "reduce" some of the still independent Indians under the dominion of the King of Spain and the Pope of Rome. So he styled it, in high-sounding Castilian; but in plain rough English, it was a marauding expedition. He had amassed in its course considerable treasures in gold and silver, a few valuable specimens of emerald and turquoise, and some other things not deserving particular enumeration. He seemed pleased to find a churchman in that remote solitude; and said he should be glad to confess and hear mass before going on his way next morning.

Fray Fernando guessed the reason for this request. Men did not usually come back from such excursions as Don Ramon's with clean hands. He naturally would find it easier to pour the tale of his sins into the ears of a stranger whose face he might never see again, than to lay it bare for the inspection of one whose accusing eye might meet his too often, and with too much meaning for his peace. The monk granted his desire, all the more readily because the morrow happened to be a saint's day—the festival of St. Joseph. The matter settled, Fray Fernando speedily quitted a scene of coarse revelry that had no charms for him.

Late as it now was, he could not sleep. But sleeplessness was no new thing with him; in broken rest he was growing continually worse. Too often did he spend the long silent hours of the night in living over the past—a record not to be dwelt on without keen and bitter anguish. At times, when sleep overcame him, he would start in terror at hideous forms and faces that seemed to stand before him. *One* especially, a face familiar and loved in early youth; but pale, distorted, and with strange fear and horror in dilated eyes. In truth, of late, since his coming to Cerro Blanco, a change had passed over him that cost him many a cold and secret shudder. Sometimes these visions haunted him when not asleep. Sometimes, while sitting with eyes open, and senses all awake, they drew near—they seemed to come within his grasp—and then would vanish—how and whither he could not tell. Even in the solitary mud-cabin called his cell from habit, he never felt alone, and least of all at night.

In order to banish these "temptations of the evil one" (as he called them), he tried fasting. This only aggravated the symptoms of his malady. He tried prayer—still they came. But his prayer was not real prayer; it was merely the repetition of a form,—a shadow, a lifeless thing.

And yet, sometimes, prayer and fasting gave relief—relief that almost grew to ecstasy. He dreamed that other visions might one day come—visions of glory, not of terror. Sinful as he was, such grace might be given him—and on some blessed day the white wings of angels might suddenly descend, and sweep away the demon host that pursued and tortured him.

35

Fray Fernando now stood at a place where two ways met. One of two destinies awaited him: either to become a saint, after Rome's most approved pattern, or—to become insane.

III

St. Joseph's Tooth

"Light for the forest child!
An outcast though he be
From the haunts where the sun
of his childhood smiled,
And the country of the free.
Pour the hope of heaven o'er his desert wild;
For what home on earth hath he?"

~ SIGOURNEY

Soon after daybreak next morning. Fray Fernando repaired to the little church—which was only a hut, larger and loftier than the rest, and adorned with a bell. He was in the habit of leaving the door open day and night; so he passed in without any delay, and walked quickly to the rough wooden box which he had caused to be erected by way of a confessional. But on attempting to enter it, he stumbled over something that lay beneath. In a moment, the Indian boy noticed on the preceding night sprang up and stood before him, with frame quivering, and cheek crimsoned beneath its olive hue. There was an evident struggle in the child's mind. Should he turn and flee, or should he dare to stay, and cast himself on the mercy of the tall dark man in gray?

Fray Fernando ended his hesitation. He did not know his language, it is true, but he knew a much more ancient language, that of nature. At least, he had known it once, and had not quite forgotten it. He drew the child towards him, and sought to reassure him by gentle and caressing gestures, patting his shoulder and stroking his long glossy black hair. And he had, well-nigh succeeded in soothing him, when suddenly the boy's expression changed to one of intense and irrepressible terror; and he tried with all his might to break away from the monk. Don Ramon's figure darkened the doorway.

"Good morning, padre!" said the soldier of fortune. "Santa Maria! what wind has blown that unlucky boy here? No doubt he has been trying to run away again. Little plague! But it shall be kill or cure with him this time."

The monk had thrown his arm round the boy's waist, partly to hold him fast, partly to keep him safe. And after a moment the child ceased to struggle, either because that grasp was so strong, or more probably because it was so gentle. But a thought flashed through Fray Fernando's mind, giving instant birth to a purpose. "The boy has placed himself, though unconsciously, under the protection of Holy Church, and it shall not fail him." He said aloud, "But what can you want with such a child, señor? He is too young to be worth much to you."

"True. But I promised to send a present of a little Indian, for a page, to a lady in the Old Country, whom I hold in great esteem. And this boy, whom fortune has placed in my power, is just fit for the purpose, with his handsome face and his bright intelligent ways. You heard me tell last night the story of his capture? No? I forgot—you retired early. *Pues,* with your good leave, holy father, I have another story to tell now. But let me first call one of my men to take that child away."

"Nay, rather permit me to keep him here for the present," said Fray Fernando, who shrank from seeing the child used with harshness, and, moreover, had further thoughts which he did not care to divulge just yet.

He tried to make the boy understand by signs that he must remain where he was. Nor was this difficult; for the 'Indian seemed already to associate some idea of protection with his presence. He lay down tranquilly behind the confessional, choosing a spot whence he could see his new friend the monk, but not his enemy Don Ramon. And then the business of the morning proceeded.

We are not going to unveil the mysteries of confession, or to violate that secrecy which the Church of Rome requires her minister to guard even at the cost of life. Nor was there anything peculiar or exceptional in the tale that Don Ramon poured into the ears of Fray Fernando. It was only the story of a young man of great energy and strong passions, sent early to seek his fortune beyond the seas, removed from every restraining influence, and with the untold riches of the New World spread out before him; all that could gratify the lust of the flesh and the lust of the eye to be had for the taking.

And yet the tale of wrong and robbery impressed Fray Fernando painfully. The monk was not hard by nature; though he might have been called a man hardened by the circumstances of his life. He had human sympathy; but it was like the drop of water sometimes found embedded in a stone. It was difficult to reach. Unknown to himself, however, a softening power was at work with him that morning. He imposed upon Don Ramon as severe a penance as he dared, for the unprovoked and treacherous slaughter of a little settlement of independent Indians, surprised in one of the oases of the great desert he had been traversing. It could not, indeed, have been much more severe, had the penitent insulted a friar, destroyed an image of our Lady, or maintained one of Luther's heretical opinions. And he told him plainly that unless he changed his present course of life, he would one day find himself face to face with certain just judgments of God against them that do such things, which neither priestly absolution, prayers, penances nor sacraments could avert.

When the rite was over, it wanted some time yet to the hour appointed for mass. Fray Fernando turned, pointed to the little captive, and said boldly, "You will gain neither honor nor profit by a prisoner taken as you took that child, Don Ramon."

"St. Jago! after all you have said, I am nearly of the same mind myself. But what can a man do? When a fair lady breathes a wish to a loyal caballero and her devoted slave, it behooves him to go even through blood and fire to fulfill it."

"Not through the blood of women and babes, and the fire of their burning homes," said Fray Fernando, perhaps a little too boldly.

Don Ramon was somewhat chafed. "I am

not worse than others, holy father," he said. "I do wrong to no christened man; and I am always careful to give the Church her due. Even now, I intend to consecrate to our Lady of Atocha gold enough out of my spoils to make a pair of candlesticks for her altar."

"In the compassionate eyes of our Lady, mercy and pity are more precious than gold," returned the monk. "And believe me, Señor Don Ramon," he continued with increasing earnestness, "your suit with the fair lady you speak of will prosper all the better if you consult the will of God and the health of your own soul in the disposition of your captives. That boy seems so much attached to his freedom, that he will either succeed in escaping you, in spite of all your precautions, or you will have to use such harsh measures to restrain him, that he may escape you in another way."

"Yet 'twere pity to lose him. He is the handsomest of his race that I have seen."

"True. And I do not care to hide from you that my heart is drawn to the child. I would gladly keep him myself, and bring him up."

Don Ramon laughed. "Commend me to the holy fathers, the sons of St. Francis," he said. "They know how to order their affairs with discretion. You have taken a fancy to my captive, padre, and you want him yourself. So you try to persuade me that I will mightily serve my soul's interests by giving him up to you. But you forget his propensities for running away."

"I do not. But I shall make a Christian of him; then if he goes, I cannot help it; if he stays, I shall instruct him carefully in the verities of our holy Faith, that he may instruct his brethren."

"A course of action like to prove very beneficial—suppose you persevere in it—to the Indians, and perhaps to your own soul also. But I know not how it is to benefit me, who have had all the toil and the fighting, not to speak of an arrow in my left leg, which might have been poisoned, for aught I knew to the contrary."

"I have not forgotten your interests in the matter, nor am I so unreasonable as to ask you to give me your prisoner for nothing. I have something to offer you in exchange worth a dozen Indian captives. Moreover, I do not insist, though I might, upon the fact that you will be doing a good work, very useful to yourself, in giving up the child to me for the purpose I have named."

"Well, well, holy father, let us hear what you have to offer. Nevertheless, the good work is the main thing. A man ought to think of his soul's salvation."

The monk drew from beneath his robe a little box of amber, with hinges and rims of gold, and with much reverence and solemnity of manner showed it to the soldier.

"A holy relic?" inquired the latter, with bowed head and voice decorously lowered, as in the presence of majesty.

"A tooth of the blessed St. Joseph, whose festival we celebrate today," said Fray Fernando reverently.

A pause followed this solemn and impressive announcement. Then the monk opened the little box, and displayed the relic to the admiring gaze of Don Ramon. "It is of most undoubted authenticity, and of very powerful virtue," he said. "And the motive which could induce me to part with it must needs be a strong one. I have kept it for many years—indeed, since my early childhood. It was given me by—" But here he broke off hastily, leaving his sentence incomplete. His eyes turned from the little amber box to the eager face of the Indian boy, who was watching them with an evident suspicion that their conversation concerned himself.

"Such a thing as that would do a man no harm in a fight or a shipwreck!" said Don Ramon. And the assertion, as he put it, was indisputable.

"It will do you good and not harm wherever you are; in the field or in the house, in the land or on the sea," returned Fray Fernando. "Always supposing"—common sense and candor obliged him to add— "that you are not engaged in any business of which the holy saint would disapprove."

"I intend to pay more regard to these considerations in future," said Don Ramon. "Well then, Holy Father, since such is your pleasure, take the boy, and I take the relic. Perhaps you would have no objection to throw me a mass or two into the bargain? Ours is a wild life— though we do good service to holy Church in fighting the infidels. And as we take care of her interests, it may not be too much to hope that she will look to ours."

Fray Fernando satisfied him on the subject of the masses; and as Pepe, who acted the part of acolyte, had by this time begun to ring the bell, he led the little Indian boy to his own cell, where he took the precaution of shutting him up, having first supplied him with food.

After mass, Don Ramon and his companions partook of a liberal breakfast, and then resumed their journey. Just before his departure, however, the soldier of fortune drew the monk aside. "Here," he said with the air of one conferring no inconsiderable favor—"here is a golden ornament which belonged to the mother of that child. I may as well give it you; perhaps it may serve hereafter to identify him. At all events, you will favor me by accepting it as an acknowledgment of your valuable spiritual ministrations. I took it, with my own hands, from her mantle, when I found her lying dead the morning after we made her and the boy our prisoners."

Something about robbery for burnt-offering flashed through Fray Fernando's mind, but he took the jewel without any other comment than a brief "Thank you." It was a large golden pin, somewhat resembling a spoon in shape, and with figures ingeniously cut all over its surface.

Shortly afterward, Fray Fernando visited his little prisoner. The child was looking out of the window of the cell when he entered; but he turned quickly round, took a mat from the floor, rolled it up to resemble a burden, placed it on his head, and then walking gravely towards his new master, deposited it at his feet.

Fray Fernando could not imagine what he meant by this pantomime; but anxious...to soothe him and to reconcile him to his situation, he drew his arm round him, and began to stroke and caress him, as he had done in the morning. Then recollecting one of the very few phrases he happened to know of the child's native tongue, the Quechua, he asked, "*Yma sutinque?*" ("What is your name?")

The boy, disengaging himself gently from his caressing arm, stood before him, with head erect, and dark eyes kindling with evident pride, as he answered, "*Viracocha Yntip Churl.*"

"God and our Lady bless thee, poor heathen child. Thou shalt have a better name than that, a *Christian* name, ere this sun goes down," said Fray Fernando.

That very day, accordingly, he baptized the child in the presence of the whole colony. He gave him the name of José, which he thought singularly appropriate, both because the boy was baptized on St. Joseph's day, and because his freedom was purchased with a relic of that saint.

Both the Spaniards and the Black people were edified by the evident willingness with which the little heathen submitted to the rite. It was not until long afterward that Fray Fernando discovered that the neophyte had put a meaning of his own upon what was otherwise meaningless to him. He imagined that this was a ceremony by which his kind protector was publicly asserting his claim to him.

But that claim had already been asserted, and confirmed by a pledge stronger than many ceremonies—by love given and returned. And it was allowed in the child's heart.

IV

Viracocha

"A child in whom childhood's life was dead,
Its sweet light marred and dim."
~ MRS. STUART MENTEITH

FRAY, RAY FERNANDO soon became aware that
he had taken upon himself a troublesome
charge. The little Indian was gentle and docile,
and he did not show the slightest inclination

to run away. But his attachment to his bene-factor took a turn that was both inconvenient and embarrassing. Fray Fernando of course intended to instruct him; but supposed that when his short daily lesson was over, he would be content to run about the galpón and to play with the Negro children. But he soon found that the dusky Indian looked on the black Africans with contempt and aversion. Whenever Fray Fernando gave him dried fruit or *huminta*,[1] he called the little Black children about him, and shared his treasures very liberally; but that done, he walked quietly away from them, and established himself on his mat at the feet of his protector. Often he sat or lay there for hours, perfectly quiet and silent. But some-times he talked to himself, or sang very sweet and mournful songs in his native tongue; and two or three times he positively frightened Fray Fernando by sudden bursts of passionate weep-

---

1. Sweet bread.

ing. On these occasions he would throw himself on the ground, wailing and sobbing without restraint, and often repeating, in tones of the most heart-rending sorrow, *"Ay, mamallay! ay, mamallay!"* And by that cry Fray Fernando knew that the orphan child was in bitterness, mourning for his mother. But as soon as the paroxysm was over, he would resume the grave and mournful silence that seemed so unnatural in a child. Fray Fernando began to fear that he might pine away and die; and was but partially reassured by Diego, who knew something of the Indians, and told him that grave silent ways were characteristic of the race.

José, as he was now called, could by no means be induced to sleep anywhere except in his patron's cell. Sometimes Fray Fernando, to whom the practice was not at all agreeable, positively refused him admittance, having first provided another resting-place for him. But in the morning he was sure to find him, no matter how great the cold might be (and he was very sensitive to cold), lying crouched at his door. Except in this one matter, he was always obedient to his protector. He learned quickly to understand what was said to him in Spanish, but was slow in attempting to speak it; whether from want of ability or want of inclination his instructor could not tell. From certain observances that he practiced occasionally—such as kissing the air and looking towards the sun, at the time of its rising and setting—Fray Fernando gathered that he had been taught to worship that luminary. By way of antidote, he brought him regularly to chapel, and instructed him carefully in the ceremonies proper to the place.

The first question volunteered by his little pupil gave the monk as keen a sensation of pleasure as the sight of the first flower of spring after the rains and frosts of winter. One day he brought the boy, who had now been several months under his care, to see the mine. He looked at everything, in his quiet, grave, intelligent way, as if he understood it perfectly.

But as they were returning he asked suddenly, "Patre" (so he always pronounced padre, the first Spanish word he learned)[2]— "patre, how did the gold get so far down into the ground?"

"God made it there, my son," said Fray Fernando.

"Yachani—I know. Pacha-camac made everything," the child returned, bowing low at the mention of the great Name, then slowly raising his open hands to Heaven, in token of adoration. "But the gold is the tears of Ynty."

"Who is Ynty?" asked the monk.

With a reverent gesture the child pointed upwards to the object of his race's homage, the glorious Sun.

"God made Ynty, and he is His servant," said Fray Fernando, not unwisely, in reply.

---

2.   No sound corresponding to the letter D is found in Quechua. Its place is supplied by T.

"Yachani—I know," José answered quietly.

Some time after this little incident, the Indians from the valley came as usual with their tribute. On these occasions José's faculty of speech never failed to return to him; he chattered Quechua with his brethren as long as they might be permitted to remain together. Fray Fernando liked to see him awakened, even for a time, from his un-childlike languor and listlessness; he therefore rather encouraged his intercourse with the other Indians.

Bitterly did he regret this indulgence afterward. A virulent fever was laying, waste the valleys, counting its victims by thousands amongst a people healthy and long-lived under favorable conditions, but deficient in strength, and with constitutions easily shattered by disease or hardship. Ere the next morning's dawn José was tossing on his mat, freezing and burning, speaking strange words in Quechua, and moaning piteously for his mother.

Fray Fernando was greatly distressed for the child. Moreover, he was alarmed, not without cause, for the health of the rest of the colony. He determined to attend the sick boy himself, and to allow no one else to approach him. Even setting aside the danger of infection, he could not trust him to the care of the Negro women, who, though kind-hearted enough, were very ignorant and stupid.

His knowledge of medicine was very limited, and he had little at command. The Indians were indeed well acquainted with the healing virtues of many of their plants, and used them with considerable skill and intelligence; but Fray Fernando had no means of communication with them. All that common sense and tender kindness could suggest, he did for his patient; the rest he was obliged to leave to nature.

Soon it appeared as though the little life, watched with such interest for well-nigh a whole year, was ebbing fast away. This did not surprise, though it grieved him. The child had been pining ever since he came to him. The slightest strain would suffice to break the slender thread. And as he sat and watched beside him through the long dark hours of the night (in that equatorial region nearly equal to the day), he thought within himself how much he should miss and mourn him. Truly the orphan had given back sevenfold the benefit received. He had made his days less dreary, less miserable, and his nights far less terrible. Whither now had vanished those visions of horror that were wont to haunt him through the sleepless hours of darkness José's presence had dispelled them, as the sun dispels the shadows of the night. Fray Fernando, as yet, did not fully understand from *what* he had thus been saved; but he felt as though the mists of a dark dread which had overhung his life were gradually clearing away—he hoped forever.

But now it seemed as if he must part with his treasure, and return to his former lonely, desolate state. The fever having run its course, the little patient lay, weak and helpless, with the look of one whose life is fading. Hoping against hope, he administered, continually and in smallest quantities, the strongest stimulant, the sora of the Indians. Anxious hours passed away with little change, yet with no visible decrease of strength. A long, weary night followed, during which Fray Fernando found it hard to tell whether José slept or waked, or lay in stupor, unconscious of all around.

At length day appeared. The sun rose suddenly, as it does in those tropical lands. José moved, looked at Fray Fernando, and smiled. He drank the cordial held to his lips, then feebly whispered something. Fray Fernando bent over him to listen. "I want to see my Father's face," he repeated more distinctly.

Fray Fernando feared the mind was wandering still. "My poor child," he said, "your father is dead—long since."

"*My* Father never dies," the child responded, with a look half of surprise, half of reproach. "Don't you know him?— Ynty the Glorious!" he added, speaking with more energy than Fray Fernando thought him capable of showing.

"When my child is better," he replied evasively, "he shall go forth and see the sunshine."

But José was not satisfied; and again, after a little pause, he pleaded, "Let me see my Father's face, good patre."

Fray Fernando, with new and suddenly awakened interest, now ventured to put a question to his child. "Does my little José then claim kindred with the princes of his people— the Incas—the Children of the Sun "For even the haughty Spanish conquerors could not withhold the tribute of their reverence from the truly royal line they had so cruelly despoiled.

"I am Viracocha Yntip Churi, in Spanish

talk, Viracocha— Child of the Sun," the boy replied.

Then Fray Fernando wrapped him gently in the soft warm skins of the vicuña, carried him tenderly out, and laid him in the sunshine.

When brought back to his couch again, the tired child whispered, "My Father kissed me;" and fell into the soundest and most natural sleep he had had since his illness.

V

Viracocha's Fathers

"The warrior kings, whose banners
Flew far as eagles fly;
They are gone where swords avail them not
From the feast of victory."
~ HEMANS

FROM THAT TIME FRAY FERNANDO took care
that his little charge should enjoy all the sunshine it was in his power to give him. And
whether the light and the fresh air, aided per-

haps by the child's superstition, really worked a cure, or whether nature, left to herself; simply rallied her well-nigh exhausted powers, it is certain that José's health improved, though slowly, and with many variations.

He seemed now as anxious to talk Spanish as he had previously been to avoid it. Fray Fernando gladly encouraged this propensity; the more so as he was now desirous of learning all the child could tell him about his own history.

One day as he sat with him in the sunshine he said to him. "You call yourself Yntip Churi, Child of the Sun. Are you, then, a kinsman of the Inca, Atahualpa, the same the conquistadors slew at Caxamarca?"

But the child's weak frame trembled at the question, which seemed to him an insult. "Oh no; no!" he answered. "Thank Ynty, I am not. Atahualpa was not Inca, he was *aucca*—how call you it?— coward— traitor. He slew the true Inca, Huascar, the great Huayna Capac's lawful son."

"But Atahualpa was also the son of Huayna Capac, was he not?" asked the puzzled monk, who could not boast of much acquaintance with the history of the conquered race.

"Yes," eagerly explained the little partizan. "But what did that matter? His mother was not *Coya*;[1] she was not even a Child of the Sun. She was only a daughter of the King of Quito, whom Huayna Capac Inca conquered. Huayna Capac was brave and gentle; and he was wont to say that he never refused a woman anything. So she made him promise to give the kingdom of his fathers to her son. And having that, he wanted all. Hence the cruel war, and the death of Huascar, the true Inca. *Alalau!*[2] never did Children of the Sun slay one another until then."

"And who taught you these things, my

---

1. Empress
2. Alas

child?"

"Mamallay—my mother."

The Inca's child was no barbarian; he was the heir of a civilization, unique indeed and partial, but genuine. No inconsiderable heritage of high heroic memories had fallen to his lot. And up to the hour when he fell into Don Ramon's hands his education had been carried on with unremitting industry. It is true that the arts of reading and writing were unknown to him; and, unacquainted with figures, he could only perform a few simple calculations by means of knots on a cord. But instead of these more mechanical acquirements, he had the lessons of a passionate-hearted, enthusiastic mother, who filled his young imagination day by day with the spirit-stirring legends of his race. These were to him religion, literature, fairy tales, all in one. No Hebrew boy, "exiled from Zion's rest," could have yearned more fondly towards Jerusalem than he did towards

Cuzco, the sacred city, where were the stately palaces of his kindred, the golden temple of the Sun, and the thrones of the beneficent Inca kings, his adored forefathers. No young Italian patriot could have learned to love his country with more passionate ardor than glowed in his heart for Tahuantin Suyu. It was by this name, meaning "the four provinces," that he always called the empire of the Incas: Peru was a word unknown to him; it owed its origin to a blunder of the Spaniards.

The strange sorrows that had fallen upon his young life—his kindred slain; his home in ruins; his mother setting herself free by death; he himself left desolate, a slave to the hated Spaniard—only served so to enamel those pictures of past glory, that the fragile vase upon which they were painted might indeed be shattered, but not a single line or hue of them could ever be effaced.

Fray Fernando was not slow in resuming

the conversation. He wished, if possible, to discover in what manner and degree his *protege* was connected with the royal family; and how he happened to be found in a place so remote as one of the little isles of verdure that dotted the great desert of the southern coast.

"Are you, then, related to Huascar?" he asked.

"All the Children of the Sun are one family," answered the boy. "But we are not of Huayna Capac's children. We are of Viracocha's *ayllu*. "[3]

"Viracocha? Who was he? I have never heard of him."

"Never heard of Viracocha the Fair-haired!" exclaimed the child in great astonishment. "Almost the greatest of the Incas! The whole world is filled with his renown. And," he added proudly, after a moment's pause, "I am his son"

"His renown has not reached Spain, however," said Fray Fernando with a smile.

3.   Tribe descendants

"I will tell you all about him," said José, nothing loath to recount a story dear to his heart, and as familiar in all its details to his memory as the simplest Scripture narrative would be to a well-instructed European child of his age." He was the seventh Inca after Manco Capac." And here he paused again with doubtful look; so strange was the ignorance displayed by his benefactor, that he would not now have been astonished if the monk had asked, "And who was Manco Capac?"

Fray Fernando knew that, however. "I have heard," he said, "that the founder of your monarchy, falsely called a Child of the Sun, taught agriculture and the useful arts to a people whom he found sunk in barbarism."

"Our Father the Sun pitied the poor ignorant people, and he sent his children to teach them" said José, telling the tale as it had been told to him, and as indeed it is still usually told to us. "Manco Capac taught the men to sow and reap and build houses; and Mama Ocella, his wife, taught the women to spin and weave. Moreover, they both taught everyone to be just and gentle, and to keep the five great laws:—' Do not be idle; Do not lie; Do not steal; Do not commit adultery; Do not kill.' The Incas who reigned after him, his sons and sons' sons, did likewise. They built temples, and schools, and forts; they made good roads and inns, and great water-courses, that the earth might be watered and bring forth fruit, and that every one might have food to eat. And they plowed the land with their own hands, that the poor man might not say the prince bade him do that which he would not do himself. They let no man want; they did justice to all; they were called the friends of the poor. That was the name best loved by the Inca' Friend of the Poor.'"

"But were they not also great warriors and conquerors?" asked Fray Fernando, thinking of the enormous tract of country over which the Inca's sway extended at the time of the Spanish conquest.

"Yes; they spread the dominion of the Sun far and wide—partly because they were brave warriors, partly because men saw that it was good to obey them, for all their subjects had peace and plenty. Often wild tribes would send messengers to the Incas, asking them to rule over them and to teach them. But even to those who fought against them they were kind and gentle; many times offering them pardon and friendship, and sparing them and showing them mercy whenever they could.

"At length there came an Inca called Yahuar,[4] who was not such a brave warrior as his fathers. He was a man sad of heart; always fearing evil. Now it happened that his son, the young Auqui,[5] behaved himself perversely, and

---

4.   Yahuar-Huaccuc
5.   Prince

the Inca was very wroth with him. He drove him from his palace and his court, and from beautiful Cuzco, the golden city; and he bade him tend the sacred llamas amongst the lonely plains of Chita. But he was a youth of much—silence, thought[6]—how call you it? He used to lie for hours on the green grass beside one of the little seas where the water-fowl dip their white wings, and look up into the far blue sky, thinking—always thinking.

"One midsummer noon he was lying thus. Everything was still and quiet; not a breeze waving the long grass, not a tiny insect's wing stirring the air. Behold! suddenly a bright figure stood before him. His dress was whiter than snow; his hair was like the tears of Ynty; his face was as a morning without clouds. The Auqui stood up upon his feet, and made low obeisance to him. Then the spirit spake, and said that his name was Viracocha; that he also was

---

6. The same word serves for both in Quechua.

a Child of the Sun; and that he had come to reveal to his brethren that all the fierce nations round, who hated their mild laws and gentle manners, had banded together to destroy them, to waste their fields, and to lay Cuzco level with the ground. 'Go,' he said, 'and tell these things to thy father. But as for thyself, be brave and strong; for I will not forsake thee; and to thee it is given to deliver thy people.'"

"What! Did he become the deliverer—he, the outcast, the evil-doer?" Fray Fernando asked, with a sudden flash of interest.

"He did as he was told," the child answered simply. "He went to Cuzco and gave his message. At first the Inca would not believe him; but too soon he found that his words were true. The barbarous tribes, many as the waves of the sea, fierce as the pumas of the mountain, were sweeping down on the sacred city. Some of them were rebels; some had never yet been tamed or conquered. The old Inca was afraid of them, and fled away weeping towards the desert. But the Auqui stood forth brave and strong in the hour of need. He unfurled the great rainbow banner of the Incas; and he bade all who loved the Children of the Sun follow him to the fight.

"Then there was a battle, fierce and long. Thousands died on the field of blood; ' for so the place has been called ever since. But the Children of the Sun prevailed at last, and put the wild hosts of the league to flight. There was no one who could withstand the conquering Auqui."

"What did he then with the vanquished?"

"What should he do? Was he not a Child of the Sun? As soon as the fight was over he passed himself throughout all the plain, giving strict command that the dead should be buried, the wounded enemies succored and cared for, the captives set free. And when, afterward, the wives and children of the rebels came to meet him, carrying green branches and imploring his mercy, he said to them, ' It was your husbands and fathers who offended, not you. And since I have already pardoned them, what have you to fear Go in peace.' Then he bade food to be given them, and great care to be taken of the widows and orphans of those who were slain in the battle. As for the chief of the rebels, he restored him to his place and his rule; and those tribes served the Incas loyally from that time forth."[7]

"A good ending to your story," said the monk, smiling.

"It is not quite the end," José answered. "The Auqui came in triumph to the place where his father was. Then the old Inca took from his head the *llautu*—the sacred crimson fringe—and the black and white wing-feathers of the coraquenque, and he put them on the

------

7. This is given as a specimen of the Inca legends and traditions.

head of the brave young Auqui; and he bade his captains bear him aloft in the golden chair, and salute him as mighty Inca, Child of the Sun, Friend of the Poor. Thenceforward the Auqui reigned gloriously. He took to himself the name of the bright spirit that appeared to him on the plains of Chita—Viracocha, foam of the sea.' He built a beautiful temple in his honor. The work was long, and took many years to finish; but he saw it finished, for he reigned until his hair was white as the snow of the Andes.

"It is told of him, moreover, that after he was settled in his kingdom, he went forth to do reverence to the Sun, as the Incas used, at the great feast of Raymi. He stood in the court of the temple before all the people, wearing the beautiful *uncu*[8] of blue wrought with golden threads, and the long mantle glittering with golden beads. But instead of making low obeisance to the glorious Ynty, he held himself

---

8.   Tunic

erect, and even dared to raise his eyes to the awful burning face of our great Father.

" 'O Inca,' said the high priest, 'what you do is not good! You give the people strange thoughts, and cause them to wonder at you.'

"'Is there any one,' asked Viracocha, 'who dares to bid me go whither he will?'

"' How could anyone be so bold?' the priest answered.

But if I bid one of my servants go here or there, will he disobey me asked the Inca again.

"'He will most certainly obey thee, Capac Inca, even unto death,' the priest replied.

'Then,' said the Inca, 'I perceive that there must be some greater Lord whom our Father the Sun reveres, and at whose command he travels every day from one end of the heavens to the other.'

"And also the great Viracocha's son, Pa-cha-cutec the Wise, and other of the Incas, in their hearts adored Pacha-camac, the Maker of the World, the eternally young, who created all things, even our Father the Sun."[9]

Here the boy ended his story, the latter part of which had evidently been taught him word for word, with especial care, as a religious lesson of high importance. Of course, it is not to be supposed that he related it exactly as here set down. He experienced much difficulty in finding suitable Spanish equivalents for the familiar Quechua phrases, and made many verbal blunders in the attempt. He managed, however, not only to make himself intelligible to the monk, but to give him not a little food for thought.

On another occasion Fray Fernando asked the child how his parents came to fix their residence in so remote a spot as an oasis in the wild desert of Achapa. It was night, and they were

9. The anecdote told above is related, by different historians, of several of the Incas. Other remarkable acknowledgments of the One True Invisible God are attributed to these heathen princes.

enjoying the welcome blaze of a cheerful fire in Fray Fernando's cell. The Indian boy, who loved the warmth, was seated close to the fire on his mat of vicuna skin; and his brown face glowed in the ruddy light, as he looked up to answer his benefactor's question. "My father and mother," he said," with other Inca children who lost their parents in the war, were taken to the desert for safety by the faithful servants of their houses. There they grew up and married; but most of them afterward went away to join our brave Inca Manco in the forests of Vilcapampa.—Manco? Don't you know he was Huascar's brother, and rightful Inca after him? Don't you remember how bravely he fought the Spaniards Our *ayllu*—that is, Viracocha's— were true to him to a man. In the last great fight at Cuzco, it was my mother's father who defended the strongest of the three forts to the very end against the Spaniard. Long did he stand almost alone upon the wall, and strike down with his club every Spaniard who tried to scale it. But they mounted the wall at last, in many places at once, and sought to surround and take him alive. Then he sprang to the edge of the battlement, wrapped his mantle round his head, and flung himself down the precipice into the Colcampata. He would not live to serve the Spaniard. And he was right."

Fray Fernando began to feel uneasy. The child's enthusiasm was of a kind that might one day become dangerous. But he was too wise to fan the flame by contradiction. He merely asked, "What became of your father? Did he, when he grew up, join your Inca in his exile?"

"No; but he went forth from our little *paucar*[10] to see the great world, and to try if anything yet remained which a Child of the Sun might do there. I do not remember his going—it was a long time ago; but I well remember the day Chaqui—that was the servant who went

10. Flowery meadow.

with him—came back alone. Chaqui told my mother that my father had gone to help the men of Chili, who were still fighting bravely against the Spaniards. And there he died in battle. My mother wept, and taught me to weep for him. But we were glad that he died fighting with the cruel Spaniards."

"José, I am a Spaniard."

"No, you are a patre. You are good." And he stroked the monk's hand caressingly. "But," he resumed, "Chaqui told us more. He told us that our brave Inca Manco was dead. Some Spaniards who had run away from their own people took shelter in his wild forest-home at Vilca-pampa. Being Inca, and Friend of the Poor, he was kind to them, and received them, and gave them food. One of them paid his kindness by slaying him. *Aucca!* After that, Manco's son, Sayri Tupac, had the right of wearing the sacred *llautu*. But to him the Spaniards sent messengers of his own kindred, who gave him many soft words and fair promises, until at last he agreed to go to their new city in the vale of Rimac,[11] there to give up to the stranger his claim to the throne of Tahuantin Suyu." The boy said this with a bowed head, and in a low sad voice, as one who keenly felt the shame of such a surrender.

He went on,—" Chaqui told us that when the Inca made the black marks that meant to say he gave up the kingdom, he wept, and taking in his hand the velvet cloth that covered the table, he said, 'Behold, the whole of this cloth belonged to my fathers, and now they satisfy me with a thread of the silken fringe!' But when my mother heard that, she was very wroth. She said he was no Child of the Sun, and his tears were worthless. And Chaqui answered her,—' But what could he do?'

'He could die,' she said. 'He *is* dead,' Chaqui told us then. The Spaniards gave him

---

11. Lima

broad lands, and gold and silver, and they allowed him to live in the beautiful valleys where the homes of his fathers were. But nothing could make him happy no, not even the fair palace of Yucay, the loved home of my father Viracocha, with the fruits and flowers of its wondrous gardens, some real, some still more beautiful, wrought out of the tears of Ynty; and its cool baths and fountains, where the water flows from the mouths of great silver llamas and dragons. The Inca pined away and died, for his heart was broken." And José ended his tale, and sat in gloomy silence watching the embers, which were dying too.

"Then, I suppose there is no Inca now," was Fray Fernando's not very prudent remark.

"Oh yes," said José eagerly "There is always the Inca. There is still Manco's youngest son, Tupac Amaru. And he will take from Spanish hands," José continued, with kindling eyes," not one thread of the crimson fringe, not one grain of the golden treasures of his fathers. He lives free in the forests of Vilca-pampa. Him we love, and him we will obey."

There was another silence. Then José said thoughtfully, "When I was a little child I used to think that the Children of the Sun reigned yet at Cuzco, and that as soon as I was a man I should go thither, and see the Inca in his golden chair, and the palaces and temples, and hear the happy songs, and join in the dances at the great feasts. But now I know that the Spaniards have swept everything away, like the great earth-overturning flood.[12] Still, for all that, one day *the Inca will reign again.*" This was said with no outburst of childish feeling, but with a quiet slow gravity, born of intense conviction. That belief was the thing that lay deepest in the young child's heart.

"How know you that?" asked Fray Fernan-

---

12. The Deluge, of which most of the American nations preserved traditions.

do, a little surprised.

"Yachani—I know," was all José would say in reply.

It was not one solitary childish voice alone that whispered, "The Inca will reign again." For long years and years was that fair hope cherished, and held close to the heart of an oppressed people, to keep it from breaking in its helpless misery. The herdsman who tended the llamas on the hills of his fathers for the food of the cruel stranger, the slave who wove their fleeces into beautiful fabrics for his clothing, or dug gold and silver out of the earth to minister to his luxuries, alike consoled themselves under toil and starvation, under stripes and torture, with that sweet whisper of hope, "The Inca will reign again." The Indian mother who sang to her babe, in cradlesongs sadder than requiems,—

> *"Seeking through the whole world*
> *I should not meet my equal in misery;*

Accursed be the night I was born;"[13]

yet taught him, as he grew, to look up to that faint star of promise, the only one that beamed on their darkness,—"The Inca will reign again."

Nor even, when the long slow years had "rolled into the centuries," was the light of that star extinguished. Still the hearts of the people yearned "with quenchless love profound" after their beneficent Incas,—after the kings who were the friends of the poor. It is not yet one hundred years since men—and women—died cheerfully, in heroic despair, with the word on their lips, "We have no king but our Inca."

Very beautiful is this tenacity of love, of faith, of hope for the future, born of the memories of the past. Are not such instincts true prophecies, though in a different sense from any of which the poor untaught Indians could dream?

---

13. From a Quechua cradle-song.

VI

Viracocha Visits His Brethren

"But what hast thou lacked with me, that, behold, thou seekest to go to thine own country! And he answered, Nothing: howbeit let me go in any wise."

~ 1 KINGS 11:22

MORE THAN SIX YEARS HAVE passed away, producing little outward change in any of the inhabitants of Cerro Blanco whom we know by name, except in the Indian boy, who has grown a fine handsome stripling. His patron is well satisfied with his development, both mental and physical. This is fortunate, for with nothing else, either within or without himself, is poor Fray Fernando satisfied. His position at the mining-colony becomes increasingly uncomfortable. Passing disagreements with Diego Rascar have deepened and widened into a standing feud. The Spaniards and Creoles take part with Diego, while the Black people count for nothing, with the exception of Pepe, and he has his own reasons for bearing a grudge against the padre. This is particularly hard, since the padre's real offense is that he has espoused the cause of the black men against the white. "A pity it is," Diego sometimes says, "that this holy man never knows when to shut his eyes."

During the last six years Fray Fernando has been growing every day more incapable of shutting his eyes to wrong and oppression. The old practice of "passing by on the other side," so safe, so easy, and so convenient, has become not only distasteful, but impossible to him. If a man chooses to act, even once, the part of the good Samaritan, he must accept the cost. He will find that he cannot, if he would, descend again to the *rôle* of the priest and the Levite.

But in proportion as Fray Fernando's own heart became softer, it seemed to him that the hearts around him grew harder. He thought that the whites were sinking gradually to the level of the Black people, their barbarous half-caste families being even more degraded than themselves. In the blacks he saw no change worth speaking of, save a change for the worse in Pepe, who, on account of his strength, intelligence, and usefulness in managing the other slaves, was petted and pampered by Diego, and allowed to indulge his vicious propensities without a check. Often did the mournful words of the prophet ring in the ears of Fray Fernando: "I have labored in vain, I have spent my strength for naught and in vain." And he could not take refuge in the strong confidence of faith, and add, "Surely my judgment is with the Lord, and my work with my God." Fray Fernando thought his work nothing—words written on water, lines traced on sand. Or, if remembered at all, he believed it would only go to swell the vast amount of his sin, that burden already greater than he could bear.

But for the Indian youth, at least, he had not labored in vain. Long ago José had displaced the clumsy Pepe as acolyte, to the great satisfaction of every one, Pepe himself alone excepted. He knew the "Doctrina de la Fe" as well as any intelligent Spanish lad of his age. He was diligent in the repetition of prayers, and the performance of every other religious duty enjoined on him. He had learned to read and write, and Fray Fernando was beginning to teach him Latin— a

necessary labor, if the accomplishment of reading was to be of any use to him, as the few books
his patron possessed *were* in that language. José
learned quickly, for his memory was remark-
ably good, and the similarity between Latin and
Spanish, which contrasted delightfully with the
utter and perplexing difference between Spanish
and Quechua, made the task a comparatively
light one.

His instructor's pleasure in his progress
might have been somewhat lessened had he
dreamed that his pupil imagined all the time
that he was learning the language of the Jews.
Was he not to read the Psalms of David in the
Latin tongue, and was not David a king of the
Jews? José believed that the Jews were a great
but very wicked people, who lived, or had
lived long ago (for his notions of chronology
were vague in the extreme), on the other side
of the Mother Sea. They were guilty, he knew,
of the awful crime of having put to death the

Son of God, and he thought that in righteous judgment the Spaniards, with the Pope at their head, made war upon them, and had driven them out of their country. He supposed the Pope to be a Spaniard, and the Catholic High Priest. He had a hazy idea that he never died, but lived on miraculously from age to age. He knew that various nations of white men, who were not Spaniards, lived beyond the great sea; and imagined they bore the same relation to the Spaniards, in power and civilization, as the barbarous tribes subdued by his Inca forefathers did to them. Perhaps Fray Fernando would not have dispelled this illusion, even if he could.

But the fact was, that at the end of all those years of loving toil and care, Fray Fernando's acquaintance with his *protége* was very superficial. He knew José well enough: the docile, affectionate child, who not only obeyed but anticipated his commands; the intelligent pupil, whose progress more than repaid the pains of his instructor. But there was another whom he knew not, who did not indeed speak with José's tongue, for that was now well used to the sonorous accents of the Spaniard, but who often looked from José's dark thoughtful eyes, and ever dwelt in the silent recesses of José's heart. This was Viracocha, the Inca's child, who cherished with passionate love the legends of his family, who still looked upon the Sun as his Father, and believed religiously in the ultimate triumph of his race. These ideas, crossed and interwoven with threads of Christian doctrine, made up a strange confused tangle of a creed, which changed its hue according as it was looked at in the light of Ynty's beams, or in that of the tapers which burned before the crucifix.

That Fray Fernando knew nothing of all this was in some measure his own fault. "Silence," it is said, "is golden;" but this is not always true. Sometimes it is sharp steel; keen to sunder bonds and separate chief friends even like the piercings of a sword. Naturally startled by the hold the ideas of his race had taken upon the mind of his little *protégé,* Fray Fernando fell into the common mistake of thinking,—"If I do not allow him to talk of these things, he will cease to think of them, and in time forget them altogether." It was easy to carry out his plan. Nothing is easier than to silence a sensitive child. Few words, perhaps none, are needed. A look, a gesture, a tone of voice, a hasty turning from the subject, will suffice to render the stream of confidence "a fountain sealed." It is the unsealing, in after-years, which will be difficult, perhaps impossible. It soon came as naturally to José to bury his thoughts as it does to his, race to bury their treasures in the earth. Thus it happened that Fray Fernando was very much surprised by what occurred on the afternoon of Christmas-day, 1570.

After performing the service, he was sitting in his cell reading, when José came in. The lad was dressed in a full suit of Spanish costume, which his kind protector had been at the expense and trouble of procuring for him from Cuzco, being anxious, not merely to give him pleasure, but also to "Spaniardize" him, as the phrase ran, in every possible way. And indeed the doublet and hosen of fine blue cloth, with white silk stockings, set off the youth's graceful figure to great advantage; and his handsome Indian face, and glossy black hair, had never looked so well as they did beneath the shade of the dark blue velvet montero.

On entering the cell, he removed the montero, and stood before the monk with a bow almost worthy of a Spanish cavalier.

"Well, my son?" said Fray Fernando kindly, looking up from his book.

"Patre," said José," it is Christmas-day; you have told me that in the country beyond the sea men give gifts to each other."

"Ah! so you want a gift, José. Speak out, my

boy; what is it?"

José hesitated; a rather unusual thing with him. He had few ways of expressing feeling, and seldom did express it at all.

Fray Fernando closed the volume he had been reading, and surveyed the youth attentively, and with much satisfaction. José was dear to him as his own son; he was yet more fond of him than he was proud of him, and that is much to say. "You make a very good hidalgo, José," he remarked with a smile. "Is anything wanting to complete your equipment? Have you set your heart upon a cloak like Diego's, or even upon a sword?"

"No, patre; I thank you. That which I desire is a thing of another kind. I desire-your leave to visit mine own people down yonder in the valley. Let the patre be good to me, his son and servant." José spoke, according to his wont, very quietly. And having spoken, he stood perfectly motionless, a waiting an answer.

But the white man started, as if he had received a sudden blow. "What is this, José?" he asked. "Why do you want to leave me?"

"I do not want to leave the patre. I want to go to my own people."

"But wherefore should you go, and to whom? You have no friends among your own people. Your father and mother are dead long ago. Besides, you are a Christian."

"The patre speaks truth; I am a Christian."

"Then wherefore forsake Christian instruction and communion? No, José; it is a vain, idle fancy. Give it up, and stay with me; for I love you, José."

José's slight fingers trembled, letting go their hold on the montero, which fell to the ground. But, after a moment's pause, he drew nearer, and knelt before the monk. "The patre has been always good to me," he said. "Let him be good to me now, and send me away, that I may go to my own people." "Stand up I" said Fray Fernando, with some displeasure in his tone. "Christian men should kneel to God alone. Wait a while; for I must think. You have troubled me, José."

José stood up, and waited. Had the padre's meditation lasted for hours, he would not have disturbed him by the motion of a limb or a muscle.

But he had not to wait so long. The padre spoke. "José," he asked, "if I give you leave to go, will you come back to me again?"

"I will surely come back to you, patre."

"You intend it. But your mind may change. I fear, if I let you go now, I shall see your face no more."

"Patre," said José, with deeper earnestness of voice, "I must needs come back. Do I not belong to you?"

"My son, we both belong to God."

"I belong to you, patre. You bought me, and

with something you were loath to part with, for I saw you kiss it ere you gave it into Don Ramon's hand."—A slight circumstance that Fray Fernando himself had forgotten—"Certainly I will return to you, patre."

"Then go, in God's name; and may He keep thee safe both in soul and body. May He also forgive me if I have sinned in giving thee this permission. For I misdoubt me sore thine errand is a foolish one."

José started at daybreak next morning. His patron gave him much good advice; fearing, and not without reason, that his inexperience and utter ignorance of the world might involve him in difficulties and perils. One of the first thoughts that would occur to a European in contemplating a journey had no place at all in the mind of José. He suffered no perplexity about ways and means; he knew that every Indian whose hut he chanced to pass would freely and gladly afford him food and shelter. He had looked at money as a curiosity, and had heard its use explained, but he had never used it or seen it used. When Fray Fernando gave him some pieces of silver to take with him, he asked what he should do with them.

"You can give them, if you like, to those who entertain you and show you kindness," said the monk.

José looked pleased. "I thank you, patre," he said. "It is good to have something to give."

The parting was an affectionate one. Fray Fernando accompanied his adopted son to the pass; there he embraced and blessed him,—and stood watching until the slight figure disappeared among the rocks. "Will he ever return?" sighed the monk. "Will my José ever come back to me again?"

The first question might have been answered in the affirmative,—but what of the second?

VII

Viracocha Comes Back

*"To be wroth with what we love,
Doth work like madness in the brain."*
~ COLERIDGE

TROUBLES THICKENED ROUND the path of Fray
Fernando during the months that followed
José's departure. Pepe had a quarrel about a Ne-
gro woman with one of his fellow-slaves named

Zillo—a quiet, rather well-disposed man. He sought to fasten upon him a charge of robbery; and Diego was quite willing to assume his guilt, and to sacrifice him to the malice of his rival. Pepe must be kept in good-humor, or everything would go wrong both in the mine and in the galpón.

Fray Fernando was roused to indignation at the thought of a man whom he believed to be innocent undergoing a terrible punishment; but his remonstrance was received with coldness, even with disdain. He was far too much in earnest, however to give up the contest. Such a monstrous injustice should not be done, if by any means he could prevent it. After exhausting all his eloquence in rebukes, persuasions, and expostulations, he drew the last arrow out of his quiver. "Señor Diego," he said, "if you do it, I lay a statement of the whole matter before your lord, Don Marcio Serra de Leguisano." A threat likely to cost him who uttered it far more than him who heard it. Nor was Fray Fernando ignorant of the peril in which he involved himself. He was alone, in the midst of lawless men, with sharp steel in their hands, and little reluctance to use it. They might well remember the Spanish proverb, "Dead men never bite." What better could the meddlesome friar expect than a dagger through his heart some dark night, and a grave on the lonely mountain summit? And who could suspect any foul play from the decorous message that would, no doubt, be forwarded in due time to Don Marcio Serra, informing him, very regretfully, that the health of the holy father had given way under the rigors of that inhospitable climate?

In former days—which seemed to belong to another state of existence—men called him who now bore the name of Fray Fernando, bravest of the brave. But for ten miserable years he had called himself coward and recreant. Still he could brave death for the sake of a poor Negro, toward whom he entertained no feeling warmer than compassion. Though, after all, not for his sake—for the sake of justice and mercy.

"If death were all!"—he said to himself, as he realized the full peril of his situation, in the lonely hour that succeeded his stormy altercation with Diego—"if death were all! But—*after death!*"This was the key-note of a long, mournful meditation, into which we cannot, perhaps dare not, follow him. At last, to relieve his burdened heart by action, he set forth upon his daily walk—never omitted—to the pass whence José might be seen returning. The Indian youth had now been more than six months away—a lengthened absence, which gave Fray Fernando much uneasiness, for José was the one solitary joy and hope of his dreary life.

It was evening—about an hour before the rapid tropical sunset. Fray Fernando soon saw an Indian ascending the winding pathway with the fleet footsteps of his race. As the wayfarer gradually drew nearer, he perceived a burden on his shoulder; and saw that he wore a white cotton tunic, fastened at the waist by an embroidered belt; a *yacollo,* or mantle; short native trousers, reaching a little below the knees; and *usutas,* or native sandals. But when his features became visible, the monk cried aloud in astonishment—for they were José's.

José, who had now attained his full height, and assumed an air of manly independence quite new to him, gravely took the burden from his shoulder, and laid it at the feet of Fray Fernando. It was the monk's first impulse to embrace his adopted child; but some momentary, unaccountable feeling, shared probably by both, checked the impulse, and held them apart.

"How is this, my son?" Fray Fernando questioned, in anxious and displeased surprise. "Where is the Spanish dress I gave you?"

José pointed to the burden at their feet. His countenance seemed as much changed as his dress. Fray Fernando thought its expression sullen, almost fierce.

"I hope," he said, "that you have not put off the heart of the Christian with the clothing of the Spaniard."

Perhaps his words were the less gentle from the state of irritation in which his mind had been left by his recent altercation with Diego.

"I am clothed as my fathers were," José answered. "I am no Spaniard; I am a Child of the Sun."

"You should be ashamed to recall those heathenish fables," the monk returned. "Have I to repeat to *you*, after seven years of careful instruction, that the sun is nothing but a ball of fire, made by God to give light to the earth, and for that purpose traveling round it every day?"

"I don't know what Ynty is. I know what

the Spaniards are; and may Ynty slay me with his arrows if henceforward I wear their dress or learn their ways!"

José flung out his words with eager, sharp abruptness, naturally increased by the difficulty with which, in a moment of excitement, he translated his rapid thoughts from Quechua into Spanish.

"José! José!" cried the monk, in angry amazement; "is this the reward of all the love and care I lavished on you?"

"I have no wish to grieve *you*, patre," said the youth, in a softened tone.

"No wish to grieve me!—yet your words are enough to bring down God's vengeance on us both. Go to! You disappoint me, José. You are like all the rest—ungrateful."

Words such as these would have brought the docile, affectionate José of six months ago to his knees, to ask forgiveness with tears. But Viracocha stood erect and motionless; in Fray

Fernando's eyes, a bronze statue of defiance. Yet, unseen by Fray Fernando, there was a quivering of the lip, a gathering mist in the eye.

"Patre," he said at length, "if you will only listen." Here he faltered—stopped—and began his sentence again in a different form. "Patre, hear what I have seen and heard, and then tell me if I ought to speak the tongue or worship the gods of the race who are trampling my people into dust."

"Nothing you have seen or heard can excuse the insolent tone you have thought proper to assume," said the monk. He continued, however, in a voice less firm, even almost hesitating—"I do not deny that there have been many instances of oppression; but still—"

"But still—they make good and just laws in the council at Seville, beyond the Mother Sea. I know that," said the Indian bitterly. "But I know, too, how those laws are kept down in yonder valleys. Cain the murderer said to God,

'I am not my brother's keeper.' But the Spaniard says to God and man, 'I *am* my brother's
keeper;' and then he slays him by the sword,' by
famine, by torture. It would be more merciful
to kill us all at once, and make the land a desert, as he has done elsewhere."

"Oh, José, you have need to repent, and to
ask God to forgive your wicked words."

"It is not your God I worship now," retorted José in desperation.

"Then what has brought you here? Better
have remained amongst your own people than
come back to insult and defy me."

"But why do you say that to me?" asked
José, with apparent simplicity. "You bought
me."

"In an evil hour. Would I had never seen
your face! Leave me, and return to your people."

And Fray Fernando turned to go. But José

placed himself before him in the path.

"Hear me, patre," he cried—"only hear me; then do with me what you will."

"Were you the José of six months ago, there is nothing I would not hear from your lips; but an evil spirit has entered into you."

"Am I worse in your eyes than Pepe or Zillo? Yet even them you would not condemn unheard."

"Speak, then, if you will; but in words fit for a Christian man to listen to."

"Patre, I went down to the valley by the road my fathers made; and I saw the water-courses they fashioned, which lead so far up into the mountains no man knoweth where they end. In the great *puquios*[1] "I could almost stand upright. I examined them well. They are all carefully and cunningly made, and lined with great stones deftly hewn and fashioned. They divide themselves into many little *puquios*—so

1. Trenches

many, that every corner of the thirsty land is watered by the streams of the snowy Antis, and brings forth maize, fruit, and flowers for the joy of man. Such things my fathers made. But the Spaniards destroy the roads, and break up the water-courses, taking the hewn stones to build houses for themselves."

"Not in Nasca," Fray Fernando interposed. "Don Marcio has strictly forbidden the practice."

José had gained his point—he was listening.

"I know it," he answered. "Don Marcio is not like others—he fears God. But they do it, all through the country; so that, where we tended gardens, our children will wander through thirsty deserts—if, indeed, there are any of us left alive. Yet the Spaniards behold these roads and water-courses with wonder and admiration. They say there be none like them in their country; all their power and all their skill could not have fashioned them."

"Yet the destruction of roads and aqueducts, though greatly to be deplored, scarcely warrants such fierce anger."

"But it is the men and women, and little children, who are destroyed throughout the land, and no man pities them. Listen, patre. I found my people down yonder in the vale of Nasca sad of countenance, though they did not complain. They miss the joyous feasts of the olden time, the frequent holidays, the dances in honor of Ynty and Quilla.[2]

Always they toil hard, often they starve, that they may pay their tribute to the Spaniards. It is very much that they have to pay, and if they fail, they are beaten and tortured. Once I came to a little village, where I found great grief and mourning. The Spaniards, who were taking up the tribute, had bound a poor, helpless boy to a tree, and were beating him most

---

2. The Moon

cruelly. The women were weeping and wringing their hands; the men—some of them begging for mercy, others searching their huts for maize, or charqui, or cords of maguey, to appease the wrath of the Spaniards. I asked what the boy had done, what law he had broken; and as I talked Spanish, the Spaniards listened to me, and told me he would not pay his tribute. I did not understand; so I turned for explanation to my own people. They said the tribute was required of all above eighteen, but that it was a common practice to demand it of boys under age, and to ill-use them cruelly till their friends paid the claim, though their own share had left them well-nigh starving. That time the silver you gave me saved the boy. But what use to save *one* —every day they do these things. "He paused for a few moments; then went on sorrowfully:—" Ere long I came to Nasca, where there is a town and a fort. There some Spaniards have come to live. May the curse of

God—"

"Hush, José! you must not curse."

José caught the edge of his yacollo with his teeth, and bit it, a common gesture with his race when moved to anger. Then he resumed:—

"In Nasca and its neighborhood I found the doors all shut and barred—a strange thing in Tahuantin Suyu. When first our people saw the Spaniards bolt and bar their doors, they marveled, and could not forbear to ask the reason—did they fear we would murder them? They answered, No; we do it for fear of thieves.' Whereat our people marveled all the more, for there were no thieves amongst them. The Inca said, ' You shall not steal.' A man who went a journey would lay a little stick, across his threshold, just to say, I am not at home; ' and although his house were filled with gold and silver, none would enter it.[3] But now—*now* all

---

3.   It is a Spaniard who tells us this—Don Marcio Serra de Leguisano, in his "Last Will and Testament"—a very noble testimony to the

is changed. Now we ourselves learn to steal, like the wicked Spaniards. O Ynty, Ynty, will you not help us?" And he turned and looked towards the sun, now descending to the west.

"Call not on Ynty, who cannot hear you," the monk interposed.

"But, bad as the tribute was," José continued, recovering calmness, and turning again towards the monk, "men did not curse it, as they did the mita. It was long before I could understand aright what the mita was. I stayed in Nasca, to learn the laws of my people from the old men there; and then I went northwards. Having crossed a desert, I came to another valley, broad and fertile. It was evening. A little village lay amongst fields of quinoa. I thought it had a lonely look. Soon I saw a group of women returning thither from their work. But I saw no men. The women walked hand in hand, chanting a mournful yaravi:—

---

conquered race.

The stranger has taken our husbands
to work in his mines,
And we toil in the fields
for our children's bread.'

When I talked with them, they told me the Spaniards take away every seventh man to work in the mines and the obregas.[4] If that is not enough, they take more. The men die quickly, and more and more are ever needed. Year after year fewer men in the villages; year after year more men in the mines and obregas.—Where will it end, patre?"

"But," said Fray Fernando," the term of their service is only a year."

"So said I to the women in my simplici-ty—' Your husbands will come back to you in a year.' And they answered, weeping, They will never come back— no, never again. They will die. Or if haply they live, the Spaniards will say—they are in debt,—and will keep them for

---

4.   Factories

yanaconas[5] forever.'"

"Is such done "asked Fray Fernando.

"Every day," answered José." At last I said to the poor women of Yca, I will go and see your husbands at the mine.' —They blessed and thanked me, and gave me a store of coca leaves to carry to them, such as I have here "(touching a little ornamental bag, curiously woven of twisted threads in different colors, which hung by his side)." One, the widow of a curaca, gave me this dress to put on; for everywhere the children fled from me in terror, because I was clothed as a Spaniard. It was the holiday dress of her only son. Two years ago a Spanish traveler had taken him by force, with another youth, to carry his baggage to Cuzco. Neither of them ever returned."

"This again is a practice forbidden by the laws," said Fray Fernando.

"What good are *your* laws? We obeyed the

---

5.   Slaves

laws of our Inca, because we both loved and feared him. But Spaniards fear nothing, and love nothing—except gold."

"José! José!"

"True, patre,—too true. As. I journeyed to the mine, I met a sorrowful company of women, some leading children by the hand. They said they were going to their husbands, at work in the obregas, else they would never see them again. When I said, I am going to the mine,' they answered me, Tell the miners to thank Ynty for their lot.' This I thought strange, for the women of Yea had talked to me of the miseries of the miners till my heart was sore. But these said, Better is it with those who dig the silver from the depths of the earth, than with those who weave the llama's fleece in the obregas.' Worked far beyond their strength, fed with food we would not offer to a beast, beaten cruelly, or else—patre, I could not tell you all. But God has mercy on them, and they die. They die soon; but others must be found to fill their places—ay, though they have to be hunted with blood-hounds. Now they take little children, six or seven years old. I saw myself—" But here José stopped, and covered his face with his hands. Soon large tears fell slowly through them. "No words!" he cried passionately; "no words. Only tears. Would they were tears of blood! And this is Tahuantin Suyu, that my fathers made so happy!"[6]

Fray Fernando was moved to compassion for the gentle unoffending race, the unresisting victims of such cruel wrongs. "A poor and harmless people, created of God, and that might have been won to his knowledge," as Sir Walter Raleigh says pathetically. He answered in a softened tone, "You could say with the prophet, ' O that my head were waters, and mine eyes a fountain of tears, that I might weep

6.   All the details given above are, of course, strictly true. The most harrowing instances of cruelty and oppression are, however, purposely omitted.

day and night for the slain of the daughter of my people.'"

"The daughter of my people!" José repeated, with eyes that turned his tears to sparks of fire. "O patre, I have not told half—I cannot! They have broken into the houses of the Virgins of the Sun. They have taken them away by violence. I know now—too well!—why my mother died rather than be captive to the Spaniard. They have left us nothing sacred, nothing holy—not even the grave. They have dug open the tombs of our fathers to search for hid treasures. They have torn the ornaments from our temples; they have turned them into stables for their horses. They have robbed our store-houses, where the Incas laid up maize, quinoa, wool, cotton, to supply the people in years of scarcity. They have slaughtered by thousands the gentle, useful llamas, that bore our burdens and clothed us with their fleeces—only that they may feast upon their brains!—Are these the favorites and messengers of Pacha-camac, sent to teach us his will? No; they are the children of Supay— the devil. I will never believe God loves them, or commands us to obey them. I will never become as one of them, to learn their ways, to wear their dress, to serve their gods—"

"José, hush!" interposed the monk. Five minutes ago those two hearts had been very near, had almost met. But José's words, blasphemous in the ears of Fray Fernando, broke down the bridge between them. "I can hear my countrymen reproached," he said, "and I sorrowfully admit there is too much cause;— but I cannot hear my Faith blasphemed. Still," he added, more gently, "I would fain believe your heart does not mean all your lips have said. Changed as you are, I can hardly think you have forgotten all the past—you whom I taught, watched over, tended in sickness. See, here is the holy emblem of our Faith." He took the crucifix, with the rosary attached, from his girdle, and held it out to José. "Take it, my son; kiss it, in token of your penitence and your attachment to the Christian faith; and I will forgive your wild words and forget them."

José took the crucifix,—but held it at arm's length.

"Kiss it, my son," said the monk.

José did not move.

"Kiss it," Fray Fernando repeated more sternly. Unfortunately he added,—"as a sign that you renounce the vain idols of your race."

What! Was Ynty an idol—Ynty the glorious? What then was this bit of wood—not even gold or silver—to which the patre bade him do reverence. José's anger was not often roused, but when roused, it was incontrollable. He made a step forward towards a steep cliff, near the edge of which he was standing. The crucifix swung and shook over the precipice in his extended hand.

"Dare you?" cried the monk, springing forward to arrest him, horror-stricken at his profanity.

"I dare!" the Indian answered, the wrongs of his race all crowding on his memory, and the cross seeming nothing, in that moment's passion, save an emblem of the creed of the destroyer. "Behold!"

The deed was done. His passion began to die away the moment it was indulged. And at the same time the last rays of the sun were dying from the sky.

Enough!" said Fray Fernando, and he spoke very coldly. The white man's anger needs no loud words, no fierce gestures for its expression." I was a fool to expect gratitude or love from an Indian. You never knew what either means, José. You have never loved me, and the love I gave to you I wasted. This is our last parting. Let me pass."

José moved aside at his command, and

stood watching him with a stupefied air, until he was out of sight.

Then he ran to the place whence the cliff could be descended with the least difficulty. Leaping and scrambling, and clinging now and then to a stray tuft of ychu, he soon reached the spot where lay the crucifix. He took it up, and placed it carefully in the little bag by his side.

From this spot he could see the valley, winding far beneath. He stood gazing until the short twilight was past, and the rapidly increasing darkness hid it from his view. Then he threw himself on the ground, and gave way to a passionate burst of weeping. For the patre had parted with him in fierce anger, telling him he had never loved him.

He had no sense of fear in that lonely spot. The tracks of the puma were seldom seen in the district; and the hardy Indian youth thought little of a bed on the alfalfa, and less of the want of food, especially whilst some fragrant leaves still remained in his coca-bag.

But he was sore in need of help and comfort, for himself and for his people. And, because he saw none, either in the darkened heavens or on the miserable earth, he wept and wailed, plucking up the alfalfa by the roots and flinging it from him in his bitter grief.

At last he looked up. Ynty was gone long ago. Not even a faint glow remained now on the horizon. He remembered the words of the great Inca Huayna Capac, taught him in his childhood. Ynty could not be lord and governor, thought the wise monarch, because so often absent from the earth; nay, he seemed like a servant who himself obeyed a master, or like an arrow shot from a bow by a strong hand. It was plain enough now that Ynty could not help his children in their hour of need. There was no one to hear and help in those cold distant heavens to which they cried in vain. Were the Spaniards right I Was God on their side I Instead of the departed sun, there burned above his head the bright stars of the Southern Cross, which the patre told him was the sacred emblem of the Christian Faith, written on the heavens in characters of fire. No hint of the true meaning of the cross had ever found its way to José's heart, though he was, of course, familiar with the historical fact. He had never heard the message of divine love.

And through the best human love that he knew came the bitterest pain of that bitter hour. The patre had saved him from his cruel enemy, tended him in sickness, fed him, clothed him, taught him. And now the patre said, "You have never loved me, and the love I gave to you I wasted."

The Indian lay quite still for a long time. Thoughts he had no power to express were struggling in his soul. José and Viracocha were at strife within him.

At last came a decisive moment. "Arri! rantihuarcca," he said, half aloud. "Yes; he bought me." That was the argument that turned the scale. José—for he it was who won the victory—started up, shook the alfalfa from his dress, tied his sandals more firmly, and again repeating, "Arri; rantihuarcca," peered cautiously around through the darkness.

An hour afterward the Indian youth was treading noiselessly through the sleeping galpón. He reached the door of Fray Fernando's hut, and pushed it gently. As of old, it was only on the latch. The monk had his own reasons for not adopting precautions that, in real danger, would inevitably prove futile. José entered. All was still. Fray Fernando lay on his pallet fast asleep, for the hour was now very late. Whereupon José, with that peculiar kind of *sang froid* characteristic of his race, turned quietly into his accustomed corner, and, as though he had never forfeited his right to be there, laid himself down to sleep.

VIII

Vindicated

"But prove me what it is I would not do."

FRAY FERNANDO RETURNED TO THE galpón sorrowful and desolate. All the tenderness that life had left in his blighted heart had been gathered up and poured forth on the head of the Indian youth, who had truly been as a son to him. He never dreamed how much he had given, until he awoke to the consciousness that all was given in vain.

Nothing, absolutely nothing, was left him now to care for. He had not a hope remaining; just then he had scarcely a fear. His heart was too weary for conflict; it only ached with a dull and constant pain. Listlessly he went through the prescribed course of his evening devotions, repeating unfelt prayers and praises that found no echo in his heart. If he had ever really prayed, he had prayed for the child he fondly dreamed God had sent to comfort him in his misery. But that was over now; José was gone back to his people and to his gods, and his work and his prayers for him—like all his other work and all his other prayers—were wasted.

In this mood he laid himself down to sleep. Of late the slumbers that sealed those eyes had been fitful and broken. But it happened that upon this occasion Nature, usually capricious, saw fit to reassert her power and exact her revenge, and ere long he fell into a sound dreamless sleep.

He awoke with a start. A sharp cry rang in his ears. The room seemed full of furious men, struggling for mastery, clinging desperately to each other's throats. Then some bright thing, a knife or dagger, known by its glitter in the moonlight, fell to the ground at his side.

Less than a minute restored his senses fully, and reduced the shadowy host of combatants to two—a gigantic negro and a slender stripling, who seemed about to pay for the frantic tenacity with which he clutched his adversary's throat, by being crushed to death in his strong grasp.

That moment Fray Fernando forgot his peaceful calling, his sacred character, everything but the youth's danger. Seizing the weapon so opportunely left at his hand, he made third's-man in the fray to such good purpose, that the Negro fled for his life, like an evil spirit of night chased by returning day.

With the dagger still in his hand, the monk stood and gazed about him in bewilderment. But he could see scarcely anything, for the moon had retreated behind a cloud.

"Much-hani Pacha-camac!" exclaimed a well-known voice. Then in Spanish, "Dios gratias!"

"José! Is it you, José? How came you hither? What is it all about?"

"It was Pepe!" gasped José. "Villain, traitor, *aucca!* May I see him hurled from the highest rock on Cerro Blanco! Patre, are you hurt?"

"No, thank God. But am I dreaming or awake? What has happened?"

"He wanted to drink your blood, but God preserved you," said José.

Then Fray Fernando had recourse to his flint and steel. But it was some time before the tiny sparks availed to kindle the tinder, At length, however, the feat was accomplished;

and a little oil-lamp shed as much light as in it lay upon the monk's perplexities.

The first thing it revealed startled him considerably. "O José!" he exclaimed in great distress, "why did you not tell me you were wounded?" For the lad's white tunic was covered with blood.

"It is nothing," said José, in whose code of morality the silent endurance of pain occupied a prominent place. "Only," he added, his dark face glowing with satisfaction, even with triumph, "the patre knows if I love him now."

"You have saved my life," Fray Fernando answered. But it was not his fashion to waste time in words when deeds were needful. He bound up José's severely wounded arm, quickly and carefully, with a piece of linen torn from one of his consecrated vestments. Then he took some wine from the little store reserved for the celebration of mass, and gave it to his patient to drink. Not until all this was done, did he ask an explanation of the events of the night.

"I came back to you," José answered simply, "because you bought me. Finding you asleep, I lay down in my place. By-and-by Pepe crept in, still and silent, as a snake creeps through the grass. I cried aloud to wake you, and sprang at his throat. What else could I do? He had a weapon, I had none. I clung to him like the puma; he struggled and struck me with his knife; but his hands were not free enough to do much harm. I pressed my fingers into his throat for very life —your life and mine. Until at last, in his pain, he lost his *think,* and dropped the knife. Then I knew you were saved."

Fray Fernando stretched out his hand to him. "You are a brave lad," he said; "God bless you!"

"Patre," said José, "say 'my son' as you used to do."

The monk was touched. "God bless thee, my son!" he answered warmly.

There was a silence; then José re-sumed,—"Patre, come with me to my people. No one will hurt you amongst them."

Fray Fernando started at the suggestion. A hasty "No" trembled on his lips; but he began to reflect that his present position was worse than perilous. What would the morning bring? Pepe's attempted crime could scarcely remain a secret. Should Diego pass it over, he would proclaim his own guilt; should he undertake to punish it, the Negro, in his despair, would re-veal everything. Clearly neither Diego nor Pepe had now any alternative but to complete their work. While a man might have repeated half a score of Paternosters, Fray Fernando pondered. Then he spoke in a decided, even cheerful tone, "José, I am going to Cuzco. Will you go thither with me?"

"To Cuzco" José cried in rapture. "Will the river go to the Mother Sea?"

"Not so loud. We must go at once, and in

silence. I must needs speak with our lord, Don Marcio Serra; and he lives at Cuzco."

"Chachau!" said José. The exclamation meant, "I am heartily willing, and very glad."

Then the monk began to put together the few articles he thought necessary for the journey.

"We need not be troubled with baggage," said José coolly. "The men will give us all we want by the way."

"And what of the way, José? How shall we find that I You know no more of it than I. You have only traveled along the coast, never towards Cuzco."

"The way, patre! How could we miss it? We have only to go by the road."

For if in the days of Roman ascendancy the proverb, "All roads lead to Rome" expressed an almost literal truth, it was yet more strictly true that in the empire of the Incas all roads led to

Cuzco. Their policy was, in the highest degree, one of centralization.

"Will you take the books, patre?" José inquired. He regarded his patron's books with almost superstitious reverence. Indeed, it is quite possible that he thought each of them possessed what his race styled a "Mother," or spiritual essence of its own.

"I will take this," said the monk, laying his hand on a Breviary. "Not the others."

Two bundles comprised all that the travelers cared to take; more indeed than José, who thought he had a child's right to everything he needed in Tahuantin Suyu, would willingly have encumbered himself with.

When his other preparations were completed, the monk took a key from the bosom of his frock, and unlocked a small strong coffer, placed for security in a kind of rude press which he had contrived in the wall of his hut. He took out some pieces of money; then paused for a moment in evident doubt. Something else was there, which he scarcely liked either to take or to leave behind; something which belonged of right to José, and which indeed his conscience told him he ought to have given him long ago. He had withheld it, fearing the memories it might awaken. But now all his precautions had been proved useless, if not worse. Better to do the thing that was right, without too much regard to consequences. "José," he said, showing him the curiously wrought pin he had received from Don Ramon, "do you remember this?"

"My mother's topu!" José exclaimed, eagerly taking it from his hand. For some moments he looked at it in silence, then he pressed it to his lips, while a tear glistened in his eye.

"Keep it," said the monk. "But we must not loiter now, for the hours of darkness are waning. Are you ready?"

"Let the patre wait but for a moment," said José. He fastened his treasure securely into his tunic; then, with some difficulty, caused by his only possessing the use of one hand, he took the crucifix from the coca-bag by his side. "This belongs to the patre," he said, with the air of a person a little ashamed of himself.

Fray Fernando wisely accepted the unspoken apology. He restored the crucifix to its place at his girdle, merely saying, "It is a precious symbol of a still more precious Thing."

Then they passed silently through the sleeping galpón; and, before the morning dawned, were far beyond the reach of the astonished Diego.

IX

The Journey

"The high Peruvian solitudes among."

~ HEMANS

Now did fray fernando and his young companion behold in all their glory "the works of the Lord, and the wonders of His hand." For their way to Cuzco led them across the mighty Andes. Of these Cerro Blanco, though in any other land it would have taken rank as a monarch mountain, was only a kind of sentinel, or advanced guard. It looked down protectively on the valleys beneath, but it looked up reverently to the white and shadowy peaks of snow which rose, one above the other, far as the eye could reach. Fray Fernando had been wont to think of the Andes as a "cordillera," or chain; now he knew them as a vast gigantic army—God's great army—at His creative word arising from the earth, and ranging themselves in what to the eye of man seemed magnificent confusion, but was majestic order in His sight, who saw the whole. "In His hand," said Fray Fernando, "are the high places of the earth, and the strength of the hills is His also. He, and He alone, telleth their number, and calleth them all by name; even as He doth the stars, which their ice-crowned pinnacles almost seem to touch."

As, in compliance with the advice of José, the travelers began their journey by descending to the vale of Nasca, in order to avail themselves of an Inca road from thence to Cuzco, they had occasion to traverse, and that more than once, each of the zones into which different gradations of altitude divide that wonderful region. They passed through valleys where tropical vegetation displayed all its gorgeous magnificence. There rose the giant palms, slender, tall, and graceful; there flourished many a wondrous flowering tree; there bloomed the magnolia, the cactus, the balsam, spreading out purple, white, or scarlet petals to the hot, heavily perfumed air; while "strange bright birds, on their starry wings," glittering with clear hard metallic luster, flitted from bough to bough, from blossom to blossom.

José, who took upon himself almost entirely the direction of the journey, gathered for his patron sweet dates, or luscious chirimoyas, looking like large green oranges. But he warned him that they must not linger in these valleys. "They are the abodes of fever," he said. And indeed Fray Fernando himself was willing enough to pass on to a purer and cooler atmosphere.

Marvelous was the beauty of their next stage. It brought them to the region of the Peruvian-bark tree, which José called quina-quina, with its light-green leaves and its little clustered flowers, rose-colored or white, filling the air with their delicious fragrance. But the cypress and the palm were the monarch trees of those primeval forests, and they gave shelter to an almost incredible undergrowth of vegetation. Their long slender stems were climbed to the very top by tangled lianas, with luxuriant leaves and gorgeous flowers. It was the land of flowers. There hung the large violet blossoms of the melastoma, there gigantic fuchsias drooped their graceful crimson bells; whilst beneath them blossoms of every hue enameled the living green of the turf. Fray Fernando could not help asking, "Is not this Paradise?"

Just then José stooped down, and from the

sweet tangle of flower-covered bushes selected and gathered a single spray. It was a cluster of curious slipper-shaped blossoms, bright yellow spotted with crimson—the calceolaria of our modern conservatories. "Amongst us," he said, "this flower means pity and kindness. With garlands of it, mingled with the can-tut[1] and the evergreen, our fathers used to crown the heads of the noble youths at the great belting festival, to teach them that as the sun brings forth flowers from the earth for the joy of man, their hearts should bring forth pity and kindness. But pity and kindness are gone now; the Spaniards have driven them away."

And then Fray Fernando knew that this was not Paradise.

Soon afterward they came to a land of giant trees. Many of them raised their mighty stems, like the pillars of a wonderful cathedral, a hundred feet in the air before they sent forth a sin-

---

1. Sweet-william

gle branch. Here a strange fit of home-sickness surprised Fray Fernando in the midst of Nature's richest glories. In the lower levels there was no perceptible change of season; eternal summer reigned supreme. But here it was autumn, and these giant trees were shedding on his pathway withered leaves, like those that used to rustle round his footsteps in the cork-groves of his native land. He began to feel an affection for them such as he never could have felt for the wonderful trees of the valley, whose great spreading branches kept their green the whole year round.

Yet another day's journey, and the travelers entered the region of mist and rain. Here were no great trees, but the perpetual moisture nourished a luxuriant growth of evergreens, of arbutus, and other flowering shrubs, in whose blossoms a bright yellow seemed the prevailing hue. José called this district the Puna, and hastened through it as rapidly as he might, un-consoled for the absence of Ynty by its numerous flowers, its verdant mosses, and its creeping mimosas.

At length they came to colder and more rugged regions, where the vegetation, at first abundant and pleasant to the eye, like that of our temperate zone, grew gradually poor and scanty. But Fray Fernando said reverently, that God had given the mountain to the beasts to dwell in. Here graceful fawn-colored vicuñas, and guanucos with long shaggy fleeces and mild camel-like faces, roamed at large, feeding on the ychu and alfalfa, that still grew in abundance. Pretty little piscaches, with bushy tails, startled by the footsteps of the travelers, ran to hide in the ychu; and here and there a plover flew screaming into the air above their heads. Once they saw a huge condor perched on an elevated rocky peak.

Thus for many days they journeyed onwards, now ascending, now in turn descending again. By-and-by they came to grassy table-lands, where herds of llamas or alpacas roamed about, either wild, or more often under the care of Indian shepherds. Where the nature of the ground permitted cultivation, the soil was well and carefully cultivated. Even on the steep sides of mountains terraces were constructed with ingenious industry. By means of these andenaria, as the Spaniards called them, many a hill, that in another country would have been a brown and sterile mass, was transformed into a beautiful hanging-garden, displaying every variety of production, from the rich tropical splendors that adorned the broad belts around the base, to the few rows of maize which were all that even the industrious Indian could persuade to take root on the narrow strip at the top.

The long journey was a very safe and easy one. For nearly all the way our travelers had only to use the excellent roads provided by the care of the Incas. Fray Fernando was not the first Spaniard who grew enthusiastic in his admiration of these wonderful works, executed without machinery, and even without iron tools. Passages leagues in length were cut through the living rock, precipices were scaled by long flights of steps, ravines were filled up with masonry, and rivers crossed by means of suspension bridges made of maguey—the native osier. At convenient distances all along the road tampus, or post-houses, were erected, where the wayfarers found shelter. José explained that, in the old times, they would have found entertainment also in many of these tampus; but since, to use his mournful and oft-repeated expression, "the Spaniards have changed all," they had usually to throw themselves on the hospitality of the Indians; and sometimes, in lonely places, to rely on the little store of roasted maize or of frozen potatoes (called *chunŭ*), which José never failed to bring as provision for the way. The

Indians were always kind and generous to wayfarers; but they had only to recognize José as a Child of the Sun, to induce them to lay the best their huts contained at his feet.

The hardihood and agility displayed by José during the journey surprised Fray Fernando. He made very little of the wound he had received from Pepe, though it was severe enough to have laid a European aside for weeks. But this was thoroughly Indian. No amount of walking or running seemed to fatigue him. Fray Fernando was by no means a match for him, and was always the first to propose a halt. José, compassionating his weakness, would frequently offer him some of his favorite coca, but this the monk always declined, from an unaccountable idea taken up by the Spaniards, that the use of the harmless stimulant was in some way connected with the superstition of the Indians.

From the extreme of supposing his pupil a child, whose simple thoughts he could read like an open book, Fray Fernando passed into the opposite one, of considering him a hopeless enigma. And, indeed, José, or rather, as the Spaniards would have called him—for they conceded the honors of nobility to the Children of the Sun—Don José Viracocha Inca, was a compound of so many heterogeneous elements, that his character might well be a perplexity. He was an American Indian, with nearly all the peculiarities that distinguish the aborigines of the New World from the natives of the Old fully and clearly developed. But races flower as well as plants. The flower of the American race—and a strange, rare flower it was—was surely that mysterious family, the self-styled Children of the Sun. Their origin continues wrapped in obscurity, but their moral and intellectual ascendancy has been written on the page of history, in the peace, the order, and the prosperity they secured to millions of their fellow-men. José was an Inca, and heir not only to the very peculiar character, but to the traditions of the sons of Manco Capac. But upon these had been grafted seven years of careful training in the white man's thoughts and habits, as well as in the white man's learning and religion. And, moreover, there was that within him for which neither race, education, nor training could fully account. Had he lived fifty years earlier, he would have been the foremost "haravec"[2] at the court of his great kinsman, Huayna Capac. He would have made sweet "yaravis "[3] for the Indian girls to sing, and more ambitious dramas to be acted before the Inca and his court. But the faculties which would then have found expression in song had now no exercise, save in the ever-recurring wail over those former days, which indeed were better than these.

This preponderance of imagination in his character was the real cause of his temporary

2. Poet
3. Songs

repudiation of Christianity (or rather Catholicism), and return to the faith of his fathers. But such a return could be only temporary, if indeed it was more than fancied. What Huayna Capac, on whom no gleam of the light of revelation ever shone, had been taught by the light of reason to abandon, could scarcely be held seriously by a youth instructed as José had been.

Fray Fernando saw with pleasure that his prejudices against Christianity were melting away, and that he was anxious to resume his studies. Often when they halted for the night he would eagerly take up the Breviary, and try to translate the Latin psalms and prayers it contained. He would frequently ask questions suggested by what he read; sometimes startling ones enough, betraying an acquaintance with facts; or rumors of facts, about the Old World, assuredly not learned from Fray Fernando. One day he asked: "Patre, do not the Jews also build great ships, and sail over the Mother Sea, even as far as this country?"

"Truly they are wanderers over the face of the earth, according to the just judgments of God," returned the monk; "but that they have come hither have I never heard. Who told you of them?"

"No one," answered José, who was caution itself in speaking of any rumors current amongst his own people. "But is it not true that they hate the Spaniards and the Catholic faith?"

"It is," Fray Fernando responded briefly. "They are an accursed race."

He did not know, until long years afterward, that José was confounding the Jews with the English!

During the past six months, José had found means to supplement the well-remembered lessons of his childhood, and to complete his acquaintance with the history, the customs, and the social polity of his forefathers. He failed not to improve the various circumstances of their journey into occasions for enlarging upon these topics to Fray Fernando. One day, for instance, an Indian chasqui, or messenger, shot past them like an arrow, his body bent forward, his burden on his shoulder, and his staff in his hand. "See the speed of that fellow!" cried the monk.

"That's nothing," said José, smiling. "In the old times, the Inca supped at sundown in Cuzco upon fish taken from the Mother Sea at Lurin the same hour the day before."

Fray Fernando knew the distance between Lurin and Cuzco—more than a hundred leagues. He said, "That is too much even for *my* faith, José."

"The Children of the Sun speak truth," returned José, a little offended. "Our chasquis," he continued," were trained to the work from their earliest childhood; and each had but a short way to run until he should be relieved by another. He had plenty of rest, and plenty of good food and chica; and he was stirred to do his utmost by the hope of reward, and of praise—that was better than reward. Was not that chasqui a happy man ever after, to whom the Inca once said with his own lips, Sit down, huanucu'?—The patre knows the huanucu is the swiftest of all creatures.—But this I say," added José with a sorrowful smile, "the Spaniards will find no man to run so fast for them, even for fear of the lash."

On another occasion they passed a melancholy troop of Indians who were being driven to their forced labor on a Spanish farm. José divided his little store of coca amongst them, and then complained bitterly to Fray Fernando of the hardship of their condition.

But the monk said it seemed not unfair that they should pay tribute in the form of personal labor. "I thought they did so," he added, "even under your Incas."

"True," replied José, " they tilled the lands of the Sun and of the Inca. But after this fashion: First, the lands of the Sun, as was meet and right. Next, the lands of the widow and the orphan, of the sick man, and the soldier who was fighting the battles of his country. Then each man tilled his own tupu.[4] These tupus were given them according to their need. If a man had a child born to him, he had a little piece added to his share of land. And they were all taught to help each other in their labor. Lastly, and not until all else was done, they tilled the Inca's land; such was the Inca's law. The work was a happy festival: men, women, and children, in their holiday dresses, thronged to the fields together; and as they drew the plow, or sowed the maize and quinoa, they chanted merry songs, or yaravis about the great deeds of the Incas. Always they had abundance of good food and chica. Neither in the field, nor in the

---

4.   Allotment of land.

workshop, nor yet in the mine, was any man's health ever known to suffer from the labor he did for his lords. And in all Tahuantin Suyu there was no man that had not food enough, and clothing suited to the climate in which he dwelt. The Spaniards know this.[5] Ask them, when you go to Cuzco, and they—even they themselves—will bear witness that never were a people more happy, more peaceful, more content with their lot, more loyal to their lords, than were we when they came to us. Why God, who governs all, let them come, He knows—I do not."

Nor did Fray Fernando. Long did he ponder over the problem thus set before him. For the first time in his life, a great grief and wrong,

---

5. "What is most wonderful is that all the labor and toil they used for their kings was their greatest delight and recreation; and such was the good rule and order observed in it that no labor was tedious, but rather of contentment and satisfaction."— Joseph Da Acosta (Other Spanish testimonies might be quoted, to the same effect.)

with which he had personally no concern, was sinking into his heart. He used to satisfy himself that the natives of the New World received a full indemnity for their injuries and sufferings in the introduction of Christianity, with its creed and its sacraments, by which their souls might be saved from everlasting perdition. But this thought was losing its power to content him. He was beginning to learn that wrong remains wrong forever, and cannot be changed into right by virtue of any benefits, real or supposed, which may eventually accrue from it.

That night, as they rested together in a deserted tampu, he said to José, "My son, it is not fit that I should conceal from you what I truly think. I think my people are verily guilty concerning yours. May God forgive us, and in His own time turn our evil into good."

José made no answer, and almost immediately went out to gather sticks for a fire. Yet never had Fray Fernando been so dear to him as at that moment. Nor had any single act or speech ever done so much to bring their hearts together as that one free and generous acknowledgment. So great is the power of truth between man and man.

X

The Dead Men Who Fought Against Spain

"If thou seest the oppression of the poor, and violent perverting of judgment and justice in a province, marvel not at the matter: for he that is higher than the highest regardeth; and there be higher than they."
~ Ecclesiastes 5:8.

THREE HUNDRED YEARS HAVE passed away since the men of the Old World spoiled and conquered Tahuantin Suyu. Those who did and those who suffered wrong have slept side by side for ages. The ancient Incas lie in glory "with kings and counselors of the earth, who have built desolate places for themselves, or with princes that had gold, and filled their houses with silver;" while their once happy subjects, doomed to toil in the service of the cruel stranger, have found repose at last, where "the prisoners rest together; they hear not the voice of the oppressor. The small and the great are there, and the servant is free from his master." And the men who robbed and tortured them, who made their fair land a desolation, until the cry of it reached unto heaven, and those who were left alive envied those whom the sword had devoured,—they also have gone to render account of their deeds before Him who is the Judge of quick and dead.

Do we still say with the Inca's son, "Why God allowed these things to be, we know not"?

Not altogether. First, let it he said, once for all, that beautiful-wonderfully beautiful-as the social polity of the Incas undoubtedly was, it was no more perfect than any other scheme which man has devised for making this earth the paradise it would have been if sin had never entered. Two defects may be specially mentioned; since these probably contained the seeds of dissolution for the whole magnificent and extensive fabric. The royal and privileged race—the Children of the Sun—stood too far above the people, and looked down on them from too lofty an eminence, as beings of quite another and a lower order. Not only had the Incas different ideas and traditions—it is said even a different language—but they had actually *a different code of morality* for themselves to that which they imposed on their subjects. Great liberties were allowed them: it is true that, in accordance with the beneficence which formed their distinguishing characteristic, they seem to have used them most mercifully,—yet still they used them. What were accounted vices in the people, were none in them; and here, perhaps, may really be found "the little speck within the garnered fruit" that, "rotting inwards," would by-and-by have slowly moldered all.

Moreover, the idea of freedom was unknown to them. While the Inca gave his subjects—and gave nobly, "as a king," to friend and foe alike—every other boon his hand could bestow, he never dreamed of giving them the rights of free men. Properly speaking, they were *not* men, they were children; to be cared for kindly, even tenderly; to be fed, and clothed, and housed; to have their work and their play, and plenty of the latter, duly apportioned them; and, in one word, to be made good and happy. It may be said, and truly, that in intelligence they *were* children, incapable of self-control and self-government. Still, the Inca's ideal fell below the Christian one in this, that he neither sought to raise them out of that condition, nor provided room for them should they desire to raise themselves. Under his system there was no growth, no freedom of choice; and there was to be none. Every man must be harm less, well-behaved, industrious, or there would be no room for him in Tahuantin Suyu. But a principle which should make a free man choose the good and refuse the evil, was amongst the things not revealed to the Children of the Sun.

But growth there must be, or decay will take its place. If the cruel white men from beyond the sea had not overwhelmed Tahuantin Suyu with swift destruction, it is still probable that the whole system would have melted gradually away, like a palace of ice, grand and beautiful, white and glistening with rainbow hues, but, from its very nature, unenduring. And the bloody civil war, which preceded and facilitated the conquest of the Spaniards, seems no doubtful indication of what might have taken place.

One such tyrant as Atahualpa [1] (who, it should however be remembered, was not a legitimate Inca) had it in his power to cause unspeakable confusion and misery, and to destroy the fruit of the beneficent labors of a long line of honored predecessors.

Perhaps, therefore, after all, it was not so dark and sad a fate for the Empire of the Incas to fall at once and in a single day almost from the very summit of prosperity, like a royal oak in the forest struck down by the tempest. If it was ever true of any empire (which is doubtful) that she "fell unwept, without a crime," it was true of Tahuantin Suyu. She and her children took, once for all, their place amongst the sufferers, not the doers, of wrong; the oppressed, not the oppressors. There can be no doubt which is the better place.

More to be desired was her doom, with all

1. Atahualpa, nevertheless, had some redeeming features of character; and it is almost certain that his cruelties were greatly exaggerated.

its anguish, than that of her destroyer and desolater, Spain. Here God's judgments are written on the page of history in characters of fire: " Woe to thee that spoilest, and thou wast not spoiled; and dealest treacherously, and they dealt not treacherously with thee I When thou shalt cease to spoil, thou shalt be spoiled; and when thou shalt make an end to deal treacherously, they shall deal treacherously with thee." As Spain did to others, so was it done to her. From the foremost place amongst the nations of the earth, she was cast into the depths of a degradation far worse, far lower than that into which she plunged the Empire of the Incas. She robbed the stores of an industrious people, destroyed their water-courses, deprived them of the means of subsistence. And from that day, even to the present, want, and scarcity, and cleanness of teeth in all her cities has been her own portion. Her very nobles, amidst their pomp and pride, have hungered and suffered thirst; the children of her chiefs and conquerors have pined away, and their eyes have failed them for want of those common fruits of the field of which, under the Inca's beneficent sway, every poor man had enough and to spare. Well have the Despoplados of Spain—bare, and brown, and barren—avenged the fertile plains of Tahuantin Suyu, laid waste by the cruel stranger.

The punishment sprang naturally out of the offense. The booty was a weight round the neck of the robber that sank him to perdition. It was the gold of Peru that ruined Spain. When she put forth her hand and took it, she took the curse of God with it. To the proud and idle Castilian, the lord of the New World, industry became the brand of slavery; commerce, a degradation; trade, the appropriate work of Jews and infidels. All those useful arts which make a people's prosperity and happiness were neglected or despised. And the treasure that undermined the life and the energy of the nation, supplied at the same time fuel to sustain the fire of that long conflict which was the passion and the doom of the Spanish monarchy.

In the contest that followed the Reformation, Spain was the great champion of Rome. Spain and England stand out before us during the last half of the sixteenth century, representatives of the principles that were contending for the world's future; and sometimes the conflict seems almost narrowed to a duel between them. Victory for Spain, meant victory for Rome; meant kingly and priestly tyranny; the inquisition, the rack, and the stake. Victory for England, meant an open Bible, free thought, equal rights, liberty of conscience.

And the tide of battle ebbed and flowed; and flowed and ebbed again. Sometimes it seemed as if the God of battles would declare for His own cause; sometimes it looked as though He stood aloof, and did not heed what men were doing on the earth.

But amidst the din and smoke of the fiercest conflict, the enemies of Spain were joined by a vast and shadowy host. Their voices no man heard, their faces no man saw, their footfalls were noiseless as the snow, "their arrows drew no blood." Yet were they valiant warriors, who did good service in the cause of England, of truth, of freedom. The men of the New World,—"the men thrust through with the sword," the men slain by famine, by torture, by excessive toil and cruel blows,—they it was who "arose, every man in his place," and fought against Spain. The tale of their wrongs and sufferings flew like fire from heart to heart, from lip to lip, and nerved the arm of the avenger. Both on the land and on the wave the strength of the Englishman became "the strength of ten," to smite down the cruel Spaniard, and to keep the fair homes of his native land from the men who conquered Tahuantin Suyu. Noble hearts, like that of Raleigh, burned over the wrongs of the conquered race, and it was their cherished dream, and his, to restore the Empire of the Incas.

But this work was not given to him, or to any man, to accomplish. In God's providence empires and dynasties pass away, and come not again. "The old order changeth, giving place to new." Yet not the less, from age to age, He is above all, the God that giveth to every man, and to every nation, "according to their works."

Still we must allow that dread mysteries, as yet but partially explained, underlie this and every other act in the great drama of human history. Questions arise within us to which man *can* give no answer, and to which God *has* given none—as yet. There are those amongst us who in secret "weep much," because the Book wherein are written the destinies of their race is sealed with seven seals, and no man is found worthy to open and to read it, neither to look thereon.

Let such accept the one thought of comfort that can avail to dry their tears: "Weep not; behold the Lion of the tribe of Judah, the Root of David, hath prevailed to open the Book, and to loose the seven seals thereof." None ever loved man as He did—He who died for man. Yet He knows *all*, from the beginning to the end. And He is satisfied.

Nay, more. He it is who shall be the Judge of man. Before His judgment-seat shall be gathered all nations—sons of Europe, who have known and dishonored Him; dusky children of the East and West, who have never heard His name. It is in His hand—the hand pierced for man—that the destinies of man are lying. Is there any heart amongst us not content to leave them there; not satisfied, to its inmost depths, by His own assurance, "What I do thou knowest not now, but thou shalt know hereafter"

XI

Across the Apurimac

An Inca king for Cuzco's throne
In victor strength shall rise.

LOOK, PATRE! WE HAVE BUT to cross yonder stream, and we shall have entered the sacred land where the golden wand of my great father Manco sank into the ground—the patrimony of the Children of the Sun. Let the patre hasten."

"I cannot hasten; I am weary." And Fray Fernando seated himself, or rather sank, upon a stone by the wayside.

The way was a steep, slippery descent, leading from the mountain's height to the

"Wide cane arch high flung o'er gulf profound,"

that spanned the rapid torrent of the Apurimac. José stopped, and looked at him with concern.

"It is a hard way, patre," he said; "but you shall soon rest. You see there is a tampu at the other end of the bridge."

"But for your help, José, I could never have come so far. To a stripling like you these mountain-paths are easy; not so to—"

"To an old man," he would fain have said; but he knew that his age, if reckoned by years, would give him no claim to the title: it was only in sorrow he was old.

"Lend me your hand once more," he added, rousing himself with an effort, "and I will try to reach the tampu."

José, who was agile as one of the vicuñas of the mountain, managed to keep his own footing in the most slippery spots, while he guided the steps of his companion to the safest places, and never failed to lend him the aid of his steady hand.

"Look there, José!" said the monk suddenly, in a tone of dismay. "Before us there is no path—no place for one; nothing but a sheer precipice. How, in Heaven's name, are we to reach the bridge? Your people must be birds, to travel by such ways."

"Our people trusted the Inca," said José, with a quiet smile; "and they knew that every way he made for them would bring them safely to the Golden City. There is a hole in the rock, and we are to go through it."

It was true. A tunnel, forty feet in length,

cut zigzag through the solid rock, and duly provided with steps, brought them safely and easily to the bridge. Even the weary monk was fain to gaze with admiration on the scene that met their view when they emerged from the darkness of the tunnel. Full three hundred feet below them the Apurimac dashed over its rocky bed between steep precipices; whilst the abyss was spanned by the graceful bridge of sogas, or cords of maguey, so light and apparently so frail that it vibrated in every gust of mountain wind, yet so strong that armies had marched over it without fear and without danger.

Nor was Fray Fernando conscious of fear, though he felt it tremble beneath his feet as he walked. He had crossed halfway when, in an unlucky moment, he looked down on the roaring torrent beneath. A sudden dizziness seized him; his limbs first lost their power, then shook with a nervous tremor that he could not control. In vain he laid fast hold on the rope of maguey, considerately hung breast-high over the bridge, and attached to it with cords for the greater security of the traveler. He could neither advance nor retreat; nor could he withdraw his eyes from the abyss, over which he seemed suspended on a thread. The sight had a fearful fascination for him. How many perplexities would be ended by just one plunge; not so much—one little step from the spot where he stood! The voice of the waters seemed to call him. But José seized his hand, and with friendly violence drew him onwards. Dizzy, faint, and sick, he reached the tampu at last.

He had been suffering all day from a severe pain in his head and neck, and now it became really agonizing. He was quite unable to partake of the roasted maize José had brought with him; and the tampu being as usual deserted, José had no means of procuring him any of the comforts he needed. He gathered, however, some of the ychu that grew near the place, and, spreading his cloak over it, made a kind of couch, upon which Fray Fernando was heartily glad to stretch his aching limbs.

"Just read the psalms for me," said the weary monk; "then I will pray, and try to sleep."

It had now become the custom for José every evening to read the psalms for the day aloud in Latin, and then, with the help of his teacher, to translate them into Spanish. By means of this simple plan, he was making fair progress in the language which he still believed to be that of the ancient Jews, and of the English. On this occasion the first psalm for the day happened to be the Seventy-first. He read it through without even a thought of its meaning, being occupied with his apprehensions about Fray Fernando. But the next—the Seventy second—arrested his attention. Glimmerings of its purport, which flashed on him through the veil of the Latin words, deeply stirred his soul. It seemed to tell of a great King—an Inca— who should rule in righteousness, befriend the poor, redress wrongs everywhere. But just as he was eagerly proceeding to the task of translation, the patre very effectually changed the current of his thoughts by exclaiming, "If this pain in my head continues, I shall lose my reason."

It was well that José's impassive Indian countenance did not betray the alarm he really felt. He had not the least idea what remedies he ought to use; and even if he had, how was he to procure them in that solitary, desolate place? He drew near, and put his hand on the monk's forehead. It was burning: so he took the cotton cloth in which he had carried the maize, dipped it in cold water, and laid it on the throbbing brow. The cool application gave temporary relief; and José, perceiving this, renewed it at intervals. As the air was chilly, he collected with considerable difficulty a supply of dry sticks (a few stunted bushes grew near), and made a fire.

After what seemed a lengthened period of restless pain and distress, Fray Fernando dropped into an uneasy slumber, which, however, grew gradually quieter and heavier. It lasted so long that his devoted attendant began to think he also might allow himself a little sleep; which he took, stretched on the ground at the sick man's feet.

The next morning was far advanced when Fray Fernando opened his heavy eyes. José, who had no doubt that he would awaken refreshed and strengthened, was greatly disappointed at the pain and weariness still too visible in his countenance.

"Where am I?" he asked feebly.

"Only two days' journey from the Golden City, patre," José cheerfully made answer.

"Many, *many* days from the Golden City—never like to reach it," Fray Fernando moaned.

"Of what can he be thinking?" thought José, in dismay. "Can he be raving?" He said aloud,—" You will reach it easily, patre, when you have had a day or two of rest. Would I dare leave you alone, and I would run and fetch help for you.

If God would but send some traveler this way! Patre, how does your head feel?"

"It still throbs wildly," said the monk, feebly raising his hand to it." What hour is it? How long have I slept?"

José answered both questions with as near an approach to accuracy as he could. Then the monk added,— "I have an impression that I talked in my sleep. Did I?" he asked uneasily.

"Never a word, patre. You only moaned, like one in pain. Patre, I wish you would eat some of my coca-leaves; they would do you good. Woe is me! I have nothing else to give you, save cold water and maize."

"Away with your coca!" said the monk sternly. "It would be a sin for me to touch or taste it."

"As the patre pleases," returned José, with apparent indifference. "But, I pray you, try to eat a little maize-just a few grains. I will make them hot for you in a minute; see what a good fire I have kindled!"

"Eat the maize yourself, my son; you must have needed it ere this."

"Oh no, patre; I have had abundance," said José, whose code of morality was not too high to permit what is often, though erroneously, called "a white lie."

The day wore on. In the afternoon the monk seemed better; and José, who keenly felt the discomfort, not to say the peril, of remaining longer in their present position, ventured to ask if he might not run at least to the nearest village to obtain food and other necessaries.

"I will run like the Inca's chasquis," he pleaded; "my foot shall not bend the blades of ychu as I pass."

He did not dream—how could he?—that

his patron was struggling, not alone with bodily pain, but with sore anguish and bitterness of soul. In this hour of weakness, Fray Fernando could not face the thought of being left to himself amidst that dreary solitude. In proportion as the world of man seemed far away, the spirit-world seemed near. José could not, at best, return before the shades of evening fell. And Fray Fernando *dared* not meet the darkness, with its strange

"Voices and visions from the sphere of those
That have to die no more,"
without the comfort and support
of a human presence.

"Wait till next morning, José," he said. "Then I shall be better or worse. In either case, I promise to let you go."

José waited, with the patience of his race. Hour after hour he sat by the fire, watching Fray Fernando as he dozed, and trying to put together the disjointed fragments of meaning gathered up from that wonderful psalm. The more he pondered, the more certain he felt that it told of an Inca— a King who should reign in righteousness, and be the Friend of the poor. But who was He? Had He reigned long ago over the Jews? Or, peradventure, was He still to come? José knew well that the Psalms contained many prophecies of future events. He would ask the patre the interpretation of this one. But he would take care so to veil his questions that the patre should never guess their real drift and object. For José, who loved Fray Fernando well enough to die for him, would yet rather have died than have allowed him to suspect certain hopes and dreams that lay hidden in the depths of his heart.

Towards evening the monk appeared so much easier that José ventured to propose reading to him.

"You may, if you like," was the answer. And

José quietly began,—"*Deus, justicium.*"

"You mistake," Fray Fernando said at once. "You read that before. This is the fifteenth evening of the month."

"Is it, patre?" José asked innocently. "Yes—no; I do not think I read this one. Not in Spanish, at least. 'Give justice, O God.'"

Fray Fernando's nerves were in that miserable condition in which the slightest jarring touch means torture. He felt it intolerable to lie still and listen to José's blunders. By way of correcting him, he began the familiar words himself,—" Give the king thy judgments, O God, and thy righteousness to the king's son.'"

"Ah, that is easy to understand," said José." But when I change the words for myself, I lose the first word before I find the second. If the patre would only go on, and recite it all for me!"

Fray Fernando had no objection. It was indeed far less troublesome to recite the well-known words himself than to hear José stumble over them. Coldly and monotonously enough, for his thoughts were far away, he repeated the words of that sublime psalm—words first of prayer—such prayer as any righteous king might fitly offer for his son and successor; then kindling and rising into a grand prophecy of a greater King than Solomon, a holier and more enduring reign than his; and ending at last with that fervent burst of thanksgiving, the noble and appropriate close to the prayers of David, the son of Jesse.

Crouched on the ground by Fray Fernando's side, and with eager eyes that never stirred from his face, the Indian youth drank in every word.

This was what he heard:—"' Give the king thy judgments, O God, and thy righteousness unto the king's son. He shall judge thy people with righteousness, and thy poor with judgment. The mountains shall bring peace to the people, and the little hills, by righteousness. He shall judge the poor of the people; he shall save the children of the needy, and shall break in pieces the oppressor. They shall fear thee as long as the sun and the moon endure, throughout all generations. He shall come down like rain upon the mown grass; as showers that water the earth. In his days shall the righteous flourish; and abundance of peace so long as the moon endureth. He shall have dominion also from sea to sea, and from the river unto the ends of the earth. They that dwell in the wilderness shall bow before him, and his enemies shall lick the dust.

The kings of Tarshish and of the isles shall bring presents; the kings of Sheba and Seba shall offer gifts. Yea, all kings shall fall down before him, all nations shall serve him. For he shall deliver the poor when he crieth; the needy also, and him that hath no helper. He shall spare the poor and needy, and shall save the souls of the needy. He shall redeem their souls from deceit and violence; and precious shall their blood be in his sight.'"

No longer could the delighted hearer keep silence. "Ranti, ranti! Capac Inca, Huacchacuyac!" (Hail, hail! mighty Inca, Friend of the poor!) he cried, springing suddenly to his feet.

"What is it, José?" asked the startled Fray Fernando, whose thoughts were recalled from the ends of the earth by this impassioned interruption.

"Nothing, patre," said José, resuming his seat, and his habitual manner. "Will it please the patre to go on? They are good words."

The patre went on: "He shall live, and to him shall be given of the gold of Sheba; prayer shall be made for him continually, and daily shall he be praised. There shall be an handful of corn in the earth upon the top of the mountains.' "— (And here the Inca's son beheld, through the happy tears that filled his eyes, the terraced hills of his fathers' land, with their waving handfuls of maize on the narrow ledges at the top, sure tokens of the industry and the prosperity of the nation.)—" The fruit thereof shall shake like Lebanon; and they of the city shall flourish like grass of the earth. His name shall endure forever: his name shall be continued as long as the sun, and men shall be blessed in him: all nations shall call him blessed. Blessed be the Lord God of Israel, who only doeth wondrous things. And blessed be his glorious name forever: and let the whole earth be filled with his glory. Amen, and Amen!'"

"Amen, and Amen!" José echoed. Then he said softly," Thank you, patre," and without another word went out.

He stood on the brink of the precipice overhanging the current. The moon was pouring a flood of light over the rocks, the mountains, the bridge; even the waters of the river, far beneath, caught the silver radiance, and glistened as they flowed along. José knew that his fathers called that stream the Apurimac—the Great Talker—because they dreamed of mystic murmurings in its noisy path, which, duly interpreted, would reveal the secrets of the future. Would that the Oracle would speak to him—but this once—and tell him who was that great Inca, that King of the East, who would deliver the poor when he cried! Had He reigned long ago, like King David, who was dead and buried in Jerusalem No; for it was said, "They shall fear Thee as long as the sun and the moon endure." Was He still to come? Or could it be that He was reigning even now? In the valleys amongst his own people, mysterious rumors passed from lip to lip about pale-faced bearded strangers, with golden hair, who should come from beyond the Mother Sea, and avenge the wrongs of the Children of the Sun upon the cruel Spaniards. Some called these people English, but perhaps they meant Jews, as when men said Castilians they meant Spaniards. The Spaniards slandered these their rivals, as was natural; saying that they were not Catholics, that they did not adore the Holy Cross, and that they roasted Indians and ate them. But those who knew better bore witness that they were always just and kind to the people of the lands where they came, and never did them any harm. Probably the tale that they were governed by a *coya*, or empress, came from the Spaniards also; for how could a woman govern a great and brave nation? Surely they must have a king! Why not the great King that David described in the psalm?

If he might only find that King, lay the wrongs of his people at His feet, implore His help for them! To accomplish this, peril would be light, difficulty nothing. Gladly would he do what none of his race had done yet of their free will—cross the Mother Sea, and plant his foot on the strange shores of which his fathers had never dreamed. Gladly would he die, slain by the sword or burned to ashes at the stake, like others of his people, if that would bring deliverance to Tahuantin Suyu, and set the rainbow banner of the Incas free once more to wave in the sunshine. Surely the Great King, if once he could but find Him, would be pitiful, for He should judge the poor and needy; and He would be strong to save, for His dominion should be from sea to sea, and from the river to the ends of the earth.

Once more he looked down at the foaming Apurimac. But in all its noisy tones there was no voice for him. Well he knew that the dreams of his fathers were but dreams, baseless and unsubstantial, to vanish when the morning light arose. Then he looked up to heaven. Quilla, the silvery spouse of Ynty, could tell him as little as the babbling stream below. But above—far above? There dwelt the Great God, who made Indian and Spaniard alike, who was blessed and praised in that wonderful psalm, and to whom, Fray Fernando told him, men might pray for help in every time of need. He knelt down, and clasping his hands, prayed his first real prayer,—"O God, teach me about the Great King, and help me to find Him."

That was all he said. But as he rose from his knees, and quietly re-entered the tampu, a calmness and a strength, never felt before, came down upon his perplexed, bewildered mind. It had its root in two persuasions, not clear enough to be expressed in words, but real enough to sink deep into his heart—that God would hear his prayer; and that he had now a purpose worth living for, and, if need be, worth dying for.

What They Did
Beyond the Mother Sea

"On my soul there fell
A horror of great darkness, which shut out
All earth, and heaven, and hope."

~ HEMANS

ALL WAS STILL WITHIN THE TAMPU, and José
had been asleep for some time, when Fray Fer-

nando softly called him.

He started up quickly. "Is anything wrong, patre?" he asked.

"No; if you are not sleeping, I should like to talk with you."

"Chachau!" (willingly and gladly!) said José, good-humoredly, as he threw the remains of his store of dry sticks on the fire, and seated himself beside it. The night was frosty, and his yacollo, or cloak, was beneath Fray Fernando.

Except for the dim light thrown out by the smoldering brands, the place was in darkness. Like most of the Peruvian buildings, it had no windows, and the door was closed.

Fray Fernando's voice came out of the gloom,—a little lower, slower, more restrained than usual. "I should like to tell you a tale of the things that happen in my country," he said.

"I like well to hear those tales patre," José answered.

"You will not like this one. It is sad as death—sadder!—sad as life."

José understood him. He knew what were the lives of the mitayos in the obregas and the mines.

Fray Fernando went on, still in the same quiet tone, like one treading the crust of a volcano with light and wary footsteps, lest perchance he should disturb the hidden fires beneath:— "In that land beyond the Mother Sea where I was born, José, is a great and fair city called Seville. There are noble churches and stately marble palaces, glittering white in the sunshine; and there are fragrant orange-groves and delicious gardens, fringing the banks of the bright river, loved of all Spanish hearts, the peerless Guadalquivir." And on that bleak mountain, at the other side of the world, Fray Fernando paid the tribute of a passing sigh to the memories of his sunny native land. "In that fair city," he went on, "dwelt the two boys whose story I wish to tell you. They were foster-brothers. One was of noblest lineage, and bore an honored name; his father's father had been amongst the conquistadors."

"I call not such lineage noble, but base," said José, forgetting for a moment his habitual caution.

"There you err," the monk returned. The conquistadors of Seville were brave men, who rescued the city from the Infidels, and planted the Cross where the Crescent had glittered for centuries, to the shame of Christian Spain. The memories of such a conflict stir the heart of youth like the sound of a trumpet, and the noble's son I speak of had his training in the midst of them. His foster-brother shared them also; his parents, though poor, were old Christians, respected by all in the district where they dwelt. That district was—but I shall have to speak of it hereafter. Pleasanter is it to speak of Melchior-gallant Melchior, with his handsome face, curling black hair, bright dark eyes, brave yet gentle heart. Fearless always, quick to resolve, strong to do and dare, impetuous yet persevering. He grew up a regular *majo*."

"What is that, patre?"

"A gallant youth of Seville, who ruffles it on the Prado or in the street, resplendent in velvet and silver lace, his dagger in his belt, his guitar on his shoulder, ready for a fight, a bull-feast, or a dance, and always ready to do homage to bright eyes and fair faces. Yet Melchior, festive as he seemed, was simple and pious, kind to his troop of young brothers and sisters, and never forgetting in his wildest moods to say his prayers, or to bring his offering to the Virgin's shrine.—Ay de mi!"

"Patre, you are forgetting the other lad, the young noble. You have not even told me his name."

"It was—Don Alfonso. Had they been brothers in blood, they could not have loved each other more. They shared the same sports, practiced the same exercises. Together they rode at the ring, wrestled, played with canes. Sometimes one excelled, sometimes the other; but they were never jealous, their love was too true. Together they dreamed of the future, and planned deeds of daring and high emprise. Sometimes Africa, sometimes Ireland or Flanders, oftener your wild Western World, José, was to be the scene of their exploits. Vain, idle dreams! One of them, at least, lived to thank God for the veil wherewith His mercy hides the coming days. But for it, life would be all suffering from its dawn to its close.

"As for Melchior, no shadowy forebodings dimmed his bright young spirit. He early gave his heart to a lovely girl, the beauty of the district where they lived, and accounted as good as she was beautiful. Great was his joy when, after an anxious wooing, he came at last to tell his friend that she had consented to bestow her hand upon him; and Señor Don Alfonso had to promise forthwith to dance the cachuco at their wedding. He was nothing loath, for he knew and liked the pretty little Juanita, and sincerely rejoiced in Melchior's happiness. He had dreams of his own at this time, moreover. There were sweet blue eyes, whose gleam made summer in his heart, and golden hair—"

"I did not think people of your nation had golden hair, patre," José interrupted.

"It is rare amongst us, and therefore perhaps more highly prized.—But to return to Melchior. Between him and the fulfillment of his hopes there was one great barrier. You cannot understand, José, how sorely, in the lands beyond the sea, men and women ofttimes suffer for the lack of those morsels of gold and silver you treat with such disdain."

"I understand very well, patre. They were poor. But why did they not ask the king? Surely he would have given them a little piece of land, enough to live upon." With José, the king was the" Deus ex machina, "who was to solve every difficulty, and set right every wrong.

"That is not the custom in Spain, "said Fray Fernando." Nor do we think it the king's business to provide for all his needy subjects."

"Then, "thought José," *he* assuredly is not the King who will deliver the poor when he crieth, the needy also, and him that hath no helper." He asked aloud," What, then, could they do?"

Fray Fernando answered,—" Don Alfonso at length suggested a plan which seemed feasible. His sisters, at his request, obtained a place for Juanita as waiting-woman to a noble lady, who was both rich and liberal; so it was hoped that after a year or two spent in her service, Melchior's bride would have something to call her own besides her velvet bodice and her silver ear-rings. Melchior, too, had his plans. He had already distinguished himself by coolness and daring in more than one bull-feast. —I have told you of the bull-feasts of Spain, José?"

"Yes," said José briefly. They were, to him, amongst the many incomprehensible things on the other side of the sea.

"Melchior dreamed of winning gold as well as glory by his feats as matador. In truth, he was far too daring. I sometimes warned him that he might tempt fortune once too often. An hour came when I wished to God that he had bled his young life out beneath the horse-hoofs on the sand of the arena!"

"Then you knew those foster-brothers, pa-tre?" asked José with interest.

"Yes," Fray Fernando answered. He re-sumed after a pause, and in an altered tone, "What comes next is not easy to tell. Yet it must be told. You know what heresy is, José?"

"Anything against the Catholic Faith— such as what the Jews believe," José replied promptly.

"Right. In Seville, just before the time I speak of, there had been many heretics, but they were discovered and punished by the Holy Inquisition."

"I pray you tell me, patre, what is the Holy Inquisition?" "A tribunal for the discovery, trial, and punishment of heretics."

"Are people, then, in your country punished for believing wrong?"

"Most assuredly. What can be more necessary and proper?" said Fray Fernando with decision, and perhaps with a little sharpness. "The lady whom Juanita served," he continued," though to all outward seeming truly pious, was in heart a confirmed heretic. And she dropped the subtle poison of her false faith day by day into the unsuspecting ear of the simple peasant-girl. Poor Juanita thought her words good and holy, and very comforting to the heart. In truth, these people often begin with good words, such as no Catholic could object to, and thus they deceive the unwary. You know what the Gospel says of wolves in sheep's clothing, José! Juanita used to remember what she heard, and repeat it all to Melchior, who dreamed of harm no more than she did. They were children, playing at the mouth of a volcano, gathering flowers unconscious of the fire that slumbered beneath, ready to break forth and overwhelm them.

"One day Don Alfonso came home from walking on the Prado. He was light of heart; the solid earth seemed air beneath his feet; for those blue eyes of which I spoke had beamed graciously upon him. He said within himself, I will cross the bridge of boats to Melchior's dwelling, and tell him.'

But as he took again the montero he had laid aside, his little foot-page came to say, Melchior del Salto is in the patio, desiring to see you.' Gladly did he go thither, but on entering, his mood changed in an instant. There sat

Melchior on the settle, his head bowed upon its oaken arm, over which his curled hair fell in disorder. His attitude spoke despair; and neither at the step nor at the voice of his friend did he move or look up. Don Alfonso's anxious and repeated questions at last drew forth the murmured answer, She's gone!'

"Gone!' reiterated the other, in utter bewilderment. Gone!—whither?—when?'

"Melchior spoke again,—' At midnight—the alguacils of the Holy Office.'

"José, you know not the despair, the dread despair, where *that* doom falls upon a loved one. They who sit and weep beside their dead,—they it is who are envied then. For we know, at least, that the dead are safe from the troubles of this miserable world—that they are in the hands of God, not of man., But years may pass before the watcher without hears so much as a whisper of the fate of him—or her—upon whom the gates of the Triana once have closed."

"O patre!" cried José in horror," is that the justice they do in your country?"

Fray Fernando now became conscious that he had said more than he ought to the unlearned Indian youth, thus "offending one of the little ones," as his class were wont to speak. So he drew the monk's frock over the man's beating heart, and hastened to explain:—"You must not think there is any injustice, José. God forbid. Their reverences, the lords inquisitors, are wise and holy men. Heresy is fearful sin, and when the Church has to deal with it, as one of her ablest doctors has most truly said, Severity is mercy, and mercy severity.'"

José listened with becoming awe. "But then, patre," he ventured to say, "that poor girl meant no harm. It seems hard she should suffer thus."

"You cannot understand," said Fray Fernando wearily. "Indians never can understand."

José was not at all convinced of the natural

disabilities or his race, but he was very anxious for the rest of the story. So he said presently, "Tell me about Melchior, patre."

"The dark hour that saw the gate of the Triana closed behind Juanita changed Melchior into another man. He grew moody, restless, sometimes even fierce. No more bull-feasts, no more festive walks on the Prado, no more dances in the evening—one absorbing occupation filled every moment snatched from work or sleep. Love alone could teach the patience with which day after day, night after night, he used to take his stand beneath the wall of that gloomy fortress. Not quite in vain. The first tears that relieved his breaking heart fell as he told his friend how he caught a glimpse of the face he loved—pale and changed—behind the bars of a grated window.

"Months passed; and Melchior's despair gave way to a fierce and frantic hope—a hope first whispered cautiously to Don Alfonso, but so eagerly shared by him that the flame was fanned to sevenfold strength. The suburb of the city where Melchior lived was close to the prison of the Inquisition, and took its name from it-the Triana. Though the Holy Office, for wise purposes, keeps its proceedings secret as possible, things must needs ooze out sometimes, and men will talk about them. At the particular time of which I speak, there was much indignation, especially in the neighborhood of the Triana, called forth by the robberies and cruelties of the head-jailer, Gaspar Benevidio—a wretch abhorred of God and man, and afterward righteously punished by his superiors. The Triana suburb abounded in lawless characters, many of whom, being of Moorish blood, were not particularly zealous for the Catholic Faith or the Holy Inquisition. Whenever Gaspar Benevidio went abroad, men scowled and laid their hands on their daggers, and women cursed him as he passed. Some of Melchior's friends of the bull-ring were often heard to murmur, "'Twere a better deed to send a lance through a hard heart than through a tough hide.' 'But what use in that?' Melchior would say. That would save no one. If now we were to attack the Triana, God only knows what we might accomplish "This was the project hinted to Don Alfonso. And he answered promptly, Do all that is in thine heart. I am with thee, according to all that is in thine heart.' Then they laid their scheme. In the midst of their madness they were prudent in details. They organized the conspirators, armed them, concerted signals, even corrupted some of the lower officials within the castle. At last came the night agreed upon.[1] Melchior and Don Alfonso headed the rioters—the latter disguised in his foster-brother's clothes, to save the honor of his noble house. There was an hour of fierce excitement, of wild fighting, of frenzied hope—then confusion, terror, despair. It

1. This riot actually took place, and from the cause assigned in the text.

was madness all—from first to last! As soon, José, might your people stand victorious against the might of Spain, as force or fraud prevail to rescue one captive from the dungeons of the Triana."

It was well, perhaps, that the monk could not see the "dark lightning" that flashed from José's eyes as he said, "Madness is strong, patre. *Did* they not rescue any?"

"None. The morning light found the rioters broken, scattered, flying. Most of them were themselves soon made prisoners of the Inquisition. Spite of all precautions, Don Alfonso's share in the matter was suspected; but his family sheltered him, and placed him in concealment. Of course, his career was ruined, his prospects blighted. And if *that* had been but all! But besides his share in the riot, a great and guilty secret lay upon his heart. He knew that in the conflict his hand had dealt a mortal blow to an alguacil of the Inquisition. That was a crime to rank with heresy itself. Like heresy, blood could not wash it out—fire must burn its stains away."

"I do not understand, patre," José said, half shuddering. The friar's answer was slow and faltering. "I mean, the punishment was—*death by fire!*"

"Horrible!" cried José. "Was Don Alfonso saved?"

"From *that* doom, yes. His relatives managed to procure for him, under a feigned name, a passage in a vessel bound for these unknown shores. It was the best they could do; and he was grateful for it—more than grateful, because they did not hate and curse him, though he had sinned against the Holy Inquisition. Father and mother blessed the wanderer—the last comforting memory left him to cling to."

Fray Fernando was silent, until at last José asked, "Where, all this time, was Melchior?"

"Don Alfonso often inquired after him;

and was assured that he was safe, and in hiding. But he believed too easily. In due time he embarked. The vessel dropped down lightly from Seville to San Lucar, a port on the coast; where she lay at anchor waiting for merchandize. Don Alfonso, standing at her side, gazed listlessly, through the golden evening light, on the quiet waters, and the low green shore, where the herds of oxen were browsing peacefully. From the shore came a little boat, with a passenger, whom business or pleasure had detained in Seville, and who, not to lose his passage, had ridden hard from the city. On board, he met an acquaintance, with whom he discussed the news of the day, walking up and down the deck, within earshot of Don Alfonso. But he heeded little; till at last a word was spoken that thrilled his soul. Today is taking place the great and long-expected *Auto-de-fe.*'"

"The—what, patre?"

José had to repeat his question. The monk

seemed unwilling or unable to answer.

"What is an *Auto-de-fe?*"

"A solemn sacrifice," Fray Fernando said at last; and he said no more.

"Let me make an end," he resumed presently. "The stranger named the names of the victims, as he had heard them from his uncle, a Dominican. Happily, Juanita was not amongst them. I suppose she died in prison. There were some notorious heretics, several foreigners. And at last—"

"Patre, what ails you? Are you ill?" asked José, who was himself trembling at the vague, imperfectly understood horrors of the tale.

"No," said the monk, lifting up his hand with a forbidding gesture, as José, now thoroughly alarmed at what the firelight revealed of his looks, seemed about to spring to his side.

He continued, though with evident effort:—" At last Don Alfonso heard the words

Melchior del Salto also is to be burned alive.' The sky grew black, and the earth reeled around him. Yet, gathering all his strength, he held himself from swooning, that he might hear the end.— Why *that* doom for him-never once suspected of heresy? '—The voices seemed to come from a great distance, but the words were clear and distinct.—' He dealt a mortal blow to an alguacil of the Holy Office. The thing was proved beyond dispute. The poor man lived two days; and though he had not seen the face of his assailant, he swore to the dress, discerned by the torchlight. Nor did the prisoner dai-ly the fact.'—At that word, Don Alfonso fell senseless. Better had he died thus,—save for his unhappy soul!"

"Patre," said José, with decision, "you shall tell me no more such stories. This one is killing you."

Fray Fernando wrestled in silence with some strong emotion ere he answered:—"

What is begun shall be ended. José, that man did not die. When consciousness returned, he would fain have thrown himself from the ship, and rushed back to Seville. But too late! All was over now, all gone—save blackened ashes. So he let the winds and waves bear him onward where they would, with broken heart, and memory filled evermore with the image of the brother who died for him."

"Did he kill himself?" asked José, whose race parted with life too lightly.

"No. He feared God, against whom, in His ministers, he had sinned most grievously. But he carried the mark of Cain on his brow—the doom of Cain in his heart. 'My punishment is greater than I can bear. Behold, Thou hast driven me out this day from the face of the earth; and from Thy face shall I be hid; and I shall be a fugitive and a vagabond in the earth.'"

"Poor, unhappy man! Does he live yet, patre?"

"It may be. To me it seems that, were he near death, he ought to confess his deed. Not simply to a priest, for his soul's sake, but also to some faithful friend, who for love of him would cross the sea, and, by revealing the truth, clear away the stain of infamy from the name of him who died in his stead."

"A faithful friend, who for love of him would cross the sea!" José repeated. "Has he such, patre? Then there is hope for him yet."

It was some time before Fray Fernando answered. When he did, his voice was choked and faltering, like the voice of one that wept. "Your words are wise," he said. "Perhaps wiser than you think. Never ask me more of this, José. Never speak of it, to me or to another."

"You may trust me, patre."

"I do. Now lie down and sleep."

José lay down obediently. But the command to sleep was more easily given than obeyed. Never in his life had he been more thoroughly awake. His mind was full of new, bewildering, fearful thoughts. What was this *Auto-de-fe*—this sacrifice which seemed a horrible execution? Did Christians then offer human sacrifices? Where and how had the patre known the Melchior—and, still more, the Don Alfonso—of his tale? Was he, perchance, the faithful friend of the unhappy young nobleman? Or—at last there flashed unbidden on his mind another thought, so frightful that he drove it away with all the force of his will, loathing himself for having allowed it even to enter his imagination.

XIII

The Doctors

"Patre," said José, as soon as the sun had ris-
en, will it please you now to permit me to run

to the nearest dwellings and seek for food?"

Fray Fernando did not refuse the desired permission; and José, delighted to obtain it, first made his patient as comfortable as he could, then started on his errand.

In a few hours he returned, accompanied by a party of five or six Indians, whom, with much apparent satisfaction and some ceremony, he ushered into Fray Fernando's presence, saying, "Here, patre, are the doctors."

The men were comfortably clothed, after the native fashion, in tunics, short trousers, and mantles, with bright-colored turbans, or caps, on their heads. But they looked worn and haggard, as men who followed a toilsome calling. Each had a kind of wallet strapped on his shoulders by a cord of maguey. The foremost of the group unbound his, and laid it at the feet of Fray Fernando, in token of his respect and desire to serve him.

But Fray Fernando naturally hesitated to

receive medical advice from those whom he accounted mere barbarians; and expressed as much to José. The latter assured him, however, that the doctors were very wise—very skilful. "They spend many months together in the forests," he said, "collecting herbs and plants of great healing virtue. Then they travel through the whole country, giving them in exchange for food or clothing, and making the sick men well. This knowledge has been handed down to them from the grandfathers of their grandfathers."[1]

Upon this, Fray Fernando, thinking it probable they would not poison him, and perhaps also thinking it little matter if they did, consented to allow one of them to examine him; which he did by feeling his pulse, not at the wrist, but at the top of the nostrils, and under the eyelids.

---

1. This hereditary guild of doctors still exists among the Peruvian Indians, and they still pursue their calling as described in the text.

José was soon informed in Quechua, which he translated into Spanish for the patient's benefit, that the patre's disease was the *sorachi,* an ailment to which travelers in those mountainous districts are liable. But the worst of the attack seemed to be over. The patient would be the better for pursuing his journey as soon as he felt at all able to do so. By the time he reached the plain he would probably be as well as ever. For his headache, he was to take a draft of herbs, and to use the powdered leaf of the *sayri,* a supply of which the doctor produced from his wallet. This was, in fact, the tobacco of modern Europe, which the Peruvians only employed as a medicine. José having hinted, however, that food was just then more needful to them than medicine, all the wallets were explored, and a sufficient quantity of parched maize, *chun□u,* and charqui (dried meat) was produced to make an abundant meal for the whole party. A portion of the latter was carefully cooked for Fray Fernando; but José and the other Indians did not use so much ceremony with their own food.

When the repast was finished, the "doctors" had some further conversation with their countryman; then they strapped up their wallets, and prepared to go their own way, from which they had been diverted by José's earnest entreaties that they would come to the aid of his sick friend. Fray Fernando asked José what recompense he ought to bestow on them. But José told him none was needed. "They are very glad to serve you," he said, "because you are my friend." There was no arrogance or assumption in this: it was the simple truth. The words, "Yntip Churi" (Child of the Sun), had a magic in them to bow all hearts in Tahuantin Suyu. Fray Fernando, however, gave the doctors a few silver coins, which were thankfully accepted; and they parted with mute demonstrations of respect and good-will.

When they were gone, José silently prepared and administered the prescribed remedies, replenished the fire, gathered together and put aside the food that had been left. That done, he sat down, and looked at Fray Fernando with the air of a person who had tidings, heavy tidings, to communicate.

"Of what are you thinking, José?" the monk inquired. He rather expected that José would urge him to get up, and to make some effort to resume his journey.

But José's thoughts were very differently occupied.

"Before they went away the doctors told me something," he said.

Fray Fernando asked rather languidly what it was.

"Nothing good," José answered sadly. "Another crime for the Spaniards, another wrong for the children of my people. The Inca is a captive."

"Whom do you mean by the Inca?" Fray Fernando might be excused for asking, since seven years had passed since José named in his hearing the exiled prince whose right it was to wear the llautu. Moreover, much confusion was created in Spanish minds by the fact that all the male descendants of Manco Capac were permitted to assume the cognomen of Inca.

"Whom should I mean but the sole Inca, Tupac Amaru? The viceroy has sent an army to Vilca-pampa. They have made him prisoner, and led him to Cuzco. Patre," José continued, with scarce an effort to conceal his deep anxiety, "you understand your own people. Tell me what they will do with him."

"How can I tell you, José?" Fray Fernando answered. And in truth it would have been hard for him to tell. But he knew something of the Viceroy Toledo, the kinsman of the notorious Alva, a stern, determined man, little likely to have taken the trouble of making the Inca a captive without a settled purpose and still less likely to shrink from executing that purpose, whatever it was.

"Three things are possible," José continued, thoughtfully, "The Spaniards may desire to wring from us yet more of those treasures they covet so madly. They are wise. If for the usurper, Atahualpa, we filled the great hall of Caxa - marca breast high with gold, we will not do less, sorely as they have robbed us since, for the true heir of Manco Capac. But my heart misgives me they have worse thoughts than that. They may keep him in captivity, or even send him beyond the Mother Sea. Either way, it would be his death; for his spirit is brave and free, like the condor of the mountain."

Fray Fernando knew there was yet another course possible to the Spaniards, but he did not care to name it.

José continued, "I can tell you at least what they will *not* do with him. What they did with

Sayri Tupac. To no deed renouncing the rights of his birth will the hand of Tupac Amaru be ever set."

"When we arrive at Cuzco we shall learn all," Fray Fernando said. "And, José, I will try to pursue the journey. I see we cannot remain here."

"The doctors have left food enough to last us for today, patre. Tomorrow, I hope, with God's help, you will be able to travel a little."

An expectation that was happily fulfilled. But Fray Fernando was still too weak to proceed far. He succeeded, however in reaching a little Indian village, where rest and refreshment were readily obtained.

Ten or twelve leagues of very mountainous country had yet to be traversed before Cuzco could be reached. It was not until the evening of the third day that the still invalided monk, with his Indian companion, stood at last upon one of the heights which overlook the ancient

City of the Sun.

Cuzco nestles at the head of a fair and fertile valley, which forms an angle between two mountain ranges. José, whose demeanor all day had been solemn and reverent, like that of one about to participate in some religious rite, long gazed in silence on the scene spread out before him. But Cuzco was not only the sacred city of his dreams; it was also the first city he had ever seen. The mass of buildings confused and bewildered him, until at last he turned with a sigh of relief to the snowy peak of Vilcanota, which rose majestically above the hills that bounded the valley on the other side. Yet he soon turned back again to gaze upon the city of his fathers—the home of his imagination, the goal of his longings. "And was *that* indeed the city? Was that beautiful Cuzco, the center and the heart of Tahuantin Suyu?" Here seemed only shapeless masses of building, tangled mazes of streets, and the flash of a river here and there amidst a wilderness of thatched roofs and tumbled heaps of stone. Nothing was like what he expected.

All at once, however, his eye kindled, his whole countenance lighted up. He laid one hand on Fray Fernando's arm, and with the other pointed to a rocky eminence on the north side of the city. It was crowned by three great semicircular walls of massive masonry, one within the other; and again within these were three lofty towers, built of light-colored stone. "Look there!" he cried in rapture. "Yonder is the great fortress of Sachsahuaman, built by my renowned forefathers. Yes, it is; ofttimes have I heard it described. Every wall, every tower, I know already." Long and fondly did his eye rest upon them; then he slowly turned his gaze to the other buildings, as if he would learn to understand them also, and imprint them on his memory. He felt no longer a stranger, but a child—a child going to his father's home.

Yet he entreated Fray Fernando to defer his entrance into Cuzco until the following day, that the Sun himself might welcome them to his own city. Fray Fernando looked on this as an instance of the childishness which seemed strangely interwoven in the tangled web of José's character with manly sense and feeling. Still, he granted the request, and all the more readily because he was very weary, and comfortable Indian dwellings were close at hand, in which they might rest for the night.

XIV

The Last Inca

"Oh, there was mourning when you fell,
In your own vales a deep-toned knell,—
An agony, a wild farewell
But that hath long been o'er.

"Rest, with your still and solemn fame,—
The hills keep record of your name;
For never can a touch of shame

Darken the buried brow."—

~ HEMANS

THE NEXT MORNING OUR travelers descended the hill, and soon found themselves within the precincts of the royal city.

As frequently happens, neither experienced just the emotions he expected. José was so confused and bewildered by the crowds which filled the street to overflowing, and thronged past him on every side, that he scarcely made an effort to look about him, and actually stood close to the temples and palaces he had dreamed of all his life without seeing them. His first impression was that the whole population of the city was escaping from some terrible calamity—a fire, an earthquake, or a flood. But recollecting that he had never seen a city before, and could not therefore be sure that this was not its ordinary condition, his apprehensions subsided, and he determined to hold his peace for the present. His fears, however, revived when he began to observe the downcast, tearful faces of the Indians, of whom the crowd was chiefly composed. Nor was he reassured on discovering that they were shared by his more experienced companion.

"José," said the monk, "something very extraordinary must be going forward here. Ask one of the Indians what it is."

Instead of making the inquiry at once from the next in the crowd, José managed to mount a large stone belonging to one of the Indian buildings which the Spaniards were demolishing, and from this vantage-ground surveyed the street. Noticing amongst the throng a white-haired, venerable-looking Indian, who wore around his head a cord of vicuna wool dyed carnation and yellow (the distinguishing badge of the Incas), he made his way, with much difficulty, towards the spot where he stood. But just as he was beginning to address him, a loud cry of terror drowned his voice, and he saw the Indians around scattering in all directions. Some hid themselves in the adjacent lanes and houses, the rest rushed wildly hither and thither-trampling upon each other in their panic.

The cause soon appeared. A young Spanish cavalier, dressed in shining armor, and mounted on a high-mettled horse, was spurring in hot haste through the crowded street, little regarding the lives and limbs of "los Indios." In any thoroughfare such a circumstance would have caused alarm and confusion, but it created a fearful panic amongst a people who had not yet overcome their superstitious dread of the "huge earth-shaking beast" that obeyed the white man.[1]

José at first gave way with the rest. But he

---

1. The ease with which the Spaniards made their vast conquests in the New World was owing, in great measure, to the awe and terror inspired by their horses, animals entirely unknown to the aborigines; it has been even said that it was the horse, not the man, that conquered America.

had seen horses in Nasca, and being naturally courageous, had successfully endeavored to
overcome his fear of them. Recovering self-possession, he looked about him, and observed
that a poor little Indian child, who had been
thrown down in the confusion, was lying almost beneath the horse's hoofs. To snatch it
from its perilous position, and deposit it safely
in the nearest of a dozen pair of arms, stretched
out simultaneously to receive it, was a minute's
work. In the next, José's hand was laid boldly
upon the rein of the reckless rider. "Have a care
how you ride, señor caballero," he said in Spanish; "we have all lives and limbs to lose, worth
as much in God's sight as your own."

The youth, for he was no more—a very
handsome young Spaniard, with fine, haughty,
aristocratic features, dark, curled hair, and the
first down on his blooming cheek—cast a look
of amazement upon "El Indio," who dared to
remonstrate with him, and in such good Cas-

tilian. Then, flushing with anger, he raised his riding-whip. "Curse your insolence!" he cried. "Let go my rein, you Indian dog."

Don José Viracocha Inca had not come to the city of his fathers to be treated as a slave. He instantly snatched the whip from the hand of the Spaniard, whose keenly-tempered blade leaped the next moment from its scabbard and flashed in the sunlight. Fatal consequences might have followed, had not one from the crowd laid a strong hand on José's shoulder, and, partly by force, partly by a few words—brief, but of momentous import—whispered in his ear, drawn him away from the scene of conflict. The whip fell to the ground, and one of the bystanders picked it up and gave it to its owner; who spurred on to the great square, lest he should incur a severe rebuke from his senior officer, and still more, lest he should miss the tragedy about to be enacted there.

Meanwhile José turned a blank, terrified

face to the old Indian with the fillet of vicuña wool—for he it was whose friendly violence had extricated him from his perilous position.

—*"The Inca?"* he repeated; "what is it you say of the Inca?"

"I say of you, that you are a brave youth, but that this is no time to show it, when the eye of every man in Cuzco is dim with tears for the Inca."

"The Inca?—Do I hear aright? Speak once again, my father."

"While I speak, they are leading the Inca to his death in yonder square."

"Alalau! Dare they do such a deed?—even the Spaniards? —What is his crime?"

"He has refused to touch Spanish gold," said the old man bitterly. "From hands red with his people's blood he would accept nothing. So at last they give him the one gift he cannot re-fuse-the stroke that sends him to the mansions of his Father the Sun."

To José it seemed as if the sun itself had suddenly become black in the heavens. To him the Inca was as truly a part of the unchanging and unchangeable order of things as the light that ruled the day. Gladly would he have laid down his own head on the block instead of his.

"Let me look on his face," he exclaimed at last; "I have never seen him."

"Come," said the other briefly; and together they threaded their way through the crowd to the great square.

In the old times, when the Inca made his royal progress, the spots where his golden litter rested took a new name from that auspicious hour. Eager thousands thronged around, rending the air, and, as the historian says, "bringing down the birds" with their joyful acclamations; and a happy man was he who was so favored as to behold the face of his prince and lord. *Now,* instead of the golden throne, there was a grim scaffold draped with black; instead of shouts of joy, there were groans and lamentations, and "noise of weeping loud." Yet the devotion of the nation's heart burned on unquenched. Because the homage rendered was not born of fear, but of love, it survived all outward change, all circumstance and pomp of golden thrones, and armed guards, and costly apparel, and was poured forth, only more richly than ever, at the feet of the despoiled and fettered captive on his way to death.

With hands bound, and halter round his neck, the son of Manco Capac ascended the scaffold. His face was calm and his step firm. He was not unworthy of his royal ancestors, who had ever braved death dauntlessly on the battle-field. Yet Tupac Amaru, still in the morning of his days, keenly felt the injustice of his doom. Looking down upon the sea of up-turned dusky faces, he raised his fettered right hand, with the palm open, then slowly lowered it again, mutely commanding silence.

And silence, sudden and complete, fell upon that great wailing multitude. It was "as if there had not been one soul left alive in the whole city." So was obeyed the Inca's last command.

"Let it be proclaimed to all the world," said Tupac Amaru, "that I have done no wrong, and that I die only because it is the pleasure of the tyrant."

Then he knelt down on the scaffold, clasped his hands, and raised his eyes to heaven. "O God!" he cried, in his native tongue, "behold how mine enemies rob me of my blood!"

There was a minute's pause; then the silent gliding forward of a hooded, black-robed figure; then the gleam and flash of steel. Then a wail of anguish—the cry of a great nation's broken heart—that arose from the crowded square of Cuzco, and swept on and on till it reached the most secluded hut of the distant Andes.

The last sands of the glorious dynasty of Manco Capac had run out. There was no more an Inca.

The murder of young Tupac Amaru deserves to be remembered, not because it was the most cruel of the misdeeds of the conquerors of Tahuantin Suyu, but because of the innocence of the victim, and because of the hopes that were buried in his grave. How, after that day's tragedy, could the Indians continue to cherish in secret the fond belief that the true heir of Manco Capac reigned still in the wild forests of Vilca-pampa, and that one day he would issue thence in victorious might to recover the throne of his fathers?

Yet hope is hard to kill. It may lie in seeming death, and be laid in the grave; but if inspired by love it will rise again, partaking of love's immortality. There was no more an Inca. But not the less did the Indians whisper to each other, "The Inca will come again." Only henceforward the restoration of the loved dynasty became not so much a political hope as an article of religious faith.[2]

---

2. The "last of the Incas," Tupac Amaru, who died as above related in 1571, must not be confounded with a far more remarkable character, the heroic and unfortunate Inca chieftain, José Gabriel Condercanqui, who assumed the name of Tupac Amaru, and led his people in their last gallant struggle for independence towards the close of the eighteenth century.

The Golden City

"How princely are thy towers,
How fair thy vales, thy hills how beautiful!
The sun, who sheds on thee his parting smiles,
Sees not in all his wide career a scene
Lovelier, nor more exuberantly blest
By bounteous earth and heaven. The very gales
Of Eden waft not from the immortal bowers
Odors to sense more exquisite than those
Which breathing from thy

> *groves and gardens now*
> *Recall in me such thoughts of bitterness.*
> *The time has been when happy was their lot*
> *Who had their birthright there; but happy now*
> *Are those who to thy bosom have gone home."*
>
> ~ SOUTHEY

THE VOICE OF JOSÉ'S WHITE-HAIRED guide mingled in the great wail that rose from the square of Cuzco. Then the old man bowed his head and wept, José also weeping with him.

"Come home with me," said the Indian noble at last, as the crowd began slowly to disperse."

"We are kinsmen," José answered, and told his name, then briefly recapitulated his pedigree.

"I also am of Viracocha's ayllu," said the Indian." My name is Yupanqui.[1] And here," he added presently, "is my house." For Yupanqui's

---

1. Literally, you shall count; but used to mean virtuous, excellent.

dwelling, like most of the palaces of the Inca nobility who resided at Cuzco, opened on the great square.

José followed his conductor into a low, one-storied building, formed of massive blocks of stone fitted into each other with wonderful accuracy. The doorway, wide near the ground, sloped gradually inwards, the lintel being considerably narrower than the threshold. A kind of passage brought them to a court, into which many similar doors opened, each leading to a separate chamber. This arrangement was rendered necessary by the absence of windows.

The old Inca conducted his guest into one of these chambers, which was spacious, and adorned with richly-colored hangings of llama's wool. There were also niches in the walls, containing a few ornaments of gold and silver—not many, for Spanish cupidity must not be tempted: the less men had, or were thought to have, the better for them in those days. On the ground were seated a group of women of all ages, weeping and wailing, and making sore lamentation for the Inca.

On a raised seat in the midst were two young girls dressed in robes of pure white, bordered with yellow, woven of vicuña wool, soft and fine as silk. Their black and glossy hair hung over their shoulders in long plaits, while the symmetry of their slight, graceful forms, and the dark beauty of their delicate features, fully justified the admiration of the high-born cavaliers of Spain for these daughters of the Sun. A delicious sensation stole over the heart of José: it was as though he heard the spirit-music of the desert of Achapa, which surprises the weary traveler at sunset, coming he knows not whence, and passing he knows not whither.

He stood apart, a silent spectator. The conversation between the old Indian, his grandchildren, and their attendants, gradually revealed to him much of their history. He came to understand that one of these girls had been destined to occupy the high position of Coya (empress, or chief wife) to the murdered Inca. But some time elapsed before he could tell which, since the grief of both seemed equal. When the younger, still almost a child, clasped her small hands, and raising her dark, tearful eyes to heaven, prayed God to avenge their prince, José said within himself, "Surely this was the Inca's choice. No marvel,—she is surpassingly lovely" But he was mistaken.

Soon afterward, turning to her sister, who sat silent, her face for the most part hidden in her robe, she said, "Sumac, my sister, above all things I pity you that you cannot die with him, as they used to do in the old days—the good ones."

Then Sumac raised her head, and in a low, quiet voice made answer:—"Indeed, Coyllur,[2]

____

2. In Quechua, Coyllur means a star; Sumac, beautiful.

that would be very sweet to me now. But—I
am afraid."

"Afraid!" Coyllur repeated in evident surprise; for never had the Children of the Sun
been known to fear death for, or with, those
they loved. "Afraid!—Of what?"

"Of the Lord Christ—that if I come to the
gate when He has not called, He will not let
me in."

"Then they also are Christians," thought
José.

But Coyllur, who evidently did not quite
understand her sister, presently resumed, in
tones of passionate grief, yet with a kind of
rhythm in her sweet voice, that made the words
half a song, " Alalau! my sister, my heart is very
sad for thee. For thou shouldst have sat on the
golden throne beside our prince and lord; sharing his dominion and his splendor, as Quilla,
the spouse of the great Ynty, shares the glory
of the sky with the lord of day. And, hereafter,

thou shouldst have had thy place on the awful thrones in the Curi-cancha,[3] where sit the Incas and the Coyas of days gone by, each with the royal robe, the llautu, and the scepter; and the grand, calm face, sealed with the majesty of death, that changes not throughout the ages."[4]

"Nay, but, Coyllur," Sumac's low voice interrupted, "do not talk thus. I never cared for being Coya; I never thought that he was Inca; I only knew that he was good and brave. Had

---

3. Temple of the Sun.
4. The Peruvians were as successful as the ancient Egyptians in the art of embalming the dead. The bodies of all the Incas, from Manco Capac downwards, were placed in the great Temple of the Sun at Cuzco. There each sat in state, in his royal robes, the llautu on his head and the scepter in his hand; his Coya being seated opposite. At the approach of the conquerors the natives removed and concealed them; but the bodies of the three greatest Incas-Viracocha, Yupanqui, and Huayna Capac-with those of their Coyas, were afterward found, and honorably interred, even the haughty conquerors baring their heads in silent reverence as they were borne past.

he been a yanacona,[5] all would have been the same."

But here José's attention was diverted from the conversation by the hospitable cares of Yupanqui, which were not forgotten or omitted even in that hour of overwhelming sorrow. The old Inca caused an attendant to bring him two golden cups, of exactly the same size and shape. These he filled with chica, and having given one to José with his right hand, emptied the other himself. José, out of courtesy, did likewise; but he declined other refreshment, for it was meet that all who loved the Inca should keep solemn fast that day.

The next morning he told his host that it would be necessary for him to go in search of "the patre," whom he had lost in the crowd on the preceding day.

"No great loss;" the old Indian remarked dryly. "If you want patres, you can find them

____

5. Slave

here, all kinds-black, white, and gray. They swarm like ants, building their nests on the ruins of our fathers' palaces."

José explained that his patre was very unlike the others, and paid a grateful tribute to the benefits he had received from him.

"He did well to make a Christian of you," Yupanqui admitted, with the sad tolerance of despair. "I also took care to have my grandchildren baptized. But for myself, I am too old to learn the white man's religion."

"My soul is ofttimes cut in two about these things," José acknowledged candidly. "Yet the white man's faith seems good to me, and I truly believe all that the patre has taught me of its mysteries."

"So say my kinsmen and my grandchildren. They have been taught by the Holy Virgins, and Sumac often prays me to listen to their words. But I answer that what was good enough for the kings and heroes who were my forefathers is good enough for me. When I die, I would rather go where they are than to the cold, strange heaven of the Spaniard.—Do you know where to find your patre?"

"I know that he intended to go to the house of a great Spanish lord, the owner of the land where we dwelt— Don Marcio Serra de Leguisano."

"Him he will not find here. His wife is our kinswoman, aunt to the children yonder."

"How that? She is a daughter of Huayna Capac."

"So was their mother, dead these twelve years. They are of Viracocha's ayllu through their father, my only son—dead also; of Huayna Capac's through their mother. Don Marcio is a good man, for a Spaniard. He prayed the viceroy, on bended knees, to spare the Inca's life. When all was vain, he would not see the crime he could not prevent. He and the princess his wife are far away."

"What shall I do then to find the patre? Must I stand in the street and watch for him? He is sure to pass some time."

Even the phlegmatic Indian could not forbear a grave smile at the expedient José's ignorance in the ways of cities suggested. "You might watch for him until the great flood comes again," he said. "Nay, like always goes to like. Seek him at the house where the monks of his sort live."

"He is a gray friar, of the Order of St. Francis."

"One of my servants shall bring you to their house. It is built, like the rest, on the ruins of an Inca palace."

"I long to walk through the city. I have been dreaming of it all my life."

"Dreaming is dangerous in these days," said the old Inca. "Yesterday's scaffold was no dream, but dreaming brings a man to that,—or worse."

"There be many things worse," José remarked. "What Sayri Tupac did, for instance."

"Well said, Child of the Sun," Yupanqui answered, with grave approval. "Come, we will walk through the city together."

Under the guidance of his new friend, José traversed the great square, the "pleasant hill" of the Incas, through the center of which the Huatanay flowed, crossed by numerous footbridges of stone. Then he ascended the height of Sachsahuaman, and explored, with mingled pride in the past and bitter indignant sorrow for the present, the ruins of the great Inca fortress. He made Yupanqui point out to him the spot whence his grandfather flung himself into the Colcampata.

Thence they looked down on the whole city, which lay beneath them spread out like a map. "There," said the old Indian—" there once stood the glorious Curicancha, glittering with gold and gems. What you see now is the temple and house of the Black Monks. Yet the wall on one side is still standing. Look, you may know it by its dark color."

"But the grand golden door and cornice, the massive golden vases, the emerald-studded sun—"

"You see all the spoiler has left," Yupanqui interrupted gloomily." Yonder was the palace of our father, Viracocha. The Christians have built their great temple on its ruins. Those lofty buildings are all theirs. They take our houses, that have better walls than they can make, and set their outlandish towers and balconies upon them, as if the roofs that sheltered princes and heroes were not good enough for them."

All this, and much more, was poured into the ears of José', while his eyes were feasted (a mournful festival!) with all that remained of the glories of the City of the Sun. When, after traversing nearly the whole town under Yupanqui's guidance, he reached at last the gate of the

Franciscan monastery, his heart was more full than ever of the wrongs of Tahuantin Suyu and the crimes of the white man.

The doorkeeper informed José that Fray Fernando had left Cuzco that morning; then asked if he were Don José Viracocha Inca, and on receiving his answer handed him a billet from the monk. This informed him that Fray Fernando, on reaching the Franciscan monastery, found a summons awaiting him from the prior of his order at Lima. The command did not brook delay; but it was a fortunate circumstance that Don Marcio Serra's country residence lay almost in his way, so that he need not forego the opportunity of obtaining speedy justice for the poor Black people at Cerro Blanco. He added, that as he did not yet know whither the prior might intend to send him, it seemed best for his dear son José to remain with the friends he was certain to find or make at Cuzco amongst his own people, till he should write directing him to rejoin him, which he would not fail to do as speedily as he might.

José keenly regretted this sudden and unexpected separation from his beloved patre. Yet, dearly as he loved Fray Fernando, that love opposed, after all, but a feeble barrier to the fascination with which his own race was once more drawing him into its bosom. The spell of its memories, full of glory—of its wrongs, its hopes, its passions—was laid upon him more strongly than ever. Day after day did he spend wandering up and down the streets and squares of the ancient city, the home of his fathers, examining, with the eager eye of enthusiasm, the ruins of temple, palace, and fortress, until he knew almost their every stone by heart. Then he would return to Yupanqui's house, to drink enchantment of another kind, as he listened to the sweet Quechua songs of the young princesses, interchanged his store of national legends with theirs, admired their skillful spinning and weaving, or aided them in their more graceful work of fashioning artificial flowers from thin plates and wires of gold and silver.

He soon became aware that the dwelling of Yupanqui was a gathering-place for those of the Inca family residing at Cuzco who still in their hearts detested the rule of the Spaniards; as was the palace of Prince Paullu on the Colcampata for those who cheerfully accepted the present state of things. Yupanqui's guests would drop in—usually by twos and threes—to share the frugal evening meal of the family, who, like all the Incas, only ate twice a day—in the early morning, and again at sundown. When, after they had partaken of the boiled maize seasoned with red pepper, the bitter herbs, and the charqui, chica was brought in, each would dip his finger in his cup and sprinkle a few drops in the air by way of thanksgiving. Then, as they drank together, their conversation was sure to turn upon the former days that were better than

these, and the crimes and cruelties of the Spaniards. José soon made friends amongst them,
and ere long was on terms of the closest inti-
macy with his dusky cousins, Don Fernando,
Don Juan, and Don Diego, whom however, he
always called by more uncouth and less familiar
ancestral names.

They had all accepted the outward badg-
es of Christianity; indeed, the rites of their
old religion were now forbidden by the conquerors. Yupanqui was almost the only person
who contrived to evade their laws; or else his
disobedience was connived at by the authorities through special favor. But in fact nearly
all the Inca Indians had received the new faith,
not only willingly, but joyfully. José, himself
a heathen in his early childhood, and of late
well-nigh moved to cast off Christianity again
by the enormities he had witnessed in its pro-
fessors, felt and expressed some astonishment
at the unaffected (though unenlightened) de-

votion of his kinsmen. But an old Inca, named Maricancha, an intimate friend of Yupanqui's, and certainly no well-wisher of the Spaniards, took him gravely to task for his irreverence. "You must indeed have been bred in the desert, young man," he said, "if you never heard the last charge of the great Huayna Capac, when, in dying, he left his peace with us. These were his words, hearken well to them: In a few years after my death a new nation will invade you, and they shall become your lords and masters. Wherefore I charge you to serve them as men; for their Law is better than yours.' It was because of these words (confirmed by many omens of strange significance,[6] which I will relate to you at a more convenient season), that, when the Spaniards came to us, we received them as messengers from heaven. We thought them the sons of Viracocha, who appeared to your father in the plains of Chita; wherefore to

6.   The Peruvians paid extreme regard to omens, and were very superstitious about them.

this day many of us call them Viracochas. And we would not hurt or offend them in any wise, but obeyed them, and believed all they told us. In truth, we were never conquered,—we were betrayed. Even at Caxa-marca, when they fell upon us without cause and without warning, in the midst of a peaceful discourse, and slew us by thousands, was there one of us that so much as raised his hand against them? Those who stood around Atahualpa (whom they esteemed for their Inca) shielded him with their own bodies, and died in silence like the rest, but never struck a blow. Since then the Spaniards have heaped upon us misery after misery. They themselves, we suspect now, are the children, not of Pacha-camac, but of Supay. Still, their Law is good and true, and it is the will of Pacha-camac that we should receive it."

Yet these Indians had but a very imperfect knowledge of the faith they professed so heartily. It had not been difficult for them to pass from one religion of forms and ceremonies and outward observances to another. Their children were sprinkled with water instead of having their first hair cut; their youths were confirmed instead of being belted; they kept fasts and festivals with different names and at rather different seasons, but much in the same manner as their fathers; they offered cakes and flowers to the Madona instead of to Quilla; and whereas they had been used to pay homage to canopas and huacas, they now adored equally numerous santos and santas. Little had been done by their instructors to stir their intellects; less to touch their hearts. Instead of the bread of life, for which they asked, the conqueror gave them a stone.

It could not have been otherwise. God honors not hands like those of the conquistadors of Peru to build His spiritual temple; nor lips like those of the notorious Valverde, the first bishop of Cuzco, to carry His message of peace and good-will to men. But it would be unjust to forget that amongst the Spaniards there were some, both Churchmen and laymen, who not only deplored in secret, but dared to denounce openly, the crimes and cruelties of their compatriots. All honor to these truly noble men, who, if they could not redeem the Spanish name from infamy and the Spanish race from just retribution, at least delivered their own souls. In rebuking the sins of their countrymen, they bear mournful and emphatic witness to the conquered race, that they were a people singularly apt to learn, if their conquerors had only been as apt to teach. "If God in past times," writes one such large-hearted Spaniard,[7] "had granted them men who with Christian zeal would have given them a full knowledge of our holy religion, they were a people very open to good impressions, as their works testify, which remain to this hour." But the burning anathe-

---

7. Sarmiento

mas that fell from the lips of divine love against those "hypocrites who shut up the kingdom of heaven against men, neither going in themselves nor suffering them that are entering to go in," belong not alone to the scribes and Pharisees of old;—they are the portion of all who tread in their footprints.

XVI

A Star

"And I—my harp should prelude woe—
I cannot all command the strings;
The glory of the sum of things
Will flash along the chords, and go."
~ TENNYSON

EIGHT OR NINE MONTHS have glided by, all too swiftly, since José Viracocha became an inmate of Yupanqui's home, and no tidings from Fray

Fernando have reached him yet.

One afternoon he turned his steps as usual to the cheerful apartment where the princesses, or *mŭstas,* were to be found. The maidens were seated near the open door; for the daylight was precious, and not too large a share fell to the lot of the Children of the Sun in dwellings built by themselves. Sumac was diligently at work on some golden flowers. Coyllur's hand was upon her much-loved tinya—the national Peruvian guitar of seven chords. Both were still dressed in soft, fine robes of gray, the Incas' mourning, for the head of their royal house; but Coyllur wore ornaments that Sumac had discarded. Bands of gold, interwoven with her beautiful hair, relieved its glossy blackness; which was still further set off by a simple yet tasteful wreath of red and white begonias.

Both sisters looked up as José entered; but Sumac immediately resumed her work, without the slightest change of expression in her worn and sorrowful face, while Coyllur's large dark eyes beamed with redoubled luster, and a visible blush kindled her features through their soft, dusky hue. José saw no one but her. He approached, and, with tender reverence in his look and manner, laid at her feet a small fowling-piece. But the young lady glanced rather doubtfully at this token of homage.

"Are you quite sure, Viracocha," she asked, "that his mother is not still inside?"

She merely meant to inquire whether the gun was not still loaded; the Peruvians styling the spiritual essence which they believed to inhabit most inanimate things their "mama," or mother; and Coyllur, not unnaturally, supposing the charge the spirit of the gun.

"Coyllur nũsta must know that her slave Viracocha would turn the fire-breathing club ten thousand times against his own breast, rather than suffer it to hurt a hair of her head," was José's answer.

"Viracocha should turn the fire against the enemies of his people."

"Perhaps, one day—if a star shines on his path to guide him."

The star beamed brightly enough upon him at that moment: though Coyllur's lips were sealed by pride and maidenly reserve, she was too young and artless to silence the mute eloquence of her eyes.

"How do you prosper in your attempt to teach your companions the use of that terrible weapon?" she asked presently.

"Well, nũsta. The difficult part of the undertaking was to teach myself first. That done, the rest is easy enough."

"I hope the place chosen for your exercise is—*safe?*"

"Safe as the rocks of the Antis. It is the field of Quepaypan, which, you know, is a good league from the city. Few save our own people ever come near it; and for fear of any surprise, we have scouts stationed all around at convenient distances."

"You should by all means procure a horse. A man looks so brave and noble upon horseback."

"You are always right, nústa. At present, however, that would be dangerous. We can learn to use our guns, and no Spaniard the wiser; but a troop of los Indios on horseback would scarcely be an agreeable sight to my lord the Viceroy—at least in his present temper."

"The bloodthirsty Toledo? May he live to see many sights less agreeable."

"Ay, nústa; but the time is not come. You remember the words of the wise Pacha-cutec— 'Impatience is the sign of a base mind.'"

Here Sumac's voice, low and soft as the cooing of a dove, broke in with the request—

"Wilt thou help me, sister? Thy fingers

shape the delicate maize-ears more deftly than mine."

"Chachau, since you wish it, my Sumac. But why such haste with the work?"

"I promised the flowers this evening to the nuns of Santa Clara."

"I am tired of the nuns of Santa Clara," said Coyllur petulantly. "I think they would have us work for them like yanaconas."

"Nay, Coyllur, they are very good to us; they teach us the holy faith. Besides," she added, in a somewhat lower tone, "you know how kind the lady abbess has been in persuading her kinsman the Viceroy to close his eyes for the present to—to what we are all sorry for."

"At least am not sorry that our grandfather will not profess what he does not believe. But give me that silver wire, and I will help you; though I had rather the flowers were for the Inca's garden than for the shrine of Saint—I forget his name.— Viracocha, will you take the tinya, and play and sing for us while we work?"

José complied; all the more readily because he had a very fine "yaravi" to sing, which he had just composed in praise of his own bright star. But his performance on this occasion was brought to a premature close by the entrance of Yupanqui, who was accompanied by two chosen friends of Inca race—Maricancha and Rimac.

Yupanqui looked upon José with that peculiar tender fondness which the old sometimes feel for the young, in whom they see their own youth reproduced, and through whom they hope to realize their own lost hopes and ineffectual longings. He marked the budding attachment between his young favorite and his grandchild even before they had become aware of it themselves; and he watched its progress with interest and satisfaction.

If the conversation, previous to his entrance and that of his friends, had been sufficiently dangerous—treasonable, in fact, to Spanish ears—it became ten times more so afterward. Since the death of Tupac Amaru, the Indians of Inca race had been exposed to much unjust suspicion, and to many persecutions from the Spaniards; treatment which, of course, aggravated feelings of bitterness where such already existed, and excited them in other cases. Some faint, floating rumor of a defeat recently sustained at sea by the Spaniards, had just reached Cuzco. In this the Indians secretly triumphed, greatly exaggerating its importance. Much discussion followed as to who the victorious enemies could be. Yupanqui and his friends had the vaguest possible ideas on the subject. No fable could have been told them too wild or too monstrous for their faith.

José, who was just one degree less ignorant than the others, was listened to as an oracle. It seemed a favorable opportunity for propounding his cherished theory about the bearded, pale-faced strangers and their great King. Not that he had hitherto been altogether silent on this topic, so dear to his heart; but never before had he spoken of it so freely.

Yet the hopes that made the young, ardent heart of José throb and bound, but faintly stirred the pulses of the aged men, whose spirits had been crushed by nearly forty years of cruel oppression. They had learned to bow beneath the yoke with sullen endurance; not acquiescent, not resigned, but sorrowfully convinced of their own helplessness and the power of the conquerors. It would not be quite true to say that they had ceased to look for deliverance; but they looked passively, with tearful, weary eyes, in which the light of hope was well-nigh quenched. Maricancha expressed the feelings of all when he said,— "These are fine words, my son Viracocha; but the Spaniards are not conquered, nor like to be, in our day. Everything bows before them. They are strong. God is on their side, and fights for them."

"I doubt that," José answered. "But the maize takes long to ripen, and God's plans may take longer."

"If what the Spaniards tell us of His plans be true, He means them to possess the whole earth."

"No, no, my fathers!" José cried with energy; "never think that. Is it not written in their own Sacred Book that the great King—who is no Spaniard, believe me—shall have dominion from sea to sea, from the river to the ends of the earth? that all kings shall fall down before Him, all nations shall serve Him? He is the mighty King, the great Inca of the East, to whom I look, and in whom I hope for deliverance. Oh, that I could but find Him!" he concluded, in tones of thrilling earnestness.

"I know who He is," said a soft, hesitating voice. All turned towards Sumac, with eyes full of curiosity and interest. "Viracocha told us those sacred words one day," she continued; "and they were sweet in our ears as the song of the tuya and wonderful as the spirit-music of Achapa. So I kept them in my heart, and asked the nuns of Santa Clara what they meant." Here she paused.

"Well, my child, and what said they?" Yupanqui asked.

Sumac crossed herself reverently. "Sister Maria told me that the great King is no other than the Lord Christ himself, the Son of God,"—she said.

But a chorus of grieved, protesting voices drowned her words. These men, so willing to hear about the Christian religion, so ready to embrace it, had yet learned from their instructors little more than a vague and awful dread of Him who is its center. They had been told of the pity and tenderness of "Our Lady," "the Mother of God." But of His pity they had never heard, save as shown through her intercession; from Him directly they expected none. Everyone except José, who remained silent, uttered some exclamation expressive of disbelief or disappointment.

"He is the Judge!" "He is the God of the Spaniards, who gave them our land and our people!" "He it is who will cast us into everlasting fire if we neglect to have the sacraments and pay the priests!" "Ay, truly!—If it were St. Christopher or St. James, one might understand. But the Son or God Himself! How terrible!"

Much more was said. But it is too painful to record such words. Indeed, they were not words so much as inarticulate cries—the cries of blind men, groping in the dark bewildered, and striking ignorantly against the Hand that would have saved and guided them—if they had but known!

"Sumac, my child—my dove! apple of my eye! daughter of my heart! what grieves thee?"—It was old Yupanqui who spoke, in the words of endearment and tenderness so richly supplied by the gentle *lengua* del Inca; for Sumac had slipped down from her seat, and was crouching on the floor, with her mantle thrown over her head, weeping quietly.

The girl's slight frame thrilled to the caressing touch of the old man, and taking his hand, she pressed it to her lips, saying with deep emotion, "Oh, my father I do not let them speak so of Him—of Him—who died for us!"

"For the Spaniards!" said Maricancha bitterly.

"For us also," repeated Sumac—her voice increasing in strength, and her eyes beaming softly through her tears;— "yes—for us also, the Children of the Sun, to take away our sins."

"The Children of the Sun do not sin, my darling," said Yupanqui. "But pay thy devotions as thou wilt to thy favorite God; no one shall speak a word against Him."

"He is the one God, grandfather. There is no other."

"No other god! What canst thou mean, my child? For whose altar are those flowers of thine? Everyone knows the Christians honor hosts of gods called santos and santas, besides the great goddess, the queen of heaven. But worship whom thou wilt, my treasure, and may all gods comfort thee." Yupanqui, and indeed everyone else, had grown very tender, not to say reverent, towards Sumac, since the great sorrow had fallen upon her life.

The girl rose, carefully gathered up the completed flowers, and glided softly from the room. Coyllur seemed to hesitate for a moment whether to follow her; but the attraction of the dreams and aspirations that were being eagerly discussed by her countrymen proved too strong, and she remained.

XVII

In the Convent Parlor

Why should I live? Do I not know
The life of woman is full of woe?
Toiling on, and on, and on,
With breaking heart and tearful eyes,
And silent lips, and in the soul
The secret longings that arise,
Which this world never satisfies!

Some more, some less, but of the whole
Not one quite happy,—no, not one!"
~ LONGFELLOW

ACCOMPANIED BY A FEMALE attendant, who carried a little basket containing the golden flowers, Sumac crossed the great square, and shortly afterward entered by a side-door the gardens which had formerly belonged to the Virgins of the Sun, but which were now appropriated to the nuns of Santa Clara. The stately terraces, faced with dark stone, and reaching down to the banks of the Huatanay, had once been adorned with all the flowers of that prolific clime, in their rich variety of form and coloring. And it is said that rarer flowers, silver pale or golden, wrought by the skilful hands of the Virgins of the Sun, mingled with the scarlet salvias, the crimson fuchsias, the variegated calceolarias, and the many-tinted orchids, looking as if they had grown up with them side by side. But now such flowers as these were esteemed too highly—not for the art that fashioned, but for the metal that composed them—to be left exposed to the changes of the elements. The terraces were beginning already to fall into ruin; and while some of the hardier flowers grew luxuriantly in sweet tangled thickets, others had perished, or become poor and scanty, under the less careful hand of the stranger.

When they entered the garden, the old Indian domestic resigned her basket to her young mistress, and then sat down on one of the terrace steps to wait, crooning a Quechua song.

Sumac slowly climbed the hill to the convent door. Even the short walk had wearied her, and the steep ascent tried her powers still further. Her breath came and went, and two or three times she stopped to rest. Reaching the door at last, she found it open, and entered.

"Tell my mother, Lucia wants her," she said in Spanish to a novice whom she happened to meet; for Sumac and Coyllur had been taught

Spanish by the nuns. They had also their Christian names, used seldom amongst themselves, but often in their intercourse with the Spaniards. Sumac's was Lucia, Coyllur's Victoria.

The novice, to whom she was well known, led her at once into a parlor, saying, "I will tell Sister Maria."

Sumac waited a while, first seated on a bench, then standing to gaze, with much admiration, on a very indifferent painting, in her eyes a wonderful work of art, representing Christ blessing the little children.

Ere long a worn and faded woman, in a dark serge robe, entered the room. She was not young, she was not beautiful—perhaps she had never been so; but when she looked at the Indian girl, there was a yearning, motherly tenderness in her face, which it may be the angels think a fairer thing than what we call beauty.

As she folded the slight form in an affectionate embrace, she exclaimed sorrowfully, "My poor child is almost a shadow now. I sometimes fear, Lucia, that you will soon vanish from our sight altogether."

"And what if I do, mother?" asked the girl, seating herself beside her, and gazing fondly into her dim blue eyes with dark ones that were all too perilously bright. "Since they slew the Inca, I have not wished to live. Tell me, mother, is that also sin?"

Sister Maria sighed, as she answered, "It is always sin, my child, if we love the creature more than the Creator."

Sumac crossed herself, and pointed to the picture. "You told me He takes away sin; you said He died for our sins on the cross."

Amidst much darkness, ignorance, and confusion, that one grand and simple truth had found its way, like healing balm, into the crushed heart of the Indian girl; for Sister Maria, having learned that truth herself, was able to teach it. In early days—days far off, and tenderly remembered now—some pure and unadulterated drops of the water of life had fallen to her lot through the ministrations of the celebrated Fray Constantine Ponce de la Fuente, in Seville. Many years since then had she lived "in a dry and thirsty land where no water is," yet, like the lotus flower, she had treasured up a little store of the precious liquid, enough to quench the thirst of a weary wanderer in the desert. Thus it was that, happily, one poor mourner was not bid to look, as too many were, for comfort, to the "Madre Dolorosa," our Lady of Sorrows, but to the Man of Sorrows Himself, who is also the Lord of Life and Glory."

Half unconsciously, Sister Maria murmured a few lines of the noble old Latin hymn, "Dies Iræ."

"What do those words say, mother?" Sumac asked.

The nun gave a free Spanish translation of

them, somewhat resembling ours:—

Think, O Savior, for what reason
Thou endured'st earth's pain and treason:
Do not lose me in that season. "

But Sumac did not approve.

"That does not seem a good prayer, mother," she said. "How could He lose me? He is God."

"Keep that faith, my child," replied the nun, a little sorrowfully.

She was conscious of many a keen pulsation of fear, not that He would lose her, but that she might somehow lose Him, which would be the same thing practically. But why should she cast the shadow of her own doubt upon her pupil's more simple trust?

Sumac broke the pause that followed. "Mother, I have now a great sin, I am afraid," she said, in faltering tones.

Upon a few occasions—very few—Sumac and Coyllur had attended confession. They had been gently dealt with; yet they both hated it. Coyllur was nearly driven to open rebellion by the requirement; while to Sumac it was a dreaded and formidable ordeal. Yet she liked well to pour her simple confessions into the ear of her chosen teacher and friend; her "mother," as the motherless girl—motherless almost since the dawn of memory—loved to call her.

"What is this sin, my daughter?" asked the nun, tenderly taking and holding the small, brown, transparent hand.

"I have much sin, because it hurts me that Coyllur and Viracocha love each other," was Sumac's faltering acknowledgment.

"What, my child! And do they?" asked the nun, with a perceptible start.

"Yes," said the Indian girl, surprised in her turn at her friend's surprise. "It is right. He is noble, beautiful, and good; and he is one of our own."

"How far has the matter gone? Does Coyllur really care for him? Is anything settled?" asked Sister Maria, with much more eagerness than might have been expected from her. She pitied the conquered race, and would fain spare them one wrong more, if she could.

Sumac looked at her, wondering. "Mother," she said, "surely you do not wish Coyllur to be a holy virgin? I might, if I live; but never Coyllur. She is too bright, too glad. She is like the little tuyas that go singing all the day from bough to bough. God, when He made her, meant her to be always happy, I am sure."

"May it indeed be so," said the nun. "No, Lucia, I do not wish to see her undertake the religious life; she has no vocation for it. But, my child, does Prince Paullu know what you have told me now? or even your aunt, Dona Beatriz Coya?"

"My grandfather will tell Paullu when it

is necessary," Sumac answered, not without a look that betrayed the distrust and dislike which even her gentle heart harbored towards the Inca who made himself the willing tool of the Spaniard. "My aunt," she added, "must be well aware of it already; they are both often at her house. And, in sooth, they never go there that I am not filled with fear lest Viracocha should fight with some Spanish caballero for paying attention to my sister."

"He could not be so mad as to fight with a Spaniard! Lucia, my child, if there be still time, if remonstrance still avails—it is for her sake I speak, and for his—"

"But what is it you would say, my mother?" Sumac asked, with momentarily increasing agitation. "It *is* too late; they love each other. Who could be so cruel as to sunder them? What have you heard? What do you know?"

"*I know* nothing, my child;"—which was true: at least, Sister Maria only knew that the

Mother Abbess was a kinswoman of the Viceroy, Don Francisco de Toledo; that three proud and needy young cavaliers—the nephews of both—were waiting in Cuzco for whatever fortune and their powerful kinsfolk might send them; and that the youngest and proudest of the three had cast his fiery dark eyes on the sweet face of Coyllur, and sworn to have her for his bride. And woe betide the Indian slave who should dare to cross the path of his master, the white man!

However, there were still a hundred possibilities in the future. Someone might change-something might happen; at all events, the trembling form, the eager parted lips, the wistful anxious eyes of her best-loved pupil were more at that moment to poor Sister Maria than any distant dangers that might menace Coyllur and Viracocha. To turn her thoughts from the subject that alarmed her, she asked, "But, my Lucia, why should it hurt you that they love each other?"

"I don't know," faltered Sumac, her head drooping more and more, until at last her face was quite overshadowed by her long and beautiful hair; "I can't tell. Only, mother," she added, looking quickly up into the nun's kind sorrowful eyes, "my heart pains me—*here*. It is hungry—it is empty—it is tired. When Viracocha speaks low and soft to Coyllur, it says within me—' *You* will never hear such words any more, Sumac —never any more!' O mother, mother! there be many voices sweet to others; one voice only was sweet to Sumac,—but it will never speak again! Dark and evil it seems to me that he is dead, and that I am left alive."

And Sumac laid herself, like a tired child, in her friend's pitying arms, and wept. It was not often that she spoke such words or wept such tears. If she had, she might have lived longer. Sister Maria mingled her tears of sympathy with the hot and passionate drops of Sumac's bitter sorrow. At last she said,— "Lucia, my child, would you desire to change your lot for that of Coyllur now?"

It was rather a strange question for a nun to ask. But Sister Maria had been a woman before she became a nun; and in spite of conventual life and discipline, the woman's heart throbbed in her bosom still.

"Oh no, no! Mother, don't you remember that *I* was to have been the sole Inca's bride?"

"Is it, then, because you esteem it so great an honor to be, as you call it, Coya—"

"Oh, hush, mother! what use is all that? Indeed, I never heeded such words when they spoke them; and I think there is much talk like the mountain snow, that melts when you take it in your hand. But, mother, you know I saw him. Once he laid aside the llautu, and the crimson tunic, and the white wing-feathers of the cora-quenque, and he put on the dress of a poor man, and came unknown to Cuzco, that

he might look upon the city of his fathers;—
that he might look too upon this poor face of
mine, that has no beauty now. And then he
said—he said—No, mamallay, I will not tell
what he said—not even to you. Those words
are all my own; they are the one thing poor Sumac has in this dark, cold world. Had he bid-
den me then, I would have gone forth gladly to
the wild desert with him—for was he not the
Inca But he did not; he told me he would come
again. He *did* come again—you know how.
They would not let me see him. Perhaps it was
best; my face might have troubled him—might
have shadowed with a thought of pain the noble calm of the look he wore, as beseemed him,
to the last. It does not matter now—for me. I
ought not to weep;—you tell me I may pray for
him. And he received Holy Baptism,—most
gladly, as they say. Moreover, he left his cause
to God;—Christ is God."

After one more gush of passionate tears

came a sudden change of tone:

"Give him—give his memory up for Viracocha! Give the emerald of the mine for one of those green leaves in the garden yonder! Not that Viracocha is not good and brave. I love him well,—as my brother. But there are ten thousand green leaves for one green stone, mother."

"So you think your own portion the best, and would rather keep it, with all its sorrow? Well, my child, I believe you are right," said the woman's heart of Sister Maria." Though, of course, earthly love is nothing, compared with heavenly—mere dust and dross," the nun interposed." Still, God knows," the woman said, taking up the parable again," it is less bitter to have once been loved, truly and nobly, and then to have been separated by man's hate and cruelty, than to find the trusted false, and to see what looked like gold fade away into tinsel."

Sumac looked up, with interest and curiosity in her tearful eyes. The old wound ceased to throb, while she wondered whether some similar scar might not be found beneath the serge robe of a holy virgin.

"I scarcely know whether I ought to tell you foolish old stories," said the nun, as the color mantled to the roots of her thin hair, touched with gray. "Of course, all is past and gone— and no matter now. It seems as if it happened to some different person, long ago, in another life. Yet, not so long, after all. It is not easy in the convent to tell how time passes. I make strange mistakes sometimes. I think I have told you that I was born and brought up in Seville."

"Seville! That is the great city beyond the Mother Sea, like Cuzco here," said Sumac, who had heard José talk of Seville.

"Not just like Cuzco; for there be many cities as great, or greater, in the Old World— though Seville is a fair city certainly."

"Viracocha has told us of it. His patre,

Fray Fernando, was born there. And I think he must be the best and kindest Spaniard that ever lived. Viracocha loves him more than any one on earth, save Coyllur."

"It was in Seville that I spent my happy childhood. Father and mother, sisters and brothers, all loved me, the youngest, and made a little queen of me. It was that they were good and tender, not that I was beautiful. Even when I was young and lively, I do not think my face was as lovely as many other faces in my native land. You might see a hundred fairer any day on the Prado. Still, God had given me the fair hair people care for in my country, I suppose because it is not often seen; and these dim eyes were what men called *zarca*. They said I stole their azure from the sky. What idle tales to tell you now! All the saints forgive me Our Lady, with the seven swords in her breast, be merciful to me! What has tempted me to talk thus to thee, poor child, whom I should be seeking to edify?"

"But, you know, I want to hear what happened," said Sumac innocently.

"*Nothing* happened, Lucia; and that was just the trouble that made the blue eyes grow dim, and took the gold from the hair you see so dull and scanty. That was the trouble too that, God be thanked, made me think of Him. Then I remembered Fray Constantino's sermons, that we used to go and hear in the great church; and then, at last, I gave Him all that was left of my poor life."

"But was there no one—," Sumac began, then stopped. "I don't know the right Spanish words to use," she said apologetically.

"Yes," Sister Maria confessed, with a faint flush on her faded cheek. "One there was who praised the blue eyes like the rest, but did not look like the rest when he praised them. Wherever I went, there he was, with that great brow and earnest face—saying so much in one word, looking so much in one glance. He was the only son of a very proud and noble, though not wealthy, family. And I thought——. But I am speaking idle words again. I will only tell you that, all at once, he vanished—without word, without sign. It was said that he had gone away to seek his fortune in this strange New World. If so, at least he might have bowed or looked farewell. He never came again. I never heard what became of him; and I shall never hear on this side the grave."

"You may be sure he was killed in battle, mother," said Sumac, tenderly suggesting what seemed to her the most honorable and enviable fate.

"I know not. I only know that I was very sinful and very miserable. I thought more of him than of God. I prayed all the saints to send him back; and I had my heart full of wicked thoughts about them, because they did not, or could not. Then other troubles came: my kind and tender parents died, my brothers were scattered over the world, my sisters were married—not all happily. One brother, my favorite, was killed in Flanders, fighting against the heretics."

"I know.—The English?"

"It did happen, strangely enough, that he fell by the hand of an Englishman. Then my proud heart broke at last. I gave up earthly hope, and turned, as I have told you, to God for comfort. My child, He does comfort the sorrowful, He does bind up the broken heart; though He takes more than a day to do His work."

"He is good," said Sumac gently. Then hearing the sound of a bell, which she knew was meant to summon the nuns to prayer, she rose to go. Remembering her basket of flowers, she took it up, and put it in her friend's hand. "Here are flowers for the holy saint, mother," she said. "I am so stupid that I have forgotten his name."

"San Martin, my child; whose feast we celebrate tomorrow. Truly, Lucia, these are very beautiful," said the nun, as she removed the fine cotton cloth that covered the basket, and took out, with admiring carefulness, the golden stalks of maize, with their rich golden grains sheathed in broad leaves of silver, and ornamented with tassels of delicate silver thread.

"San Martin. Was he the good man who, you told me, gave his cloak to the beggar? Will he be pleased with our flowers, do you think, mother? I am glad. But, mother, I want to make some now for our Lord Christ Himself. May I?"

"When it comes near Easter time, you shall. But now, dear child, the Lady Abbess bade me tell you she would fain you wrought a few for us, that we might send them to Spain, as an offering to the Mother House at Valladolid."

"You shall have them, mother," said the girl. "But I would like, best of all, to make some to give to our Savior."

"Give Him your heart, my child. That gift will please Him more than any other," said the nun, as she kissed her affectionately. "Now I must hasten, or I shall have to do a penance for coming late to prayers."

XVIII

At Home

"Trust!—the blessed deathly angels
Whisper Sabbath hours at hand.
By the heart's wound when most gory
By the longest agony,
Smile!—behold, in sudden glory
The Transfigured smiles on thee:
And ye lifted up your head,
And it seemed as if He said-
' My beloved, is it so?

> *Have ye tasted of my woe?*
> *Of my bliss ye shall not fail.'*
> *He stands brightly where the shade is,*
> *With the keys of Death and Hades."*
> ~ E.B. BROWNING

IT WAS MIDDAY. SUMAC LAY sleeping, or seeming to sleep, on a low couch, called a pununa. A favorite attendant sat near, converting a little heap of wool into delicate threads by means of a spindle which she turned with a curiously-carved handle, and looking from time to time, with a mute and wistful sorrow, on the wasted face of her beloved nusta.

It has been said that some women "have no language at all for their profoundest experiences, except to pine away and die." Of such was Sumac. We have little right to look down from the proud height of our "Aryan" or "Caucasian" superiority upon our dusky brethren and sisters, as though their love and sorrow, compared with ours, "were as moonlight unto sunlight, or as water unto wine." Well have the race to which Sumac belonged asserted their claim to the love that proves itself stronger than death. Of Sumac's own kindred was the Inca girl, Manco's young wife, who endured every torture the Spaniards could invent without groan or murmur, and died at last smiling—because she died for him. Which of us could do more for earthly, not to say for heavenly love? And frail and shadowy as Sumac looked, within her slight frame there dwelt a spirit capable of the same devotion.

Viracocha entered the room gently through the open door, opposite to which Sumac's couch had been placed. He was now dressed in full Inca costume. Above his uncu, with its belt of embroidered cloth, he wore a short mantle of vicuña wool, white and very fine, and adorned with a broad yellow border. On his head was a stately cap or coronal of egret's feathers, bearing underneath the much-prized sacred cord of yellow and carnation, the insignia of the Children of the Sun. Viracocha was "a very handsome youth, well-shaped, and of a lovely countenance, as were all the other Incas."[1] His chest was broad, his limbs slight, his head well-formed and graceful, his complexion a comely olive-brown; the oval face smooth as a maiden's, yet thoroughly manly in expression-the parted lips revealing snow-white teeth—the nose aquiline-the eyes black and piercing, but capable of the tenderest softness—the black hair worn short according to custom, but very abundant and beautifully fine and glossy.

No wonder that such a youth was considered a highly ornamental addition to the numerous and splendid religious processions, upon the effect of which the Spanish friars seem to have placed their main reliance for the conversion of the Indians. He was also received

---

1.   Garcilaso de la Vega

into the best Spanish society Cuzco afforded, and pronounced by the Dons whom he enjoyed the privilege of meeting at the house of Dona Beatriz Coya and elsewhere, "*Homo tan formal y complida que Nosotros*"—(As formal and well-bred a man as Ourselves)—a high eulogium from Spanish lips. The Inca's son was a gentleman as truly as any European prince or noble. He had not to learn courtesy from the Spaniards; he had but to translate its outward expression from the language of one set of observances into that of another. Moreover, Viracocha was born a poet; and the perilously sensitive and susceptible organization has its compensating advantages. At least, it enables a man to adapt himself to circumstances, not hypocritically affecting what he does not feel, but throwing himself readily into different forms of feeling. Ministering to Fray Fernando, pleading with unaffected eloquence the cause of his people, planning their deliverance, making love to Coyllur, taking part in a Corpus Christi procession, or exchanging Castilian courtesies in pure Castilian speech with the gentlemen of the Viceroy's suite, Viracocha was still, for the time being, "a whole man to that one thing," doing it with all his heart, and consequently doing it well. But this, though it was not hypocrisy, might yet easily become so.

All this time he is standing motionless, patiently waiting to be assured whether Sumac sleeps or not. At last his patience is rewarded—the girl opens her large languid eyes, and looks the question she does not need to speak.

"Dear nũsta, I have not been successful," said Viracocha gently, as he came to her side, "although I preferred my request to the great mother of all the holy virgins."

"To the Mother Abbess?"

"Yes. I entreated her, for the love of God, to allow Sister Maria to come and see you. But she refused me. She says it is against their law for any holy virgin to leave the house."

"So near—only a few steps from their garden gate to this!" said Sumac plaintively.

"The Mother said that to permit it would be a great sin. But to speak plainly, nũsta, I think she is no better than an ugly old toad. If sin there be, what should hinder her doing penance?"

The Lady Abbess, it must be owned, had not been particularly courteous to Viracocha, whom she regarded as her nephew's rival; nor very anxious to grant the request of which he was the bearer from the sister of Coyllur, who had of late bestowed sundry spirited rebuffs on that young nobleman.

"Then I shall never see Mamallay again!" said Sumac sadly, large tears gathering in her eyes. Presently she spoke to the attendant, "Amancaes,[2] bring me my book."

Sumac possessed a book, which she regard-

2. Lily

ed with half-superstitious awe as a wonderful and mysterious treasure, and with intense affection as the gift of her beloved "Mamallay." It was a small, brown, well-worn volume—"The Sum of Christian Doctrine," by Fray Constantino Ponce de la Fuente. Sister Maria had taught her to read, but she was far from perfect in the art; and if she had been, much that the book contained was quite beyond her comprehension.

She took it reverently in her thin hands and opened its first page. Some faded writing was there, upon which she pressed her lips fondly once and again. Then, showing it to Viracocha—"That is Mamallay's name," she said; "the name she had before she became a holy virgin."

With some difficulty Viracocha read the name, which was traced faintly, in a delicate female hand—"Dona Rosa de Mercedes y Guevara."

"Yes, that was her name—Rosa. It is the

name of a fragrant flower that grows beyond the Mother Sea,—they say nothing like it was ever seen in our country till the Spaniards brought it over. The book was made by a good man—a great speaker, who used to tell the people to be good, as the Dominicans do in the great church on saints' days. Mamallay loved his words; she says no one else ever spoke to her heart as he did. But afterward he did something wicked: I know not what, I only know they put him in prison. Yet the book is very good, and full of words about our Lord. His name comes often. I cannot read the hard words; but I can read *that,* and it does me good. "She paused to take breath, then resumed—" But you are wise, Viracocha. You know the white man's learning. So I wish you, when I go away, to have my book for your own. My other things (they are not many) my grandfather will have, and Coyllur. But my book shall be yours, because you can read it, and because I love you, brother."

"I thank you, dear nūsta. But I hope you will live a long time yet."

"It is not best for me to live. The Lord Christ knows that. How good He is! He saw me standing, all this time, outside the gate. He knew I longed—oh, how sorely!—to go in. But I would not until He called; no, I would not! Now He has called. Mamallay said so the last day I saw her. She told me His words,—' Come unto me, all ye that labor and are heavy laden, and I will give you rest.' His own words, Viracocha!"

But Viracocha cared not for them just then. He did not labor, nor was he heavy laden.

Sumac presently resumed—"My brother, since I have grown too weak to walk to the convent garden, I have much time for thinking. And as I think, things grow clear to me. Best it seems to me now that you should wed my sister."

"That is my dearest hope—one day."

"But, Viracocha, life is too short to be waiting for one day.' Why not ask my grandfather to give her to you now?"

Viracocha's black eyes became coals of fire, and his cheek burned through its olive hue;—but he was silent.

"Well?"—Sumac whispered.

"Ask him to give me Chasca, the evening star, from the sky! No, nusta,—no! Not till I shall have done that which may give me right to claim a boon so priceless."

"What is it you want to do?" the dying girl asked wistfully "Nusta, you know."

"I am not sure I do, you talk of so many strange things. Yet I can guess. You want to cross the Mother Sea, Viracocha."

"Arri! arri![3] And to come back with an English army, sent by the great King, to restore the Inca. And then, as the deliverer of my people, to kneel and claim Coyllur nusta."

3.   Yes. yes.

"Viracocha! Viracocha!" said the dying girl, raising herself upon her couch, and looking with imploring earnestness into his face,— "I know where that will end. And I know, too, how the Spanish steel wounds—not the flesh it falls on—*that* pang was short, thank God!— but the heart that loves. One of us is enough to bear that, Viracocha; do not lay it upon Coyllur."

"God knows I would not cause her a pang for all that earth contains."

I see great sorrows, like great clouds, hanging over you," Sumac went on sadly." That Spaniard wants to have Coyllur."

"Aucca! I will fight him some day, and with his own weapons. The Spaniards shall see for once how an Inca can use them. The first time I met him, he would fain have struck me with his whip." (For the young cavalier whom José had encountered the day of his arrival in Cuzco, proved to be no other than Don Francisco

Solis de Toledo; a circumstance which intensified their mutual distrust and dislike.) "It was—that, however, does not matter now," said José, checking himself suddenly as he remembered *what* had taken place that very day.

"But he will not fight you, Viracocha. He knows better He will have you killed. The Spaniards do what they please. They are strong."

"God is stronger, Sumac nũsta."

"He is," Sumac answered quietly." But He did not bid you fight Don Francisco; nor go in search of the English."

"That I question. I believe He calls me to seek the great King who will deliver the poor when he crieth."

Here the conversation was brought to a close by the entrance of Coyllur, who had been visiting her aunt, and brought to her sister delicious Spanish sweetmeats flavored with orange-flower water, the gift of that kind-hearted lady.

Never again had Viracocha opportunity for quiet talk with Sumac. From that time she grew rapidly worse. Pain and weakness claimed her for their own. She bore them very patiently, and faced the quickly-approaching end with a calmness more gentle and tender than the usual stoicism of her race.

Almost to the last the frail wasted fingers sought the familiar work, and feebly twisted the threads of golden wire. If Coyllur or her attendants remonstrated, she would say, "You know they are for the Lord Christ. They must be ready for Easter."

They were ready for Easter. They filled a place among the glittering decorations of the high altar in the Church of Santa Clara. But ere the Easter bells began to ring, the gentle Inca girl had closed her eyes upon a world she was little loath to leave.

Every rite of the creed she professed had been duly afforded her. She confessed, communicated, and had extreme unction with all the proper forms, but with a very misty and imperfect apprehension of what was being done for her. If these things cannot help, neither may they hinder, the soul that trusts in God's mercy through Christ. As the dew ascends from earth to heaven, unbidden, uncontrolled by man, so poor Sumac's simple prayer ascended straight to the throne of God—"Good Lord Christ, take me to Thyself."

Old Yupanqui, who hid a broken heart beneath a coldly impassive exterior, could not refuse his beloved grand-daughter's last request—that he would receive Christian baptism. Accordingly he submitted to the rite on Whitsunday—though with little comprehension of its significance.

"I will do what she wished," he said to Viracocha. "And after all, if I were now to go and dwell with my fathers in the Mansions of the Sun, they might not know me, or they might look upon me with scorn, because we are not what we were, in the old days when they ruled the land."

"At least, my father," Viracocha answered, "you cannot doubt it would be well for all of us to follow whither she is gone"

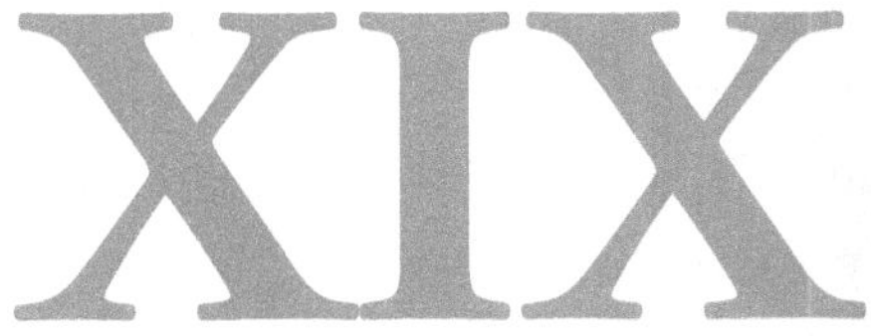

The Star Shines

"From the beautiful face of my love,
They call her Coyllur.
It was by reason of her beauty
A harmonious name.
Like the moon in its splendor
Is her bright forehead,
When it shines in brilliancy
In the highest heaven."

~ From "*Ollanta*," an Ancient Inca Drama

Coyllur's grief for her sister was poignant. The girls were tenderly attached to each other, and had never since infancy been separated for a single day.

Sumac's sorrow bound them only more closely together; and during her long illness Coyllur had waited on her with the most assiduous affection. She was in consequence little able to bear the severe fasts and strict seclusion which the Peruvian customs imposed upon mourners; and erelong old Yupanqui began to look with keen apprehension on her drooping form—dreading, not without reason, lest the last joy and solace of his declining years should be taken from him. Viracocha's alarm was not less than his.

Both welcomed the gentle authority with which Dona Beatriz Coya insisted on removing her niece to her own more cheerful dwelling. For the Inca buildings, admirable as they were for "simplicity, symmetry, solidity,"[1] and wonderfully fitted to resist the ravages of time and the shocks of earthquakes, were rather dull places of abode for ladies.

It was new life to Coyllur to welcome the flood of sunshine through the strange luxury of windows; or, seated in the pleasant balcony, to contemplate at her ease the never-ending marvels of the square below. There the stately church processions wound along with all their glittering show; there the Spanish soldiers mustered in shining armor; and, best of all, there rode the splendid, haughty Spanish cavaliers, managing their noble steeds with consummate ease and grace, not quite unconscious of the dark eyes that were watching them with interest. Moreover, Coyllur nŭsta had a pretty sleeping-chamber in her aunt's house, which boasted a window also. It was pleasant, in the delicious tropical nights, to lie waking on a couch draped

---

1.   Humboldt

with dainty stuffs from Spain, and to listen the while to sweet music—more scientific and harmonious than that of the ruder instruments of her native land—from the guitar attuned by a skilful hand to the melodies of Spain.

Had such reached the ear of Viracocha, they would have moved him to indignant sorrow. Better far for both had he laid Sumac's warning to heart and acted upon it; but sentiments of honor, which ruled his soul as absolutely as that of any "preux chevalier" of the Old World, utterly forbade his claiming the prize he longed for until he had won it by some deed of signal merit. Nor would Yupanqui, in all probability, much as he loved him, have allowed his suit if preferred too soon.

While awaiting the opportunity for this, he bent all his energies to the task of making himself worthy of Coyllur. The grand-daughter of the great Huayna Capac stood very near that golden throne, which, though it existed in imagination only, was about the most real thing in earth or heaven to José Viracocha.

He studied diligently, learning "the Humanities," as taught in Europe, from a Dominican monk, and the more mysterious and difficult science of the Quipus from an aged Indian, who had been a Quipu-comayoc [2] in the days of the Incas. He procured one of the rare and costly maps of the period, which, full of blunders as it was, yet gave him a better idea of the world he lived in than he had before. Lastly, he became a more accomplished marksman with the Spaniards' own formidable weapon than many of the Spaniards themselves, and learned to compete successfully with the best of them in fencing and cane-playing.

All this time he had not forgotten Fray Fernando. Not a day passed in which the man who for more than seven years had been to him as

____

2. Officer whose duty it was to preserve and interpret the Quipus.

a father was not present to his thoughts. Warm and grateful affection, not unmixed with reverential compassion for sorrows vaguely guessed, gathered around his image. Yet not the less did Viracocha belong to his own people and to Coyllur. His place and his work were with these, not with the Spaniards.

It may seem strange that he did not try to communicate with Fray Fernando by letter, since he could write very well; but the idea of writing a letter was so foreign to all his habits and associations, that it never occurred to him. And had he thought of it, whither was he to send the letter when written Even if the monk's present address had been known to him, only half of the difficulty would have been obviated; for under the Spanish government no regular system of posts had replaced the admirable and efficient chasquis of the Incas.

Shortly after Coyllur's departure to the house of her aunt, Viracocha left Cuzco on a mysterious errand. The Spaniards were informed he was going to visit his friends and kinsfolk at Nasca. And not even amongst themselves did the Indians speak freely of his objects or destination. Only the initiated knew that he was to pass in disguise up and down the country, to ascertain the real state of the minds of his people, and to reawaken slumbering hopes of the restoration of the Incas. He had also to give signs and pass-words, to collect and transmit tidings, and to arrange secret meetings; but all these things were shrouded in the greatest possible mystery.

He may have had something both to ascertain and to command on the subject of the hoards of gold and silver which were buried by the Indians at the conquest, to be disinterred whenever a prince of their own race should require them, and not till then. But whatever might be doubtful about Viracocha's mission, one thing at least was certain,—the young envoy went forth taking his life in his hand.

Ere he left Cuzco, he paid a farewell visit at the mansion of Data Beatriz Coya., And here, on entering the low and sloping doorway which formed part of the original Inca building—the ground-floor of the present mansion—he encountered his rival, Don Francisco Solis, who was just passing out. They exchanged a cold and haughty salutation; each regarding the other with cordial hatred. Viracocha saw the Spanish knight vault lightly into the saddle of his noble steed, held for him at the door by a mulatto page, and for the hundredth time envied him his mastery over the proud and beautiful creature. Then turning, he sought the apartment where Coyllur was to be found; and as fortune favored him, she was alone.

His lips at last unsealed by the approaching separation, and the consciousness that he was about to hazard all for the cause dearest to the hearts of both, he said a thousand things in the soft musical "lengua del Inca," which would not bear translation. The hour was rapturous, but all too brief, and bounded by that terrible parting. Already he had risen from his place at her feet, and received the pretty Spanish "Vaya con Dios," which she added to the Quechua "Paccaricama," when his eye rested on a pair of perfumed Spanish leather gloves, embroidered with seedling pearls, lying beside the guitar, her aunt's recent gift. Instinct revealed the donor: he saw in them the homage of his rival, and the countenance of Viracocha fell.

Coyllur noticed the change, and said, not without confusion, "They are pretty, Viracocha. He would leave them;—but I do not value them."

"They are not worthy to touch the pure hands of my nūsta," said Viracocha, with a scornful glance at the dainty trifles. "No Child of the Sun is ever adorned with pearls, since they cannot be obtained without risk of life."

(A beautiful trait, recorded by Garcilaso de la Vega of his Inca forefathers.)

But Coyllur thought not of the old Incas, her forefathers—she thought only of the young Inca standing before her, whose looks were far more eloquent than words.

"I care nothing for such Spanish trumpery," she said, as, taking the gloves, she flung them from the open window, over the balcony, down into the square beneath.

Viracocha's countenance softened—brightened into restful assurance. "It is well," he answered. "Now I go. Will my nústa give me a token—a flower to keep for her sake?"

And selecting, from a vase which lay before her on the table, a rich crimson tintin, or passion-flower, Coyllur placed it in the hand of Viracocha, who kissed it and laid it in his bosom. So they parted.

The Star Sets

"Untrue! untrue! O morning star—O mine!
That sitteth secret in a veil of light
Far up the starry spaces—say untrue!
Speak but so loud as doth a Tyrrhene moon
To wasted waters."

~ E.B. BROWNING

ABOUT TEN MONTHS AFTERWARD, Viracocha came back. He bent his steps, in the first instance, to the dwelling of Yupanqui. But there all was changed, except the familiar walls,—those adamantine Inca walls, which still defy the hand of time, and the far less gentle touch of man. Even these, however, were hardly visible through the heaps of stones, of timber, and of mortar that lay around them. With these materials, a second story, after the Spanish fashion, was being added to the Inca's house. A Spanish master-builder was overlooking the work, and directing the labors of a crowd of Indians and Black people. But no one could give Viracocha any information about the former occupants of the dwelling, turning away from them, he crossed the square towards the mansion of Dona Beatriz Coya. On one of the stone footbridges he encountered Sumac's old attendant, Amancaes. The poor woman threw herself at his feet, and kissed his dress. He raised her, spoke a few kindly words of greeting, and asked for news of the household.

Soon all was told. Less than a month after Viracocha's departure, old Yupanqui was found one morning, lying dead on the blanket of biscache wool that served him for a couch. But his death was opportune, and saved him much sorrow. Almost immediately afterward, the storm that had been gathering over the Inca family since the apprehension of Tupac Amaru, broke at last. The suspicion of the Spaniards and the tyranny of the Viceroy found expression in a severe decree, banishing nearly all the Children of the Sun from the beloved city of their fathers. Dona Beatriz Coya took the dejected and sorrowful Coyllur to her own home. Her grief for her grandfather was wild; but her aunt comforted her as best she could, promising to supply the place of a parent to her. From that day forward, the orphan girl was of necessity thrown entirely upon the protection and guidance of Dona Beatriz, and of the Spaniards, or Spaniardized Indians, who surrounded her. So the end could not be wondered at. The next day, in the Church of Santa Aria, Coyllur was to give her hand to the Spanish cavalier, Don Francisco Solis de Toledo.

Don José Viracocha Inca did honor to the memory of his ancestors by his manner of receiving this intelligence. A Spaniard would at least have sworn by all the saints in heaven to have his rival's blood. But the Inca's son had trained himself "the fierce extremes of good and ill to brook impassive." Therefore he spoke no word; he gave no sign. He silently emptied his coca-bag into the withered hands of the poor woman; then he walked quietly on to the door of the stately mansion of Don Marcio Serra de Leguisano.

The door-keeper was an Indian; which is equivalent to saying that he was the humble servant of Viracocha. From him he learned that the nūsta was at that moment in the court yard. "I would go thither, my brother," said Viracocha; and the Indian of course admitted him.

The taste of Dona Beatriz had transformed the courtyard into a pretty garden, rich with tropical glories, and having in the center a fountain of limpid water. Coyllur, who was gathering flowers, still wore her graceful national costume; but a Spanish head-dress of black silk and lace hung down over her pure white mantle of vicuna wool. On seeing Viracocha, she allowed the flowers to fall from her hands, and, trembling from head to foot, cried out in Spanish, "Santa Maria!"

Viracocha approached, knelt before her, and kissed her passive hand. Then he rose, and quietly withdrew a few paces.

"Coyllur nũsta," he said, of course in his native tongue, "I know all.—But will you, for the sake of the past, answer me one question this day? That done, I shall trouble you no more."

Coyllur hung her head; and clutched nervously at the graceful bells of a tall fuchsia, near which they were standing. A spray came off in her hand, and she tore it to fragments.

Viracocha stood motionless, patiently awaiting her reply. It came at last:—"Ask what you will of me," she murmured.

"Is this thing your own free choice, Coyllur nŭsta?" Viracocha asked, with almost as much outward calmness as if merely inquiring what she meant to do with the flowers that lay neglected at her feet.

"Why ask that?" she faltered, in a very different tone from his.

"Because—if *Yes*—I go home, never more to see your face. If *No*"-his dark eyes kindled, and unconsciously he advanced one step nearer,—"I fling this mantle round you, and thus I bear you safe to the dwellings of my people, let who will bar my way. Coyllur, star of Heaven, trust me—I will save you."

She shrank a little, as if frightened by his vehemence; and José, instantly recollecting himself, recoiled also.

"I am afraid for you," she faltered. "If *he* should come and find you here, he would kill you."

"Let him try," said José with a haughty smile. "But fear not. In your presence there shall be no bloodshed. Nũsta, I await your answer."

Coyllur wrung her hands, as one in pain. "O Viracocha, Viracocha!" she cried at last, "why have you come to torture me? Why do you bring the old times back again to me? And yet—and yet—"

José took from his bosom Sumac's little book. Carefully preserved and pressed between its leaves lay the crimson passion-flower. This he gently removed, and placed in the trembling hand of Coyllur. "If you think the heart next which it has lain ever since worth your keeping, keep it," he said. "But if indeed you have given yours to the Spaniard, then give it back to me, for it will be all that I have left on earth."

Minute after minute passed away, and still the shadows chased each other over the agitated face of the Indian girl, whose heart was torn by contending emotions. But at last the fight was over; the day was won. It was the proud Castilian knight who proved the conqueror;—with his fair face and splendid courtesy, and the masterful ways wherewith he seemed to rule man's will and woman's heart as easily as he controlled his noble steed. Pity, esteem, and old familiar kindness Coyllur still felt for the son of her people;—but she loved the Spaniard. Silently, tremblingly, with bowed head and sorrowful heart, she gave the withered flower back again to Viracocha.

Without a word he replaced it in his bosom. Then he said, calmly enough, "God bless you, nustallay," and turned to go. But, turning again for a moment, he added, "I shall see your face no more. Unless, indeed, you or yours ever need the help of the children of your people. Then I will know it, and be near you."

Coyllur watched him until he disappeared in the long dark passage that led to the outer door. Then she fled for refuge to her aunt, whom she actually terrified by an outburst of passionate weeping.

Doha Beatriz Coya, who had labored much to bring about this Spanish match, soothed and comforted her niece by every tender art in her power. "You have no idea, my child," she said, "with how many sad misgivings of heart I gave my hand, in my day, to the stranger. Nor was I quite so fortunate as you are. Everyone knows Don Francisco Solis is of the best blood in Spain—blue blood, as they say;—while Don Marcio Serra (whom the saints preserve!), you know, was—was not—well, no matter now; he is as good as the best of them, and better. But was it not told you how I braved the anger of Paullu, and of all my kindred, because I could not endure the thought of him? And at last, all that Paullu could wring from me, by prayers and threats and promises, was just this, 'Perhaps I will have him, and perhaps I will not.'" And the good lady indulged in a laugh at the recollection of her own girlish willfulness. "But there was no perhaps with my Uncle Paullu," she continued. "At that time he dared not, for his head, disoblige one of the conquistadors. So I was married, in spite of myself; to the best of husbands. And I have had, since then, everything my heart could desire; besides the power to help my people, which I have not failed to use, God and the saints enabling me."

Whilst Coyllur was thus receiving from her kind-hearted aunt the time-honored conventional consolation,

> *"She herself was not exempt,*
> *Doubtless she herself had suffered,"*

Viracocha was wandering, with his broken

heart, amongst the ruins of his ancestors' fortress on the Sachsahuaman hill.

At length he threw himself down amongst the tumbled stones, on a patch of emerald grass variegated with blue and golden wild-flowers. Then came his hour of weakness. All his proud stoicism gone, he bowed his head and wept—such tears as a man may weep un-blamed who has just lost everything that made life precious.

What dried his tears at last was not any thought of comfort, but the fierce and passionate hatred that like a bitter flood rushed over his heart, leaving no room for softer feelings there. How he hated these enemies of his race—these cruel Spaniards! His own gentler language supplied no words fit for his rage: he was fain to curse them, and that aloud, in the tongue they had taught him to speak. The crushing sense of their all-conquering power, and his and his nation's impotence, only intensified his hatred a thousandfold.

Now for the first time he thoroughly rec-ognized and acknowledged to himself the strength that God had given to the white man. It was not their fire-breathing clubs, not their horses, not their iron tools, it was their strength that won them the victory—strength not of limb and muscle alone, but of heart and brain. They were not better than his own people,—not braver, truer, kinder,—far otherwise,—but they were stronger. And before this terrible strength, this force and weight of manhood in the pale-faced stranger, had perished, or was perishing, all the gentle grace and beauty of the old time; so fair even in its ruins, yet powerless to touch the hearts of the destroyers.

Viracocha's outburst of agony ended in a dumb, crushed hopelessness, worse than agony. Wherefore contend with this resistless might? It was the vicuña in the paw of the jaguar, the gentle dove in the talons of the mighty condor of the Andes.

Then came softer thoughts. Had all men united to tell him Coyllur could have proved untrue, he would have flung back a scornful denial. Even now, scarcely her own lips could convince him—lips that had spoken the soft musical "Vaya con Dios!" that haunted his memory still—that would haunt him forever. O Coyllur, Coyllur! Star of his life, set forever! And again his tears fell like rain, as over and over he murmured the beloved name.

Yet those tears relieved him; they did him good. They gradually recalled him to himself. He remembered his promise that she should see his face no more. This was the last service he could render her. He would leave Cuzco— and depart—whither? He knew not—he cared not. But ere he went, it behooved him to render account of his stewardship, and make full report of all he had seen and heard during the last ten months. Amancaes had informed him that Maricancha, in spite of the decree of banishment, contrived still to linger in Cuzco, under cover of a disguise, and she had told him where to find him. To him therefore he must go, and at once.

He rose and retraced his steps to the city. He was successful in finding Maricancha; but when his interview with him was over, he wandered once more towards what had been Yupanqui's house, feeling utterly desolate and alone. But near the door he met a young son of Dona Beatriz Coya's Indian porter, who had evidently been sent in search of him.

The boy brought him a sealed letter, which he said had been left for him some time ago at his master's, by a messenger from the house of the gray monks.

It was addressed, "A Don José Viracocha Inca, h. Cuzco." José cut the silk that secured it with his useless Spanish sword, and read these words:—

"MY SON,—I am sick in body and sick at

heart. Come to me if thou canst. I need thee. Ask for me here at the Franciscan monastery.

"Thy unworthy father in God,

"Fernando, Brother of the

"First Order of St. Francis.

"Given at Ciudad de los Reyes, on the vigil of San Antonio, in the year of grace 1573."

Nearly a year ago! Late in the day as it was already, José Viracocha had put three good leagues between himself and the Golden City ere he saw the sun drop in flame behind the snowy peak of Vilcanota.

Old England

"That mother's face,
Its grave sweet smile yet wearing in the place
Where so it ever smiled."

~ HEMANS

IT NOW BECOMES NECESSARY FOR US to pass, with the rapidity of thought, from one side of the globe to the other, that we may visit for a little while the shores of "Merrie England"—

the England of Queen Elizabeth and the Reformation.

It was a glorious hour in England's day—the hour that followed the sunrise. Everywhere life was awakening—life of the intellect and imagination, and, through God's blessing, that yet higher life which is his best and purest gift. Therefore living works were wrought, of which the memory shall last as long as this earth endures.

But our concern is not now with the brilliant workers of that busy age. We shall not visit the starry court of the maiden Queen, nor allow ourselves to linger fondly over names—such as Raleigh, Spenser, Sidney, Shakespeare—which have become "music more than any song" to every English ear. Rather shall we glance at the interior of a modest home, where dwelt in those days an English matron, who, though unknown to fame, was truly one of the noble band without whom the England of Elizabeth and the Reformation never could have been.

In the weald of Kent, where the trim hop-gardens flourish now, there stood at that time a half-ruined keep, built in the stormy age of the Wars of the Roses. It was much out of repair, and quite destitute of what were then accounted modern improvements. Its principal apartment was still the great hall, which was heated by a fire on the hearth, strewn with rushes, and furnished with massive, quaintly-carved oaken benches, cupboards, and tables.

But some women have the faculty of transforming any place, however dreary, formal, or comfortless, into a home. Of such was Marion Gray, widow of Walter Gray, a gentleman of Kent, of ancient lineage and good repute.

It is evening; and Marion Gray sits at the center table, an oil lamp illuminating the space around her, but leaving the greater part of the gloomy hall in twilight. She is busy adorning the sleeve of a cambric shirt with very fine "pearling;" her deft fingers moving rapidly, while her eyes are seldom raised from her work, save for a hasty glance at the lamp, which scarcely affords the amount of light needful for such delicate embroidery "Shall I trim it, mother?" asks her companion, a fair boy, who does not seem equally loath to look up from the pages of a great book he has been reading aloud. The volume, "imprinted at London, by John Day and William Seres," consists of the collected theological writings of the Reformer Thomas Becon, and certainly is not just what an ordinary boy would have chosen for his private enjoyment. But Walter Gray is not an ordinary boy; and if he had been, those were days in which young people did the pleasure of their elders, not their own.

"I think it needs not," the mother answered. Then, perhaps surmising that the boy was tired of reading, she asked him, "Dost remember any of thy cousins, Walter?"

"None but George, mother. Do you not mind the year you had the great fever, and my aunt came here to tend you'? How she brought George, a ten years' bairn, with her; for she said he was so masterful, and of such high stomach, none of the maids durst attempt to keep him under? And a proper life we led each other, he and I. The very night he came we fought together. He called me an outlandish imp, and no true Englishman, because I was born at Geneva; and I for answer fetched him a buffet on the cheek."

"Ill-conditioned boy! Even at seven years old, you should have known better than to strike your little guest."

"Marry, mother, he paid me, and with usury," laughed Walter. "But if I had had the wit, I might have given him a better answer. I might have said he would have been born at Geneva too, an his father had not thought more of his silks and satins than of his conscience."

"Therein thou wouldst have shown thine foolishness as well as thy discourtesy. In Queen Mary's days thine Uncle Noble did not yet know the gospel; how then could he go into exile for it? In truth, it was what he saw, in those evil times, of the faith and patience of the saints that, with God's blessing, won him to a better mind. I have heard him say so myself. And as for thy comrade George," she added more lightly, "I daresay his love of fighting stands him in good stead now, when he meets the Dons upon the high seas."

Walter's face, naturally fair and pale, was overspread in an instant by a crimson flush, telling of some strong hidden feeling suddenly awakened. But it passed as quickly as it came; and he said, in his ordinary tone, "Mother, I pray you, tell me the names of all my cousins. 'Twere as well I knew them, at least after a fashion, ere I saw them."

"Willingly, my boy. Thine aunt hath said

so much of them in her letters, that I almost think I can see the six stalwart lads gathered round her, with the one fair girl they are all so fond and proud of. First, then, there is Thomas, good steady lad, as for old times' sake they call him still, though he must be near his thirtieth year now. He is his father's right hand and faithful helper. Next comes Harry, the soldier; he has volunteered, I told you, in aid of the persecuted Protestants in the Low Countries. Your uncle can send him thither better furnished forth than many a peer's son. Will, the third in age, is 'prentice to Master Nevet, the jeweler."

"'Prentice!" cried Walter in high disdain." O mother! Only think of one of our blood standing at the door of a shop, and crying ' what do ye lack; what do ye lack, my masters?' as Sir John Carr says the London 'prentices are wont to do."

Mrs. Gray looked steadily at her son with her clear, soft blue eyes, and said, flushing faintly, "Then what think you, Walter, of one of our blood sitting up whole nights to work English broidery on the robes of a Geneva citizen's dame, carrying them to her with her own hands afterward, and taking thankfully the silver she gave in payment?"

"And did you do that, mother" asked Walter, with softened look. "What dreadful times they must have been!"

"Not dreadful *then,* for God sent them, and each day had but one day's burden to bear. But sometimes now they seem dreadful to look back upon.—Of whom was I speaking? Of Will? George the sailor comes next in age. And I suspect Master James will never rest till he follows the same way of life,—for all his father's talk of needing his help himself."

"Has James then told his father that he wants to go to sea?" asked Walter abruptly, and in a tone more blunt and eager than that in which he usually addressed his mother.

"He has spoken of his wishes more than once, I believe; but he obeys his father, as in duty bound.—Take care, Walter; you will spoil my book. Pity lads are not taught to sew, since it is hard to keep idle hands out of mischief.—After James comes the fair maiden Lilias, the pet and pride of all her brave brothers; she will be about thy age, I reckon. Lastly, there is little Ned, the scholar of the family; he was thirteen at Christmas. Be kind to Ned, Walter, and let him look to you as to an elder brother; for I wot his father means to send him to Oxford, and you may be a good friend to him there, being the elder by three years. There,—that is finished, and makes the eighth of your new shirts.—Be very careful, Walter, whom you trust for the washing of them; for cambric and Holland are light to rend and ill to mend."

"Yes, mother," said Walter, with a sigh.

The next day he was to leave the home of his childhood and to begin a new life amongst strangers. Yet dearly as he loved his mother (and good right he had to love her dearly), it was not the thought of parting that wrung that sigh from the boy's heart. He was thinking of what had just been said about his cousin, James Noble.

Walter Gray's life hitherto had been rather a singular one for a boy. He was born at Geneva, during his parents' exile for conscience' sake; and he barely remembered their departure from that friendly city, and his father's death on the homeward journey. The young widow and her orphan boy were most kindly received in London by the worthy merchant to whom her sister had been induced to give her hand, at a time when everyone thought she sorely disgraced her family by so doing. But now the wheel of Fortune had turned so far that good Master Noble, mercer and warden of his craft, had more to spend on the education of any one of his six sons than sufficed Mistress Marion

Gray to maintain the state of a gentlewoman in the home of her husband's ancestors.

It was well that she was not obliged to delegate the important task of her only son's education to any hands but her own. Like many noble women of the sixteenth century, Marion Markham and her sister Lilias had received from their father an excellent classical education. So good a teacher was she, and so apt a pupil did Walter prove, that when at length, distrusting her own powers, she sent him to the vicar of the parish, Sir John Carr, to be examined in Greek and Latin, that worthy gentleman, whose store of learning was not ample, found the scholar of fifteen quite too much for him. He prudently sent him back to his mother with a highly complementary letter, in which he compared her to Minerva, to Cornelia, and, what was more to the purpose, to the sainted "twelve days' queen," her husband's distant relative.

Nor were studies yet more important than Greek and Latin forgotten. Walter was made familiar from his earliest childhood with the Book that his mother held dearer than life, and constant were her prayers that its holy lessons might be written on his heart.

Walter had another teacher, moreover, a stern but very efficient one. In the school of poverty he learned self-denial; and well has it been remarked that "the worst education that teaches self-denial is better than the best that teaches everything else, and leaves that out."

And yet, in spite of all, there was one defect—only one, but that a great one—in Walter's education. The boy had no boyhood. A truly healthful, happy childhood he had enjoyed in its season; for the child dwells in his own little world, safe as the fairy in her crystal globe from the cares and sorrows and most of the dangers of maturity. Almost all the little child really needs is love. Give him *Mat,* and no matter how poor and bare and narrow his surroundings may be, imagination will make them a kingdom. But it is otherwise when

"Shades of the prison-house begin to close
Around the growing boy."

Then, in proportion as his wants increase, his dangers multiply. His animal nature grows and expands, while imagination pales and fades, leaving him very dependent on the common world that surrounds him, often very curious about it, asking a great deal from it, and influenced by it in ten thousand ways. Through this stage he must needs pass, if he is to prove hereafter a complete and well-developed man.

Walter Gray, however, was expected to grow at once, and without any interval, from the thoughtful child into the thoughtful man. Boyhood, with "its unchecked, unbidden joy, its dread of books and love of fun," was not for him. Instead of sharing the sports of merry schoolmates, this boy shared his mother's cares and anxieties as her friend and confidant, sometimes even already her counselor. Instead of planning victories at prisoner's base and trap ball, and raids upon orchards and nut-woods, he planned how to find bread and beer enough for their household, and still to have somewhat over to give to him that needed. Virgil and Plato were to him what "The Seven Champions of Christendom" were to other boys. It is true that he was taught to ride, and to shoot with the bow and arrow, and he could do these as well as any lad of his years; but he did them, as he did everything else, gravely and with a purpose. They were part of his education.

It is not easy to defraud Nature of her due. Often, for the time, she seems to acquiesce,—at least she takes it patiently, and makes no sign. But she silently keeps account of every debt; and it is well if some day she does not suddenly present a bill for the sum total, and demand an acquittal, admitting of no denial.

Late that night Walter sat in thoughtful mood upon his trestle bed. His chest, packed by his mother's careful hand in readiness for the morrow's journey, lay so near, that his feet, as he swung them back and forwards, sometimes touched it. His doublet was off; his fair hair, tumbled by his restless hands, fell in disorder over his neat Holland shirt. There was no light in the room, save what the moonbeams shed through the narrow, unglazed slit that served for a window.

The boy was asking himself a question, often well-nigh the most important a boy can ask, "Shall I tell my mother?" He asked it the more sincerely and earnestly because he had just been repeating the evening prayer his mother taught him, and not without some simple additions, the promptings of his own heart. And now he had a great mind to delay no longer, but to step softly to the door of his mother's room (where he well knew the light would still be burning), to seek admittance, to kneel down beside her chair—just as he knelt when he learned his first prayer—and to tell her all.

But *what* was that "all"? What had he to tell?—As well to find that out first. And really it was difficult to find out;—it perplexed him. There he sat, feeling as though some weighty, half-guilty secret lay upon his heart, something that he was almost acting a traitor's part in keeping hidden there, and carrying away with him un-confessed. Yet, when he sought for words in which to tell it, *what* had he to say? Only that upon every excuse (and often indeed without excuse), he used to loiter about the stall of the village blacksmith—once a seaman, and sharer in some of old John Hawkins' most desperate enterprises;—that he was never tired of listening to his wonderful tales of daring deeds wrought by English hearts and hands upon the high seas, where the small, slight vessels of English merchantmen so often measured their strength against the stately caraques of the Don;—that he cared little to ride anywhere save to the crest of the hill, whence he could see the far-off waters sparkle in the sunlight, and sometimes watch a white sail gliding slowly by, wondering if it was bound for that great mysterious West, the land of his romance and enchantment. That was all he could find to say; and what was there in that to trouble his mother with at midnight?

But beneath there was a blind, dumb instinct, a great passionate longing, for which he had no words. Perhaps it was a heritage from some far-off Viking ancestor, whose slender, snake-like galley had pushed its prow into unknown seas in search of fame and plunder. Walter had no names for the thoughts and feelings that for more than a year had been troubling him so strangely, growing every day more frequent and more keen. He only knew that he would have given all the world to change his fine cloth and velvet for a pea-jacket, his Holland shirt for a Jersey, his scholar's pen for a stout cutlass. But what use in crying for the moon? Work of a different sort was cut out for him. Tomorrow he must go to London, to visit his kinsfolk in the city; and after that to Oxford, to study hard (he liked study well enough, when ships were not sailing away westward before his mind's eye), to win honor, fame, and wealth, and at last—perhaps— if God willed and made him worthy—to take holy orders and preach, like Sir John Carr.

What folly he had been thinking! He felt quite ashamed of himself. He would go to bed, sleep, and forget it all. The sooner the better, for the nights were cold (it was early March); he should freeze if he sat there much longer. He must rise before daybreak; but he was sure old Dickon would call him in good time; *he* was never late.

So Walter Gray paid the tribute of a sigh to his boyish dreams; then he went to bed and to sleep, nevertheless he did not forget them all.

His Own Way

WALTER HAD NOT BEEN LONG ASLEEP, when loud knocking at the great door awaked him. Saying to himself, "They might knock till

Doomsday for old Dickon—early to bed and early to rise is his motto," he rose, and putting on his clothes hastily, went to see who was there.

It was Sir John Carr, who good-naturedly had ridden two or three miles out of his way from the neighboring town to bring Mrs. Gray a letter, left there for her by means of that as yet rude and primitive institution, "Her Majesty's Post." It would seem, indeed, that common humanity demanded this service, since the letter bore the following quaint addition to the ordinary superscription:—"Haste! Haste! Haste! Post, haste for thy life! See thou tarry not!"

Walter, reading this, and not being aware that such exhortations were quite customary, "by reason that the posts be so slow nowadays," brought the letter in some alarm to his mother, who, late as the hour was, had not yet retired to rest. "I fear there is something wrong with my uncle's folk," he said.

Mrs. Gray broke the seal and read in silence. "All is well, thank God," she answered. "But your uncle feared the letter might not come till after you had gone. There is a ship, in which he hath a venture, lying at Sheerness, and now ready to go up to London. And he thinks it will save expense and trouble for you to ride thither, and take advantage of the ship."

"I have no objection," cried the delighted Walter. "And indeed, mother, for that matter—," he continued, with a flushed face and nervous air.

But just at that moment Mrs. Gray's little oil lamp went out suddenly, so she did not see the boy's face. And she knew it was past midnight, that Walter ought to be in the saddle by five in the morning, and that young eyes need long sleep. So she kissed him, and bade him go to bed at once.

Walter's happiness may be guessed when, in due course, he found himself at last on board a real ship. The *Royal Tudor* was a Turkey-merchantman, just returned from the Levant, well laden with the rich silks and cashmeres of the East. But she was something more. Great guns showed their black muzzles from her portholes, and stem and stern were garnished with what, to Walter's inexperienced eye, looked like fortresses, small but strong. Every man on board was a soldier, prepared to do and die in defense of the ship and the ship's freight. The *"Noli me tangere"* of the Scottish thistle would have been an apt motto for the English ship; though the converse, "I will not touch you," would have been far from applicable. Woe to the trader or man-of-war—whether Spanish, Flemish, or Portuguese—which should dare to interfere with her, or, even without interfering, should cross her path by accident! Already she had given a good account of more than one "caraque" or "caravel," over which the yellow flag of Spain should never float again. And everyone on board, from the captain to the cab-in-boy, considered such "spoiling of the Egyptians" not only perfectly lawful, but a highly meritorious and satisfactory doing of their duty in that state of life unto which it had pleased God to call them.

All this and much more Walter learned, before he had been four-and-twenty hours on board, from his cousin George. The light-hearted, good-natured sailor-lad did the honors of the ship, his pride and joy, in first-rate style to his gentlemanly cousin; nor was he by any means insensible to the profound admiration with which the young scholar regarded him. This admiration might have become mutual, not without advantage to both, had not Walter's evil genius prompted him to show off the fragments of nautical knowledge he had picked up from his friend the blacksmith. In his enthusiasm he ventured upon some ill-advised observations about "cobridge-heads," "skyscrapers," and "mizzen-masts," which provoked George to peals of laughter, and unnecessarily loud assertions that "Master Walter might be a fine scholar on shore, but he did not know a main-mast from a marlin-spike on board ship."

Walter ought to have- joined in the laugh, or found a good-humored retort. But it is hard to be taunted with ignorance of what we love. So he changed color, and, with some irritation of manner, vowed that he would soon know everything on board as well as George himself. And he was as good as his word.

When the ship arrived in London, the welcome he received from his uncle and aunt and their family was all that could be desired. Thomas Noble was a good specimen of a fine class, the merchantmen of England, who were then beginning to be what they have been ever since, "the honorable men of the earth." Like so many of their brethren in the Low Countries and elsewhere, they had espoused, almost universally, the cause of religious truth and freedom, and they maintained it often with great courage and liberality. There was not amongst them all a more zealous "Gospeller" than Master Noble, Warden of the Mercers' Company, and some time Sheriff of London Town.

He dwelt on London Bridge,—like the well-known cloth merchant, Master Hewit, whose young daughter the apprentice, Edward Osborne, saved by his celebrated leap from the kitchen window into the river below. All things had gone prosperously with Master Noble. He had the blessing that makes rich, and no sorrow added with it. His six brave sons were doing well, each in his own way. Gentle Lilias was a flower scarcely opened, fair and pure as a spring lily. At the time of Walter's visit, it happened that all were at home, or within easy reach of it, and often gathered around the cheerful, plentiful board where their father presided.

Walter was very happy amongst them. His

days and weeks glided rapidly by amidst novel sights and exciting occupations. He saw the Queen ride in state to old St. Paul's, amidst transports of the loyal ardor that was such a characteristic feature of the times. He saw St. Paul's itself; and Westminster Abbey, and the Tower, and the shops, and the fields where the young men and apprentices played games, and practiced archery; and he sent out his own cloth-yard arrow very creditably amongst the rest. What was better than all, he bore part in a healthy, kindly family life, where peace, order, and plenty reigned.

It was strange enough that his most intimate friend amongst his cousins should be the one that he had come prepared almost to despise-"'prentice Will," in his plain blue gown and close-cropped hair. One evening at supper George was vaunting the glories of the *Royal Tudor*, when Will (who was frequently permitted to join the family meal, his master being an old and valued friend of his father's) looked up quietly from his trencher of powdered beef, and remarked, "She's well enough, brother George; but call me knave and Papist if the *English Merchantman* does not beat her as clean as Harry beat that great lubberly lout of a draper's lad last Saturday at the butts in Finsbury fields."

"Speak of what you understand, my lad of watches and finger rings," George retorted contemptuously. "Would you wish a craft built for running to and fro in the Mediterranean to look like a cruiser for the Spanish main?"

"Is the *Royal Merchantman* to sail the Spanish main?" asked Walter in an eager, nervous whisper.

"The *English Merchantman,* an it please you, cousin," Will corrected aloud; "though, indeed," he added mysteriously, "if all were known, the other name might not come so much amiss. My master more than hints there be high and mighty personages with him in his venture."

"Will," said his father, "don't speak evil of dignities."

"Where's the evil, father?" Will asked briskly, yet respectfully. "Everyone knows my master's good conditions; and that which, in the way of gain or profit, would not soil *his* fingers, is clean enough to be touched by the Queen's gracious Majesty herself, God bless her."

"Amen" said Harry the soldier. "Will, my lad, ne'er fash thyself with scruples about the *English Merchantman*. Let her cleave the waves as merrily as she lists. Ay, and let her crew seize Spanish treasure,—what is that but robbing the robber, and spoiling the spoiler? And if they cut the throats of the men—say rather of the fiends—that guard it, they will serve them better than—"

"Harry! Harry!" It was his mother who spoke, and in a tone of grieved surprise. "Are these fit words for a Christian man to speak?"

"No fit words for you to hear, at all events; so I crave your pardon, mother," he answered. "Yet, if you knew what I know of deeds done by the hands of Spanish men, I think that you-even *you,* could not weigh and measure out your words when you spoke of them."

"Will," whispered Walter, "will you take me to see the *English Merchantman?*" "With all my heart," Will answered.

He was quite ready to fulfill his promise. The next Saturday afternoon, the holiday of London 'prentices, was the time fixed upon. Will asked his cousin's leave to bring with them his fellow-apprentice, and Walter somewhat reluctantly consented. He found Eustace Jenkyns, however, a notable addition to their party. He was a bold, merry scapegrace, who, to Walter's surprise, seemed quite an authority upon nautical matters; but, as Will privately informed him, was "nowhere" in the business, and just now in disgrace with his master for

sundry acts of gross inattention and careless-
ness. Naturally idle and restless, he had fallen
in with some of the wild speculations current
at the time, and these had filled his head with
visions of money-getting, far more rapid than
any the workshop or the counter could realize.
He talked of the gold to be won in the far West
by brave hearts and ready hands, even alluding
to the legend, already well known to Walter,
of the lake of Parima and the golden city of
Manoa or El Dorado. Walter believed, for his
part, that the Incas who had been dispossessed
by the Spaniards were still reigning there in
barbaric splendor; and many and many a time,
as he sat in the window of the old hall in his
childhood's home with some early narrative of
travel borrowed from the vicar before him, had
he dreamed of finding and restoring them. Eustace Jenkyns did not care in the least for the
lost Incas, but he cared for gold and for glory.
Of these he talked, while Walter listened—and

the poison shot through his veins like fire. Gold would be welcome, of course, to one who knew so well the pains and privations of poverty. But glory!— that was the bait that drew him irresistibly on.

He was not greatly shocked when at last Eustace trusted him with his grand secret. "I was not made for crying, ' what do you lack, my masters? ' or for twisting steel wires and copper filings either," he said. "My Christmas box is broken and spent long ago, my credit gone, my master turned against me.

'Twere no great matter to break my indentures too, and slip oft in the dark next Friday se'nnight to the *English Merchantman*. So Master Nevit would lose a bad 'prentice, and the service would gain a good sailor. And what would you think, Master Walter, of flinging off that pretty scholar's gown, crying, ' He, for the high seas!' and joining me?"

"Fie on you, Jenkyns!" cried Walter, turning away half angry, half amused. And yet the shaft hit.

A chain of circumstances, slight, yet strong, had woven itself around him, and by this he was being gradually drawn onwards to a deed from which, if boldly proposed to him at first, he would have turned away in horror. And yet, if his heart had not yielded already to temptation, these circumstances would have been as powerless to draw him as threads of gossamer.

It was quite natural that pretty Cousin Lilias should receive a large share of Master Walter's attention and admiration. As the time was drawing near when he ought to quit his uncle's hospitable roof for Oxford, it occurred to him to beg one of the young lady's top-knots for a keepsake. This was fair enough, since he had spent much more than he should have done upon ribbons and trinkets for her. Happening to find her one evening alone—she was standing in a kind of lobby that had a window, with a balcony outside, overlooking the river— he modestly preferred his important request. At first he played the grown-up cavalier, made her the fairest compliments he could think of and even indulged in some of the "euphemisms" which were then beginning to become fashionable.

But gradually his boyish nature reasserted itself, and forgetting his assumed manliness, he sprang forward and deftly tried to snatch the precious knot of blue ribbon; which, however, Lilias, for fear of surprise, had already taken from its place, and was holding high above her head. And thus for a minute's space or so they fenced and parried, laughing lightly at their sport, like the children they really were.

So absorbed were they in their play that George drew near unnoticed. The young sailor was very proud of his sister, and had never been quite cordial with Walter Gray since he observed his attentions to her. He showed, therefore, more indignation than the occasion seemed to demand. "Sister Lilias, you are too old to play with unmannerly boys," he remarked in an elder-brotherly tone of reproof. "Our mother is asking for you in the parlor."

Lilias took the hint and vanished; although she did not present herself in the well-lighted parlor until she had cooled her burning cheeks with fresh water. George meanwhile gave Walter the full benefit of his angry scorn.

"You poor little scholar boy!" he cried. "Prithee, keep to your Latin grammar, and leave ladies' top-knots for those who can win them in something better than child's play. If you had not been all your life tied to your mother's apron, you would know by this time that my sister Lilias—"

"At least I know what you, sir, seem to have forgotten-that your sister is a lady," interrupted the indignant Walter. "How dare you chide her as an ill-conditioned child? And as for myself, though I have the misfortune to be a scholar, I hope at least to show you that I am a man. Will you fight me, sirrah"

"I'll put thee in my pocket, and carry thee over the Bridge and along Cheapside, with all the 'prentice lads and serving-lasses to look on and cry Lack-a-day!" returned George, laughing heartily. "Nay, nay," he added presently, glancing at Walter's flushed face and lowering brow, "'tis but sailor's nonsense, Cousin Walter. I mean no harm. There, give me your hand. One must be careful of a girl like Lilias, though."

But Walter turned haughtily from him, and leaning against the casement, looked out upon the waters of the Thames, gliding peacefully far below.

"The lad is dumpish," thought George. "Well, I can't help that. Tomorrow I will buy for him that book I saw him eye so lovingly in old Spicer's booth the other day, to show I bear no malice." Comforting himself with this resolve, he walked away, carelessly whistling some sailor's melody.

Walter stood and gazed—in a listless, unhappy mood, discontented with his lot in life, angry with everyone, but most of all with himself. If he could but go away, win gold and glory, and then come back and show his cousins the worth of the "little scholar boy" they despised! What was it that just then shot noiselessly from under the arch of the bridge? A wherry, barely visible through the darkening gloom. But he marked it as it glided past; and he knew its errand well. Had not Eustace Jenkyns told him all? What mattered the details of the plot—how serving men and lasses were bribed, and the suspicions of the city watch laid to rest by a plausible story, accounting for the appearance of the wherry at that unseasonable hour? All he cared to think of was the rapturous joy with which the freed apprentice would set his foot that night on the deck of the *English Merchantman.* And then,—away to the distant West, to the land of gold and glory, of romance and dreams!

Why should Eustace Jenkyns, the goldsmith's runaway apprentice, taste that joy, and Walter Gray, scholar and gentleman, be shut out from it all? Was not his own life in his hand to do what he pleased with? For one delicious maddening moment he seemed to feel the spicy gales from those distant shores already fanning his cheek. And then his eye rested on the boat, gliding slowly past once more, *two* men in it now.

Another moment and the opportunity would be gone-gone forever. There was no time for thought. From the ship he would write to his mother, explain all, and excuse himself-if he could. Now he must act; now or never. He took out a white kerchief, and waved it. The signal was noticed by the men in the wherry—one of them raised his oar to a perpendicular position by way of answer.

Now, what should he do? At this hour the doors would be shut and all the lower windows of the house securely fastened, nor could he open them without attracting attention. But he remembered that George had once descended from the balcony to the river,—a perilous, but practicable feat, which he had heard him describe, with all its circumstances, for the benefit of James and Ned. Walter, naturally brave, was capable in this hour of excitement of the wildest daring. His head was steady, and his limbs were light and agile. In a moment he was out on the balcony, over it, clinging to it with both hands while he sought foothold beneath. He had not, fortunately, to entrust himself to a trim, modern building, smooth as glass from attic to basement. The kitchen window, an old statue of a saint in a niche, uneven stones here and there, tufts of grass, weeds, lastly the bridge buttress, gave him the support he needed, and enabled him at length to drop exhausted, but unhurt, into the dark cold waters beneath. He was soon helped into the boat by the astonished, but admiring Eustace Jenkyns.

And thus Walter Gray, by one egregious act of folly, or rather of madness, falsified the promise of his thoughtful childhood and precocious boyhood, gave the lie to all his past life, and utterly changed all his future.

Where It Led

"Oh! what a tale to shadow with its gloom
That happy home in England. Idle fear!
Would the winds tell it?"

~ HEMANS

THREE YEARS HAVE PASSED AWAY since Walter Gray so suddenly and strangely forsook his home and his ' friends. During that time he has had his heart's desire—in part, at least. He has seen how the sunlight glistens on the waters of the Spanish main, his foot has pressed the flowery shores of unknown islands, and his hand has borne part, not unworthily, in England's great naval contest with the enemies of her creed and her race.

But for all this he has paid a heavy price. He has taken his own way, and whither has it led him? Haply to an early grave, amongst the shells and sea-weed, fathoms deep below the blue waters he so longed to look upon? Had such been his fate, many might have mourned, but some would have envied him; and certainly, no forebodings of an early, honorable death would have done aught to deter him from the path he had chosen. But the English mariner who in those days dared to invade the Spanish main, the Pope's gift to his favorite son, had to brave dangers far more terrible. The Holy Inquisition stretched its ghastly arm over half the globe, and with a touch, "cold, strong, passionless, like a dead man's clasp," claimed and held every English prisoner that fell into Spanish hands.

Rashly— perhaps too rashly— the *English Merchantman* measured her strength against a great Spanish galleon and two smaller vessels, with which she fell in off Juan Fernandez. Gallant was the fight maintained by the English ship, but it was too unequal even for that day of marvelous naval achievements. After five hours' hard fighting she was glad to get away, crippled and sorely raked, yet unconquered. But Walter Gray was reported missing. No man saw his face again, after that first mad rush upon the enemies' deck in which he had borne his part so bravely.

And could his comrades have seen his face six months afterward they would not have recognized him. Well would it have been for him had he died of the wound that separated him from his countrymen, and left him a helpless captive in the hands of the Spaniards, and at the mercy of the Holy Inquisition. By that hideous magician the bright-eyed, fair-haired English youth was soon transformed into a gaunt skeleton, old in misery, if still young in years. In pursuance of his sentence at an auto-de-fe in Lima, he took his place on the narrow wooden bench of a Spanish galley, and chained to three other wretches, toiled with them at the task of moving one of its forty great oars.

Here—it is a fellow-sufferer who speaks—his food was a scanty allowance of "coarse black biscuit and water, his lodging was the bare boards and planks of the galley, and hunger, thirst, cold, and stripes he lacked none."[1]

But, it will be asked, had Walter Gray no alternative? Did men come forth from the gates of that gloomy "Santa Casa," only to take their places in Spanish galleys? Not always. Some there were who wrestled boldly with the Inqui-

---

1.   "Narrative of Job Hortop, in "Hakluyt's Voyages."

sition fiend and overcame him, finding man's worst God's best, and death the gate of glory. But each of these crowned conquerors possessed a talisman, whose marvelous virtue bore them through the fiercest conflict,—even that white stone "wherein is written a new name, which no man knoweth save he that receiveth it."

Walter Gray had not this talisman. Yet for the honor of his country, for the remembrance of the lessons learned beside his mother's knee, he had borne much, and with heroic spirit. He knew that the creed he had been taught in childhood was true. But then he did not know that its promises were true *for him*. Perhaps they were, perhaps they were not; and like far wiser men, Walter Gray found it "hard to die for a perhaps." So at last his heart failed him. He became a Penitent; and he experienced the tender mercies of the Inquisition towards returning penitents. He was sent to the galleys—

for twenty years, or for life. He scarcely knew how the sentence ran; and in fact it did not matter.

Here, at first, he breathed rather than lived. He took no note of time, for "his soul was black, and knew no change of night or day." His fettered limbs moved at their hateful task like parts of a machine, and thus he suffered little beyond the mere outward bodily miseries of his lot. He might have died thus erelong; and then, his chains loosed at last, he would have been flung into the sea with no more thought or ceremony than a dead hound. But he was roused at last from his torpor by a slight accidental circumstance.

One day the commissary, or overseer of the slaves, was as usual walking up and down the narrow gangway that separated the two tiers of benches on which the rowers sat. Something was amiss with the handle of the great Manita whip he carried in his hand, and he took out a strong knife to mend it. But the blade snapped across near the haft and fell down amongst the slaves, close to the place where Walter sat. He had often, in a vague, dreamy way, wished himself dead and out of his misery. Now the thought flashed across his mind that with this weapon he could kill himself. He snatched it up, and hid it in the sleeve of his tattered red jerkin. As at that moment the attention of the commissary was diverted to something that was taking place on the other side of the vessel, the action passed unobserved, at least by him.

Walter had now a definite purpose, and his mind awoke from its lethargy to deliberate on the best means of executing it. The desire to die actually helped to bring him back to life. He would kill himself, and be done with all this pain; no further did his thoughts travel. But how to do the deed?

It seemed very easy; now that he was provided with a weapon, it might be done at any moment. But he could not dismiss the fear that his ever-watchful enemies might by some means or other bar even *this* door of escape from their cruelty; indeed, the instinct of a hunted, baited creature was sufficient in itself to make him conceal his movements. So he determined upon waiting until nightfall, when the miserable slaves, bending over their oars, snatched a few hours of comfortless repose.

Night came at last. All was still on board the galley. Walter looked cautiously around him—then took out his weapon. For one moment, and no more, he hesitated: by this time he was naturalized to horrors, and deliberately and of set purpose "his soul chose death rather than life." But the broken blade hurt his hand; and he lost another moment, in the very act of turning it against his own heart, in trying so to grasp it as to avoid this trifling pain. So ineradicable is the natural instinct of self-preservation.

In that instant his arm was seized somewhat roughly, and *the* voice of the slave who sat next him whispered in his ear, "Camerado, what are you doing?"

"No harm to you," answered Walter, who had by this time been schooled by hard necessity in the tongue of the stranger. "No good to yourself," rejoined the other; and he wrenched the broken blade from the poor boy's nerveless hand, and flung it overboard.

"Oh! why did you take it from me?" cried Walter. "It was cruel!—I needed it." And leaning over his oar, he gave way to a passionate fit of weeping.

Since he came on board the galley, he had not shed a tear. Nor could he have told anyone why he wept now. He would have said, if asked, that his tears were for the lost fragment of steel, for which he felt an unreasoning, childish regret.

The weather-beaten slave beside him laid a fettered, bony hand on his. The gesture was friendly, but friendly gestures were so strange to Walter now, that he started and sobbed in his alarm, "Do not betray me."

"God forbid!" replied the other. "I have not spent fifteen years at the oar for nothing. Do not weep, camerado. Pray God to forgive your sin, and go to sleep."

"I cannot sleep," Walter answered. "Would to God I could die!"

"When your time comes, He will call you. Perhaps tonight. The more need you should ask His forgiveness."

Walter feared to be drawn into any talk about religion, lest he should implicate himself by some unguarded word, and fall again into the cruel hands of the Inquisition. So he only said, rather sullenly, "I am an Englishman."

"Englishmen pray to God, and He hears them. I once saw two Englishmen die, and I am very sure God was with them."

"Where was that?" asked Walter, with some faint stirrings of curiosity, and a strange feeling, half pleasure half pain, at the mention of his countrymen.

"At a great auto-de-fe. They were burned alive—"

"Hush!" Walter interrupted with a shudder. "Don't talk of that."

"Not if it troubles you, señor." This fellow-slave of Walter's knew him to be a gentleman, and addressed him as such; an attention not without its effect on the mind of the unhappy youth. "Yet that was no worse than this," he added,—"not so bad, as I think sometimes. I was very near proving it too."

"Why, what have you done?"—Walter had often heard the other slaves talk carelessly, and even boastfully, of their crimes; but he never knew this man to make the slightest allusion to his past history.

"I was thought to have done something

which had almost lit the pile for me. I might have shared the fate of those two Englishmen—well if I had shared their hope."

"Are you not afraid to talk thus?" Walter asked. "Is it not dangerous?"

"You speak of danger!—you, who tried just now to kill yourself! Had you succeeded, where would you be?"

"At least not in the Inquisition," was Walter's murmured answer.

"O camerado! don't you know that it is a fearful thing to fall into the hands of the living God?"

"I ought to know it," Walter answered sadly. "Has He not sent me here for my sins?" With a long shuddering sigh he thought of his treason to his mother, and his weak denial of his mother's faith. And again he wept—wept and sobbed aloud. For after a long drought the rain-clouds are apt to hang heavily; and it is not the first shower or the second that will clear the sky.

"Weep on," said his comrade. "God has set you two lessons. One—your own sin—you are learning now; the other He will teach you by-and-by."

But though Walter's right hand neighbor desired him to weep on, his "oar-fellow," who sat on the bench above him, was of another mind. This man, who had been captain of a gang of robbers in the wilds of the Sierra Morena, bestowed a hearty kick and curse on his young comrade. "Hold your peace, English heretic," he said; " else I will call the commissary, and put it to his conscience as a good Catholic, whether it is not penance enough to be beaten all day like a hound, without being kept awake all night like an owl."

Walter thought it best to take this gentle hint. He rested his weary head upon his oar, the only pillow it had known for months, and tried to sleep.

But sleep would not come to him. Thoughts came instead, crowding thick and fast upon him-thoughts of home, of his mother. No wonder that he wept on still, though noiselessly, lest he should awaken his companions.

At last he raised his head quietly; and through the mild gloom of the tropical night, which was not darkness, he looked cautiously at his right-hand neighbor, or—as in thought he had already begun to call him—his friend.

Doubtful whether the thin gray hair that fell over the oar concealed the face of a sleeper, Walter gently touched the ragged sleeve.

"*Quién va?*" the Spaniard responded, turning to him at once, with a questioning look in his keen dark eyes, where the fire burned still, undimmed by the sorrows that had turned his raven hair to gray, and worn his stalwart frame to a skeleton.

"That *other lesson?* What is it? Tell me, camerado."

For a minute's space the galley-slave was silent. Then, in a voice scarcely raised above a whisper, but so clear and distinct that every word stood out as if read by a lightning flash, he repeated,—"'The Lord is nigh unto all them that call upon Him, to all that call upon Him in truth. He will fulfill the desire of them that fear Him, He also will hear their cry, and will save them.' Ay, señor, even in the galleys!"

At the Oar

"Old faces look upon me,
Old forms go crowding past."
~ AYTOUN

WALTER GRAY SLEPT AT LAST; weariness of body gaining the victory over sorrow of heart. He was wakened from a dream of home, more vivid than any he had known for months, by curses and blows and cries of pain, the usual matins of the galley-slave.

He put his stiff and weary limbs into the position necessary for their accustomed toil, and grasped his oar. But he did not escape a rough admonition from his comrade the bandit, seasoned with a couple of oaths.

"Look alive there, Englishman, and take your own share of the pulling; else you are pretty likely to take your own share of the lash by-and-by!"

It happened, however, that they received orders to pull gently. There was no occasion for haste, for the sea was calm, and they were near land. If he pleased, Walter might look about him as he rowed.

And right glorious was the sight that greeted his dim and tearful eyes. The water beneath was a sheet of liquid light, silver and rose; and before him stretched the green and pleasant shore of the Bay of Callao, with the giant Andes towering far above in the distance, the cold of their everlasting snows kindled into flame by the magic of the sunrise.

It was long since the crushed heart of Walter Gray had thrilled to the beauty of earth and sea. But this morning, like the Ancient Mariner, he "blessed them unawares;" and, like him, he felt the blessing return into his own bosom.

"Look, camerado!" he whispered to his friend, taking his right hand from the oar to point to the snowy mountains.

"*Quiton!*" murmured his older and more cautious companion—for the commissary was near. Too late! The cruel lash swung, quivered, descended. Walter's cry of pain rang through the clear morning air, startling his own ear with its echo, and making him ashamed of his weakness. Next time, he vowed, he would give no sign.

Already a change had begun in him; he was growing gradually more like his former self. And as days passed on, life and feeling returned to him, slowly but surely. It was a fettered hand, like his own, that had plucked him back from the gates of the grave. And that hand had also pointed upwards to a star of hope. Again and again did Walter's pale lips murmur over those words: "He also will hear their cry, and will save them '—even in the galleys."

But with hope came memory—fast-thronging memories of the past-of his home, his mother, his faith. Sharp, sudden stings of remorse followed. Conscience spoke aloud, and would not be 'silenced; telling of his home abandoned-his mother wronged and deceived, perhaps heart-broken—his faith forsaken, his God denied. Could there be forgiveness for such as he?

For a considerable time the *San Cristofero* lay quietly at anchor in the Bay of Callao; so he had leisure enough for thought. Indeed, we are assured by no less an authority than that of Cervantes, that there was "plenty of leisure in the galleys of Spain."

His look of deep dejection, and the tears that often, at this period, fell silently from his eyes, were not unnoticed by his compassionate comrade. This man went amongst his companions by the name of the "Matador;" for almost all the galley-slaves had quaint *sobriquets*, by which they were distinguished, their real names being rarely known, and still more rarely used. Nor could Walter help remarking that he was singularly unlike the rest. He never joined in the revolting blasphemies with which the rowers' benches so often resounded; he never tried to evade his share of the work, but rather exerted himself to shield and spare his weaker companions; and neither under the blazing tropical sun nor the drenching rains, neither in toil, in hunger, nor in pain, was he ever heard to murmur. By degrees Walter began to talk with him, to confide in him. And one day he abruptly uttered the substance of many a brooding thought,—"I hope they think me dead in England!"

"Why hope that, señor?"

"Better dead, than *here.* Better dead twice over, than a slave—and an apostate." The last word, it need scarcely be said, was breathed in a low and cautious whisper.

"That depends,"—the matador replied, with equal caution. Walter felt sorry he had ventured so far, and held his peace.

But the matador resumed presently, of his own accord, "Life is better than death, señor."

"This is not life; it is living death," Walter answered.

"Not so, my young camerado. It is written, 'The dead cannot praise Thee.'"

"*Praise!* If you spoke of prayer, I might understand you. But who ever yet praised God in the galleys?"

"One, at least, señor. A poor man who,

long ago, in the depths of his despair, cried, and the Lord heard him, and saved him out of all his troubles.'"

"Do you mean—" Walter stopped and hesitated. "I wish," he continued, looking at him with interest," I wish you would tell me who you are; and what misfortune—crime I cannot believe it to have been-has brought you hither."

"Whereto would that serve, señor? Mine is an humble name, unknown to fame. And I do not, like you, suffer for my faith. I am here for the deeds wrought by my own right hand."

These words destroyed a hope, or rather a surmise, about the matador, that had of late been growing up silently in the mind of Walter. The old galley-slave went on,—

"Do you think, my young camerado, that no man save yourself ever cursed the day of his birth, and sought death and found it not? The first year I spent at the oar, I would have thanked any man to give me a heave overboard, or to pass a sword through my body."

"The first year!" Walter echoed, with a long sigh. "I have been but seven months here, and they seem a lifetime. More years to follow!—More years! God help me!"

"Amen. God comfort you, as He has comforted me."

"How?"

"By showing you Himself; señor Englishman,—Himself, the God of all comfort, the Savior from sin and sorrow, the Lord who binds up the broken in heart;" and the worn, bronzed, weather-beaten face kindled and glowed at the words.

Walter asked in surprise, "Where—how did you learn all this?"

"Where? Sitting on this bench, chained to this oar. How? Through the goodness of God in bringing back to me what I heard, but little heeded, in happier days."

"Heard, but little heeded," Walter sighed again. "Just my own case. But—one thing perplexes me."

"What is that?"

"From whose lips *you* can have learned all this." For Walter believed, and not unnaturally, that there was only light in the land of Goshen, the countries of the Reformation, and that all the rest of the world lay in Egyptian darkness. Of the gleams that here and there illumined that darkness he had never heard.

The matador smiled, a little sadly. "Perhaps," he said, "I would scarce tell you *that* did I not think my own hour near—my hour of deliverance. We feel the water calm and calmer under the keel as we draw nigh the shore. What could not be spoken once, for tears, is easily enough said now. She taught me, whom I loved best on earth."

His quiet tones sounded more sorrowfully in Walter's ears than a burst of emotion would have done. It may be sadder to walk dryshod over the deep channel of a great grief passed away and done with, than to cross the shallow, noisy stream of a present sorrow. "It is bitter," he said falteringly, "to be parted forever from what we love. I too—I—"

"Shall meet the loved again—up yonder," said the matador, pointing with his fettered hand to the cloudless azure above them.

"It was all my own folly, my own sin! Ah, you know not how deeply I have sinned!"

"But God knows. Arise, and go to your Father, and say unto Him, Father, I have sinned against heaven and before Thee, and am no more worthy to be called Thy son."

Walter's tears flowed too fast to allow him to utter the answer that trembled on his lips. But eyes and thoughts were raised upwards, and the cry that reached no mortal ear was heard by Him who bindeth up the broken in heart, and giveth medicine to heal their sickness.

Some days afterward the matador seized a quiet moment in which to whisper to his friend, "I have been asking God to comfort you.—Has He?"

Walter answered with brightening eyes, "Not yet with the best robe, and the ring, and the fatted calf. But even now with the word, '*This, My son.*' And that is enough."

The Friend of the Poor

"We two walk on in our grassy places,
On either marge of the moonlit flood,
With the moon's own sadness in our faces,
Where joy is withered, blossom and bud."
~ JEAN INGELOW

IF MENTAL ABILITY IS UNEQUALLY distributed, so
also is that energy of character without which

it is of comparatively little use, and which, indeed, sometimes supplies its place. Some men are so largely endowed with this valuable quality, that, after ordering their own affairs, they have abundance remaining to bestow upon their neighbors; and, fortunately for society, energy and benevolence are qualities very often found in combination. But these benevolent persons occasionally violate the sacred rights of individuality by taking the concerns of others too unceremoniously into their own hands; consequently it is their trial—and a very keen and bitter one—to find their excellent arrangements too often set aside, with or without good reason, by the very persons for whose benefit they are designed.

Don Fray Tomas de San Martin, prior of the Franciscan Monastery at Lima, was a man of this temper —at once energetic and benevolent. And it must be allowed that for such the Church of Rome makes admirable provision.

As the head of a wealthy and influential religious house in the capital of the New World, Fray Tomas found ample exercise for his gifts; and eventually they were brought under the notice of his ecclesiastical superiors during a mission to Spain, which he undertook for the purpose of obtaining the establishment of a university in Lima. Shortly afterward he was appointed to a post calculated to afford them yet wider exercise—the bishopric of Chiquisaca. This was an onerous charge, especially in a country that had yet to be reclaimed almost entirely from heathenism.

It was to his credit that, amidst his preparations for undertaking it, he found time to recall to memory the pale, fiery-eyed, thoughtful-faced young monk whom he had sent eight or nine years ago to the heights of Cerro Blanco. He considered Fray Fernando just the material out of which a model missionary to the Indians might be molded. Hence the summons that awaited the monk at the Franciscan convent in Cuzco.

When Fray Fernando at length presented himself before the prior of his Order, Fray Tomas received him very cordially, and explained to him, with much affability and condescension, the important part he intended him to perform in spreading the faith amongst the Indians of his new diocese. For this work he conceived him eminently fitted by the zeal and the talents he had observed in him during his novitiate; and no doubt he would find the Indian youth, whom he had with so much Christian charity redeemed from slavery, baptized, and educated, an efficient interpreter. For the Indians of Chiquisaca had, fortunately, been subjects of the Inca, so they all spoke the "lengua general."

He then proceeded to display before the eyes of Fray Fernando a vista of future usefulness combined with peril and adventure, and showing at the end some far-off glimpse of a possible crown of martyrdom. If he had been dealing with a Churchman of an ambitious, worldly temper, he would have substituted the more material attraction of a bishop's miter; but he told himself that he "knew his man."

It was soon evident, however, that he did not know his man at all. Fray Fernando stood before him—paler, more fiery-eyed than ever, and with some traces in his raven hair of the snows he had dwelt amongst. He was respectful, for that was his duty; obedient, for he had sworn to obey. He thanked the prior for his remembrance of him, his commendations, and his confidence; for he could do no less. But his thanks were too plainly words of course—withered flowers, out of which the sap was dried and the coloring faded. He only acquired a little animation of manner when he went on to say, that while prepared to obey his lord the prior in everything, he would yet make his very humble supplication that the duties of a preacher might not be imposed on him, as he did not feel himself capable of fulfilling them.

"Some scruple of conscience, no doubt," thought the half-offended but still patient and considerate Fray Tomas. "Poor man! he has had little to do on that lonely mountain save to set up scruples and to knock them down again, else he might have died from sheer inaction. I ought to deal gently with him."

Scruples are weeds that luxuriate in the soil of monasticism. It is full of the elements that minister to their growth—idleness, solitude, introspection, and the habit of magnifying trifles. Don Fray Tomas was well acquainted with every variety of the species-foolish scruples, morbid scruples, honest scruples, and the not uncommon kind that may truly be called dishonest, since they are used to lead the thoughts away from some real sin which the heart is not willing to surrender. As he abounded both in tact and kindness, he was quite an adept in the art of uprooting these troublesome weeds; and he had no objection to use his skill in the service of Fray Fernando.

But the younger monk was impervious to his well-meant hints: he would neither give confidence nor receive consolation. He even turned a deaf ear to the intimation that his superior would be quite willing to become his confessor. Fray Fernando had not confessed once for the last sixteen years without believing that he committed mortal sin by abusing a sacrament of the Church. He neither wished to do this oftener than he could help, nor to impose an incomplete and therefore invalid confession upon a man so astute as the prior.

So the patience of Fray Tomas came to an end at last. He thought Fray Fernando brainsick and conceited, both in the old and the modern sense of the word. He regretted the trouble he had taken in summoning him from

Cerro Blanco, and made up his mind that he would get the Indians converted without his help. Yet he was too benevolent to send him back, or to consign him to his monastery under circumstances that might leave a slur upon his character in the eyes of his brethren. He procured for him therefore the office of attending to the spiritual wants of the seamen who frequented the port of Callao; and Fray Fernando, really grateful for this undeserved kindness, addressed himself to his new duties with diligence and zeal.

But the extreme heat of the climate—the burning suns, and the heavy clinging mists—told upon his constitution, now accustomed to a clear and bracing mountain air. It was not until he had more than once had the calenture severely, that he yielded to the longing, often felt, for the presence of his adopted son; and, as we are already aware, the letter that summoned José to his side lay unclaimed at Cuzco for nearly a year. When at last the monk and his adopted son met once more, the Indian youth, according to his character, expressed but little, either joy or sorrow; yet not the less did he feel profoundly that his father and teacher was bound, at no distant time, for that far-off, mysterious Christian heaven, of which he had heard so much and knew so little.

A circumstance that occurred shortly after his arrival confirmed his forebodings. José never spoke of Coyllur—never even named her, if he could help it; but he was quite willing to talk about the gentle Sumac, and to tell Fray Fernando the story of her life and death. He dwelt especially upon her strong attachment to the Christian faith, and how that faith had enabled her to die in peace; and with a reverence not altogether free from superstition, he showed his patron the little book which had been her dying gift.

Fray Fernando took it from his hand, and

looked at it with interest.

"I have heard Fray Constantino preach in the cathedral of Seville," he remarked presently; "and a wonderful preacher he was. Pity that his heart was lifted up within him, and so he fell into the snare of the devil! He became a heretic, and ended his days in the prison of the Inquisition.—But lend me this book for a little space, José; I should like to read it."

Pleased to give him pleasure, José complied, and, leaving Fray Fernando to read at his leisure, wandered out to the bay to feast his eyes upon the marvels of the shipping. On returning to the humble lodging of his patron, he was greatly alarmed to find him lying senseless on the floor. But he had seen Sumac swoon, and he knew what remedies to adopt. He ran for cold water, bathed the monk's forehead with it, and chafed his hands. Fray Fernando ere long recovered consciousness, looked about him, drank the water José raised to his lips, and told him not to be frightened. Then, availing himself of his help, he rose and placed himself in his usual seat.

"What has happened, patre?" José asked affectionately. "Are you ill?"

"No," the monk answered slowly, as with eye and hand he sought for the little book. It had fallen to the ground, but José picked it up and gave it to him.

"Tell me"—he began, but his voice faltered—died away. He paused a moment, then resumed more calmly, "Tell me—who gave this book to the Palla?"[1]

José opened the first page, and pointed to the inscription, "Dona Rosa Mercedes y Guevara."

Fray Fernando gazed on the faded writing with eager kindling eyes;—gradually they

---

1. The Spaniards called all the Indian princesses Pallas, though the title properly belonged only to the married ones amongst them.

changed, softened, grew dim with a mist of gathering tears. At last he said very gently, "That name was once dear to me." And he said no more.

But José drew nearer, and of his own accord put his arm round his neck, laying his hand on his shoulder.

By-and-by the monk inquired, still with the same gentleness of manner, "How did the Palla become possessed of that book?".

"Dear patre," José answered, "I will tell you all I know. Sumac Nuśta loved to go to the House of the Holy Virgins—the nuns of Santa Clara. This book belonged to one of them, who was Sumac's dear and chosen friend. Sister Maria was her holy name; the name she had from her father and mother was—what you find written there."

"Enough, José; my past comes back to me. The happy, happy past before— Strange—wonderful—that we have been near each to other, have breathed the same air, trod the streets of the same city-never knowing! Well—better so! Both dead—dead hearts in living bodies."

Then silence fell on the two. José stood like a statue of bronze; Fray Fernando sat, and dreamed of the past.

At length he spoke again. "José, is there anything I have for which you would give me this book in exchange?"

José smiled as he answered, "Nothing, patre. Take it from the son to whom you have given everything. Sumac Nūsta would wish you to take it," he added, seeing the monk hesitate.

"Thank you, José," said Fray Fernando, grasping the Indian's slender hand. "What I have said is safe with you," he added, and the subject dropped—forever.

How was it in the meantime with José himself? He was passing through the furnace of a bitter anguish. Many men, whose love was true as his, have had to do the same. But few come forth from that furnace unscarred, scarce one unscathed. Some hearts its fire burns hard, turning them to stone; some hearts consume in it like dry wood, leaving only ashes behind; while some, perhaps, are melted there, that they may be refined and purified like gold.

José could not forget. There was in his nature a dumb, persistent tenacity, both of purpose and of affection. The river might flow for leagues underground, yet its still, strong current would know no change. He rather brooded than thought, rather dreamed than reflected. After that one outburst of fierce agony on the Sachsahuaman Hill, he uttered no complaint, even to himself. Perhaps eventually the doom of his race might come upon him, and stoicism pass gradually into apathy.

A Spaniard in his circumstances would have acted differently. Had the rival of Don Francisco Solis been of his own race, the successful suitor would have worn a shirt of mail beneath his broidered doublet, and barred his windows well. For "Honor," that idol of chivalry—a bloody idol, too, propitiated by many a costly hecatomb—sanctioned almost every kind of treason and violence when glozed over by the name of love. It was fortunate for Don Francisco that he had not torn his prize from a Spanish hidalgo, but from a simple Inca Indian, who reverenced from his heart the Quechua laws of his ancestors, and the Ten Commandments he had learned from Fray Fernando.

Quietly, and without a word spoken on either side, José resumed his old position towards Fray Fernando; only he was, if possible, more assiduous than before in rendering those personal ministrations which the monk's feeble health now made doubly acceptable. A prince amongst his own people, he had yet no sense of degradation in performing even the lowliest offices for his adopted father. He loved him; that was enough. Moreover, in common with all his race, he held the paramount sanctity of the bond of ownership, believing that it ought to supersede, not only every personal consideration, but every other claim. "I am his; he bought me," was a plea strong enough to justify the most unbounded devotion.[2]

When Fray Fernando was engaged in his spiritual ministrations, José always accompanied him as his acolyte; and from this office he reaped the great advantage of being able freely to visit all the ships in the bay. It was not long until his attention was arrested by the miserable condition of the slaves on board the galleys. Not all the wonders of the great galleons, with their tall masts and spreading sails, and their strange monstrous guns, could turn his eyes and his thoughts from those black unsightly hulks, where sat the long and serried

---

2. This fidelity of the Peruvians to any master to whom they had once yielded them, selves, is described in very striking terms by Garcilaso de la Vega.

rows of degraded wretches; brown, haggard, filthy, fettered to their places. "Are they men?" was his first question to Fray Fernando. When told they were criminals, enduring a severe but well-merited punishment, he remarked, "The king ought rather to kill them. Why does he not?" For José was himself the son of kings, whose stroke often dealt death, swift and remediless, but who never knew the fiendish delight of torturing their victims.

Then Fray Fernando said, "We will bring alms to the slaves on board the galleys."

"Chachau!" José answered. "My Fathers were the Friends of the Poor." And they did so.

The Fruits of West

"And when you see fair hair, be pitiful."
~ GEORGE ELLIOT

THE GOOD GALLEY *San Cristofero* was doomed to lie at rest for a lengthened period in the port of Callao. She needed repairs; and since these repairs had to be accomplished by Spanish hands, and "Tomorrow is the god of the Spaniard," a great many tomorrows came and went before they were completed. And even when at length they had come to an end, the galley had still to await, for an indefinite time, the pleasure of the stately man-of-war she was destined to escort.

These delays were no cause of regret to the slaves on board. They gained thereby some trifling alleviation of the miseries of their lot. The rowers who sat on the first bench, and who had the severest toil, but the greatest privileges, were often permitted to go on shore; their peculiar dress, and the iron anklet they always wore, being considered sufficient securities against the possibility of an escape. Although this welcome relief to the monotony of their life was not usually granted to the others, they also sometimes received small sums in charity, which their more fortunate comrades used to lay out for them. Moreover, there was little to be done. The rowers might sleep through the sultry hours of the tropical day, or sit idle, leaning against their oars, and gazing on the fair sights that met their eyes—the crystal waters, the green shore, the white and distant mountains.

One very hot day a cry ran along the benches that the commissary had fallen down dead. And almost immediately afterward the slaves saw him carried along the gangway into the little covered recess in the forecastle. No very kindly interest in a man from whom they had received little save curses and blows could be expected from them; but in their present state of inaction any event was sure to be eagerly discussed. By-and-by they learned that he was not dead, only suffering from a sunstroke. But his condition was thought sufficiently dangerous to require the immediate services of a priest.

There stepped on board accordingly a Franciscan monk, accompanied by a handsome well-dressed Indian, who carried the little silver bell intended to warn all who heard it of the presence of their Creator. Even the slaves were expected to prostrate themselves at the signal. The matador had, apparently, no scruples about this ceremony; but to Walter Gray it was a bowing of the knee to Baal, which in his heart he detested, though he was not yet strong enough to challenge martyrdom by a refusal.

He was not particularly pleased to meet the keen dark eyes of the Indian fixed upon him with an earnest and, as he fancied, a suspicious gaze. Nothing, indeed, could be more unlikely than that an Indian should observe his reluctance or scrutinize its motives; but he had suffered so much that his apprehensions were not always under the control of his reason.

The slaves maintained a respectful silence, or conversed only in whispers, until the monk had performed his ministrations, and with his attendant re-entered the boat that was to convey him on shore. They then began to discuss the occurrence amongst themselves. Did you see the monk's face, comrades?" one of them inquired." On my faith, he might be a brother of ours. He looks as lean and hollow-eyed as if he had sat for a twelvemonth at the oar."

"Yet what an eye he has, the holy man!" remarked Walter's oar-fellow, the Quatrero." He looked at me for a moment, and I had to turn away lest he should begin to reckon up to me on his rosary all the sins of my life."

"If he began *that* bead-roll he would be here till sundown, and not half through then," said another dryly.

"Hush mates!" a third interposed. "Here comes the dark-faced sacristan again, and with a basket of fine fruit on his arm. Enough to make us all die of thirst this burning day. What lucky fellow has got a real to spend?"

"What good in that? He will serve our betters first. Well if he comes our way at all."

And now the "dark-faced sacristan" stood on the deck, holding parley with a soldier who acted as sentinel. All took notice of his gallant air and manly bearing, and saw that he wore his handsome national costume with as much stately grace as a Spanish cavalier could wear his cloak and sword. "A fine bird that, and in fine feathers," muttered the Quatrero. Meanwhile the soldier conducted José Viracocha to the captain, of whom he made some request, which appeared to be granted immediately. The captain politely accompanied him to the gangway, and by a motion of his hand indicated that the slaves were permitted to hold communication with him.

José stepped at once to the bench where sat the English youth, whose golden hair and fair complexion rendered him conspicuous amongst the swarthy Spaniards and dusky Creoles and Mulattoes. With a bow and a smile he placed his basket of fruit in his hand.

Walter, in his surprise, at first took it mechanically. Then reflecting that the Indian probably wished to sell, and that he had no money, he tried to convey as much by signs.

"Perhaps, señor, you speak Spanish?" said José, making use of that language.

"I do," Walter answered, more and more surprised.

"Then I pray of you to accept my gift, Señor Englishman," the other said, adding the last two words in a low voice. Some of the more forward amongst those around beginning to beg from him, he responded at once, "Yes, yes, poor fellows, you shall all have something." And he scattered small pieces of silver with a liberal hand amongst them, taking especial care that the feeble, worn-out men who sat on the bench next the water should have their full share.[1]

Both Walter's disposition and his interest led him to share the Indian's gift very freely with his comrades, of course not forgetting his

---

1. The precious metals were very plentiful in those regions, and prices, of course, proportionally high.

special friend the matador. And the sweet and luscious chirimoyas proved very acceptable to men obliged to sit unsheltered under the fiery blaze of a tropical sun. Every one supposed that the Indian was the dispenser of his master's charity, though for what reason either he or the Franciscan monk should have singled out Walter Gray as the chief recipient of their bounty could not be surmised.

The young Englishman's story was known to all on board. But, fortunately for him, the captain of the galley was no bigot; he was a thoughtless, idle young prodigal, the son of a respectable merchant, sent to sea in despair by his relatives, whose interest procured him the situation he filled. The commander of the troops on board, on the other hand, was far too fine a gentleman to have any concern at all with the slaves, beyond holding his men in readiness to shoot them down if they attempted mutiny. Thus, whilst every one believed, as a matter of course, that Walter Gray, the English heretic, was infinitely worse than a thief or a murderer, no one thought much about him.

The Indian came again the next day with a larger supply of fruit, which, however, he gave to the soldiers. But the disappointment visible in the longing eyes of the thirsty slaves as the store quickly disappeared was soothed by charity of even a more acceptable kind. Many blessings were invoked both upon himself and upon "his reverence the holy father," whose emissary he was supposed to be—nor did he contradict the supposition. But he contrived, whilst giving silver to the others, to slip a broad piece of gold into the hand of Walter. The Englishman was about to express aloud his astonishment at this liberality, but the Indian caught his eye and whispered, *"Tace."* As may be imagined, the Latin word, spoken by such lips, only changed Walter's look of surprise into one of amazement.

After the Indian's departure he expressed his wonder at the circumstance to his friend the matador.

"Depend upon it, Englishman," said the old galley-slave in reply, "the good friar has taken pity on you for your youth and your gentle looks, which would strike a stranger, like the sight of a fair green sapling amongst a bundle of dry brown fagots. One can read in his face that he has known much sorrow himself, and therefore, perhaps, his heart is tender for others."

"But the Indian," said Walter. "Do you know, matador, that was a *Latin* word he spoke to me?"

"Why not? He is the servant of a churchman; and he that measures oil gets some on his fingers.' Though," he admitted, "he seems wondrously wise and civil—for one of the wild men."

A concession that moved Walter to draw

upon old stores of information, and to talk of the strange civilization of the New World, and the splendors of the two great empires that had already been discovered there. Growing more and more interested as he went on, he conquered Mexico with Cortes, overran Peru with Pizarro, and was making rapid progress towards the discovery of El Dorado, when at last the matador brought him to a pause.

"I used to know all these things long ago," he said. And this was true. Time was when such themes never failed to bring the blood to his cheek and the light to his eye. But now the dry embers were not even stirred by the old fire. "I have done with Golden Cities now," he went on. "The only one I am ever like to see will not be found beyond those white mountains, but higher up—beyond the stars. Your words, that glitter like gold themselves, mind me of other words heard years and years ago, out of the one story that is all true;—about a City that hath foundations, ay, and streets of gold and gates of pearl."

The extensive and accurate knowledge of Scripture that Walter had acquired in his childhood was now proving a great comfort to him. He gladly shared his stores with his companion, who listened to the words of Holy Writ with an intense and unflagging interest, contrasting strangely with the seeming indifference with which he heard Walter's other narratives.

Walter Gray was not now the miserable, dejected wretch, passively accepting his life of suffering, that he had been a short time before. The light of heavenly hope had arisen upon his soul, making all things new. It was worthwhile to live, since he might live unto God—even in the galleys. Many things in his lot were still hard to bear; but nothing was intolerable, since the worst could only mean death, and death was the gate of everlasting life.

And, as it is God's will that little things

should often contribute not a little to the help and healing of sorrowful hearts, the visits and kindnesses of his Indian friend, which were continued from day to day, proved a wonderful tonic to Walter Gray. The very occupation they gave his mind was a much prized relief from the dreary monotony of slavery. The visits were something to expect, to long for, to think over. It was good also to be able, even in the midst of his poverty, to minister to the need of others; and thus he began to find positive enjoyment in sharing the liberal gifts he received with his less fortunate comrades.

The true explanation, however, of the strange partiality José evinced for him was this. Whilst looking with a pitying eye along the rowers' benches of the *San Cristofero,* his glance had been suddenly arrested by Walter's fair, or golden hair. Now, in José's eyes, fair hair had wonderful significance. It was linked in his thoughts with the Sun, his great Father; and with his ancestor Viracocha, called the fair-haired. And yet more, it was bound up with all those dim, mysterious prophecies— those faint rumors floating amongst his people—of the bearded strangers, wise and mighty and strong to deliver, who were to come to them from beyond the Mother Sea; and for whom many of them had at first mistaken the Spaniards— to their own undoing. The hopes dearest to José's heart were built upon the fair-haired Englishmen.

Great was his joy, therefore, when he ascertained that Walter was in very deed an Englishman. And he was confirmed in more than one fond delusion by finding that when he addressed a Latin word to the captive, the latter, though naturally surprised, evidently understood him.

He soon found, however, that it was better on the whole to communicate with his new friend in Spanish. And he directed all his address to the task of opening up and improving the means of communication with him. This did not prove so difficult as he had anticipated. Even on board a galley a man's gift maketh room for him; and José had both the means to offer very acceptable gifts, and the tact to offer them in an acceptable way. It is true that in losing Coyllur he lost also the secret hoards of Yupanqui; a loss for which he grieved little; far less than he rejoiced that they were saved from the covetous gripe of Don Francisco Solis. But Maricancha, who was childless, made him welcome to all that he had. At their last interview, he had pressed upon him as much gold as he could carry, with several valuable jewels.

It was not hard for José, thus amply supplied with the sinews of war, to gratify the officers and soldiers of the *San Cristofero*. They— as well as the galley-slaves—looked upon him as the Indian servant of a Franciscan monk; a character of all others the least likely to excite suspicion. And as José knew well enough that Franciscan monks had not usually the means, even if they had the inclination, to exercise unbounded liberality, he soon gave his friends to understand that his master was the almoner of a rich and pious lady, who had great compassion upon poor galley-slaves, and moreover wished to benefit her soul by works of charity. But it was his finest stroke of policy to bring on board the galley frequent supplies of a fragrant brown leaf, which proved a most welcome gift, to all—from the señor commandante, who was not too proud to thank the Indian with an elaborate Spanish bow, to the poor rowers, who begged for it piteously to comfort them under their miseries. If the bearer of such treasures chose to amuse himself for half an hour chatting with the slaves, it was no one's business to hinder him, and consequently, no one did it.

So José's friendship with Walter Gray grew and prospered, though under difficulties.

XXVII

The Matador

"Some murmur when their sky is clear
And wholly bright to view,
If one small speck of dark appear
On their broad heaven of blue.
And some with thankful love are filled
If but one gleam of light,
One ray of God's good mercy, gild
The darkness of their night."

~ ARCHBISHOP TRENCH

YOUTH DESPAIRS EASILY. The young, unused to sorrow, sink beneath a burden that the aged would bear without a murmur; unused to life, they put the cup aside as soon as the taste grows bitter. But the rebound is easy also. At any moment hope may revive; the flowers may bloom and the birds sing again.

It was wonderful, considering all the circumstances, that Walter Gray did not die. But since life remained, it was not wonderful that even in the galleys his crushed heart began to recover itself, under the combined influences of heavenly hope, and of the thoughtful and generous ministrations of his new friend.

It had at first been no trifling ingredient in his cup of bitterness that the robbers and murderers amongst whom he toiled looked upon him as a wretch infinitely more degraded than themselves. Even the Quatrero was wont to play the Pharisee, and, crossing himself devoutly, to thank God that he was not as this English heretic. But things were altered now. He was beginning to be regarded by his comrades as a person of distinction rather, and one whose intercession might upon occasion do them a good turn. At least he could and did procure for them, or share with them, many a valued gift, including the much-prized tobacco. They thought he owed the special favor he enjoyed to his extremely youthful appearance; José always called him "El Mozo"—the lad.

"Ask our Indian, next time he comes, to tell us his master's name and his own," said Walter's comrades to him one day. And Walter did so.

José smiled at the question; and very readily informed him that his patre was called Fray Fernando, and "a man more like a saint there never was in the world," he added. But when pressed to tell his own name, he returned an evasive answer, saying that the rowers ought first to tell him theirs. It was wonderful how far José contrived to lay aside the reserved and stately dignity of his ordinary bearing, and to assume a frank and friendly, even a jovial manner, in talking with these poor men. For it was absolutely necessary to his plans that they should all regard him with confidence, as a friend. Yet he drew the line somewhere; he never touched them.

They complied, gladly enough, with his request; the more hardened telling him their *sobriquets* with coarse jests and oaths, which he fortunately did not understand. At last, however, it came to the turn of Walter's special friend, who said simply, "I am called the matador."

"Matador!" José repeated. "That means—man who slays a bull."

Great was the astonishment and admiration with which this evidence of José's knowledge inspired the galley-slaves; and it was certainly remarkable in an Indian.

"And did you really slay a bull, señor matador?" he questioned with interest.

"No, Señor Indio. I only wounded him, and saved a gentleman from being gored."

"Tell the story, matador," cried several voices.

"There is none to tell," said the matador, who, except to his immediate neighbors, rarely spoke at all, and still more rarely spoke of himself. Being, however, urged by José to relate the circumstances, he did so briefly. "Some twelve years ago," he said, "before we came to the New World, when my arm was stronger, I sat on the first bench, and had leave to go on shore at Carthagena. There was to be a bull-feast the next day; and they were driving the beasts into the city—all the world out to gaze at them, of course. In old days, I knew something of the ring myself. So I must needs stand and gaze with the rest. The first bull was stupid, and made no sport. But the second was an ugly-looking beast—a dry, tough fellow, lean and sharp-horned—"

"Ay, ay," cried one Spaniard after another, in high delight at hearing once more the language of the sport all had loved in former years; "we know that sort. Hard to kill. No flinchers."

"Pries," the matador went on, "the poor beast was driven mad by the shouts of the bystanders, and the blows of their goads and sticks. He broke out of the line; and, not knowing his real tormentors, stood roaring and pawing with fury. At last he put his head down as if he meant mischief, and made a determined rush at a dainty young hidalgo who had been doing nothing at all, but who happened to be dressed that day in a new scarlet doublet with a montero to match. He was a brave man, and had his tool ready in an instant. Still, it might have gone hard with him, only that I, knowing the business, snatched a long knife from a butcher who stood at the door of his stall, and turned the creature's rage against myself. I managed to keep him busy till they rescued me.

I could have killed him, of course; but I knew better. Who, I pray you, was to pay for him if I did?"

"I hope the gentleman you rescued paid you!" Walter threw in.

"Oh yes; he behaved well to me. He would gladly have ransomed me, but that could not be. So he lined my pocket with good gold doubloons, and procured me every favor and indulgence in his power. But, enough of me.—Señor Indio, your turn is come now. Slaves though we may be, we like to thank our benefactors, and it is therefore only in reason that we should know their names."

"'You will be little advantaged by knowing mine. Your countrymen call me Don José Viracocha Inca."

From the much prized Spanish title all present gathered that their Indian friend was a person of distinction; but the rest fell unnoticed on every ear save that of Walter, who started and looked up, with curiosity and interest in his face.

It is not true that romance dies quickly, blighted by the frosts of cold reality. On the contrary, no part of our being is more tenacious of life. It partakes of the nature of perfume, — spiritual, intangible, apparently evanescent, yet lingering strangely and mysteriously in the withered leaf or blossom long after the bright colors have faded, and the very garden where they bloomed has become a desolate waste. The Indian's quaint, high-sounding name had in it a perfume of old romance that brought back the thoughts of Walter Gray to the familiar room where he had first read the story of Pizarro's daring and his guilt, and where his young heart had first kindled over those wild, splendid dreams of the lake of Parima, and of the golden city of Manoa. He had a hundred questions to ask the Indian, who soon afforded him an opportunity of putting them, by passing along the benches to distribute the contents of his fruit basket, and stopping, as he always did, near Walter.

José briefly satisfied his curiosity. Yes, he was really a Child of the Sun. Was he proud of his origin? An expressive smile was the answer. Did he worship the sun? No, assuredly; he was a Christian. "But," leaning over Walter and whispering, "I have hopes of obtaining from the señor commandante permission for you to come on shore. Then I will tell you of my people; and you, in return, will tell me of yours."

"Don José Viracocha Inca, what has moved you to show me such singular kindness?"

José lowered his voice still further. "You are an Englishman, therefore the Inca's friend," he murmured.

Walter looked up wondering. "If in any way I could reward you—," he began.

"That you can. When you regain your freedom and go home, tell your King what I have just said."

He was gone ere Walter could answer that he was never likely to go home.

"Matador," he said that night to his companion, "I am troubled about our Indian friend. What can I do to recompense him? I shall never see my home again—how, then, can I tell king or queen of his strange kindness and friendship?"

"Tell it to the great King," said the old galley-slave in reply.

XXVIII

The King of the East

"*He who trod,*
Very man and very God,
This earth in weakness, shame, and pain,
Dying the death, whose signs remain,
Up yonder on the accursed tree,
Shall come again, no more to be
Of captivity the thrall,
But the one God, all in all,
King of kings and Lord of lords,

As his servant John received the words,
'I died, and live for evermore.'"
~ R. BROWNING

JOSÉ'S HEART WAS GLAD WITHIN HIM. For Fray Fernando had at last obtained permission for the slaves of the *San Cristofero* to come by turns to his lodging that they might make confession of their sins, and receive private religious instruction and consolation. It is true that the señor commandante had shrugged his shoulders rather scornfully at the request; while the captain had hinted that the trouble the good friar was taking about the souls of the rowers was nearly as superfluous as that of "the over-clean Harcajo people, who wax their asses' feet." But both had very good reasons for not crossing his whims, even if they had been still more unaccountable. Nor was there really anything objectionable in his proposal, since he made himself personally responsible for the safe keeping of all the prisoners.

So the poor wretches were allowed to come, two and two together, to the humble lodging of the friar; and many a fearful tale of guilt and shame did they pour into his ear. They were a motley crew. Some of them were Spaniards from the mother country, but a large proportion were Creoles, and there were some Mulattoes, and even two or three Black men amongst them.

"Poor fellows!" said José compassionately, "one can give them at least a bath, a change of clothing, and a good meal!"

"It is easy for you, José. You only see those low wants of the body that you can supply, or at least alleviate," Fray Fernando answered sadly. He was sitting at the table, his head resting upon his hands—an image of despondency. "Who will find me a bath for those sin-stained souls—clean raiment to cover them in God's sight and their own—bread for their bitter hunger of heart?"

"But, patre," said José again, "you surely can do all that yourself. Else, why are you a patre? Are not the Sacraments for that?"

Fray Fernando sighed. A chill misgiving, that the remedies did not after all reach the seat of the disease, was sinking gradually into his soul. Those degraded beings, into the core of whose hearts sin had eaten like a canker—was any moral restoration possible for them? And without moral restoration, could the spiritual cure he professed to work be real or effectual? What good in giving them absolution from the blasphemies of yesterday, when, through the partition that divided his chamber from José's, he could hear the new score begun almost ere they had left his presence! Could the conscience indeed be cleansed whilst the heart and the lips remained so fearfully unclean?"

Amongst the saddest moments in a man's life are those in which he begins to suspect the sovereign efficacy of those remedies for the ills of humanity in which hitherto he has trusted without question. They may not, perhaps, have availed for him; but that, he has told himself, is his own fault—he has not applied them rightly. An undercurrent of hope remains that he may do so yet, or that others may do it for him. He may be dying of thirst, yet still the waters of Shiloh go softly; his wound may ache un-healed, yet still there is balm in Gilead. But who shall bring help or comfort to his despair-ing soul if once he surmises that the fountain is not in Shiloh, that there is no balm in Gilead, nor any physician there?

Hitherto Fray Fernando had blamed him-self; he had not doubted his Church. Her mystic sacraments brought no mystic blessing to him, only because he did not fulfill the in-dispensable conditions of blessing. That they could bring no blessing to others was a new, and, as it then seemed to him, a still more ter-rible thought.

"Patre," José resumed, little guessing what was passing in his patron's mind—"patre, *my* friend comes today. I know you will be very kind to him for José's sake."

"For *your* sake, surely! But a galley-slave is a strange friend for Don José—the Child of the Sun. What have you seen in this youth?"

José answered evasively, "He is so young, patre, to have suffered so much. And he has hair like the tears of Ynty, and eyes the color of the cloudless sky. Moreover, he is gentle; and he never uses oaths or evil words."

"Ah! I have observed that myself. I know something of his story: his case is a singular one."

Fray Fernando was aware that Walter Gray had been a prisoner of the Inquisition. And he surmised that the "penitence" that saved his life was not, probably, the most sincere in the world. If he were a Dominican friar, with heart and soul devoted to the interests of the

Holy Office, he might seek for symptoms of a "relapse"—but he was nothing of the kind; he had no wish to meddle in such matters. Whatever he might suspect, or even ascertain, the poor lad should be safe with him, unless he should prove himself unworthy of favor. He said aloud: "You may trust me, José. I will be kind to your friend."

"Thank you, patre.—Ah! here they come. That tall, brown, bent man is called the matador. He and the Englishman are friends."

Fray Fernando went to the door to meet his guests, whom he welcomed with the customary *"Pax vobiscum."* They bowed; the old man bending low, the younger slightly, like an English gentleman acknowledging the salutation of an equal.

According to custom, José set a substantial meal before the visitors. It was not, indeed, usual to partake of food before attending the confessional; but the case of these poor half-starved galley-slaves was peculiar, and in Fray Fernando's judgment it required peculiar treatment. Whilst they did ample justice to the repast, he would enter freely into conversation with them; and endeavor, in a friendly manner, to learn something of their history. Generally they were disposed to be communicative; being pleased to find themselves listened to with interest, and not without hope of future benefits. But these two were very silent. Walter's mind was greatly disturbed, on account of the impending interview with the monk. Most gladly would he have avoided the visit, if he could have done so without exciting suspicion, or rather, without actually proclaiming himself a heretic, who refused the sacraments of the Church. But as it happened, this scheme of his Indian friend, devised for his special benefit, was but too likely to prove his undoing. During the meal, he ate little and spoke less, awaiting, with mingled feelings, the dreaded summons to the confessional.

The matador, from long habit, was silent; but his eyes often sought the face of the monk, as if finding a strange attraction there. Something, indeed, there was that affected him like the strain of some half-forgotten melody, which the memory can neither wholly grasp nor let altogether go.

Fray Fernando did not pay any particular attention to him, but observed the young Englishman with much compassion. Guessing pretty accurately what was passing in his mind, and willing to end his suspense, he departed from his usual practice by giving precedence to the younger. "I see, my young friend," he said, "that you have finished your repast. I will therefore hear your confession first. Come with me." And, rising from his seat, he led the way into the inner chamber, where was his oratory and confessional.

Anxiously had Walter prepared himself for

this hour. He had planned and pondered, and formed many a resolution, which he dismissed, and then formed again, as to how he should speak, how he should act, when the important moment arrived. But now all vanished utterly from his memory. A strength and calmness, never felt before, descended suddenly upon him. No thought of fear occurred to him, nor indeed any thought at all save the one which wholly filled his heart. He was called to confess. And like a lightning flash, came those words across his mind: "He that confesseth me before men, him will I also confess before my Father and before the holy angels." Repeating them over to himself, he followed Fray Fernando into the inner room.

José kindled a light for the matador, and supplied him with tobacco, and with a quaint cumbrous pipe covered with Indian carving. From what he had seen of the man, he respected and liked him; but neither had any wish to converse with the other. So they sat together in perfect silence, quite content to wait, and to enjoy their own meditations.

They could hear the voices of the monk and his penitent plainly enough, the thin partition being of cane covered with plaster. First, that of the young Englishman—calm, earnest, solemn—"I desire to confess"—but the end of the sentence escaped them. Then Fray Fernando's voice, earnest also,—not quite his ordinary professional tone, which was well known to José. Then both, succeeding each other rapidly, sometimes even mingling, as the voices of men who dispute, and rather hotly. Then a brief sentence, mournfully spoken by Fray Fernando. Then, once more, the voice of Walter Gray, so full, so calm, so harmonious, that José thought he must be reciting some sweet yaravi of his native land, instead of making confession of his sins. Then a pause, followed by some low quiet words from Fray Fernando. These appeared to end the interview. A movement was heard within, and in another moment Fray Fernando opened the door. "Remember, I give you time," they heard him say. "You are under my instruction. I must see you as often as I can."

Walter Gray bowed, and walked into the outer room. Released from the hateful oar, he looked tall and stately; and in spite of his ragged jerkin and fettered ankles, a true English gentleman—"a Child of the Sun," José called him in his heart He placed himself in the seat at the table from which the matador had just risen, and resting his face upon his hands, seemed lost in thought.

The silence that followed was really hard for José to bear; he had hoped such great things from this interview, and taken such pains to procure it. Yet he respected the Englishman too much to intrude on his meditations. He waited for some time with exemplary patience; but at last, growing desperate from the fear of losing altogether the only opportunity he might ever enjoy, he ventured to ask,—

"Señor Englishman, will you speak with me?"

Walter Gray started, uncovered his face, and turned his frank blue eyes upon José, whose presence, up to that moment, he had completely forgotten.

"I should be ungrateful indeed if I would not, Don José," he answered. "What do you want with me?"

"I have somewhat to say to you; somewhat also to hear from your lips," said José, in his grave, sententious way. Then rising from his seat, he stood before the Englishman.

For a minute's space each gazed at the other in silence. They were a strange contrast—the Inca Indian and the Anglo-Saxon,—the heir of a civilization that had played out its part in the world's history and was now fast fading, and the representative of the great race that held the world's future in its hand, and was destined to slay the slayer, and to spoil the spoiler, of Tahuantin Suyu. It was like the morning sun looking in through unclosed windows on the pale tinted gleam of an alabaster lamp, accidentally left burning still—though its work was done and its use over.

José, like Walter, had prepared diligently for this hour; but unlike him, he did not at the critical moment forget all he had to say. Still it was with something like hesitation that he began,—"Señor Englishman, you inquired my name the other day—"

"And gladly do I offer my grateful thanks to Don José Viracocha Inca for a thousand kindnesses," Walter said heartily.

"Listen! There are three names there. *Don José,* my Spanish name, is like that." He unclasped his mantle and flung it from him, standing before Walter in his simple tunic of fine white cotton, fastened at the waist by an embroidered belt. "It is an outside garment, assumed, thrown off, as lightly. And no dearer do I hold my Spanish manners, and tongue, and learning. Then, there remains *Viracocha,* the name my mother gave me when she had my first hair cut. That is my own name,—myself. It means Foam of the Sea.' Well, let that go too! Let the foam flash and fade and die away into nothing! Who cares? It was never meant to last. But there remains still the best, the most precious name of all.—No nobler, I think, is spoken anywhere on earth.—That shall last, when all the rest have perished. I am *Inca,* Child of the Sun.

"Yes, Señor Englishman, I repeat it proudly, Child of the Sun. I know what I say. In the midst of our sorrow and degradation, I can smile myself for very scorn at the insolent scorn of the Spaniards, who call this a vain heathenish superstition of ours. How are children known save by their likeness to their father? And my race bore their father's image, plain as the light of day. Like Ynty the glorious, they shed abroad life, joy, fruitfulness, far and wide, wherever their sway extended. I tell you, Englishman, in days to come, you will find our tongue spoken, our name honored, our laws reverenced, far away amongst wild tribes you have not dreamed of yet. For we were great kings and mighty conquerors; and it was our glory that we did not reign or conquer for ourselves.

"But the Spaniards came, few in number, yet so strong. Why has God given the white man such terrible strength? They had fire-breathing clubs, and horses, and great ships. But more than all these, they had strange craft and cunning, wherewith they deceived us. They called themselves messengers of God, and we believed them." José paused sorrowfully.

"I know the story of the conquest of Peru," Walter threw in, thinking to spare him a painful recital.

"Peru!" José repeated with a smile. "What is Peru? That barbarous word was not known amongst us until the Spaniards came. Yet it is meet they should call the land by a new name. Tahuantin Suyu, the empire of my fathers, they have never known,—and never shall they know! But again I tell you, Señor Englishman, Tahuantin Suyu is not dead. No! though they have laid waste her fair fields and terraced hills, and destroyed her roads and water-courses— No! though they have steeped the land in blood, from the Mother Sea to the White Mountains, and again from the White Mountains to the pathless forest—No! though they have taken the true heir of Manco Capac, and dragged him to Cuzco, and though I have seen—I myself— his head fall beneath the Spanish ax. No!—*The Inca will reign again.*"

José's hope was buried, but it was still there. Like the treasures of Yupanqui, of which the secret hiding-place had been revealed to him by Maricancha, who had himself helped to inter them, he knew where to find it, and could produce it when he chose.

The firm conviction and the intense earnestness that breathed in his every look and tone, impressed Walter Gray. He asked, as Fray Fernando long ago had asked, "How know you that?"

José took up a curious, many-tinted shell which lay on the table. "There, put that to your ear, Señor Hualter" (the nearest approach he could make to the pronunciation of "Walter"). "Do you hear nothing?"

"I hear a murmur, like that of the ocean."

"What does that murmur say?"

Walter smiled as he answered, "I scarcely know. Perhaps —that it has come from the ocean, its home."

"True," said José. "And thus I too have put my ear to the beating heart of my people. I hear a murmur there, never ceasing, never changing. That murmur says, 'The Inca shall reign again'"

There was a pause. Walter looked at him, wondering, interested, yet bewildered.

"Shall I tell you something else which is murmured in the heart of my people?" José resumed. "There are dim prophecies floating here and there amongst us, of strangers, great and brave—fair-haired, bearded, children of light—yet to come from beyond the Mother Sea, who shall avenge our wrongs, and help to restore our ancient dominion."

Walter's eyes kindled, but he did not speak.

"Señor Englishman, I read in your face that you understand me."

"Yes—oh yes! Would that we could help you!"

"You *can* help. All is not yet told. I have learned, by long silent thought and study, that the Spaniards too have prophecies—strange prophecies—telling of a king to come, and from you."

"From us? From our nation? Do you mean an Englishman"

"Yes. An Englishman-a Jew. A son of David, your king."

Walter looked blank astonishment. "You are under some strange delusion," he said. "We are not Jews; nor was David our king."

"You are heretics, are you not? And heretics are Jews."

"Heretics indeed they call us; but we are not Jews. Don José, did your padre teach you this?"

Walter's surprise was not unmixed with amusement; but José was profoundly earnest, and moved to his inner depths. "The patre," he explained, "is wise and good. But he dared not teach me, what none of his people would wish ours to know, that there will yet be a greater king than theirs. Nay, it may be that they themselves do not understand, or believe, that their boasted empire is doomed one day to fall in the dust before that great Inca of the West, who shall have dominion from sea to sea, and from the river even unto the ends of the earth!'"

A faint glimmer of light now began to break on Walter's mind. "You are quoting Holy Scripture," he said.

José sought Fray Fernando's Breviary, and opening at the Seventy-second Psalm, he pointed to it, saying, "You will understand it, because it is written in your own language."

"Latin is not my language," explained Walter, "but I can read it." And his eyes rested on the page, whilst his bewildered mind strove in vain to find a clue by which to unravel José's tangle of ideas.

José drew nearer. "Kind and good Englishman," he entreated, "tell me who that king is, and where I shall find him."

Walter looked up from the book, and gazed at him intently. "Do you indeed desire to know?" he asked.

"Does the thirsting earth desire the rain of heaven? Have I not made a solemn vow that I will lay the cause of my people at his feet, and implore him to do justice and judgment between us and the Spaniards?"

Walter pondered. "I fear you will be troubled, disappointed, when you hear all," he said at last.

"Only try me."

"That King," said Walter gravely, "is reigning even now; though not in England, nor in Spain. Hearken, Don José. Long ago He came to the people of His choice. But they rejected, insulted, slew Him. Yet He will come again, perhaps soon; and take to Him His great power, and reign in righteousness over all the earth, from the rising of the sun till the going down thereof. Of that reign, all kings who have ever reigned in righteousness and judged the poor and needy—as David and Solomon; even, for aught I know, as your own Incas—have given the world imperfect images, and a faint shadow. All the hopes they have awakened He will fulfill."

"They slew Him?—yet He will come again?" José questioned, his eyes intently reading the face of Walter.

Then there was a pause. At length, drawing from its place in his chuspa, or coca-bag, a little crucifix Fray Fernando had given him, he kissed it, laid it reverently down, and made the sign of the cross upon his forehead.

"Yes, you are right," Walter went on. *"He* is the great King. He it is who shall judge the people with righteousness, and the poor with judgment. The mountains shall bring peace to the people, and the little hills by righteousness. He shall judge the poor of the people, He shall save the children of the needy, and shall break in pieces the oppressor."

Here he stopped suddenly; for two large, heavy tears fell from the dark eyes of José, blotting the pages of the book.

"Why do you weep?" he asked kindly.

José's words came slowly out of a depth of quiet despair,—

"For my lost hope. I thought there was a real king. But it is only a mystery of the Faith.—One said so to me long ago. I ought to have believed her."

"O Don José, you do not understand! He is truly all—more than all—your heart desires. And as surely as tomorrow's sun shall rise, He will come again, and reign upon this very earth on which we stand now, to make an end of sin, and to bring in everlasting righteousness."

"But He is the Judge of all. He is the God of the Spaniards. He takes their part now— hereafter, perhaps?"

"Hereafter the proud Spaniards and their master, the Pope of Rome, shall lick the dust beneath His feet. Their plagues shall come in one day—death and mourning and famine; and the word shall be fulfilled to them, Rejoice over her, thou heaven, and ye holy apostles and prophets, for God hath avenged you on her.'" Then, with a sudden change of tone, and growing pale,—"But I should not speak thus. I forget myself. Don José, I have put my life into your hands. You will not betray me?"

José placed his hand in his.

"Do not I also hate the Spaniards?" he said. "But your words cut my heart in two, like a sword. I thought I had grasped a strong hand to help my people; and lo! it is but a dream—a shadow. There is no help for us, in heaven or on earth."

"Do not think so. The King will help you, if you come to Him."

"How can I come to Him?"

"Has not the padre taught you to pray?"

"Surely. But what use in that? It is only speaking words. As well might I speak to the spirits of my ancestors—and better, since they are my own race: I know them."

"And Him you do not know? Ask Him, Don José, to reveal Himself to you. He loves you—died for you."

So engrossed were José and Walter Gray in their conversation, that it occurred to neither to observe the very unusual length to which the matador seemed to be protracting his confession. Instead of wondering, as they might well have done, at the delay, they felt like men suddenly awakened from a dream, when the slight cane door of the partition was thrown open, and the matador came forth. He looked, Walter thought, as though he had been weeping; yet his brown cheek was flushed, his eyes were bright with animation, and his bent form seemed for the time to have regained the erect stateliness of youth.

José, for his part, did not spend a thought, scarcely even a glance, on the matador. He had abundant occupation for his thoughts at home. Yet, preoccupied as he was, the moment he saw Fray Fernando, he was struck by a strange alteration in his appearance also. Bidding a hasty, though warm and grateful, farewell to Walter Gray, he turned, full of affectionate solicitude, to his adopted father.

The monk, however, put him aside with a gesture. He said "I will walk down to the *San Cristofero* with—my *friend.*"

After Many Days

"Think! the shadow on the dial,
For the nature most undone,
Marks the passing of the trial,
Proves the presence of the sun."
~ E.B. BROWNING

FRAY FERNANDO HAD NOT BEEN unmoved by his interview with Walter Gray. The young Englishman had avowed to him, frankly and fearlessly, that he had been taught to confess his sins to God, and to Him alone. And yet, he added, to such a man as Fray Fernando, who had shown him much kindness, and who for years, and he doubted not for wisdom also, might be truly called his father, he would not refuse, nay, he should be glad to make a candid confession of his past misdeeds, which were many. Fray Fernando thought this speech evinced some hopeful dispositions, but at the same time great ignorance, if not willful misunderstanding, of the true nature of confession. He therefore essayed the necessary explanations; and these in turn gave rise to numerous questions from Walter, most respectfully and even deferentially worded, yet very difficult to answer satisfactorily. Fray Fernando found it a hard task to prove the necessity of confession and the virtue of penance. For Walter had been taught controversy almost from his cradle, and did no discredit to the teaching.

More than once Fray Fernando had well-nigh lost patience with him; but his utter helplessness, and the terrible penalties that hung suspended over his head, moved the compassion of the friar, and made him forbearing. And at last he succeeded in winning from the lips of the Englishman the admission, that although his scruples as to some parts of the doctrine and discipline of the Church were as yet un-removed, he was desirous of receiving instruction upon these subjects. Professing himself contented with this *for the present,* he agreed to postpone the ceremony of confession to a future occasion; and in the meantime to allow Walter to tell his story, not as penitent to priest, but as man to man.

The simple narrative, frankly and naturally told, was not without its effect upon the monk. Of the horrors of the inquisitorial dungeon Walter said little, almost nothing-and yet Fray Fernando shuddered. Good Catholic as he had lived up to this hour, and thoroughly free, in thought and word, from the stain of heresy, he still regarded the prisons of the Holy Office with terror, not quite unmixed with a strange fascination. Perhaps this was because his own faith was so far above suspicion, that he could freely afford to pity the victims of heresy. Or perhaps it was because his heart, or that of someone he loved, had once bled beneath the relentless sword of St. Dominic.

But whatever he felt on the subject, he said nothing. He merely observed, that a mark of divine grace had already been bestowed upon "Señor Valter" (as he called Walter), in that he had been outwardly reconciled with the Church; and he doubted not that He who had begun the good work would complete it in due time. For his own part, he would use all his influence with the authorities to obtain for his young friend ample opportunity of receiving such instruction as might remove his scruples and promote his edification in the faith.

And with these words he dismissed him, and summoned the matador.

For some minutes Fray Fernando sat in silence, pondering Walter's case, and scarcely heeding the poor man who stood before him, patiently awaiting his pleasure. Looking up at last, he saw a tall, stooping, emaciated figure, a face nearly as brown as José's, thin gray hair, and a long gray beard. "My friend," he said compassionately, "I can see that yours have been lengthened sufferings. But Holy Church is a tender mother, who abandons not the most unfortunate or the most erring amongst her children. I trust her consolations are not unwelcome to you."

The matador, who, since he entered the apartment, had scarcely averted his dark eyes for a moment from the face of the monk, made answer instantly: "They are most welcome, reverend father." The faith upon which he lived was, in truth, the same as that of Walter Gray; but he had not enjoyed the same opportunities of instruction. Those gleams of light that had sufficed to illuminate this world and the next for him had come to him from the Lutheran Church of Seville; and up to the last, the members of that Church had been forced to continue in external communion with Rome; nor, it seems, had the consciences of the greater number amongst them reproached them for so doing. How could the poor galley-slave see farther than his teachers, or attempt the task of bringing the articles of his creed into logical consistency with each other. But if there was some confusion in his head, there was no contradiction in his heart. He knew that God had forgiven his sins for His Son's sake; even though he did kneel down meekly before Fray Fernando, and submit himself obediently to all prescribed forms, taxing his memory to recall the most trivial words and deeds recorded there, in the hope of receiving an absolution of which he had no need.

But the substance of his confession caused Fray Fernando great surprise. He felt like one who has prepared himself to drink a bitter potion to the dregs, but finds the draft instead some rare old wine, fragrant with the sunshine and the dews of the summers of long ago. It was no pleasant task to hear the confessions usually made by the galley-slaves. But the soul of this poor man seemed sensitive to the touch of sin, as polished metal to the lightest sullying breath. He did not, like the others, regard his sins as so many debts, to be paid somehow or somewhere, lest disagreeable consequences should follow. He had learned to look upon his sin as something which interposed an unwelcome cloud between a reconciled Father and a loving child. Indeed, he spoke as one who knew a secret, which, to say the truth, was as yet unrevealed even to his earnest and conscientious father-confessor.

Fray Fernando listened with compassion and interest, not unmixed with a strange kind of reverence. The very dialect in which the matador spoke deepened the impression of his words. It was the soft liquid "Andaluz," which he himself, in his early days, had been accustomed to hear spoken in his native city of Seville.

Willingly, and with slight penance imposed, he bestowed his absolution and his blessing. And when the matador had risen from his knees, he said to him, "Stay a minute,—I would willingly know something more of you. I think you are not destitute of the grace of God, who giveth to all men as He will."

The matador, be it observed, had not in his confession revealed his real name, or the crime for which he suffered. Such a revelation, though usual, was not obligatory; unless it happened to be the penitent's first confession since the commission of the crime.

"God has been very good to me." he answered quietly. "I am, moreover, grateful to you for your kindness, holy father."

"I have done little for you; I would willingly do more, if I knew how. Something occurs to me at this moment. I have no doubt you are from the old country? Probably a native of Seville?"

The matador bowed.

Fray Fernando checked some remark that rose to his lips, ere he said, "My position here gives me many opportunities, did I care to use them, of holding communication with Spain. It may be you have friends or relatives yet living there to whom you would gladly send a letter. Can you write?"

"I could write once, your reverence; but my hands have held the oar too long to hold the pen now."

"I will then, if you wish it, write at your dictation."

"I thank you, reverend father," the matador answered, slowly and rather doubtfully.

Fray Fernando rose to procure the necessary materials from the next room.

But the matador stayed him. "If you please, father," he said with hesitation, "I do not think—I do not know"—and he slowly raised his worn right hand to his forehead, and held it there horizontally, lightly touching his brow with its fingers.

Something in the slight action struck Fray Fernando. One whom he knew long ago had been wont to use it. Exactly thus: the brow just touched, not pressed; the eyes—dark, thoughtful eyes—not covered, but looking out, as it were, a great way off. Of what was he dreaming? And why did the patio of his father's house at Seville, with everything it contained, from his father's portrait by Juan de las Roelas down to the least ornament, rise suddenly before his eyes?—But this must not go on. With an effort he dispelled the vision, and once more saw the matador standing before him. "Consider what you wish to do, my friend," he said kindly.

"I have considered, reverend father," the matador answered, removing his hand and looking earnestly at the monk, who felt every moment more tormented by thronging memories of the past;—until at length there came a flash of relieving thought—

"Last night I must have dreamed some vivid dream of my early home. Doubtless it is that which haunts me now, though memory fails to recall it distinctly."

Meanwhile, the matador was saying, "It seems to me that it is not well to write. All those I knew think me dead long ago. Perhaps they are dead themselves; for I have been in the galleys nigh upon twenty years.—No, not quite—sixteen years last December. I had my sentence at Seville, in the great *auto-de-fe.*"

"You are then a prisoner of the Holy Office?" Fray Fernando asked, with a vague unaccountable feeling that his dream was coming back to him, and that the scene in which he was acting was a part of it.

"Yes; I hope your reverence will not think the worse of me for that?"

"No; you have probably been drawn aside from the Faith by the subtleties of some designing heretic"

"That was not exactly my case, father. My crime was not heresy, but daring resistance to the Holy Office."

"How?" asked Fray Fernando, now thoroughly awake, and startled—nay, alarmed. What if one, concerned in *that* enterprise, were suddenly to appear and, even in this remote corner of the world, to recognize—

The matador spoke again: "We essayed a

desperate deed. We—for to you I fear not to confess all—we dared to attack the Triana itself."

The blood forsook Fray Fernando's cheek and lips as he questioned,—"*We!* Who?"

The matador, embarrassed by the question, not only from the abrupt and startling way in which it was proposed, but from the difficulty of answering without naming names guarded by his loyal heart in sacred silence, replied after a pause,—"I was the leader—I myself."

"You! ' exclaimed the monk, fastening his eyes upon him in amazement." *You!*—'Tis false.—'Tis not true!"

"Father, I am God's free-man, though the king's slave, and I speak the truth as in His presence," said the matador, with gentle dignity.

Fray Fernando was no longer pale, he was ghastly, and his lips trembled as they faltered, "Your name?"

"At the service of your reverence—Melchior del Salto."

As one possessed, Fray Fernando sprang from his seat, seized the poor man's arm, and in tones not loud, yet fierce and wild, exclaimed, "Man, 'tis false! You—whoever you are—you are *not* Melchior del Salto—An evil spirit takes the form to mock me—*He* was burned to ashes at the stake."

"On the faith and truth of a Christian man, Melchior del Salto stands before you. But—but—"

It was the matador's turn to tremble now and falter. When he spoke again it was with low, imploring voice. "Father," said he—"*Senõr*—for Heaven's sake take off your hand—sit down—let me look you in the face."

He need not have so entreated. The friar's strength was failing through intensity of emotion. He sank unconsciously into the seat. "I am losing my reason," he murmured. "What did you say?—Who are you?"

"I am Melchior del Salto, reprieved at the last moment, because their reverences received information that it was another hand than his which struck down Tomas Varguez that fatal night. And you— you?—*Nay*, señor, not one word.—You are *Señor Don Alfonso!*"

"Melchior!—Brother risen from the dead 1" exclaimed Fray Fernando; and in another moment two hearts that had long been sundered were beating against each other. Then they "lifted up their voices and wept."

When words were possible, they were broken, faltering, in.

"Now I know why I loved you from the first," Melchior del Salto murmured. "I used to listen for the sound of your voice, to watch for the very shadow of your cowl. But, ah, how altered,—señor, my brother!"

"Throughout these long years I believed my brother died for me—the death of fire."

"And *you,* instead, lost all for that brother's sake."

"Oh no; the crime for which I suffered was my own.' And you, my brother—you have suffered—how sorely! Sixteen years in the galleys!"

"God has not forsaken me. His goodness and mercy have followed me every step of the way. Till now—at last—He has given me this great crowning joy,—to see your face again!"

Thus they talked, and might have talked till midnight, had not the new bell, recently brought from Spain for the church of Callao, rung out its musical summons to prayer at the vesper hour.

Fray Fernando heard not the sound; but upon Melchior del Salto it had a magical effect. It transformed him instantly into the galley-slave and the matador. "Our hour is long past," he said. "This must not be. The Englishman will share the blame that is due to me. Besides, the privilege another time may be withheld."

The thought of sending back his newly-found brother to the cruel slavery in which he had pined so long, seemed absolutely horrible to Fray Fernando. Still, it was inevitable. They must part. Sorrowfully acknowledging the necessity, he accompanied the two galley-slaves to the *San Cristofero,* and excused them to the captain, taking upon himself the blame of their late return. "I will see you tomorrow—early," he said, as he bade Melchior del Salto farewell.

The Magic Stone

"Every man is a friend to him that giveth gifts."
~ Proverbs 19:6.

FRAY FERNANDO'S THOUGHTS were very busy during his five minutes' walk from the *San Cristofero* to his own humble lodging. He came to the determination that he would tell José everything that had happened. He had great reliance on the Indian's tact and skill in dealing with those who held the destinies of the galley-slaves in their hands. But, independently of this, his adopted son deserved his full confidence, and he should have it.

"José," he said, "I have something to tell you."

José, at a moment's notice, buried the treasures of new knowledge he had just received from Walter Gray, and was longing to examine, in some deep place within his heart, and stood prepared to listen.

"Do you remember the tale I told you in the tampu beside the Apurimac?" asked the monk.

"Every word of it."

"Shall I lose forever your love and your reverence, José, it I confess to you that the Don Alfonso of that tale stands before you now?"

José's countenance showed no emotion; neither horror nor amazement, not even surprise, was depicted there. It was, in fact, no more than for a long time he had suspected. At first the suspicion brought keen sorrow and perplexity to his loyal heart; but he had, fortunately, been able of late to persuade himself that the patre was quite justified in his resistance to Spanish cruelty and oppression. How he reconciled this belief with his respect for the Catholic faith and the authorities of the Church, it is impossible to say. But indeed there were so many unreconciled contradictions in the mind of José, that this one might well pass unnoticed amongst them.

He said very quietly, "I always knew that the patre was a noble amongst his own people. And what did he, in fighting for the deliverance of the oppressed, save to show himself the friend of the Poor—like a child of the Sun?"

Then, in words few and broken by emotion, Fray Fernando told him the strange sequel of the story. But, to his amazement, José listened with cold incredulity. Was the patre quite sure that there was no mistake, no delusion—that the galley-slave was in very truth the person he represented himself to be?

Now, if the patre had told him that he had just been honored with a visit from the Virgin Mary, José would have received the communication with the deepest reverence and the most unquestioning belief. For it would then have been "a mystery of the Faith;" and José was in the habit of divesting himself of his reason and common sense whenever he entered the temple of the supernatural. Scarcely any marvel could be proposed to him there to which he would hesitate to give implicit credence. But upon the platform of this world and its affairs, and within what he considered the legitimate domain of his reason, he was a shrewd and careful investigator of facts. He inherited the practical ability of his fathers, who were accustomed to decide hard cases, and to do justice and judgment between man and man.

The half astonished, half angry Fray Fernando found he had no alternative save to set his doubts at rest by a full and circumstantial account of his interview with the matador.

This could hardly fail to convince the most skeptical; and once convinced, José was ready to prove himself an invaluable ally.

"We will save him," he said. "Spain is far away; Spaniards will do anything for gold."

Fray Fernando pondered. "But I have no gold," he objected.

"I have," José answered quietly. "Moreover, the time is favorable. The Commandante has gone to Cuzco. Only the Capitano remains. He has his price. Let me treat with him, patre. Nothing easier for him than to give out that the men are dead."

"The *men?*"

"Yes; the stake I mean to play for is the

deliverance of both—the matador and the Englishman."

"For Heaven's sake, José, beware what you do," cried Fray Fernando in alarm. "You will peril all. The Englishman is a prisoner of the Holy Office."

"So is the other."

"Ay; but consider the difference. Melchior was condemned to the galleys full sixteen years ago, in Spain. The matter was never known here; and by this time is well-nigh forgotten everywhere. But Walter Gray—fresh in every man's mind and memory, and under the very eyes of their reverences who pronounced his sentence!—No, no, José; unless you want to ruin us, you must leave him alone."

"Well, I can wait," replied the imperturbable José. And rising from his seat, he began to prepare their frugal supper.

But Fray Fernando could not eat. Out of the fullness of his heart he talked to José of the former days, and of Melchior del Salto; until it became absolutely necessary for him to attend to his evening devotions. When these were over, José prevailed on him to lie down, and at least endeavor to take some rest. Sleep was not possible to him; but it was good to lie motionless in the dark on his mat, to think over the past and the present, and to thank God for His great mercy.

José, when left alone, meditated for a little while on the patre's strange history, then disinterred his own treasure, and began to examine it.

The bitter disappointment that he felt at first had by no means passed away. He quite believed all that Walter Gray had told him. This, from his point of view, was both natural and reasonable. His forefathers had gone forth to propagate the worship of the Sun, as the best and purest religion they knew. And yet that worship had not wholly satisfied the more intelligent amongst them; and they had turned readily, nay, eagerly, to the Spaniards as the depositaries of a more satisfying faith, which they gladly learned from them. But José had had abundant cause to suspect that the Spaniards were not what they professed to be, the chief favorites of the true, invisible God, nor their kind of worship the most acceptable that could be offered to Him. What more reasonable than to suppose that the wise and powerful English, from whom he hoped so much, would be better instructed?

But, granted that Walter's words were true, what they revealed was still "a mystery of the Faith," and nothing more. And in far more educated minds than José's mist and mystery are closely allied. The hopes that had seemed so real, so substantial, so near, were relegated at once to the land of dreams and shadows. Hence the chill disappointment, the utter helpless sadness, that settled down upon his soul.

After a long interval of desultory brooding, that did not deserve the name of thought, he roused himself, trimmed the lamp Fray Fernando had left lighted, and sat down to read over, yet once more, that sublime psalm—the song of the King who should reign in righteousness.

With kindling eyes, and a beating heart, he followed the description of what the King should be. Step by step his soul seemed lifted upwards, until at last it reached the footstool of God Himself—"The Lord God of Israel, who only doeth wondrous things."

"Blessed be His holy name forever,'" José read half aloud, "and let the whole earth be filled with His glory. Amen, and amen!' His glory—whose? The great King's? No, God's—the God of Israel's. And yet the great King's also, if Señor Hualter's words be true—for He is God—God and man—Sufferer, Savior, Redeemer, King." Thus for the first time, in all its grandeur, the great Truth broke upon his mind.

It was like the uprising of the sun-a rapid tropical sunrise.

Would that King then, he questioned with himself, really come in His glory, take the part of his people, and avenge them upon their enemies, the cruel Spaniards? Might not this, after all, be possible? And if so, what a vengeance His would be! José was neither merciless nor bloodthirsty; he desired no wholesale massacres, no tortures. And yet, as he sat there with the Breviary still open before him, a vivid panorama rose before his eyes. He saw the great square of Cuzco filled with Indians, mounted upon splendid horses, and carrying fire-breathing clubs,—all guarding a grim scaffold draped with black, where a stately Spaniard, with the features of the Viceroy Toledo, was about to bow his haughty head beneath the fatal ax.

But a loud knocking at the outer door dispelled his vision into air. He hastened to unbar it, and confronted a sunburnt mariner from the

San Cristofero.

At the same moment he became aware that his lamp was useless,-the day was breaking.

"One of the slaves is very ill," said the mariner. "Will the padre come and see him, for the love of God? Ask him also to bring 'su majestad,' for the man seems to be dying."

"I will waken the patre," said José. "Tell me the name of the sick man."

"He is called the matador."

Fray Fernando came forth from the inner room. "I have heard all," he said, looking greatly agitated. "You need not have asked the name. I knew it."

Quickly and silently he made the necessary preparations. No wonder that José, in his ignorance, looked with trembling awe upon the little silver box, which he was taught to believe actually contained his Creator and his God! Upon this occasion, however, the thought flashed through his mind—"Was the King of whom Señor Hualter spoke really there? If so, how could He be gone away into heaven '?" But it soon gave place to a reflection of a more practical kind,—"The patre has had no food since yesterday forenoon. If he goes forth fasting he may take the calenture.—Patre," he said aloud, ' I pray you drink at least some of this chica ere you go."

Fray Fernando shook his head. "I shall communicate with him," he said.

Nothing more was spoken until they were on their way, Fray Fernando bearing the precious viaticum, and José the little silver bell with which he failed not to warn bystanders to show fitting reverence.

Then Fray Fernando said, "If it be possible to remove him, we must do it."

"What becomes of galley-slaves when they are ill?" José asked.

Fray Fernando sighed. "The only place for

them is the hold," he said. "And that is so dark, and withal so horribly unclean, that, I have heard, many die at the oar rather than enter it."

"Surely the chihuayhua flower, the emblem of pity, does not grow on your side of the Mother Sea," said José with quiet bitterness.

"But sometimes there is leave given to bring them on shore to the prison, or to some hospital," Fray Fernando resumed.

"This man shall come on shore, and neither to prison nor hospital," José answered determinately. "Here we are, patre. Look, there stands the captain by the helm. I am to deal with him, you understand? But he must bring me to his cabin. I can do nothing within earshot of his men."

So successfully did José deal with the captain of the *San Cristofero,* that in less than an hour the sick man was taken gently from the dark and horrible hole into which he had been thrown to die, placed on a rude litter made out of a couple of spare planks covered with José's mantle, and borne carefully to the lodging of Fray Fernando.

"You succeeded marvelously—how did you manage?"—the monk asked of José, so soon as he had rendered Melchior the cares his situation immediately demanded, and had seen that he was slumbering from exhaustion.

"I had, in the clasp of my yacollo, a certain magic stone, which I did but show the captain, and the sight of it bowed his heart at once."

"And what said he to you?"

"Many things, which seemed utter unreason. Such as these: Pray devoutly and hammer on stoutly.' That the golden load is a burden light,' and that he was not like the tailor of Campijo, or Campillo, or some such place, who wrought for nothing, and found his customers in thread."

"What answer made you to his litany of proverbs?"

"None; save to give him that glimpse of the magic stone. And to tell him I knew the poor fellow was dying (which in truth I know not at all); and that if he died on shore, there would be no man the wiser—but one man the wealthier. But had I known these were proverbs, I might have favored him in return with one of ours, from the lips of the wise Inca Pachacutec: 'Anger and passion may be cured; but folly is incurable.' And of all the follies under God's heaven, the worst, as I think, is that of the white men, who will do nothing for pity and for mercy, for the fear of God and the love of man; but everything for gold and silver, or for children's toys of colored or sparkling stones."

Fray Fernando sighed. "You have done well, José," he said. "But I fear the deliverance has come too late."

"Nay, patre. Our people indeed die easily; but the white man is strong, and he clings to life as the lianas cling to the forest trees. With care and God's blessing, I think we may save him yet."

The Years That the Canker-Worms Hath Eaten

*"Tell him, when he is a man, to reverence the
dreams of his youth."*
~ Schiller

MELCHIOR DEL SALTO FELT AS IF heaven had
begun already for him. It was no wonder.

His limbs, freed from their galling fetters, lay in luxurious rest on a couch of vicuña-skin; his toil-worn, well-nigh crippled frame was stretched at ease the whole day long; and his ears, so sadly used to blasphemies and cries of pain, had only to drink in the gentle tones of Fray Fernando, or the quiet words of José. He was very happy, and deeply thankful. Still, he did not recover. He had no disease; he was only worn out— "used up." It was time. Sixteen years was a good term of service at the oar, even for a strong man.

Melchior's strength had been failing for more than a year; though the lengthened swoon, that drew attention to the fact, was caused by the agitation of his interview with Fray Fernando. He afterward told his foster-brother that deliverance from bondage had come to him just at the right moment: not too soon, else he might have had to return to a strange un familiar world, like a ghost come back from the dead; not too late, since it was good to rest for a little while, ere he went forth on his journey to that home wherein he should rest forever.

Only one regretful thought troubled the calm of those declining hours. And at last, one day, when José had gone to Lima, and Fray Fernando alone was sitting by his side, the secret sorrow found words.

"Do you want anything, my brother?" the monk asked tenderly, noticing that Melchior's eyes were fixed upon him with an earnest inquiring gaze.

"Nothing, Señor Don Alfonso. Except what I am trying to find, and cannot."

"Perhaps I could find it for you."

"Would to God you could!" Melchior answered with a mournful smile. "I am looking, in that worn, old face of yours, for the dear, young, noble face my heart so loved and reverenced in the days gone by."

"Then indeed you look in vain, my brother. Don Alfonso Garcia de Fanez is dead and buried long ago; and he who sits here is only Fray Fernando, the Franciscan friar."

"But this I would fain know, señor, and my brother—where is Don Alfonso buried, and what has he left behind him? He should not have passed away without mark or remembrance. For he was made for great things."

"So seemed many another who has come to ruin, as he."

"There was no other like Don Alfonso.—Nay, let me speak, señor. In the galleys I spoke but little, and very soon I shall speak no more. You were the passion, the idol, of my boyhood and my youth. And even now I do not wonder. You learned with ease all that other men learn with pain. You knew a thousand things I had never dreamed of yet you knew all I knew also. You did all that I could do, and better than I."

"You say too much for me, Melchior."

"I say the truth, señor. Always you made us feel that you were more than you did; that the ready stroke and spring at the bull-feast, the thrust and parry in the tilting-ring, were but earnests given of great deeds yet to be. O brother, brother, do you not remember all those old talks in the orange-grove by the river-side? All those plans, that came to nothing How you were to raise a corps of volunteers, and help to rend Ireland (that fair jewel, you called it) from the crown of the English usurper And how you were then to settle and colonize, taking me with you, and getting for me also a grant of land among the saffron-kilted kernes? My brother Francisco was to be our priest, and Miguel and Ruy to till the ground."

"Dreams—all dreams!" Fray Fernando answered sadly. "They are no more to me now than the tales José loves to tell us of his Inca forefathers."

"But, señor, my brother, you yourself told

me long ago that the dreams of youth are the flowers, the doings of manhood the fruit. Woe for the flowers that they have fallen, and left no fruit behind!"

"The tree was blighted, and is dead. Whence, then, could the fruit come?"

"That work was mine. There, señor, is the thought that wrings my heart."

"Put that thought away from you, dear and generous brother," Fray Fernando eagerly interposed. "It was not your work; it was my fate."

"What do you mean by that word fate,' señor? I am a poor ignorant man, yet I know this: it was no fate that happened to me, but the will of God. How much more you—wise, learned, and a churchman!"

"I am learned in nothing, Melchior, save in sorrow.—But this is ungrateful," he added presently. "God has healed my worst sorrow in giving you back to me."

"He will heal the rest too," said Melchior. "And though the flowers faded so long ago, I think the fruit will come yet." Fray Fernando sighed. Then his own secret trouble rose half unconsciously to his lips. "I am not at peace with God," he said. "I have trifled with His grace in His sacraments."

"I know but one way of making peace with God, señor. That is through Christ. He is our way, and He is our peace."

Fray Fernando looked somewhat surprised. "How do you know that, Melchior?" he asked.

"Because, Señor Don Alfonso, I have trod the way, and I have found the peace."

Just then José entered, carrying a pataca, or covered native basket, from which he produced some articles of food and other things that he had purchased in the city. Amongst them was a flask of wine from the old country, which he gave to Melchior, saying, "My Father smiled upon the fruits of your native land, and they have sent their best juices hither to make sick men well."

"Don José, you are very good to me," said Melchior gratefully.

"I ought to be good to everyone today," José answered, as he seated himself, and loosed the fastening of his yacollo, which was now a simple golden pin—his mother's tupu—instead of a large and lustrous emerald, Yupanqui's gift. "I have heard such good tidings. But I ought first to tell you, patre, that I failed to do your errand at the Franciscan monastery. The monks would not trust me with the Book, without a written order from yourself."

Fray Fernando had sent to request the loan of a copy of the Vulgate. Perhaps his motive for this request might have been found in certain conversations he had lately held with Walter Gray, who was now permitted to come to him three times a week for religious instruction.

José went on: "Whatever may have caused

their hesitation, it was scarcely the value of the Book, since I offered to leave them my gold bracelet in pledge for it. I think they feared I might do myself or someone else a mischief with it, as if it were a carbine or musket. It reminds me, patre, of the old times in Cerro Blanco, when I stood in such awe of your Breviary, believing that a spirit dwelt in it, which spoke to you when you read it."

Then Melchior said reverently, "It is quite true, Don José, that a Spirit dwells in the Book you were to have brought today; and He will speak to you, if you read it with prayer and humility."

"You are making pictures, Melchior," José answered readily —"I see." He himself was quite as anxious for the Book as Fray Fernando, because he thought it would tell him of his King.

"But you have not yet told us the good tidings, José," Fray Fernando resumed presently.

José's black eyes kindled with a vivid inward fire, but no other feature of his face showed emotion, and his voice was calm, even low, as he spoke. "Some Spanish soldiers have just come back to Lima from the country of the Chunchos, which you call the Montana. They have brought with them —sore wounded and sick unto death—Don Ramon de Virves. It was at his own earnest request they brought him so far, for he thought to embark for Spain. But he will never see Spain again. God has visited his iniquities on his head."

"Take care, José," said Fray Fernando gravely. "Long ago the wise man said, 'Rejoice not when thine enemy falleth, and let not thine heart be glad when he stumbleth: lest the Lord see it, and it displease Him, and He turn away His wrath from him."

"Who is Don Ramon de Virves?" Melchior asked with interest.

José turned to him and answered, still in

the same low quiet voice, "When I was a child I dwelt with my kindred in a little green spot in the great southern desert—a paucar,' we call it. One day that Don Ramon de Virves came thither with his Spaniards. We were mostly women and children; we neither could fight with them, nor desired to do it. So we gave them to eat and to drink, and let them lie down in our huts to sleep. But while we slept they arose, drew their Spanish steel, and slew all— men, women, and little children—without re- morse or pity.[1] That was their way of 'reduc- ing' Indians to the obedience of the crown of Spain and the faith of Christ. Yet it was well for those who died. Thrice more unhappy were the two spared—my mother and I. Bound and guarded, we watched the flames that burned our home to ashes. But the Children of the Sun know how to die. When night came again,

____

1. A hundred such stories could easily be gathered out of the blood-stained records of the Spanish conquests in America.

my mother kissed me, and said, `Pacha-camac cares for the wild beasts on the mountain,[2] he will also care for thee, my child. Then she bade me go to sleep. When I awoke, she was dead. I am a man now, and I thank God that she won her freedom thus; but I was a child then, and I wept and wailed over her lifeless form in the bitterness of my anguish. Yet I too would have died, rather than be Don Ramon's slave, if the patre had not bought me. Judge whether or no I have cause to rejoice that Don Ramon is dying now in pain and misery—forsaken of God and man."

"José, my son José!" Fray Fernando interposed, in a tone of grieved surprise. "Remember that vengeance belongs to God, not to us. To Him we ought to leave it."

---

2. The Incas believed that "Pacha-camac had appointed the same care to be taken of the wild as of the tame flocks;" for this reason they would not hurt or destroy them, except so far as was necessary for the food, the clothing, or the safety of man.

"I have left it to Him," José answered calmly, "and He has taken it."

"But did you never hear," said Melchior, raising himself and looking earnestly at the Indian youth— "did you never hear that our blessed Lord Himself, when He hung on the cross, prayed for His murderers, and said, 'Father, forgive them, for they know not what they do'?"

"No?" José said, interrogatively, and with a perplexed, discomfited look.

"How can you say 'No,' José?" Fray Fernando asked, a little jealous perhaps for his reputation as instructor. "You have heard it a hundred times. And what says the Paternoster, —almost the first thing I taught you?"

José struggled with a thought he did not choose to admit, and putting it from him with an effort, answered doggedly, "It says, Thy kingdom come.'"

"It says also, Forgive us our trespasses, as we

forgive them that trespass against us.'"

"And," Melchior added, "none have part in the kingdom that is to come save those whose trespasses are forgiven."

José received these sharp arrows of truth without remonstrance, but without acquiescence. He bore their sting as he would have borne physical pain—silent and unmoved, though keenly sensible. In any other case he would have been very angry with the hands that winged them; but he knew not how to feel anger towards a dying man like Melchior, still less towards the patre. But how unreasonable, how unjust, how cruel the requirement!

Whose requirement? That he did not ask himself just yet. With a lowering brow and a heart full of bitterness he went forth; nor did either Melchior or Fray Fernando see him again that night.

XXXII

Walter Grey's Advice

*"Forgive!—for 'tis sweet to stammer one letter
From the Eternal's language: on earth it is called
'Forgiveness.'"*

~ LONGFELLOW *(from the Swedish)*

JOSÉ VIRACOCHA WAS NOT AT ALL more vindictive than other men. He inherited from his ancestors no implacability of disposition, no burning thirst after vengeance. On the contrary, it was their special glory—a glory that ought to last when other glories fade away—that they saw the beauty of fair Mercy, and wooed and won her to sit beside them on their golden throne. Many a deed of generous magnanimity had place amongst his cherished traditions. He could not remember the first time he had heard how the Inca Mayta caressed and fed the little children of his enemies; how the Inca Huayna Capac taught and acted upon the noble maxim, "We ought to spare our foes, for they will soon be our subjects." But he had now come to a point at which these traditions could not help him. Although the clemency a monarch extends to despairing suppliants at his feet is a fair thing to look upon, and very grateful to eyes fatigued with the monotonous crimson of battle-fields and massacres, still it is not the forgiveness of keen and cruel personal injuries. As surely as the crystal rings when struck, so surely does human nature respond, with the sharp cry of hatred, to the stroke of wrong. There is only One Hand whose touch can bring peace and make silence there.

José could not forgive Don Ramon: he had no wish to do it-his soul rose in rebellion at the very thought. He saw clearly all that it involved. If he pardoned Don Ramon, he must pardon also all his enemies, with all their injuries, public and private. He must pardon Don Francisco Solis; and him he hated quite as bitterly as he hated Don Ramon. And there were times when his resentment against both paled and faded before the intensity of his indignation against the spoilers of Tahuantin Suyu. Them also—even *them*—he must pardon! Impossible! Yet a suspicion, gradually becoming a conviction, was stealing over his heart. It was no other than the King whom he sought—the Divine Monarch and Deliverer, the great Inca of the East—who required this thing of him, who demanded it as the test of his allegiance.

If, instead, He had but asked his life-blood!

In his sore dismay and perplexity, he bethought himself of Walter Gray, to whom he was becoming every day more strongly attached, and to whose comfort he ministered in every possible way. Walter would give him the English view of the matter; and that, most probably, would be the true one. So, after Walter's next visit to Fray Fernando, José returned with him to the beach; and standing before him as he rested for a little in the welcome shade of a rock, he briefly acquainted him with the strange demand that had been made upon him.

"If," he said, "I proposed stabbing the man through the back, or setting fire to the house where he lies wounded, I could understand the King having somewhat to object. Nor, indeed, would the Incas have approved such practices. But to bid me forgive him from my heart! How can it matter what I feel there? Whose business is that, save my own?"

"It is God's business, José;—and the King is God." "I know it," said José reverently.

"God sees your heart, reads it through and through, claims it for His own."

José lay down on the sand, and turned his face away from Walter. At last he said,—"I almost wish I had never met you, Señor Hualter." "And why that, Don José?"

"You trouble me. Better not to know the King, than to know Him and not to obey Him; and He is hard, *hard* to obey."

"Oh no!"

"But yes. I know now why none of the Spaniards really obey Him, though they pretend to do it,— They cannot. Nor can I; I am afraid of Him."

"You ought not. He loves you, He died for you;—and He only wants you to be like Him."

"Well, if need were, I could die for Him. But" (a tremor shook his whole frame; not violent—none of his movements were that—but telling of intense repugnance) "this thing I cannot do;—I will not. What use to try? I could never forgive that man, unless I were taken to pieces and made over again."

"'Except a man be born again,'" said Walter Gray, "'he shall in no wise enter into the kingdom of God.'"

"Who says that?"

"The King Himself."

"I do not understand.—Stay, I do!" he added, after a thoughtful pause. "I remember the patre said those words to me. He told me they meant my baptism. He said I was born then into the Christian Church."

"You remember your baptism?" asked Walter.

"Of course I do; I was ten years old."

"What did you feel? Did you receive a new heart, and begin a new life then?"

"In one way, yes. I felt great love for the patre, who, I thought, was claiming me for his own by certain mystic rites and ceremonies; and I gave myself up to him very gladly. But as for thoughts of God or the Church, I had none. Until long afterward, I worshipped my Father the Sun."

"It is very plain that you still need to be born of water and the Spirit, and to receive the new heart which God alone can give you. And He will. You have only, on your part, to `give yourself up to Him very gladly,' as you did to the padre.—Don José," said Walter Gray, starting up suddenly, "I could talk to you for hours; but I dare not linger. Look yonder! The sun touches the sea already; and ere it sinks, I am bound to be on board. There is not a moment to waste; the sunsets are so rapid here. Wonderful, like everything else in this wonderland of yours!"

"I am with you, Señor Hualter," said José,

suiting the action to the word.

As they walked along together, Walter remarked: "I dare not make the captain angry by delay, lest he should deny me leave another time; and few other times may be left to me now, Don José. The Commandante returns from Cuzco tomorrow, and it is whispered he has orders for us. I fear we may be sent to some distant shore, where I shall never see your face or that of Fray Fernando again. It is so lonely on board, now the matador is gone; though, God knows, my heart rejoices at his deliverance. Farewell, Don José!"

Next morning José said to Fray Fernando: "Patre, I am going to the city to visit some of my people. Will you give me a letter to the monks, and I will bring you back the Book you want?"

"Willingly, my son. But, I pray of thee, come back thyself as speedily as thou canst; for since yesterday there are five men ill of the calenture, and two of the Creoles from San Domingo are dying, as I fear."

"I will hasten."

"Hasten thine errands in the city—not thy footsteps by the way; for the heat is fearful to-day, and I would not have thee get a sunstroke."

"No fear of that. My Father never hurts his own; he only smites the Spaniards," said José, as he started at a brisk pace on his seven miles' walk.

His assertion was not strictly true, however; for the burning sun of Lima proved fatal to many of the Inca family exiled by Spanish tyranny from Cuzco and its neighborhood, and forced to take up their residence on the hot, unhealthy coast.

That day José brought back with him in triumph a formidable-looking volume. Fray Fernando laid it aside until the evening; but when the door of their humble dwelling was barred for the night, and the lamp was lighted, he set it on the table before him, and began to read. Melchior prayed him to read aloud, translating the Latin into Spanish as he read. There were few things which he could have refused Melchior; so he turned from the Epistles of St. Paul (which he had been exploring to test the accuracy of Walter Gray's quotations, and to discover, if possible, some key to the perplexities they awakened), and, rightly judging that the Gospels were the best food for the unlearned, he found the opening page of the New Testament, and began to read "The Gospel of Jesus Christ, the Son of God."

No man had ever two more attentive hearers. Melchior was soon to know more than even that Book could tell of Him whom his soul loved. Yet every word it revealed was precious. What if, ere long, he should drink from the fountain-head? Hitherto only a few drops in a tiny cup had been borne to his thirsting lips; therefore for the present it was joy enough to stoop over the running stream and drink, and give God thanks for the draft.

José, meanwhile, had not yet drunk; though he was sore athirst, and the water was near him. From the day when he learned who the King was from Walter Gray, until that other day when the summons to forgive his enemies smote him to the heart, José had occupied somewhat the position of a devout Jew "waiting for the consolation of Israel," looking with earnest faith for a national Messiah, a great Redeemer and Deliverer, who should save his beloved people from all their enemies. Such a Deliverer he was prepared to welcome and to obey, even to the death. But now a lightning flash, scathing and burning while it illumined, had revealed to him the necessity of another deliverance, hitherto undreamt of,—a personal deliverance from sin. He was learning that the Son of God must be sought as the Savior of the soul, or He will not reveal Himself as the King of the nations. Even the question, "Will He restore the Incas?" was postponed, of necessity, until their child found an answer to that other question, "Will He receive me, and make me over again, so that I can serve and please Him?"

He who read was seeking as earnestly as those who listened. Fray Fernando's difficulties were far more complex than those of José. He needed everything—truth, peace, light, pardon. There were times when the last seemed the most pressing need of all. If each had tried to condense his longings into a single prayer, that of Fray Fernando would probably have been, "Wash me thoroughly from mine iniquity, and cleanse me from my sin;" and that of José, "Create in me a clean heart, and renew a right spirit within me." Though it is likely José would soon have added, "Do good in thy good pleasure unto Zion" (meaning what stood for Zion in his mind); "build thou the walls of Jerusalem."

The King Found

"He came to me in Power; I knew Him not.
He came to me in Love; and my heart broke;
And from its inmost depths there rose a cry—
'My Father, oh, my Father, smile on me!'
And the great Father smiled."
~ NIGHT AND THE SAUL

A QUIET MONTH GLIDED BY, BEARING the *San Cristofero* away to more northern shores; and

slowly—almost imperceptibly—drifting another bark, long tossed by storms, towards
the haven of welcome rest. So gradually was
Melchior sinking, that although Fray Fernando
watched him, hour by hour, with the devoted
love of a brother born for adversity, and José
with tender kindness, it was probable that the
coming Visitant, the shadow of whose presence
any stranger might readily have seen in his face,
would take them both by surprise. The more
accustomed they grew to the pleasant office of
tending him, reading to him, talking with him,
the less they seemed to think that all must have
an end, and that shortly.

By this time they had read the Gospels
through—and not once or twice. They had
read the Epistles also; they had explored the
narratives and prophecies of the Old Testament; they had even, to José's intense delight,
made some acquaintance with "the book of the
Golden City," as he called the Apocalypse. But

always they turned back to the Gospels with fresh wonder, interest, and joy. What one of them, at least, found therein, will appear in the following conversation.

It was a close and sultry afternoon. Fray Fernando had gone out to perform the duties of his office towards some poor fever-stricken mariners, who lay in a rude shed on the beach, called by courtesy the Hospital. José sat beside Melchior, gently fanning him, and, as he did so, chanting in a low harmonious voice some melody of his people.

"Ancha Incay Hocca?" Melchior repeated, opening his eyes with a smile. "If I were you, Don José, I would rather sing a psalm than those heathen words."

"The words I sing are a psalm to me," José answered; "but if they trouble you I will stop."

"Oh no. But I did not think there were any psalms or sacred songs as yet rendered into your tongue."

"Nor are there, so far as I know. These are words from a Play which my fathers used to act before the white men came."

Melchior heard him with indifference. What were plays to a dying man? He had done with "vain shows;" where he was going all would be real. Still he felt that a little interest in what interested his Indian friend was the least proof he could give of his gratitude for a thousand benefits; so, when José said, "Shall I tell you about it?" he answered promptly, "If you please, Don José."

José, with evident pleasure, began his story. "There was once," he said, "a great and brave chieftain, whose name was Ollanta. He rebelled against his lord the Inca; he took for himself the province given him to rule over; and he slew those who were sent against him. For he would fain obey no lord, but be lord and Inca over all himself. But, after a long time and a grievous war, in which many men were killed, he was overcome and made prisoner; and his friends, who aided him in his rebellion, were taken also. With their hands bound and their eyes bandaged, they were led to Cuzco. Then, at last, the bandage was taken away. Behold! they stood in the presence of the sole Inca. He sat on his golden throne, the high priest on his right hand, the great general whose valor had won the victory, on his left; and standing around him, like stars around the sun, all his glorious court. He looked awful in his majesty. Right sternly he asked the trembling captives, 'Why have you done this thing?' But they only bowed their heads and answered, Father, we have nothing to say.' Then the Inca turned to the high priest, 'What do these men deserve?' he asked. Too well the high priest knew the answer, but his lips refused to utter it. 'The Sun has given me a merciful heart,' he said. So the Inca looked from him to the victorious general, whose heart was cast in a harder mold.

And he spoke out boldly, Inca, these men have slain our fathers; they must die. Let them be tied to stakes driven into the ground, and let their servants, who fought for them, be made to march over their bodies. Then let those servants also be slain with arrows.' Then the Inca looked upon the captives; and his face was sad and stern; 'You have heard your sentence,' he said.—' Take them away.' And the servants wept and wailed and made sore lamentation. But Ollanta and his friends spake never a word; for they knew that their doom was just. As they had sown, they must reap. Only they looked up to the glorious Sun, and around them on the fair earth, as men who take their farewell look of all.

"Then once more spake the Inca. 'Stay,' he said. 'Unbind those men. They shall not die, but live. Ollanta, I forgive thee.' And turning to the guards that stood around, he added, Bring the golden helmet, the mace, and the arrows.'

(These were the signs of Ollanta's forfeited honors.) Give them back to him. And to his friends likewise restore their maces of office, their arrows, and their bracelets.' Moreover, forasmuch as pardon is not complete without trust restored, he said to him, Ollanta, thou shalt govern Cuzco for me when I go forth shortly upon my warlike expedition to Collasuyu.' And he sealed all with the generous word, ' I shall go with joy; leaving, to govern here, my faithful Ollanta.'

"Oh, my friend! Ollanta's eyes were dry at the terrible death-sentence; but I tell you he wept then! Ollanta never knelt at the Inca's feet to implore his life; but I tell you, when the Inca forgave him thus, he flung himself in the dust before him, and swore to be his slave forever! And, at last, the grateful, reverent love that overflowed his heart, found voice in the words I sang just now.

"O Inca! this is too much
For a man who is nothing.
Mayest thou live a thousand years.
I am as thou makest me;
Thou dost give me succor:
Crippled, thou makest me stand;
Fallen, thou raisest me tip;
Poor, thou enrichest me;
Blind, thou givest me sight;
Dead, thou restorest life;—
Thou, indeed, teachest me to forget."[1]

"What, Don José, are you weeping at your own tale?" asked Melchior, wondering at the emotion that filled the eyes and well-nigh choked the voice of José.

The Indian dashed the unbidden drops away. "Not often do we weep, we Children of the Sun," he said. "Yet Ollanta wept at the In-

---

1. See "Ollanta, an Ancient Ynca Drama, Translated from the Original Quechua by Clements R. Markham. C. B."

ca's pardon; for his heart grew soft within him, like the heart of a little child. And I too—O Melchior, can you not read the meaning of my tale? Listen, then. I am Ollanta, the rebel. I did not know my King, my Inca. I would not obey Him; I fought against Him; I wanted to be lord and ruler myself, and to do my own will, not His. But He conquered me, and took me, and led me step by step, as it were with bandaged eyes. And now, at last, the bandage is taken away. I have seen Him. First *there,*" indicating with rapid gesture the Book on the table; "then *here,*" laying his hand on his heart. "He has pardoned me—pardoned, blessed, restored; made me His free, happy servant; told me to live and work for Him.

> *"O Inca! this is too much*
> *For a man who is nothing.*
> *I am as thou makest me;*
> *Thou dost give me succor:*
> *Crippled, thou makest me stand*

Fallen, thou raisest me up.
Poor, thou enrichest me;
Blind, thou givest me sight;
Dead, thou restorest life:—
Thou, indeed, teachest me to forget.'
Ranti! Ranti! Capac Inca! Huacchacuyac!"

There was a long silence, filled with happy thought. Then at last, Melchior asked gently, "What of Don Ramon de Virves *now*, Don José?"

"Have I not said, Thou, indeed, teachest me to forget'?" José answered. Presently he added, with a smile, "It is not told in the Play; but for my part, I have always believed that Ollanta stretched out his hand that day to the general who was his enemy and sought his life, and said to him, Let us be friends for the Inca's sake.'— But I am sorry for Don Ramon de Virves. He is gone where my pardon cannot reach him. I have told all to the King; and I have asked Him to let me show some of them how He teaches to forget."

"Don José, you ought to tell Fray Fernando what you have just told me. I would die without a shadow on my heart if only he—he too—"

"*He?* the patre? Of course he has known all this, and far more, for many a year—from his childhood, I suppose. I wish indeed from my heart that I could tell Señor Hualter, who is far away from us now. He it was who first told me about Christ the King. Instead of the gem I sought—the hope or deliverance for my people—he put that day into my outstretched hand a little seed, like a grain of sand. I was grieved and angry, for to my eyes it had no beauty: it did not burn and quiver in the light like the stones of fire. But I buried it in my heart; and lo! it sprang up and grew, until at last there came forth a living flower, brighter and more glorious than a thousand cold dead stones.—But the patre, oh—he knows every-thing!"

"I am sure God has marked him for His own," said Melchior—"' chosen him in the fur-nace of affliction,' as he read yesterday from the good Book. But if it were not for the hope in Him, life would be a sad thing enough for my brother and for me, Don José. Does he seem to you an old, broken, world-weary man, with the wrinkles on his brow and the gray streaks in his hair? In years he is yet almost young. If he has numbered eight and thirty, it is the utmost."

"I know he has suffered as few suffer, even in this sad world."

"You may well say that. Think of those long, dark, weary years! And now I go hence—I who have cost him so much, and been able to give him back so little. But I turn to you, Don José. All that I would have been to him, all that I would have done for him, and never can be or do, I leave to you—you, his adopted son. I pray you to help him, guard him, watch over him."

"I vowed to do that, Melchior, ere I ever saw your face." "Yet promise now once more, to please a dying man."

"With all my heart I promise. Perhaps," he added, "you may be able to watch over him yourself, from your place in yonder sky."

"I do not think that, Don José. What do we know, after all, save so much as that Book tells us? And it tells us scarce anything of the dead, but that they are 'with the Lord.'—Ah, there is Señor Don Alfonso at the door. I would know his step amongst a thousand."

Another was at the door also, though neither José nor Fray Fernando heard his footsteps. But at midnight he entered unbidden, touched Melchior with his shadowy hand, and whispered the gentle yet imperative summons, "Arise, and go hence." Not always without a struggle does the flesh leave the spirit free to obey that call. With Melchior the struggle lasted "until the breaking of the day." But in the end there was peace. For the last time on earth, the foster-brothers held converse together. What passed was unheard, even by José, who kept watch in the outer room. If "the rites of the Church" were administered, José did not know it, and was amazed at the apparent omission.

And when the sun arose in glory, the weary spirit won its freedom. There was one more look and smile for "Señor Don Alfonso," there was a murmured word of grateful farewell for José, and then the brave and faithful heart of Melchior del Salto ceased to beat.

Fray Fernando closed his eyes, and sat down and wept beside him.

But José said, "You should not weep for him, patre. He sees the King in His beauty."

Yet Fray Fernando did well to weep. There are tears that bring help and healing with them. Of such were the tears he shed over the lifeless form of the brother whom God had given back to him so strangely from the dead. Instead of the thoughts of restless anguish, of remorse and shame, that had haunted him for sixteen weary years, he could think of Melchior del Salto, now and henceforward, with tender regret; not indeed unmixed with pain, but still calm and soothing. Meanwhile, for himself, the long conflict of his life seemed over. Peace and reconciliation had come to him at last, breathed softly by dying lips. And with peace there came strength also. Possibilities of new life, of a life of healthful, holy activity, began from that day forward to open out before him. Even yet he might serve the God to whom Melchior del Salto had lifted up his heart in the hour of need, and who had heard him, and saved him out of all his distresses.

XXXIV

The King Followed

"So I go on not knowing;
I would not if I might!
I would rather walk in the dark with God,
Than walk alone in the light;
I would rather walk with Him by faith,
Than walk alone by sight."

~ ANONYMOUS

A YEAR HAS PASSED AWAY SINCE all that was
mortal of Melchior del Salto found a quiet

resting-place beneath the shadow of the new church of Callao. To Fray Fernando it has been "the beginning of years," the first year of a new life. Its days and nights have been filled to overflowing with thought and action. Inward change and progress have kept pace with outward activity; "great searchings of heart" with valiant work of head and hand. And yet the Fray Fernando who raises his eyes from his book, with a pleasant smile of greeting for José as he enters, looks a healthier, happier, and even a younger man than he who brought the dying galley-slave to his home. Nay more: Fray Fernando looks younger now than he did when he bought the best blessing of his life, some fifteen years ago, from Don Ramon de Virves with the tooth of St. Joseph.

The book he is reading—his favorite, almost his only study—is still the Vulgate. From its pages he has learned many things.

Important side lights have been thrown

upon their teaching by numerous conversations with Walter Gray (now once more at Callao, after a long coasting expedition)—by the simple faith that upheld Melchior del Salto in the hour of death—by Fray Constantino's well-worn volume. But another light, without which these would have been useless, has illumined the sacred page for Fray Fernando—even "the candle of the Lord," which is his Spirit. The result of all may be briefly told:—at the year's end his faith differed widely from the recognized creed of that Church with which he still remained in outward communion.

No man who thinks profoundly and feels keenly can change his ancestral faith for another without many a fear and misgiving and many a pang. In deep soil the roots strike deepest: even to lay the branches low the tempest must put forth the fierceness of its strength; what then if the roots be torn away? Surely the soil will come up with them—the heart itself be convulsed to its depths.

Yet Fray Fernando, who had suffered so much already, suffered less than might have been expected during the progress of this momentous change. It was in his favor that he had grasped truth with a firm hand before he felt the call to abandon error. Moreover, action was with him not only the companion of thought, but its precursor. The cumbrous armor of superstition was not torn from him by violence so much as laid down voluntarily piece by piece, as he found that it hindered instead of helping him in his daily conflict with sin and ignorance. Experience taught him, also, that the truths his own soul lived upon were life and peace to the sick and dying to whom he ministered continually—to the crowd of Black people, Creoles, and mariners to whom he preached on the shore every Sunday and holiday; and that whatever was not found in the Vulgate was not good for them any more than for himself.

And, added to all, he had José—José the most appreciative of scholars, the most sympathetic of friends—"answering him like silver bells lightly touched." Everything he learned was imparted almost immediately to José, and the joy it gave more than doubled by the process. José himself would have originated nothing in this line. He was content, and would have been content, to the end of his days, to eat the heavenly manna as his fathers ate their maize, simply as they got it, without the aid of the stones that bruise or the fan that winnows. He would have gone on, satisfied and happy, loving his King, living for Him, and willing at need to die for Him, but never suspecting the mode of worship he had learned at Cerro Blanco not to be altogether well pleasing and acceptable in His sight. If anything he had been taught had ever chanced to perplex him, as appearing contrary to some other thing that his heart held dear, he would have told himself,

"It is a mystery of the faith," and have rested satisfied.

What Fray Fernando taught him, however, he understood thoroughly, and felt profoundly. Moreover, he was the safest confidant the monk could have chosen. No man ever knew better how to keep his mouth and his tongue, and in so doing to keep his soul from troubles. He was the guardian of many deadly secrets about his own people; and he was just as likely to betray Maricancha or Rimac to the Viceroy, as he was to compromise Fray Fernando with the Inquisition.

His own life at this time was quite as busy, and probably quite as useful, as that of his patron. Most of the surviving members of the Inca family, who had been banished from Cuzco and its neighborhood, were forced to take up their residence at Lima, where, severed from the associations dear to their hearts, and exposed to the influences of an unhealthy climate, they withered away like trees transplanted into un-genial soil.[1]

Every hour that José could spare from attendance on the patre he devoted to the task of comforting and ministering to these his brethren. It is true that the common wants of the body, such as food and clothing, he seldom had to supply. Impoverished though the Incas were, they still had treasures at command in the love and reverence with which every Indian heart regarded them. "We were wrong, indeed," said the baptized Indians, when taunted by the Spaniards with having worshipped their ancient kings—"we were wrong; for now we know they were not gods, but men. Yet, having received so much good from them, we cannot think them less than of divine race; and if you show us such men now, needs must that we pay them the same veneration."

---

1. Out of thirty-six persons who were thus banished at one time, no less than thirty-five died within the space of two years.

Yet much remained that José could do for his friends. His familiarity with the white man's language, learning, and habits, enabled him to perform many important services for them. But best of all was his power to comfort them with strange sweet words spoken in the tongue of their fathers, and linked in a thousand ways to all their cherished thoughts and traditions, yet strong with a strength and wise with a wisdom that was not theirs. Earnestly did he labor to inspire the hearts of his brethren with his own passionate love and reverence for the King, the great Inca of the East, upon whom all his hopes were resting.

To return to that particular evening, just one year after the death of Melchior del Salto. José came in, hot and tired, from a walk to Lima, undertaken as escort and guide to a Dominican friar, newly arrived from the West Indies. The monk had spent the preceding day and night with Fray Fernando, being ill from the effects of a long and uncomfortable voyage. He was not too ill, however, for much conversation, or rather controversy, with his kind-hearted host.

"Well, José, did you deliver up your charge in safety?" Fray Fernando asked with a smile.

José's face wore a rather curious expression as he answered, "I did. Two years ago, patre, I should have been pleased to see a Spaniard treat his own countrymen as Spaniards everywhere treat Indians."

"I had hoped, José," said Fray Fernando a little sadly, "that those old thoughts of bitterness were of the past."

"The old bitterness, yes; the old thoughts—*never*!" José was silent a moment, then resumed in a different tone. "This good friar seems to imagine that we of Rimac are all fast asleep, and that he has come to wake us. He thinks we are poor, silly, ignorant folk, understanding nothing; just as the Spaniards think of my people. All the time it is *they* who cannot understand.

How can they, when they despise us We know secrets that are sealed from them forever."

"Did you follow our long argument today, José?" Fray Fernando asked somewhat anxiously.

"I followed you," said José, "and I went before you, and all round you, and away from you, and back again to you, twenty times, at least, while you were talking."

"Ah, José! I shall never get the slightest idea of logic into your head. How could you possibly think out a chain of reasoning after that fashion?"

"I do not think my thoughts, patre, in chains, with one link holding on to another. My thoughts grow up like flowers—here, there, anywhere they list."

"Then read this, and tell me what thoughts 'grow up' in your mind about it." And Fray Fernando handed him a letter, a fair, well-written document, with a miter on its seal. It was in Latin, but that was now no impediment to José.

He laid it down again with a look of satisfaction. Evidently "the words of the wise had been heard in quiet;" the fame of the patre's simple yet fervid eloquence had reached at last the dignitaries of his Church, and induced them to pay him a high, but well-merited compliment. "My heart is glad," said José. "You will make the walls of that great cathedral echo to grand, glorious words of truth. And on Easter-day, too! You will tell them Christ is risen!"

But Fray Fernando's face did not reflect the joy that beamed from the dusky countenance of José. On the contrary, it wore an expression of anxious thought. "How can I tell them Christ is risen," he said, "without telling them also—Oh, my son, do you not perceive the strait I am in?"

José understood him; and the gladness faded from his face. But he placed his hand on

Fray Constantino's book. "Have you not told me that *he* preached for years in the cathedral of Seville, and no man even suspected him of believing as you do?"

"Not quite as I do. That last terrible mystery"—his eyes sought the little silver casket, rarely used of late—"having dared to let *that* go, José—"

"We keep Christ, the King. He will guide us," José said reverently.

"Perhaps it were best to accept this call, and, once for all, tell out all the truth in the face of the great congregation!"

José shuddered inwardly. He knew the Holy Inquisition as a vague, dark shadow, nothing more. Neither Walter Gray, nor Melchior del Salto, nor Fray Fernando himself, would ever talk of it. Presently he drew close to the patre, laid his hand, as a son might do, on his shoulder, and began to speak—eagerly, fluently—in low, soft, pleading words, that fell from his lips like ripe fruit "dropped in a silent autumn night."

Tears glistened in Fray Fernando's eyes. "My son," he answered tenderly, "it must be God's will even before yours. If He has given me back—after all those years of anguish—light, joy, hope, liberty,—is it too much that I should bring Him a thank-offering?"

"Many thank-offerings you will bring Him, patre; such as the soul of that poor man who died yester-even calling upon Christ the Savior."

"It may be He has other work for me. But I know not. Rest content, José; I will go no-where, I will do nothing, save as He leads my footsteps."

"I ought to rest content with that, patre. The King will lead you, and by the right way."

There was a pause, which Fray Fernando broke at last. "José, do you remember—long ago, on our journey from Cerro Blanco to

Cuzco—that moment when, suddenly emerging from the darkness of the rock-hewn passage, we came in sight of the deep ravine of the Apurimac, spanned by the bridge of sogas "I remember it well, patre; but what brings it to your mind just now?"

"At first I knew not. In an instant I saw all-mountains, rocks, river tumbling at their base, slight strong bridge of osiers —as if revealed by a lightning flash. But now I know. It was some chance words of yours, spoken then, ' Our people trusted the Inca. And they knew that every way he made for them would lead them safely to the Golden City.'"

José smiled, then murmured softly, "Yachani" (I know). He had still a habit of dropping a word or two in his native tongue when anything touched his heart. "I know" in Spanish only meant "I am aware." "I know" in Quechua meant, *"1 feel, I am satisfied."*

XXXV

Easter Day

"Christ hath sent us down the angels
And the whole earth and the skies
Are illumed by altar candles
Lit for blessed mysteries;
And a Priest's hand through creation
Waveth calm and consecration."
~ E.B. BROWNING

IT WAS EASTER-DAY IN THE City of the Kings, the capital of the New World. The bells of the

Christian churches rang out glad peals of triumph; banners and tapestry adorned the principal streets, which were thronged by Spaniards, Creoles, and Indians in their gayest costumes. But in the great Square the throng was thickest, and all were pouring onwards in a steady stream towards the new cathedral. This singular building stood before them, in all the glory of its painted facade of glaring red and yellow, its lath and plaster towers, and its three wide green doors, now thrown open for everyone to enter. But once within, the bad taste that planned the exterior was forgotten, and nothing felt but admiration. Decorations of the most costly kind abounded in rich profusion; and the numerous altars literally groaned beneath the weight of silver vessels, massive enough for a monarch's ransom.

It was very early, yet the spacious building was already filling rapidly. Perhaps rather with eager sight-seers than with devout worshippers or attentive hearers. For there was much to be seen that day, if there was also something to be heard. Places were reserved in the nave for the friars of the four great monasteries—the Dominicans, the Franciscans, the Augustinians, and the Mercedarios; and by-and-by they defiled slowly in, wearing their appropriate costumes. The Franciscans looked the best satisfied and the most interested: the sermon of the day was to be preached by a Franciscan monk.

Few Indians were visible; not that they would not have liked well enough to witness the pageant, but the Spaniards and Creoles, as was natural, had the best places, and left little room for their dusky brethren. One Indian enjoyed, however, by special favor, an excellent seat, whence he could both see and hear everything.

With a heart full of the deepest anxiety, José (who, with Fray Fernando, had come in from Callao the day before) took his place amongst the hearers of his patron's Easter sermon. He knew that for some days previously the monk had been continually in prayer. But he had spoken little, indeed nothing whatever, about his own intentions, or the possible issues of the day.

High Mass was first celebrated, with more than the usual pomp attendant on that chief ceremonial of the Roman ritual. The solemn tones of the organ, recently brought from Spain; the sweet chants of the white-robed choristers; the gorgeous dresses of the priests, with the bright harmonies of their varied coloring; the beautiful children swinging censers; the clouds of fragrant incense;—all these filled the soul of José—keenly susceptible of such influences—with exquisite pleasure. He gave himself up without reserve to the spell that stole over him. For the time—only for the time—he forgot all Fray Fernando's anxious questionings, all his great searching of heart, about the sacrifice of the Mass; and at the elevation of the Host he bowed himself to the ground with as little scruple or hesitation as any man in the vast congregation.

And very soon afterward he enjoyed the proud triumph of seeing the patre—still in the simple dress of his order, though waited upon by gorgeously attired acolytes—ascend the stately pulpit in the sight of all.

For a few moments, heedless of the crowd beneath, Fray Fernando lifted up his heart in silent prayer. Then in a voice, apparently not loud, but clear enough to be heard throughout the great building, he repeated the few simple words he had chosen for his text, "The Lord is risen indeed."

The Lord is risen—the *Son of God.* Therefore all He said is true, and His claim to Divine Sonship established forever.

The Lord is risen—*the Redeemer of man.* Therefore the redemption is accomplished, the debt paid to the uttermost farthing. For the prison gate is thrown open, and the Surety has gone forth in triumph.

The Lord is risen—*the First-fruits of the Resurrection.* Therefore all shall rise; earth and ocean shall give up their dead; not one lacking of the countless millions that are slumbering there. For "since by man came death, by man came also the resurrection from the dead."

The Lord is risen—*the Head of the Church.* Therefore those who are His body, made one with Him by a living faith, are already by faith risen with Him. Let such "seek those things that are above, where Christ sitteth at the right hand of God."

These were the thoughts that, clothed in a rich drapery of imaginative, perhaps even to a modern taste fanciful illustration, Fray Fernando presented that day to thousands of wondering hearers. The manner was not strikingly unlike that of his brethren—the gift of fervid eloquence was shared by many amongst them—but the matter of the sermon was new and startling.

Yet two at least of the truths he told, Rome has preserved well and carefully amidst all her errors. Nor were the two others, as he stated them, in any open contradiction to her teaching. But the utter absence of much that they were wont to hear—and, even more, the power and vital force that dwelt in what they heard—awed, impressed, amazed the intelligent amongst his audience. If the comparison be not derogatory to such high personages as the Archbishop and Chapter of Ciudad de los Reyes, it may be said that they felt as felt the witch of Endor, when at her call from the earth arose—no counterfeit, no pale shadowy image,—but dread reality, the very prophet of Israel, come from the world of spirits with a message of doom for those that awaked him.

José's simple heart, meanwhile, beat high

with exultation. Those truths, whatever they might be to others, to him were life and joy and peace. Christ was risen indeed for him.

The preacher also had a place in his thoughts. *Now,* at last, would all men see how great, how wise the patre was! And, casting a triumphant glance around, he read admiration in a thousand faces, whilst his own was saying, "Is not the patre great?"

But amongst the faces upon which his eye rested, he marked *one*—unlike the others—that of the Dominican from Cuba. It did not speak admiration: it was doubtful, dark, anxious. And José felt as if from that moment the light grew dim; and a chill mist of fear rose up and overshadowed everything around.

In his cell in the Franciscan monastery, he had a strange dream that night. He thought that it happened to him to go with the patre on board a ship which lay at anchor in the bay. Alone, they drifted somehow out to sea together. No mariners, no rudder, no compass there. Nothing but white sails set, wild waves around, fast fading land behind. And they looked each on the other in blank dismay.

Then suddenly, as things happen in dreams, the storm arose, the wild wind shrieked and howled, the ship tossed helplessly.

José stretched forth his hands and cried aloud, "Lord, save, or we perish!"

When—behold! a Form appeared, treading the stormy deep. And a Hand touched his;—with the thrill of *that* touch José awoke, and lo! it was a dream.

But he could not forget that dream.

José's Mistake

"Dark lowers our fate,
And terrible the storm that gathers o'er us;
But nothing, till that latest agony
Which severs thee from Nature, shall unloose
This fixed and sacred hold. In thy dark pris-
on-house,
In the terrific face of armed law,
Yea, on the scaffold, if it needs must be,
I never will forsake thee."

~ JOANNA BAILLIE

ABOUT SUNSET ONE EVENING, a little more than a fortnight afterward, Fray Fernando and José were seated at their frugal meal of maize-flour bread and fruit. "O José!" the monk exclaimed suddenly, laying down his knife and looking at his companion with an air of distress, "I have quite forgotten that starving family at Chorillos. I promised to bring them food today. *Vae meâ culpa!* God grant some of them are not dead by this time. I must go to them immediately." He rose, and began hastily to empty their little store of maize into a cotton cloth.

José rose also, and quietly put on his cap and mantle. "I think I had better take a little flask of sora; someone may be ill," he said.

"*You!*" exclaimed the monk, looking up from his task of tying the corners of the cloth together. "I am going myself."

"Excuse me, patre; you know of old I run like the huanucu."

Under the circumstances, this was an unanswerable argument. José was permitted to depart, well-pleased to save the patre, who had had a hard day's work already.

Very quickly did his fleet footsteps traverse the rank grass and reeds of the green fields, overhung with drooping willows, that separate Callao from Chorillos, a little hamlet nestling beneath the bold cliff of Marro Solar. He easily found the poor family of Mestizos, for whom the food was intended, performed his errand of mercy, and set out on his homeward way.

But although he made good speed, the hour was late when he returned. Still, he was rather surprised to see no light in the little latticed window of Fray Fernando's room. "The patre must have been tired," he thought, "or he would not have gone to rest ere my return. I am glad I saved him the walk, which, for him, would have been a very long one."

He knocked gently, and presently heard the approaching footsteps of the old mulatto woman with whom they lodged. Instead of opening the door at once, she stood and asked, with unusual caution, "Quién va?"

"I—Don José." The door opened. José entered, and passing at once into their little sitting-room, requested a light.

When it was brought, he looked around him in surprise and dismay. Where was the patre's cloak? Where was the Bible —the "Sum of Christian Doctrine"—the little box of sandalwood, the gift of a grateful mariner, in which the patre used to keep the few papers he had I "What has happened?" he asked.

"About half an hour ago, two hidalgos came here and took the padre away with them," said his sable hostess.

"Hidalgos!" José repeated in amazement. "Friars perhaps you mean?"

"Friars, indeed! I hope I know a holy friar when I see him. I was a Catholic Christian before you were born, young sir; and I have

Catholic blood in my veins, which is more than some can say who put 'Don ' before their names. I tell your Excellency they were Spanish gentlemen, with swords and cloaks."

"Someone ill, doubtless, on board one of the vessels," thought José, as he sat down to await the patre's return. "I wish, however, they could have waited till the morning.—Did he give you any message for me?" asked José as the woman was leaving the room.

"Yes; I was forgetting. It was not much, at all events. He just bade me say to you, 'Every way He makes for us leads safely to the Golden City.'"

A pang of vague uneasiness shot through the heart of José. He feared—he knew not what. He watched anxiously for the patre's return. But hour after hour passed away, and he came not. At last it was morning. José threw on his yacollo, and went down to the beach. Few were stirring at that early hour; and none could give him any tidings of Fray Fernando.

"He must have gone to the City," he said to himself. "At the Franciscan monastery they will surely be able to tell me what has become of him. Perhaps he has suddenly received orders to go to some distant place." But his alarm was increasing every moment.

José had frequently visited the Franciscan monastery, both with Fray Fernando and by himself; and he was very favorably regarded by its inmates, as an interesting specimen of the educated and Christianized Indian. Two of the brethren readily came to speak with him.

In his usual calm, unimpassioned manner, he told his story; but his hearers gazed at him and at each other in evident blank dismay. Then a rapid Latin colloquy passed between them: they were not aware that José understood the language.

"I have feared this for some time," the elder whispered. "Too clever—too mystical! Ah! the spite of those Dominicans!"

"Had he worn the black cowl, instead of the gray, he might have preached with impunity all the heresies of Luther," returned the other. "Well, the Holy Office never had a better man or a truer Catholic in its dungeons."

"Still, you cannot deny that he was very imprudent. *Miserere me!* We are helpless as sheep against these sons of St. Dominic. If good Fray Tomas de San Martin were but here!"

"He could do nothing in a case of this kind. But—*tace!* we are forgetting our dark-faced friend."

"Better he should not suspect the truth. Let us tell him quietly to go his way.—My son," he said, addressing José in Spanish, " we are led to believe, by what you have told us, that the holy father has been sent, by his spiritual superiors, on some mission of importance requiring haste and secrecy.

Where do your kindred reside? Be advised

by us, and rejoin them for the present. The Fray's absence may be lengthened, for anything we know to the contrary."

José bowed. His lips were silent; nor did his impassive Indian countenance express either the anguish or the resolution that filled his heart. But he said within himself, "God do so to me, and more also, if I go to my people and leave my father alone amongst his enemies."

From the gate of the Franciscan monastery he went direct to that of the grim dark pile of building called the Santa Casa. Here he rang the bell, and requested an interview with one of their reverences the Lords Inquisitors.

A request heard with surprise, yet granted promptly enough. The Indian might have evidence to give, perhaps important revelations to make.

José glanced coolly around the room to which he was conducted, with its somber furniture and black tapestry. When the inquisitor, a Dominican monk, made his appearance, he bowed like a Spanish hidalgo, and then with the utmost self-possession preferred his petition. He was Fray Fernando's servant, he said. The holy father was used to his ministrations, and could not well do without them, more especially as his health was feeble. Might he entreat, therefore, to be per mitted to share his imprisonment and to wait on him?

José would gladly have stooped far lower to aid or comfort his adopted father; for love casts out not only fear, but pride.

Whatever astonishment the inquisitor might have felt at his request, he expressed none. He answered courteously that the petition should receive the earliest attention of their reverences, and that he would himself use his best interest to further it. He then asked several questions, which José answered truly, but cautiously, for he was fully alive to the danger of compromising the patre by his admissions.

"The honorable Table of the Holy Office sits today," said this urbane specimen of an inquisitor. "We will try what can be done for you. We hold the character of Fray Fernando in much esteem, and are desirous of showing him all the kindness and consideration in our power."

"I have been, perhaps, needlessly afraid of these inquisitors," thought José, who had never heard of "the iron hand within the velvet glove." He said aloud, "When may I have the honor of waiting on your reverence, in order to be informed of the decision of the holy fathers?"

"You may call tomorrow morning, an hour after matins. Good-day, Señor José." The last words were spoken with a slight but observable hesitation. The holy father intended to be courteous, but he was really at a loss in what manner to designate a person who adopted the style and title of an Inca, yet described himself as the servant of a Franciscan monk "Señor José" was a harmless compromise between the much coveted and high-sounding "Don José" and plain un-prefaced "José."

Next morning, José presented himself at the Santa Casa precisely at the appointed hour. Few ever entered its gloomy gates before or since so willingly. He did not even shudder as he heard them close behind him, he thought only how soon he might be permitted to see the patre.

Unaccountable folly!—are we ready to exclaim, with our ideas of the Holy Inquisition. But from José's point of view it was nothing of the kind. He knew very well that the Holy Office could pretend to no authority over Indians; the Bull to which it owed its existence in the New World having expressly exempted them from its jurisdiction. Had he chosen to profess a hundred heresies, the dread tribunal could not legally have called him in question for one of them. He had, therefore, on his own account no apprehensions whatever, whilst for Fray Fernando his apprehensions amounted to an agony of fear. He was fully aware that his patron was really guilty of what the inquisitors called heresy, and therefore in deadly peril. Being, moreover, profoundly ignorant of the modes of proceeding adopted by the Holy Office, he could only transfer to it his own ideas of courts of justice and of criminal trials. He supposed that judgment would be given and punishment inflicted speedily and sternly, though possibly in secret. What then remained for love to do save to gain access to the captive, to console, to strengthen, to minister to him—perhaps even (who could tell?) to suggest and carry out some plan of escape? This was the one faint hope he still dared to cherish.

The warders and turnkeys of the Santa Casa would surely be of Spanish blood? And might not they be bribed It never occurred to him

that their reverences the Lords Inquisitors, being of Spanish blood, might be bribed also. So
mean a thought of the mysterious dread tribunal he would not have dared to entertain, This
was his fatal mistake. When he relinquished his
liberty, he relinquished, by the same act, his
one real chance of rendering effectual help to
Fray Fernando.

He did not enjoy the privilege of a second
interview with the suave and courteous inquisitor who conversed with him the evening before. A familiar, in a kind of semi-clerical dress,
waited upon him in his stead. This official informed him that his petition had been heard
favorably, and then conducted him into a little chamber resembling a monk's cell. Here he
was locked in, and left alone hour after hour,
to his great perplexity and annoyance. Evening
brought another familiar, who supplied him
with food; and of him he inquired the reason of
this strange treatment, but was told in answer

that the servants of the Holy Office were not permitted to converse with the prisoners.

"Prisoners!" José repeated in amazement. "I am no prisoner. I have come here of my own free will."

But the familiar was not to be entrapped into the violation of a prison rule. He shook his head and left the cell, muttering, as he did so, "Then go away of your own free will."

As José had come to the Santa Casa with the intention of remaining there (though certainly not as a prisoner), he had brought with him a few necessaries for himself, and some comforts for Fray Fernando. He brought writing materials also; nor did he omit to conceal about his person a sufficient store of the gold he esteemed so necessary to his plans.

Accordingly, the next morning he gave the attendant a little note, praying him to have it transmitted to any one of their reverences the Lords Inquisitors. As the request was not unlawful in itself, and was accompanied by a present, it was not refused; but no answer came, either to that or to the numerous other notes that José sent in the same way, first supplicating, then demanding, explanation and redress.

In this manner weary days passed away, growing at length to long, slow weeks of misery. And José began to give way to despair. He made frequent inquiries about Fray Fernando; and by dint of bribing the familiar who attended him, succeeded in extracting a little information—just enough to increase his uneasiness. The padre had been ill, but was better now. He had undergone two examinations, both of them since José's incarceration. No one had the least idea what his fate might be. José might be allowed to send him a few trifling presents; but to see him was impossible. It would be as much as the attendant's life, not to say his place, was worth.

José writhed and struggled like a wild creature caught in a net. It only mocked his misery that he was well fed and carefully attended, and that the few personal requests he thought it worthwhile to make (as for fresh water and clean garments) were promptly granted. The silence which reigned around him grew insupportable. Often did he compare himself to a traveler in the desert suddenly enwrapped in the folds of a thick mist,—hemming him in like a wall, clinging round him like a garment; while in his wild alarm he calls, and calls again—but in vain—no voice replies, for no human ear is reached by his despairing cry.

Did the last words that had come to him,—that perhaps would ever come to him,—from the loved lips of his father and teacher, return upon his bewildered mind in those dreary hours of pain and perplexity—"Every way He makes for us leads safely to the Golden City"?

A Disappointed Man

"Within my breast there is no light
But the cold light of stars;
And I give the first watch of the night
To the red planet Mars."

~LONGFELLOW

PART OF THE SANTA CASA was fitted up, with due
pomp and luxury, as the dwelling-place of his
Reverence the Lord Inquisitor-General of the

Indies; and was not infrequently the scene of a stately hospitality becoming the high position of its occupant. One day his lordship enjoyed the honor of entertaining several distinguished guests. The party consisted of the archbishop and a few of the canons, the priors of three of the great monasteries, with a sprinkling of military and official personages of exalted rank. But the place of honor was occupied by a young man, a stranger in Lima, to whom all present seemed to pay considerable deference.

The inquisitor's guests did ample justice to a luxurious repast. They ate the savory flesh of the huanucu, the Peruvian partridge and wild duck, the brains of the llama, the delicate "Manjar blanco"— compounded of the breasts of capons beaten up with rose-water and white sugar—from dishes of gold and silver; and they drank the choice and costly wines of Spain cooled with the ice of the Andes. They were cheerful, even festive, though within the limits of decorum and of stately Spanish reserve and dignity.

At last, however, they ceased even to toy with the luscious grapes and fragrant melons that, newly introduced into that distant land, had a sweetness far beyond their own for the lips of exiles. The table was deserted, and most of the guests sought the garden, where the evening breeze was blowing cool and fresh from the snow-clad mountains. But the stranger lingered still, standing in the deep embrasure of a window. He looked about thirty, but was really much younger;—a handsome man, with a high, narrow forehead, scornful, petulant lips, and brows so often knit in anger or impatience, that the contraction had almost become permanent. Presently the sleek, good-humored, sensual, yet intelligent Lord Inquisitor glided softly to his side; the black cowl and white frock of the Dominican making a picturesque contrast with the purple velvet and gold lace of the Castilian noble.

They conversed together upon such topics as the inquisitor thought likely to interest Don Francisco Solis de Toledo, nephew of the Viceroy of Peru, now about to take command of the troops on board a stately Spanish man-of-war.

Such an appointment was not considered derogatory to a person of high birth; though not exactly the provision the world might have expected the Viceroy to make for his sister's son, But Don Francisco Solis was not a man easily provided for. He was overbearing, impracticable, and obstinate to a degree which made him the terror of his friends and patrons. These qualities were in some degree inherent in his character; but a different training might have subdued or softened them. It ever the wholesome discipline of a life amongst equals might have been beneficial to any man, that man was Don Francisco Solis. But it had never been his. Ere his boyhood was over, he had been sent out to the New World to play the tyrant;—a conqueror amongst a nation of slaves. And the curse of the tyrant fell upon him, and ate into his soul. He became at last unable to do anything, save to tyrannize.

Repeated experiments convinced the Viceroy, to his cost, that his brave and gifted young kinsman— for brave and gifted he really was— had utterly incapacitated himself for any career that necessitated his working under any one, or with anyone. An exploring expedition into the interior of the country might have brought him fame and fortune, but it could not be undertaken without money and without companions. What was to be done with a man who was sure to quarrel with the moneylenders, and to fight duels with the gentlemen who volunteered to serve under him? Rich as the Viceroy was, he could not provide each of his needy kinsmen with a silver mine for his sole private use. He was glad, therefore, to relieve himself at last of the troublesome Don Francisco by appointing him to the command of the *Trionfo.*

To return then to the inquisitor. He had just been asking, with much courtesy, after the health of his Excellency's noble lady, the Princess Dona Victoria,—by which stately name Coyllur nūsta was now known.

Having expressed his gratification at the intelligence that the lady was in good health, the churchman continued, "A young Indian nobleman has been brought under my notice lately, who is, as I believe, a relative, or at least a connection, of the illustrious princess."

Don Francisco, who regarded all his wife's relatives with profound disdain, looked just the degree of interest that politeness demanded, and played with the costly lace ruffle which half covered his white hand.

The inquisitor resumed, "I must not conceal from your Excellency that the young man I speak of is in rather an unfortunate situation at present. It has been found necessary to place him, for the good of his own soul and the interests of Holy Church, under a degree of restraint."

"I thought," said Don Francisco, who would not have cared if the inquisitor had announced that it had been found necessary to hang him,—" I thought your august tribunal did not interfere with 'los Indios.'"

"True," replied the churchman." We cannot prosecute an Indian as a criminal; but we may lawfully employ one as a witness,—and for that purpose we may detain him, if necessary. At first it was in that way that we found it convenient to place the young man I speak of under a light and temporary restraint; but the case in which we expected to require his testimony having taken a turn that renders it superfluous, he might have been set at liberty, but for certain weighty considerations."—Here the churchman paused, heaved a little sigh, and looked as if doubtful whether he ought to proceed any further.—However, he presently added," His name is Don José Viracocha; and he claims the right to quarter the sun proper on the shield tierce in fess.[1] Do you know him, most illustrious señor?"

Don Francisco started, and the color flashed to his white face. "I have reason to know him," he said. "He is my enemy."

"Indeed!" returned the inquisitor, with just as innocent a look of surprise as if he had not been aware of the fact, and made the communication for that very reason. "Don Francisco Solis pays the Indian a higher compliment than any of his race could have expected ever to deserve, when he condescends to call him *his* enemy."

Don Francisco bowed, then smiled bitterly. "We have good authority, reverend father," he said, "for esteeming serpents the enemies of

---

1. The arms granted by Charles V. to the Inca family.

the human race. Indians wound like serpents. I believe that young man—who, I have heard, had once the intolerable presumption to consider himself *my* rival—could give account, if he pleased it, of certain treasures which ought to have been my wife's portion."

"Ah, how is that, señor? But forgive my curiosity, if, unfortunately, it should appear impertinent."

"No forgiveness needed, father. I am not ashamed of aught that concerns me. I leave that to those who climb up to heaven upon crooked ladders." (He did not mean anything personal by this remark.) *"Pues,* reverend father, I heard a great deal about the golden hoards of the old Inca noble, my wife's grandfather and guardian. He was called Yupanqui, or some such barbarous name; and he remained a pestilent heathen almost to the end of his days. And I, as a Christian gentleman of Spain, thought that those heathen spoils of his would come well to hand, and in good time, to give retaining fees to a hundred stout free lances, and to find them arms and horses, for a little expedition I contemplated. St. Jago! with a troop like that at my back, I might have shown my illustrious uncle that there are men yet left alive, though Cortez and Pizarro and Hernan de Soto are with the saints. Perhaps, too, that there are barbarian kings and kingdoms yet to conquer, though Tupac Amaru has lost his head,—as he well deserved. But the malice of fortune, who has always shown herself my enemy, would not permit me so much satisfaction. Of old Yupanqui's boasted treasures, all that ever came my way was a dungeon of a house, all walls and no windows, and a few paltry gold and silver ornaments."

"Does the noble lady, your Excellency's wife, know nothing?"

"*Nothing.* That was soon ascertained."

"Who were most in the confidence of the

old Inca?"

"This Viracocha was as a son to him."

The inquisitor paused. Then he said, very quietly, and without looking at Don Francisco—" For many reasons, I think it will be our wisest course to send the young man to Spain. I have ascertained that he is in the confidence of all the members of the Inca family who are here at present; and that he spends much of his time in secret cabals and consultations with them, Such proceedings *must* be stopped.—You understand me, señor?—Yet we have no authority to deal with him after any summary fashion; while to detain him in prison here would cause remark and inquiry, perhaps create a scandal. It is an evil world, Señor Don Francisco. We are closely watched, and have to be careful— very careful— not to expose our Holy Office to obloquy by the slightest, the very slightest over-stepping of our legitimate powers. Wise as serpents'— you recollect, señor? Furthermore, there is another prisoner also, whose case we may see it advisable to refer to the authorities at home. The Trionfo is to form one of this year's Plate fleet, I believe, most illustrious señor?"

Don Francisco bowed.

"For humanity's sake," the inquisitor continued, in a low voice, and still without looking at Don Francisco—"for humanity's sake, I could wish to send these unfortunate persons to Spain in a good and large vessel. The voyage is long, and the precautions rendered necessary by their unhappy position—"

Here Don Francisco said, suddenly and sharply, though still with an air of affected indifference, "You had better fling the wretches into the sea at once, and have done with them. They will never survive such a voyage under such circumstances."

"I should be sorry to think that, señor and your Excellency," said the Dominican. "For I have quite a personal regard for the last-mentioned prisoner, who is a Spaniard and an ecclesiastic. Since we are speaking freely and in confidence, I may acknowledge that it is from motives of clemency, and to give him a chance of saving his life, that we have decided upon referring his case to the Table at Valladolid. As to the Indian"—the inquisitor mused a little—" if he could only be removed to a safe distance from his brethren—sent amongst the barbarians, for instance—nothing more would be required. We really wish him no harm; our object is to get him out of the country without creating a scandal."

Perhaps it was the position in which he stood, with his back turned to the light, which gave a pallid look to the face of Don Francisco. Yet this could not account for the sudden flush that passed over it, vanishing again as quickly. But after a moment's pause he answered, in tones of icy coldness, "If your reverence thinks proper to send prisoners to Spain in the *Trionfo,* I shall do myself the honor of introducing the master of the ship to your notice. You can communicate with him at your pleasure. I hear he is a very worthy fellow, well acquainted with his business." Then he added languidly, "How hot it is, father! Has not this been a very unhealthy season in Ciudad de los Reyes?"

The inquisitor understood that the subject was dismissed, and performed his part in keeping up the conversation which Don Francisco thus directed into another and indifferent channel. Less than half his active mind sufficed for the effort, leaving the rest at liberty to pursue more interesting subjects. Whilst therefore he talked of the weather, the mists, the sunstrokes, and the calentures, an undercurrent of thought ran on, somewhat after this fashion: "Don Francisco Solis is scarcely grateful for one of the fairest chances a man was ever given of recovering a lost or buried fortune. Still, he is a Toledo; one may trust his honor. If he gets the truth out of this Viracocha, whether by fair means or by foul, he will not forget Mother Church. And he shall not want a broad hint or two on the subject of her claims, seasonably administered.

"As to poor Fray Fernando—unhappy man!—it is the only way of saving him from the fire, into which he is too willing to throw himself, even without the friendly aid of some of my colleagues, who have more zeal than discretion. A curse on their officiousness, beginning with that of our meddlesome brother from Cuba! What good end will it serve to bring upon us and our holy tribunal the suspicion and of all the Franciscans in the country? And what harm could the poor friar's heresies have done to a pack of black people and Indians? The sacrament of baptism is valid, even though administered by a heretic; and that is all they require."

Don Francisco meanwhile was thinking, for his part: "I wonder who was his reverence's grandfather? Some low person, I doubt not, with a taint of infidel blood in his veins. Every nobody from the Old World sets up here as 'Don,' and 'Excellency,' and 'most illustrious.' Probably he was engaged in trade. This reverend father, beneath his black cowl, has the soul of a trader. As for that Viracocha,—I hate him. I could better pardon him for hiding the old Inca's treasures, than for his insufferable presumption in supposing that I. —*I*—would actually have condescended to fight with him! If los Indios begin to take such airs, to Spaniards and gentlemen, this country will very soon become—" (Here Don Francisco said a strong word to himself.) "The inquisitors might as well stretch a point, for once, and fling the wretch into the fire for worshipping his abominable idols, as no doubt they all do in secret. Still, he may burn, hang, or drown, for aught I care. I shall not soil my fingers with him. No! my Lord Inquisitor forgot whom he addressed, when he presumed to hint that I might degrade myself to the part of torture-master, to wring from this luckless wretch the possession of his secret. No I not for all the gold in Peru. My life for gold, any day; my honor for gold—*never!*"

Other Castilian nobles, in Don Francisco's place, might have read differently the laws of honor. The means that Spanish knights and gentlemen did not scorn to employ in seeking for the hidden treasures of the New World, are not pleasant to contemplate: witness the well-known story of the heroic Mexican Emperor Guatimozin.

The light by which Don Francisco Solis guided his footsteps was a dim, earth-born glimmer. It was not sunlight, not true starlight even; only the gleam of the red planet Mars, called the "star" of chivalry. Yet, for once, it suf-ficed to make him aware of a deep pit of moral degradation cunningly dug right across his path. And it taught him to avoid it.

Fray Fernando's Words

"'Twas still some solace, in the dearth
Of the pure elements of earth,
To hear at least each other's speech,
And each turn comforter to each."
~BYRON

José's long agony of suspense had an end at last. One evening after nightfall, the familiar who attended his cell conveyed to him a courteously worded but peremptory order to put on his cap and mantle and follow him forthwith. José obeyed, wondering; and was yet the more surprised to see the attendant make a package of the clothes and other matters belonging to him which were lying about the cell, preparatory to taking them away.

"Are they going to set me free at last?" he asked.

But, as bitter experience might have led him by this time to anticipate, he received no answer. The familiar, carrying a torch and the packet he had made up, conducted him to a side-door of the Santa Casa. This was opened immediately, and he saw—though dimly, for the night was dark—a little troop of horsemen waiting outside. Then a horse, ready saddled, was brought to the door, and a person who seemed to be the leader of the band directed him to mount; adding, however, as he hesitated a moment before obeying,—

"Be not afraid, Indian; one of these gentle-men shall hold your bridle."

"I am not afraid," said José, who, though he had never been on horseback in his life, scorned to show reluctance or timidity before these strangers; "but I should like to know whither you are about to take me."

The officer bent down from his saddle, and whispered—"Let well alone, Indian. You have been most mercifully dealt with by their reverences. Learn that 'silence is holy,' and that your tongue may hurt but cannot mend your case."

Having given José this significant hint, he turned to the still open door, where the alguacil was standing, torch in hand.

"How long are we to be kept waiting here?" he asked impatiently.

"He is coming, señor," said the attendant.

José mounted without further demur.

Then another horse was brought to the door, and held in readiness for another rider. After a brief delay, one came slowly forth, wrapped in a Franciscan monk's gray cowl and mantle. José half uttered a cry of surprise, perhaps of joy. It was the patre. But the officer again interposed. *"Quiton!"* he said, and touched his sword.

Nor was Fray Fernando permitted to utter a word. The rapid ride from Lima to Callao was accomplished in perfect silence. The two captives soon found themselves on the seashore. They were then transferred to a little boat, which conveyed them to a stately galleon lying moored in the bay. They were put on board; and a guard of soldiers received them. One steep ladder after another had then to be descended by their unwilling footsteps, until at last the ship's hold was reached,—and there they lay in midnight darkness, and for a time, it may almost be added, in despair. Even their reunion, after so long a separation, failed to kindle joy or hope: they seemed brought together again only to die. Fray Fernando was the first to recover himself so far as to speak.

"*You* here, my son José! Why this? Of what have they accused *you* he asked.

"In truth, I know not," José answered, in a weary, hopeless tone. "I was never informed-never tried-never judged."

"What never even examined? That, indeed, is strange."

I had an interview once with two black monks."

"Well, and what said they to you?"

"They asked if I could repeat my Credo. I answered,—'Will your reverences hear it in Quechua, in Spanish, or in Latin?' In the next place, they inquired if I knew the doctrines of the Catholic faith. I told them they might question me therein. Then, did I detest the wicked idolatries for which my forefathers had gone into everlasting fire? I made answer promptly—' As for my forefathers, Christ shall judge them, not you; as for myself, I thank His grace that I have turned from dumb idols to serve the living and true God.' Then—But what does it all matter now?" said José wearily, while the momentary animation of his tone and manner quickly died away.

"It matters much to me, José; for I fear it is on my account you have suffered all this misery."

"Nay, patre; do not think it. It was—But why seek for reasons I Enough—I am an Indian. The hatred they bear my race—my poor doomed race!—accounts for all."

After a gloomy pause, he resumed—"And you, patre? You have been ill. I fear—"

"Fear nothing for me. I am well—now," said the monk. But his faint and broken tones gave the lie to his words of cheer.

Then José shook off the dull lethargy that

had well-nigh overpowered him, and roused himself to attend to the one duty that yet remained to him. He drew close to the patre, embraced him tenderly, and from that moment took him completely into his charge. With some of his own clothing he managed to contrive a tolerably comfortable resting-place for his wasted form. He bathed his burning brow; he held his hand in his; he bore the jar of water that had been left in their dungeon once and again to his fevered lips,—but he scarcely spoke a word.

They had before this become aware that the vessel had weighed anchor, and was in motion. By-and-by food was brought to them, and José requested the use of a lamp. He had still the means of bestowing a bribe, as the usual custom of searching prisoners on entering or leaving the Santa Casa, and depriving them of their money and valuables, had been dispensed with in his case. The lamp made its appearance accordingly; a supply of oil was even promised. But at first the light that revealed their faces each to other appeared, a doubtful boon: so ghastly, worn, and death-like did Fray Fernando look to José; and such settled, hopeless sorrow did he read in the dusky countenance of his Indian friend. Yet between the two there was a marked difference—like the difference between the morning and the evening twilight. Ill and feeble as Fray Fernando was, he seemed to carry some light within that, as time passed on, kindled into greater brightness hour by hour; while José simply faded.

"Have you no wish, José, to learn whither we are going, and with whom?" Fray Fernando asked, wondering at his apparent indifference to all things save one—Fray Fernando's own bodily comfort and well-being. "I can tell you somewhat;—though but little, it is true. My case, I have been informed, has been referred to the Table of the Holy Office at Valladolid;

though how and wherefore you have been involved in my misfortunes, I am ignorant as yet. But this, at least, I know: we are at present in the *Trionfo*—a great and brave galleon, which is making her voyage, with the rest of the Plate fleet, to the mother country."

"We shall never reach it," said José.

"God only knows," Fray Fernando answered; and the conversation dropped.

A day or two afterward Fray Fernando resumed it:—

"One of us, at least, will scarcely see the shores of Spain. José—my son José!"

"I am here, patre, close beside you."

"Come closer yet. Take my hand in yours; let your loving eyes look into mine. I have somewhat to say to you."

José obeyed. His hand did not tremble and no tear dimmed his eye as he answered. "Speak on, my father."

"Some there are who die in the face of day, ten thousand eyes to witness their suffering and their patience, ten thousand hearts to judge their cause. José, for years and years my thoughts dwelt upon such a death. I feared it—shuddered at it—fled from it. Ay, when God sent you to me first, a little child, your innocent talk dispelled many a frightful vision of the hideous zamarra, the gazing multitudes, the burning pile. You know all now, José. It is true, you cannot know—but you can guess, far off and dimly—the dark remorse, the haunting terror, of those dreary years.

"Then at last, through God's great mercy, the burden was lifted from me. I was no murderer. The mark of Cain was gone from my brow. I could go forth erect, and walk amongst my fellow-men, no longer a solitary being, held apart by the awful loneliness of a great crime and a bitter retribution. 'And then, as if all this had been little in His sight, He gave me more a thousandfold than deliverance, than liberty, than even the brother of my heart restored to me from the dead—He gave me Himself. You know how the light of His presence dawned, grew, brightened around me. You know, for you shared that light. But a strange thing was wrought within me that was hidden even from you, José. The doom that for years had been the haunting terror of my life came back again upon my mind,—but transfigured; no more a terror— a secret thrilling hope. It was as if some veiled, shadowy form, that I thought a demon, had haunted my footsteps night and day, and then suddenly coming up beside me, dropped off the shrouding veil, and stood radiant, an angel of light. No longer did the burning pile mean shame and horror: it meant glory, martyrdom, an abundant entrance into the home and the kingdom prepared for me. It meant His seal-the signet of the King whose purpose none may change-set at last upon my poor spoiled life, in token that He claimed and owned it. It meant fire from heaven consuming the accepted sacrifice. Even when I stood very close to it I felt no fear. And, José, I tell you now, that it was well worthwhile to stand there face to face with death. God was so near—nearer far than you are—though your hand holds mine, and your breath is on my cheek.

"But after that there came a bitter hour. A dark cloud rose up suddenly and hid Him from me. They, who thought themselves the arbiters of my fate, determined, in mercy as they believed, to spare me the doom of fire. Instead of pronouncing my sentence themselves, they would send me a captive to the mother country. Of course, in this dungeon, and to a man whose strength is wasted as is mine, that means death,—unless God should work a miracle for me. José, I longed to die for Him; but in my own way, not in His. I longed to show forth His mercy and truth with my last look, if not with my last breath, in the great congregation. With the lot that He appointed for me I was not content. Fain would I have escaped it by any means—save *one*. So I mourned bitterly before Him. Then He turned away His face from me, and my heart was cast down within me.

"But He is wiser than I,—and oh, how tender with His wayward child! The first word by which He brought me comfort was thine, José: ' Every way He makes for us leads safely to the Golden City.' Still, though comforted, I was not at peace, until at last there came another word, borne softly into the depths of my heart—a brief, simple word, but a word of His—' Come unto Me.'—' Unto Me.' That is enough. That one thought fills all my soul. I care not for the way, since He—He Himself— is the end. I am satisfied. I need no more. Thou hast dealt well with Thy servant, O Lord, according to Thy word!"

XXXIX

José's Words

"Who hears the last shriek from the sinking bark
On the mid sea, and with the storm alone;
And bearing to the abyss, unseen, unknown,
Its freight of human souls?—
the o'ermastering wave,
Who shall tell how it rushed, and none to save?"

~ HEMANS

WITHOUT A WORD OF LAMENTATION, without
a tear or sigh, José heard all. He fully compre-

hended the patre's situation, and his own. He believed that he must soon close the eyes of his father and his friend; and that duty done, that he must linger on in his frightful prison alone, until Death, the deliverer, should come to him also. It never occurred to him that, after all, he might live to see those distant alien shores towards which his enemies were bearing him. No Child of the Sun, he told himself, could live on for dreary months and months without his Father's smile, deprived of light and air and liberty.

Fitful longings for these common but most precious boons came and went, troubling with passing storms the deep and bitter waters of anguish that filled his soul like a flood. Often would he start from dreams of the glittering ice-crowned heights of the Andes, as he used to see them from Cerro Blanco; or of the cool interior of Yupanqui's house, with some melody of his native land, breathed by the lips of Coyllur, still sounding in his ear. Often, again, the great green leaves of the tropical forest would droop over his head; he would touch them, pluck them, feel their moist coolness, watch the sunbeams flicker amongst them, see some bright bird with radiant plumage flit through their overhanging branches, and be wakened by its song, or by the murmuring sound of running waters.

Thus brought back to his misery, he would rise from his place without moan or murmur, trim the lamp, give Fray Fernando food or water, or do for him, most tenderly, any other little office that love and watchful care suggested; but, except to answer his questions, and that briefly, he scarcely ever spoke.

At last a circumstance occurred that partially broke down this mournful stoicism. The position of the prisoners in the dark damp hold was necessarily one of great misery; but they were not treated with intentional inhumanity by those who had the charge of them. Their food was sufficient, though coarse; and if their allowance of water was scanty, so also was that of the ship's company, and José contrived that the privation should be little felt by the patre. As time wore on, the soldiers whose duty it was to guard them and supply them with necessaries became gradually more friendly and communicative. A belief was gaining ground amongst them that the captives, though prisoners of the Holy Office, were not heretics, but political offenders of some kind; for it was well known that such were occasionally apprehended and punished by the Inquisition. The pious deportment and devout language of Fray Fernando favored this supposition; but still more the presence of José, since it was inconceivable that an Indian could be a heretic.

Moreover, the soldiers of the *Trionfo* were sorely in want of interest and occupation during the long voyage, which at best must oc-

cupy many months. They were all "señores caballeros," who would not, to save the ship from
sinking, haul a rope or climb a mast. Except in
the improbable event of an enemy appearing
in sight, these two hundred and fifty hale and
active fighting-men had literally nothing to do
save to burnish their armor, to play cards with
each other, to quarrel with the Flemish gun-
ners, or to tyrannize over the mariners, who
were treated like slaves, and "made to toil and
moil for all the rest."

Those therefore who attended the prisoners
were very willing to vary the monotony of their
lives by exchanging a few words with persons
who, for many reasons, excited their curiosity.

Fray Fernando and José soon learned that
the señor commandante was at deadly feud
with the captain of the ship, an officer who in
an English vessel would have been simply called
the sailing-master. The soldiers, of course, took
part with their commander; and to the surprise

of Fray Fernando, who had been told that the ship was an excellent one, railed continually, and "in good set terms," against the unfortunate Trionfo, with all her appurtenances and appointments.

"Is she not a swift sailer?" inquired the captive, naturally anxious to encourage conversation.

"Oh yes. Swift enough, to be sure; everything sacrificed to speed, and to the stowage of her merchandize. See her decks I All for space: not an inch of shelter or vantage-ground where a man could cover his head from an enemy's fire. Not too sea-worthy either, for all the gallant show she makes. Well we are with the Plate fleet, or we would not sight a hostile flag for ten thousand pieces of eight.' Worse luck! If on the contrary the ship were what she ought, and the captain anything but a hen, with low wretches of mariners without honor or valor, no sight would be more welcome—not even the shores of old Spain."

Fray Fernando remarked afterward to José,—" The galleon may be a fine ship for all that. It is evident that the soldiers take their cue from their commander. He must be, as I think, a man of strong though rather peculiar character. I doubt that he is much beloved. His men all fear him, evidently.

I should not be surprised to find that some of them hate him."

"They never mention his name," said José languidly.

"Who is he?"

"What! Do you not know? He is the Viceroy's nephew, Don Francisco Solis de Toledo."

José uttered a piteous cry, as one surprised by sharp, uncontrollable anguish.

"What is it, my son José?" Fray Fernando questioned tenderly. But José could not speak. After that one involuntary cry he could only lock his lips with stern resolve. Had he allowed a word, a moan, or even a sigh to escape them, there would have ensued a passion of weeping, to shame his manhood, and—far worse—to alarm and distress the patre beyond description.

The last time Don Francisco Solis and Don José Viracocha met face to face was at the door of Dona Beatriz Coya's stately mansion in Cuzco. That day, as they exchanged formal salutations, José, strong in the favor of Coyllur, felt his proud triumph over his Castilian rival, and scorned him in his heart. Where was now that old happy, hopeful time? Where was that sweet face—those dark eyes, from which his soul had drunk enchantment? Where were the dreams that filled his heart,— of great deeds to be done for his people, and deliverance to be won for them, perhaps by his arm?

Gone from him, and forever. He lay in that dismal hold, a captive, with Death already in his heart. The Spaniards had the dominion over the land of his fathers. Don Francisco Solis had the beautiful bride that should have been his; and, as if that were not enough, it seemed he had even the key of his rival's dungeon—a thought that added the last drop to José's over-flowing cup of bitterness.

What had he left him now to show that the past was not all a dream? Only this. He still wore about his person, carefully wrapped in a morsel of parchment, the withered passion-flower He took it out, and held it near the lamp; a poor, crushed, faded thing, meet emblem of his own crushed hopes and faded life.

"What is that you have there?" Fray Fernando questioned. José allowed him to take it in his hand. "It has a story" said the monk. "Tell me, my son, if you will. We are all the world to each other now."

"The story of one I loved—and lost," José murmured, in a voice like the ghost of his natural one. "It was Don Francisco Solis who robbed me, making my life desolate. As, every day, his people rob mine. And," he added yet more sorrowfully, "Christ, the King, does not help us!"

"José, José, come near to me."

José came near. The monk raised himself, drew his arm tenderly round him, and held him to his heart. "Oh, my son," he asked very gently, "can you not trust Him still?"

"Still,—even still,—I hold the Savior. At least, I hope He holds me. But the King—"

"Is strong to save us yet," said Fray Fernando.

"To save *us*?—It may be. But what are we two, down here in the hold, with only two lives to lose? It is my people I think of—my people! For them my heart is heavy as stone, cold as ice of the Antis. Day and night, patre, I see visions and dream dreams. Faces look upon me—dark faces, growing ghastly in dungeons like this—

agonized faces—faces of the tortured and famine-stricken, of the women and little children who weep in secret places, and there is none to pity them."

"None—upon earth," Fray Fernando interposed. "But, you know—"

"I *know* nothing. I try to believe, even yet, that He cares," said José, whose heart was sickening now with the sorest of all doubts. "Ay, patre," he went on more earnestly, " He said, I have compassion on the multitude.' In those happy days at Callao, when I came to know Him first, I put my finger on that word, I knelt down and pleaded it with Him—for my people. And I believed surely that He would do them right at last. It was so well with me that I never doubted it would be well with all I loved. But in those dreary weeks, shut up in that hateful Santa Casa, hope faded from me day by day. Not hope for myself. Still, when He calls, I can give my soul up to Him without fear. But my people—my people! Who shall show me any light or hope for them? Must wrong and cruelty go on forever and ever—none to help, none to save?"

Fray Fernando's heart went up in an agony of earnest prayer for his beloved son, in this hour of sore and bitter need. At last he said, "But where you trust your own soul, José, you can surely trust all else that your heart holds dear?"

"I suppose so," José murmured. "At least I ought. But all is dark—dark. Wrong triumphs always. Nothing seems to come right."

Fray Fernando had reached the place of sunshine, far up on the mountain summit, very near the sky. But José was still in the *Puna,* the land of mist and rain, where no sunbeams pierce the thick dark veil of clouds.

"José," said the monk once again, "I pray you, do not think of men. Think of Christ. Look to Him."

"Patre," José answered, with infinite sadness in his voice, "speak no more to me. God knows you are dearer than my life—dear as my own soul. But even you cannot help me now. I sit beside you, your hand in mine; but I am alone. My ear hears your voice; but my heart hears nothing. Nothing—except the wail and dash of waters, and the voice of those who cry, as from a sinking ship. Who cry to a King—*a King!* —far away in the distant heavens. And He is silent."

Soon that happened which made José's allusion to a sinking ship seem like an awful prophecy.

The terrors of a storm at sea, always great, were multiplied sevenfold to the unhappy captives who lay in darkness and the shadow of death. Vainly did they try to guess, from the wild, discordant sounds that met their ears, mingling in tumultuous confusion, what might be the fate in store for them—what horror, of all the horrors that threatened, would be the first to lay its spectral grasp upon them, and claim them for its own.

The storm raged on; the timbers strained, and the waters surged around the floating prison, which rocked and shook with their violence. The captives began to fear—and not without reason—that they would force an entrance, and drown them as they lay in the dark, clasped in each other's arms. For now their lamp had expired, and no one brought them oil. Nor food; an omission that soon added another terror to those that oppressed them already. What if, in the general confusion, they should be forgotten and left to starve? Better let the waters find them where they lay; better sink with the sinking ship.

Fray Fernando called on God. Even in this dark hour his faith did not fail. Sorely tried indeed it was, by Nature's shrinking from a terrible death that had no glory in it, and must be faced in darkness and loneliness. Still, he could take comfort; and even give it to his companion in distress. "God is with us, José," he murmured. "He stilleth the raging of the waves. And all His ways lead us safely to the Golden City. Fear nothing."

But for José, Fray Fernando would have died, over and over again. He held him in his arms, or, weak as he was, he would have been dashed against the wet planks bound with iron that formed the sides of their prison, by the lurching of the tempest-tossed ship. He covered him with his own garments from the damp, death-like chill, as unlike the healthful natural cold of the outside air, as the noisome hold was unlike the breezy height of Cerro Blanco. And from time to time he fed him with the morsels of food that still remained to them, dipped in the one precious cup of water to which at last they were reduced. If, meanwhile, he himself felt hunger, thirst, cold, terror, at least he made no sign. And to the patre's inquiries he always answered—far more cheerfully than he had spoken before the storm—that he was well, and that he needed nothing.

After this agony had lasted for what seemed to both of them a long lifetime, but those who could see the face of day would have reckoned about three times four-and-twenty hours, Fray Fernando suddenly raised himself, and exclaimed, "José, do you hear those cries? The ship is settling—we are going down! Let us commend our souls to God!"

A dreamy languor had been stealing over José for some time past, despite his utmost efforts. Rousing himself with difficulty, he answered, "I do not think it. I think the storm is passing."

"Hush! Listen!"—There were confused noises,—shouts, the clanking of chains—uneasy trembling and swaying of the ship; then— at last—the shock of a strange stillness after tumultuous motion. "We have come to land," said José.

"'So He bringeth them to the haven where they would be," Fray Fernando murmured, sinking back.

To José the words came faintly, as if from a great distance. He tried to fix his attention, fancying that the patre still continued speaking—failed—tried again—could hear nothing except a bewildering murmur as of many waters—then lapsed into utter unconsciousness.

José's Words Again

"And now He pleads in heaven above,
For our humanities,
Till the ruddy light on seraph's wings
In pale emotion dies;
They can better bear His Godhead's glare
Than the pathos of His eyes."

~ E.B. BROWNING

WHEN CONSCIOUSNESS RETURNED to José, he was surrounded by what seemed to his dazzled eyes a flood of light. Yet, in fact, he was only lying in the gloomy, dimly-lighted space between decks. An agony of burning thirst was his first feeling; and, as his eyes gradually recovered their powers of vision, he instinctively looked around him for the means of quenching it. A pitcher of water lay near; but when he moved to take it, someone raised it for him, and bore it to his lips. Then he drank, and never had he enjoyed so delicious a draft. After this, his thoughts grew clearer.

"Where is the patre?" he asked.

"I am here, my son," said the voice of Fray Fernando; for he it was who sat by his side, and who had raised the water to his lips.

"Where are we? What has happened?" questioned José, in a tone of bewilderment.

Fray Fernando explained:—" They have put the ship into a bay, a kind of natural harbor, on some lonely island-where, probably, the foot of man has never trod since the making of this world. The storm is over; and the lives of all on board are saved, thank God." "And you, patre?"

"I am better. They have brought us here, between the decks, whilst the hold is being cleansed, and some leakages repaired. Most of the soldiers and the crew are on shore. Even so much of God's free light and air as we enjoy here seems to bring new life to me. Now I return your question. And you, José?"

"I? Since I drank that water, I am quite well. How cold it is! Easy to tell it has come fresh out of some deep fountain in God's own blessed earth."

"Drink again. There is no stint now, thank God. They have found spring water, and are bringing an abundant supply on board."

And José drank again—deeply, as one who had thirsted long and sorely.

Then Fray Fernando prayed him to eat. Food was at hand,—not coarse, hard biscuit, but cool and luscious plantains and bananas, fresh gathered from the luxuriant grove that filled three-fourths of the little island.

José ate, and was refreshed. "How long shall we stay here?" he asked.

"For several days, at all events, we must stay. Some damage has been done during the storm to the rigging, and especially to one of the great sails, which must needs be repaired before the ship can put to sea again."

"How has the storm dealt with the other ships that were with us?"

"That we cannot tell. We have been separated, by the stress of weather, from all, except one. One vessel has taken shelter in the same bay, and is near us now. One for which we have good right to care. Guess its name, José."

"Is it a galley, patre?"

"Yes—a galley."

"The *San Cristofero!* O patre, if only we

might see the face of Walter Gray once more!"

But Fray Fernando shook his head. "Our making inquiry after him could do us no good, and might do him cruel harm," he said. "He would come again under suspicion, as the friend of prisoners of the Holy Office."

For the space of a week, and rather more, the captives were permitted to enjoy their comparatively comfortable quarters between decks; and their lot was further alleviated by good food, delicious fruit, and an abundant supply of fresh water. But this little gleam of sunshine soon faded. Both the commander and the captain of the *Trionfo* were very anxious, and with good reason, to overtake and rejoin the Plate fleet. They were therefore of one mind in desiring to hasten the departure of the galleon from the friendly shelter of the island; though they were by no means so unanimous in their ideas of the share that the soldiers and the mariners ought respectively to take in the preliminary labors rendered necessary by her condition.

The captain was reported to have said one day, in the bitterness of his soul, that he supposed the "señores y caballeros," who did him the honor of walling up and down the deck of the *Trionfo,* would rather go to the bottom at once, or fall alive into the hands of the English pirates and cut-throats, Draco and Achines (he meant Drake and Hawkins), than demean themselves so far as to roll a single water-cask on board. And that, as for himself, he was a plain man, and must speak his mind, if the señor commandante were the Lord Viceroy's nephew ten times over; ay, and if he were to run him through the body the next minute.

To whom the señor commandante made answer, with cool contempt and well-bred scorn, that the worthy señor capitano very far mistook if he imagined that anything he could possibly say or do could induce Don Francisco Solis so far to forget what was due to himself as to honor him with his sword.

In spite, however, of these bickerings, the work was done at last; and, accompanied by the *San Cristofero,* which had waited to attend upon the larger vessel, the great galleon bade farewell to the peaceful shores of the friendly island. In return for Nature's profuse hospitality,—for the cold fresh water bubbling in crystal streams, for the golden juices of the delicious fruits, for the wild birds all the more easily snared and taken because unused to the destroyer,—surely the best thing her first visitants could have wished the little isle was so to slumber on for ages yet to be, unsullied by the foot of man, who has so often turned his rightful lordship over creation into cruel tyranny.

If such thoughts did not occur to Fray Fernando and to José, it was because they had never seen the island. And now they could only think that they should never see anything on God's free earth again; they could only feel the crushing, stifling misery of their return to the hateful dungeon of the hold, the scene of such bitter suffering.

But to each other they gave no utterance to what they thought or felt. Indeed, at this time they spoke but little. Sometimes, however, Fray Fernando repeated psalms or other passages of Scripture suited to their condition; and often he prayed, for himself and for José.

As weary nights, and days which were nights in all except the name, wore on, the gloom around them grew and deepened, until at last it seemed to pervade everything, and to shut their very voices in like a thick and heavy fog. Gradually, silence as well as darkness was establishing her dominion over them.

They were losing the desire to move, as well as to speak. Both often lay for hours motionless, as if in stupor.

Yet night and silence frequently cover, with their veil of mystery, the slow quiet growth that tells of the presence of life. Over the chaos of one heart, at least, the Spirit of light and liberty was brooding throughout the great darkness of those gloomy hours.

Much was Fray Fernando surprised, when one day José suddenly raised himself, and with considerable energy began to speak:—"In the old days of the Incas—"

Never before, in that dreary prison, had José named his heroic fathers—a significant and mournful sign. When the lute thrills no more to the master's touch, when the heart responds no longer to the theme that always awakened its deepest harmonies, there is room to fear that both are broken. Fray Fernando felt a throb of joy at hearing the familiar words once again; and had he been even in the act of death, he would have roused himself to listen to what followed.

"In the old days of the Incas," José said— and though his voice had certainly a muffled sound, it was unfaltering and full of purpose—" the eldest son of the sole Inca, who should be his heir, was prepared for his high inheritance by severe and arduous exercises. He had to suffer pain and weariness, to fast long and often, to go unshod and in poor mean clothing, to sleep on the bare ground. All this, that when he should behold himself on the throne of his majesty, he should look down from thence with a compassionate eye on the poor, in remembrance that he himself was one of them.'"[1]

Fray Fernando feared his companion's mind was wandering. He scarcely knew what to answer. At length, however, he said, "That was a noble thought."

But after a short pause José went on, in a measured musical tone, almost a kind of chant:—"In after-days, when the poor man came to the Golden Throne with his tale of wrong and woe, he would bend low before

---

1.   Garcilaso de la Vega

the sole Inca, on whose head was the crimson llautu and the white wing-feathers of the cora-quenque. ` Inca, Child of the Sun, Friend of the poor! 'he would say, ` I pray thee, look on me. I hunger. Thou hast hungered too. I have no place to lay my head. Nor hadst thou. My feet are weary, and they bleed; for the paths are rough and stony. So were the paths thou didst tread in once.'"

Here again José paused, and Fray Fernando suggested, "Then the Inca would have pity on him?"

José's voice rose higher—though still it was soft and harmonious—as he glided insensibly from the parable into the interpretation. *"Pity?* No. It was not pity He gave me. Shall I tell you, if words *can* tell it, what He said, stooping down from the throne of His majesty? He said, Come near to Me,' and I came. Then He said, Child, it is true. My unshod feet have trod that rough and thorny way. My heart has hungered and thirsted-even as thine. I too wept over My people-bitterer tears by far than thou hadst ever need to weep over Tahuantin Suyu. Hast thou forgotten that great and bitter cry," O Jerusalem, Jerusalem, thou that slayest the prophets"? Yet I remember all.' "—Here" José paused, overcome by his emotion.

But "a breath and a beam of heaven" passed through the weary heart of Fray Fernando, as he asked, with eager interest, "Has He then taken the burden from you, José?"

"No, He has not; He has shown me more love than that.

He has said, 'I bear it with thee,'—a better word, ten thousand times, than 'I take it from thee.' Don't you know sharp pain can become highest joy sometimes? With us, the crowning glory of the Belting festival for the noble youths who stood victorious and approved, was when the sole Inca pierced their ears with his own right hand. How the touch of that hand thrilled them through with pride and rapture! And now—His hand touches me—His voice whispers, "Once I suffered all; now I know all. Wait. Trust me. My name is Secret. Believe, and thou shalt see the glory of God."

"And you *can* trust Him now, José?"

"With all my heart and mind and soul and strength. I only grieve now for my past distrust of Him. I know not what He will do; but I know *Him.* I give my people up to Him, as freely and joyfully as I give Him up this life of mine. He is the King. He is coming, and that soon. He shall right every wrong.   He shall deliver the poor when he crieth, the needy also, and him that hath no helper. And His dominion shall be from sea to sea, and from the river even unto the ends of the earth.' Ranti, ranti! Capac Inca, Huacchacuyac!"

Fray Fernando could only say, from the depths of his heart, "Thank God!" And so Peace came down to that gloomy dungeon, and spread her white wings over the desolate captives there. Nay, the Son of Peace Himself was with them. And whenever His voice should summon them, they would come forth out of the darkness "into the sudden glory" with instant readiness and glad confidence. Surely soon now—any day, any hour, any moment—might that thrice welcome voice be heard, calling them home, to dwell with Him forever.

José Is Avenged of His Enemies

'The spirits of your fathers
Shall start from every wave,
For the deck it was their field of fame,
And ocean was their grave."
~ CAMPBELL

HARK, JOSÉ! WHAT IS THAT? "Only the wind,
patre," José answered, in a languid, dream-like

voice.

"No! Surely not the wind. Hark, again!"

"Thunder, patre? The God of glory thundereth."

"It may be—yes. Yet, no, no! Too continuous for that. Listen, José."

"They are putting the ship about. Take care, patre, you will be hurt. Turn your head the other way."

With some help from José Fray Fernando changed his position.

"José:" he said again, "that sound we hear is the boom of great guns. We are attacked by an enemy; God have mercy upon us!"

"Christ have mercy upon us!" José echoed. Then both were silent, in the solemn hush of inward prayer.

José was the first to break that silence. "Now, indeed, patre," he said, "the great Inca sends His messenger Death to bid us drink with Him."

"Well, we are ready."

"*Ready?*—Is it not His own cup, from which, first, He drank Himself?" [1]

For days, weeks, months perhaps, they two had lived in continual expectation of death, "dying daily." And when now at last they saw death face to face, they felt no terror—no, not even fear—but a still and reverent awe, befitting those who stood in the presence of the minister and messenger of the great King.

Meanwhile the boom of the guns went on, and "the voice of them that shout for mastery, and the noise of them that cry, being overcome," reached the hold where the captives lay. Until at last all manner of fearful, discordant sounds seemed rolled and mingled together in a con-

---

1. Alluding to a graceful custom of his royal forefathers. When they desired to honor any man, they would send him a cup exactly the same as that from which they drank themselves with the message.— "The Inca drinks with thee in this cup."

tinuous uproar. Now and then a crash, like the fall of a mast, was heard; or the heavy thud of a cannon-shot perilously near their dungeon.

As they sat hand in hand, listening breathlessly, José whispered, "Would we even knew who our enemies are!"

"They are pirates, doubtless. They will not try to sink the ship, their object being, of course, to get possession of the treasure on board."

"Thank God for that. Perhaps, after all, we may see the sun before we die."

"But think of the gallant soldiers and the poor unhappy mariners, José. Let us ask God to have mercy on them."

"With all my heart. No doubt, by this time, many a brave man is lying low."

They prayed silently for all on board; for the commander, the captain, the soldiers, the mariners. While they were thus occupied, the noises grew fainter, or perhaps they heard them less.

At last there came a deafening shout that seemed to burst at once from a hundred throats. Neither José nor Fray Fernando had heard anything like it in their lives before. "God help us!" said Fray Fernando. "We are overcome." For he knew that was a shout of triumph, and one which did not come from Spanish lips.

No further firing was heard; only confused noises of various kinds,—and voices. After a delay, long to their anxious suspense, steps drew near.

"They are going to rifle the hold where the treasure is," said Fray Fernando.

Without consulting him, indeed to his surprise and dismay, José, with considerable effort, stood up, and placing his lips as near the hatchway as possible, raised a loud shrill cry, as one who called for help.

"O José! beware what you do."

"Why, patre? Wherein can our condition be worse than it is? Who can be more our enemies than the Spaniards?"

Once again he cried aloud, throwing all the strength that months of suffering had left him into that cry.

Not in vain. The hatchway was torn up rudely; and someone called out in Spanish, though with a foreign accent, "Quién es?"

Then they heard the voice of a Spaniard, evidently giving some kind of explanation. Then a brief parley ensued. At last a ladder was put down through the hatchway, and the prisoners were ordered to come up.

An order more easily given than obeyed by men who by this time were scarcely able to stand. Two or three sun burnt bearded faces looked down from the hatchway; and their owners, convinced that either the will or the power to ascend the ladder was wanting to the prisoners, speedily descended, and with small ceremony helped or dragged them to the light. One strong fellow put his arm round José, and fairly carried him up the ladder. Still up—up—up—until at last he met a blinding blaze of sunlight, and a gust of sea wind, "shrill, chill, with flakes of foam," swept over his bewildered, throbbing brow.

Presently someone held to his lips a cup of the commandant's rare old wine. Revived by the draft, he looked around him, shading his eyes from the light with his brown transparent hand. He was lying on the deck of the *Trionfo.* But his first distinct impression was of the blue sea, its waves tipped with foam; over them a white-winged sea-bird; in the distance one black hull—was it the *San Cristofero?* Turning his eyes to the other side, he noticed a strange-looking ship, apparently fastened to the *Trionfo,* but much smaller, and in form and fashion quite unlike anything he had ever seen before. But what was immediately around him soon drew his attention, blotting out all else from his sight. There—on the deck—horrors undreamed of met his view. Blood everywhere, and men lying dead: some as if in quiet sleep; and some, with clenched hands and agonized faces, whose last struggle seemed scarcely over yet. Rough uncouth figures moved to and fro amongst them, most of them carrying burdens. But Fray Fernando was nowhere to be seen.

The man who had given José the wine made some remark in a foreign tongue, which, from its tone, was evidently designed to encourage him, and assure him of safety. But before he had collected his scattered senses sufficiently to attempt a reply in Spanish or Latin, his new friend was called away to another part of the ship.

So he lay still where he was, in utter bewilderment—trying to think, trying to comprehend.

At length a suppressed moan close beside

him reached his ear, and brought him to himself at once. The low sound was more effectual to rouse him than the thunder of all the ship's guns would have been.

It was a moan evidently wrung by overpowering agony from a brave man's reluctant lips. José looked. Not two paces from him lay a wounded cavalier, his splendid dress all torn and blood-stained, his face ghastly, his hand upon his breast, as if to stay the streams of blood that were bearing life away.

A moment more and José, strong enough now in his heart's tenderness and pity, was kneeling beside his enemy, Don Francisco Solis. Raising him gently in his arms, he tore his own tunic to bind his wound, and put the wine-cup to his lips from which he himself had drunk so lately.

In vain. At every breath the blood welled faster. The hand of Death was on the proud young cavalier. Yet not all in vain. He tried to speak. "Call some of my people," he murmured. "Varco—Rodriguez—Martin—what has become of them all?"

"I believe the ship is in the hands of pirates," José said. "The soldiers, no doubt, have been slain or made prisoners. Anything I can do for you, I will."

"Who are you?"

"One who bears you good-will. You are sorely wounded, I fear."

"I am slain. With this blood my life flows out. Call me a priest."

"That I know not how to do. Put your trust in the mercy of God—in the blessed Savior who died for you."

Don Francisco feebly raised his hand, seeking something suspended round his neck. José found it for him, and put it to his lips. It was a small gold cross, with a costly jewel in the center, beneath which was inserted a relic of inestimable price, a fragment of "the true cross." "Oh, Señor Don Francisco!" said José earnestly, "look with your heart to Christ. He can pardon your sins. He can save you, and take you this day home to Himself. Think of Him."

But it was a thought of earth that filled the heart of the dying man at that moment. "Will you show me Christian charity for the love of God?" he murmured.

"For the love of God—I surely will."

"Then bring—or send—this cross to my beloved wife, Dona Victoria Solis, at Cuzco.—But what is this?" he faltered, making an effort to look up. "Your tongue Spanish, your face brown—who are you, in Heaven's name?"

"One who will do your errand faithfully, Don Francisco Solis de Toledo—though he grieves that it is so sad a one. Is there any message you desire to send with the cross to Coyllur?"

"Tell her—ah, my breath is failing—tell

her I did my duty —like an honorable and valiant noble of Castile—and that I truly loved her—thought of her to the last. Although—Tell her—"

No more was to be told. Already the mists of the great darkness were gathering over the eyes of Don Francisco. Still he tried to murmur something, which José's utmost efforts failed to catch. But he held the cross before him, that his last conscious look might rest upon the symbol of divine love and forgiveness. And thus, with his head pillowed on the breast of his enemy, and the hand he had disdained to fight ministering tenderly to his last earthly needs, the haughty spirit of Don Francisco Solis passed away.

José, scarce willing to believe that all was over, still held him in his arms, when a tall, strongly-built man, not without a rough stateliness and dignity of manner, came up the companion-ladder, stood near the two figures, the dead and the living, and looked thoughtfully at them. His hair and beard were black, and his complexion well sun burnt. His dress was plain,—a buff leather jerkin, evidently the worse for the recent fight; but a sword with a jeweled hilt was stuck in his belt;—it had no sheath, and was still bloody.

"My poor fellow," he said to José, in imperfect Spanish, "your master is dead."

"The señor commandante was not my master," José answered, looking up." He was my enemy."

Your enemy!" the other repeated in surprise." In that case you have proved yourself a Christian, and a good one. You are one of the two prisoners whom we found in the hold?" "Yes, señor."

"You are free now. We Englishmen set the captives free, and deliver the oppressed, wherever we go."

"*Englishmen!* Are you indeed Englishmen?

Then I thank God that I have lived to see this day."

"I am glad you have such a good opinion of us. And I hope we shall give you no reason to change it. We are ready to welcome you on board our good ship yonder, the *Sea Snake,* of London. Your fellow-captive is there already."

He turned, apparently to bid one of his men conduct José to the English ship. But in the moment that he did so, something met his eye that changed the current of his thoughts. It was the black hull of the galley, the only ship in sight, which was now no longer lessening to a speck on the horizon, but very rapidly growing larger.

Brief orders in a foreign tongue were issued to those around; and José soon saw the strange uncouth figures swarming like bees up the ladders and from every part of the *Trionfo,* back to their own ship, each bearing his burden.

He could not in the least comprehend what

was going forward; the whole scene in which he moved was a bewildering mystery to him. One thing alone he realized: yonder was the galley *San Cristofero,* and Walter Gray, a captive Englishman, sat chained to one of its oars.

He gently laid down his lifeless burden, and springing forward, threw himself in the way of the personage who had ad' dressed him, just as he was about to leave the deck of the *Trionfo.* "Señor and captain," he said, "in yonder galley there is an Englishman—a slave."

The English captain thundered some explanation in his own tongue, and laying his hand on his sword, looked at the galley as if the fire in his eyes would alone suffice to destroy it. But he had not an instant to lose. Pointing to José, he spoke three words to a young man who stood beside him, and was on his own quarter-deck ere their echo had died away.

The young sailor gave José to understand by signs that he had been told to conduct him to the English ship. José gazed sadly on the dead face of his enemy, then closed his eyes, and taking off his own yacollo, laid it decently and reverently over him. That done, he followed his guide from the deck of the *Trionfo* to that of the *Sea Snake*—then down a companion-ladder, to a small, dimly-lighted cabin. The Englishman being apparently under an impression, not altogether unfounded, that the Spaniards starved their prisoners, quickly set before him a huge platter of boiled beef, a mountain of biscuit, and a great leathern jack of strong ale. That done, he disappeared in a moment, leaving José very thankful for what seemed a marvelous providential deliverance, but much perplexed by the whole affair.

It was a most joyful surprise to hear the voice of Fray Fernando out of the gloom. "I am glad you have come, José."

The monk was lying on a mattress which had been laid for him in a corner of the cabin;

but so imperfect was the light admitted by the one small window of thick horn, that José had not perceived him until then. He explained: "Between the unaccustomed sunshine and the feebleness of my long unused limbs I contrived to slip, and hurt my ankle. It will not signify. They laid me here very kindly, and they have given me everything I needed."

"Can you comprehend what has befallen us, patre?"

"I have learned somewhat from the padre of the English, who paid me a brief visit here—' Sir Thomas,' they call him. He seems to be a good, humane man."

"I suppose we are in the hands of English pirates—buccaneers?" said José.

"That certainly cannot be doubted. They call their ship a merchant vessel, and avow that they have come to the Spanish Main to trade for sandal-wood. Of course their trade is in itself contraband, even if it were not merely a cloak to cover piracy. The Trionfo, laden with gold and silver, and separated from the Plate fleet by the recent storm, was only too tempting a prize. They bore down upon us, all sails crowded, determined to fight."

"But, patre, the *Trionfo* is five times the size of this little ship."

"True; but size is one thing, and strength another. I have heard it said ere this that our ships are built for carrying treasure, theirs for winning it by force of arms. You are aware the *Trionfo* was always accounted unwieldy, and not over well appointed. Moreover, the damage she received in the gale was scarce repaired as thoroughly as might be. The English guns did great execution upon her, her huge bulk exposing her the more; while the small craft of the pirates, bristling with fortifications from stem to stern, took little harm from all our firing. The *San Cristofero* came near to help us, and indeed gave the enemy volley after volley, but not, it seems, to much purpose. We had several shots between wind and water, and at last our mainmast was cut away. It was feared the ship would sink, with all on board; so the captain and others prayed the commandante to lower his flag. He treated the proposal as an insult, and swore to slay the first man who should name surrender in his hearing. But, shortly afterward, a mortal wound laid him low. Almost at the same moment the buccaneers threw out their grappling-irons, and prepared to board our ship. Then the captain and two or three of the officers hoisted a flag of truce. The buccaneers only wanted plunder—our great ship, if they had it, could serve them nothing—so it was not difficult to come to terms. The English call the capitulation an honorable one for us— but God help Captain Manuel Sergaz, and the officers who took part with him, when they get to Spain!—if ever they reach it, which the present state of the ship renders, I fear, very doubtful. They will probably make once more for our friendly island, that they may repair damages and refit for the voyage."

"Patre," said José," Don Francisco Solis died in my arms." He paused, overcome by emotion of many kinds; nor could he regain sufficient composure to pursue the subject. Presently he added, "At all events, we are free. Let us thank God for that."

"Amen!"

"Patre, I saw the captain of the English. He spoke to me. He is not like what I expected: not blue-eyed and fair-haired, like Walter Gray."

"The English priest tells me he is a brave man, and a good Christian. Though how the latter can be consistent with his buccaneering exploits, I confess I scarcely understand. His name is Captain George Noble, and he is the son of a wealthy merchant of London."

Here their voices were drowned by a shrill, horrible, deafening cry—such a cry as José, at least, had never heard before. He gazed at Fray Fernando in consternation.

"That must be the *chamado,* the cry of the galley-slaves when they advance to the attack," said the monk.

José was greatly excited. "Patre, forgive me," he exclaimed. "Needs must that I go on deck and see what is happening there. I will bring you tidings."

Joyful Meetings

"O give thanks unto the Lord, for he is good: for his mercy endureth forever. Let the redeemed of the Lord say so, whom he hath redeemed from the hand of the enemy."
~ PSALM 107:1, 2.

THE COMMANDER OF THE *San Cristofero*, while he seemed to be leaving the *Trionfo* to her fate, had been only making use of a stratagem. He sheered off from the English ship, and rowed to a considerable distance, fully intending to return so soon as the mariners, engaged in boarding the great galleon, should have left their own vessel deserted and defenseless. Then he hoped, with some help from the survivors of the *Trionfo,* to sink or take her without difficulty. But the cowardice (as he esteemed it) of those who commanded the galleon, in capitulating to the English, somewhat disconcerted his plans. On seeing the white flag put up, however, he at once ordered the slaves to row back to the scene of the conflict. This was done with the rapidity and directness which gave the galleys, in their independence of the action of the wind, such an advantage over sailing-vessels. Then he issued orders for an immediate onslaught. But he did not find the English as utterly unprepared as he expected. Moreover, the *Trionfo* failed to co-operate with her ally. Already she had moved away; and either honor, prudence or most likely the absolute necessities of her own situation, prevented her return to help the San Cristofero. So it was possible that, ere the end of that day's conflict, the commander of the galley might have occasion to recall the Spanish proverb about those who "go out for wool, and come home shorn."

By the time that José, not without difficulty, climbed the ladder and stood on the deck, the English had already driven back their assailants, and pursued them on board the galley— roused to tenfold fury by their captain's hint that an Englishman was chained to one of its oars. Eagerly did José gaze at the *San Cristofero,* but to his unpracticed eye it presented nothing save hideous and bewildering confusion. Those uncouth figures, roughly clad, simply armed, swarmed all over it, with strong cutlasses in their hands, hewing, smiting, struggling, in fierce conflict with the stately, well-appointed Spanish soldiers.

But anon something happened that even José understood full well. The first care of the English, on boarding the galley, had been to supply the slaves with the means of freeing themselves from their fetters. Now the work was accomplished, and with one fierce yell the gaunt figures arose, each from his place, and sprang upon their hated tyrants like bloodhounds on their prey. The vengeance of years was in every blow they struck. José distinctly saw the quatrero—the captain of Walter's oar—seize the commissary, and after a moment's desperate struggle, whirl him round and fling him over the galley's side into the seething depths beneath. Then he saw the young sailor who had been his own guide on board the English ship stand for one moment face to face with Walter Gray—then put his arm round him, guard him through the *melee,* and lead him to the spot where the captain was.

But what followed utterly baffled José's

comprehension. It was not until afterward that he learned that the soldiers of the *San Cristofero,* now attacked at once by two terrible enemies, feared their own slaves more than the English, and were glad to yield to the latter, and to be taken on board their vessel as prisoners of war. That done, the liberated slaves, who were now the masters of the galley, returned once more to their oars and rowed away, free to go whithersoever they pleased, provided only they came not within the shadow of the yellow flag of Spain.

But little did José care whither they went,—in that rapturous moment when he grasped once more the hand of Walter Gray, and knew that his friend was a free man now and forever. He had thought it impossible to be further surprised at anything, that day of surprises. But he was certainly astonished to see the English captain take Walter Gray in his great blood-stained arms, kiss him mouth to mouth, and then, throwing off his cap, and raising his eyes to heaven, thank God solemnly before them all. The rough mariners who stood around seemed to share his emotion: they also bared their heads and added a reverent "Amen" to the thanksgiving. Then a few anxious words, spoken hurriedly by Walter Gray, won a brief but apparently satisfactory answer from the captain. Then the young sailor, José's guide, came forward also and embraced his rescued countryman. And at last the strange proceedings concluded with a ringing, vociferous English cheer which made José's heart leap to his lips.

Before its echo had died away he was going back to the cabin to tell the patre all, when Walter Gray intercepted him, embraced him affectionately, and taking his hand, led him to the captain, to whom he spoke a few words in his native tongue.

The captain immediately stretched out his own right hand to the Indian. "Don José," he said, in his imperfect Spanish, "Master Walter Gray, who is my dear friend and kinsman, tells me that you have been a true brother to him in the time of his adversity; and that, but for you, he would not be here alive this day. I owe you more thanks than I can speak in a breath. Come and sup with me. Our worthy chaplain is fluent in your tongue, and will find words better than I can for what I wish to say to you."

About an hour afterward a select party assembled in the state-cabin of the *Sea Snake.* It consisted of Captain George Noble; two or three gentlemen-volunteers on board his ship, including his own younger brother and José's guide, James Noble; the chaplain, Sir Thomas Hartfield; Walter Gray, dressed now like an English gentleman; Fray Fernando; and, lastly, José. The commander of the *San Cristofero* had been courteously invited, but had excused himself, to the comfort of all.

The viands were indifferent; but the wine,

which was part of the spoil of the *Trionfo,* made amends, and was duly appreciated by most of the party. But whatever else the little festival lacked, in one thing it was favorably distinguished from many more pretentious entertainments-every man who took his seat at the board had a truly happy and thankful heart. Even although the attack of the *San Cristofero* had prevented their rifling the *Trionfo* as thoroughly as they would otherwise have done, gold and silver enough had been won that day to make the fortunes both of the owners and of the crew of the *Sea Snake.* If it was not strictly true of the latter, that "the youngest cabin-boy amongst them might be a captain for riches," the glowing hyperbole was little more than a natural and pardonable exaggeration. Perhaps only those who have greatly dared and greatly suffered can taste the full joy of such success, more than crowning their utmost hopes.

Yet this was the least joy of that joyful day.

When the meal was over, the captain filled a cup of wine, and, addressing Fray Fernando and José in the best Spanish he could muster, said, very simply, "Señores and true brothers, I desire to pledge you this day in grateful friendship. First, however, I would fain let you know what I and others owe to your kindness. I have not much Spanish, as you perceive; but our good chaplain, who has the tongue of the learned, shall speak for me."

"Nay," said Walter Gray, with eager emotion, let me speak.

I know all."

"Tell your own tale, if you will, my boy," said the captain, looking at him affectionately. "Mine you cannot tell, for as yet you know it not."

"And mine," Walter acquiesced, "our dear friends know already."

Here the chaplain, a quiet, good-looking man in a cassock, took up the word, addressing himself in very fair Castilian to Fray Fernando and to José:-" Señor Walter Gray, as doubtless you are already aware, is the only son of his mother, and she is a widow. You also know, probably, in what manner he left his home, and why."

"That," Walter again interposed, and in English," I have not shrunk from telling these my friends, humbling and painful as was the confession. Yet," he added, with crimsoned cheek," for the sake of others who are here present, I repeat it now. Allured by vain dreams of gold and glory, I selfishly and wickedly forgot all that I should most have remembered—my mother, my duty, my God."

"That is but one side of the story, and not too fairly put either," said the captain. "Sir Thomas, obey orders, and speak out without fear or favor. Let these, our Spanish friends, know that it was not altogether through Master Walter's own demerit that he proved a runagate."

Sir Thomas resumed his interrupted discourse in Spanish:—" The captain desires me to inform you that he considers himself the person most to blame for the fact of Señor Walter's flight, which took place from his father's house in London." "*You* to blame, Cousin George! No—a thousand times, no!" Walter cried; but there was a look in the bronzed face of the sea-captain that warned him to be silent, and to hear the rest.

"The captain says," continued the patient narrator, "that although he was well aware of his young kinsman's passion for the seaman's life, he yet took no pains either to win or to keep his friendship and Confidence. On the contrary, he treated him with scorn, as a child, a book-worm, a landlubber; though all the time in his heart he envied his superior bearing. He rather made-believe to despise him, Jest he should be despised by him. At last they had an open quarrel; and a very foolish, childish quarrel it looks now."

"So it was, on my part," was Walter's commentary.

"Worse on mine," said the captain. Then, in his eagerness, quite forgetful of the effect of the confusion of tongues, he finally discarded the chaplain's mediation, and spoke in his own language and his own person:—" Cousin Walter, I mocked and taunted you, and that bitterly. I was sorry a moment afterward, as I tell you now. I need tell no man whether I was sorry when I knew you were gone—driven from us, likely enough, by those angry words. I laid the sin from that moment at my own door. And your letter, which you wrote to your mother from the *English Merchantman,* only made matters worse with me. Had I not been as blind as a mole, I could have guessed what was likely to happen, and might have hindered it. But I said nothing to any man; and a few days after, we weighed anchor, and off with us to the Turkish seas. A man is apt to forget things, knocking about the world, as I have done from my childhood. Yet, should I reach the age of the patriarchs that lived before the Flood, never—never shall I forget my last home-coming. The *English Merchantman* touched London Quay a matter of three days before us. She brought home that tale about you, left on the deck of the Spanish ship—whether living or dead, no man knew for certain. If you had seen my father's face when he told it to me! Woman's tears are bad enough-and neither my mother nor Lilias spared theirs-but man's grief is worse to see. And my father blamed himself; though, indeed, *he* was blameless in the matter. All made their minds up at once that you were dead. But, for my part, I never thought so. And by-and-by I learned what made me certain you were not. My mother went to yours, to comfort her in her sore anguish. When she came back to us, these were her words: My sister lives, because she hopes and prays still.' Then I took my resolution. Straightway I arose, and went to my father, and told him everything. 'Father,' I said, I drove Walter away. Therefore I should peril goods and life to end this horrible suspense, and bring back—himself, if it may be; if not, certain tidings of him. Do not withhold me. It is borne in upon me that I should do this thing.' But he shook his head, and with deep anguish told me, what he hoped the sorrowing mother knew not yet—the frightful claim of the Inquisition. His best hope was your death. As for your rescue, no wilder dream could enter the imagination of man. 'Still,' I pleaded, 'in any wise let me go.

Wild dreams come true sometimes. At all events, my heart burns within me. I must needs fight the Spaniards—and avenge him, if I cannot deliver him; or I will die.' Then he said,— Walter, you know how good, how generous he is. And you also, my friends,"—glancing round the table—" you know him well. This was the outcome of all: I went to Kent, Walter, and I saw your mother face to face." Here, for a moment, George Noble's voice trembled; and the blunt, simple frankness of his manner was almost swept away by a rising tide of emotion." No; I cannot tell you what she said to me. But this I will say," he added reverently." When a woman's tender heart is bowed to the will of God, He puts a strength and calmness there of which we men could not dream unless we saw it; and we are better men all our lives for having seen it once.

"At last, I laid my hand in hers, and I said, Mother, if he lives, I will bring him back to you, God helping me.' How I came to promise that, without fear or faltering, dead against all human probability of fulfillment, to this hour I know not. The words seemed put into my mouth; I could not but speak them. I knew she knew *the worst;* and whether or not my rash promise gave her any comfort, I could scarcely tell. But you all know, comrades, a promise is a promise. If a man cannot redeem it, he can die in the effort; and death wipes all scores out. So I sold my share in the *Royal Tudor;* and it brought me a goodly sum, for God had prospered us. We bought the *Sea Snake,* then almost ready for the Spanish Main. My father helped largely therein; and, moreover, invested a share for my brother James, who must needs go out with me. These gentlemen, my friends, have shares also. We were chartered for the Pacific, to get sandal-wood."

"Ay, sandal-wood, to be sure! and *nothing* else!" It was young James Noble who spoke, glancing round the board with a significant smile.

"Hold thy tongue, lad" said Captain Noble. "Nothing else that matters now,—especially in the presence of these honorable gentlemen;" and he looked at Fray Fernando and José.

"Who, as our captain seems to have forgotten, do not understand a word he has been saying for the last ten minutes," said the chaplain.

"Indeed, I did forget," said Captain George Noble, looking disconcerted. "Prithee, Sir Thomas, ask them to pardon me. Say to them what I would say in their own tongue, if I could. We owe it to their Christian charity that Cousin Walter was kept alive until deliverance came to him. But for them, he tells us, he would have sunk long ago under his bitter and cruel bondage. Thanks, first to God, from whom all goodness comes; then to these, His servants—' This our brother was dead, and is alive again; was lost, and is found.'"

Sir Thomas Hartfield interpreted what was said to Fray Fernando and José. But the hearty clasping of hands and drinking of healths that followed, with true British cheering, needed no interpreter.

One word more in Spanish was addressed to

the strangers, and this time it was Walter Gray who spoke. "I have told Cousin George, and all our friends here present, that you are truly one with us in faith and hope. You will come with us to England? And as surely as friends, homes, welcomes await us there, so surely all these are yours as much as they are ours."

With glistening eye and quivering lip Fray Fernando thanked him, and accepted his offer, for himself and for José.

Foam of the Sea

"Ask'st thou my home?
My pathway wouldst thou know,
When from thine eye my
floating shadow passed?"

~ SCHILLER

IT WAS NIGHT—GLORIOUS tropical night-surely "not made for slumber." There was no moon, but her place was well supplied by the soft radiance of large luminous stars—Argo in the zenith, the Southern Cross near the horizon, while, far away towards the north, "the stars of the Great Bear shone with almost fearful magnitude."[1] Nor was the deep that lieth under less marvelous for glory and for beauty than the sky that stretched above. Beneath the vessel's keel burned a sheet of living fire, kindled by mysterious phosphoric lights. Jets of flame—blue, and red, and purple—flashed out here and there; while a shoal of dolphins, sporting about the ship, cut the waves in long circling lines, that gleamed and sparkled with prismatic hues.

Two, perhaps three, were enjoying this sight from the deck of the *Sea Snake*. Fray Fernando and Walter Gray sat together, now talking in low quiet words, now silent, but always in true communion each with the other. A little further off José stood, leaning against a mast, either wrapped in his own thoughts or sharing

---

1.   Humboldt

those of his friends.

The strength of all three had been sorely wasted by previous sufferings; but quiet of mind, fresh sea air, and unbounded care and kindness from everyone on board the English ship, were gradually restoring them. Even Fray Fernando, whose recovery had at first been looked on as more than doubtful, both by others and by himself, was now improving day by day. A little while ago José,—who, as ever, waited upon him with the most devoted love,—said to him, his dark face glowing with thankful joy, "I knew it, patre, from the very hour they rescued us; you will not die, but live, and declare the works of the Lord." Only his limbs, enfeebled and well-nigh crippled by long confinement, had not yet regained, if ever they would regain, their former strength and activity. Two or three turns up and down the deck were still abundant exercise for him.

And now Walter Gray was pouring into

his sympathizing ear a detailed description of the quiet English home, "among the rose-hung lanes of Kent," that would, he hoped, be his home also. He was confident that his mother and Fray Fernando would thoroughly understand and admire each other. He could talk and think of that mother now, not indeed without deep penitence for his wrong-doing, but without the aching remorseful pain, the great shadow of doubt and dread, which had lain on his heart so long. He thanked God for keeping alive her hope for him throughout those sad years. For he knew that, with her, hope meant prayer; and he believed that, but for the prayers which, like unseen angels, kept guard about him, he would not now be sitting on the deck of the *Sea Snake* a free and thankful man, but dead long ago in his despair and anguish.

Something of this he even ventured to hint to Fray Fernando; for in starlight much may be spoken that the glare of day would frighten into silence.

"Yes," Fray Fernando answered, after a thoughtful pause, "I do rejoice, Walter, at the prospect of seeing your happy English home. If a measure of strength is given back to me— and I begin to think God means to give it—He will find work for His servant, with whom He hath ever dealt so graciously, beneath the stars of the northern hemisphere, as well as under the Southern Cross—and for my José too."

"Ah! as to that," said Walter, in a lighter tone, but very heartily," Don José Viracocha Inca will be a great hero amongst us. We shall never keep such a wonder in our quiet home. The Queen and the Court will rob us of him all too quickly."

At that moment the captain's loud, cheerful voice was heard from the fore-deck, "Cousin Walter, I want you here."

Walter rose, saying to Fray Fernando, "I will come back as soon as I can."

When he was gone, José came slowly forward and stood before the monk.

"Patre," he said, and his voice was low and sorrowful,— "patre, listen to me."

"My son, what is it'?" Fray Fernando questioned, startled by his tone.

"My father, be patient with me. I have that to say which wrings my heart." Here he paused; then, suddenly pointing to the luminous waters, he exclaimed, "Look there, patre!" A sportive dolphin had described a larger circle than usual; it burned for a moment, a diamond ring of flashing foam, then faded quickly away. "Viracocha is but the foam of the sea. He comes and goes like that."

"I do not understand you, José. What are you talking of?" asked the bewildered Fray Fernando.

"My father, if Christ the King were now to call your son and servant to His home, instead of yours, would you not give him up?"

Fray Fernando trembled and grew very pale. "What mean these strange words?" he faltered. "Are you ill?"

"No, patre."

"I know well you have suffered, and far more than you would ever acknowledge. But surely life is coming back to you, as it is to me. Is it not so? Speak to me, José—my son José!" There was anguish in his tone.

"Yes, patre, life is coming back to me; and with life, a message from my King. Patre, patre,—I know not how to tell that message. Yet, woe is me if I withhold it—if I fail to obey!"

"A message! What message, José?"

"Go home to thy friends, and tell them how great things the Lord hath done for thee, and hath had compassion on thee.'"

Fray Fernando started—shuddered, as if an arrow on an errand of death had suddenly pierced his heart.

"José, you may be deceived—mistaken," he said hurriedly. "When first did you feel or fancy this?"

"Patre, when I lay in the dark hold of the *Trionfo,* He stooped from His golden throne, looked with pitying eye upon my great anguish for my people, and gave me rest and peace. Even with that peace came that message first. But I only smiled in my heart, and said to Him, ' Inca, thou knowest all. I would speak for Thee if I could, but Thou art calling me instead to die for Thee.' But when He took us both out of the horrible pit, gave me the dying charge of Don Francisco Solis to deliver, and then restored you to life, I heard his voice again. —Patre, it is just this way with me. In my sore hunger and thirst He reached me, with His own right hand, golden fruit from the tree whose leaves are for the healing of the nations. I ate, and thirst and hunger passed away. I was satisfied. But within the golden fruit the seed lies hid; and he who eats the fruit must needs plant the seed. That charge is laid upon him."

"And you would leave me, José?" The words were quiet, but depths of tenderness,—of anguish,—of entreaty, lay veiled beneath them.

José's dusky countenance grew pale, and his steadfast lip trembled. Unconsciously he wrung his hands together in the bitter pain of his heart. "Had the King asked my life," he said with deep emotion, "it were given readily. Now, He asks more. But He cannot ask too much—not too much!" After a pause he added, in a more natural voice, "Still, I have no right to make my burnt-offering of that which belongs to another man. Nor would He accept such. Wherefore, patre, if you—you who bought me, you who own me—if you forbid me to do this thing, I yield, and I go with you to England."

Fray Fernando's heart leaped to his lips. The dreaded separation averted, José his—his altogether, his forever—all for one word I And yet, sorely as he longed to do it, he could not speak that word. He dared not.

At last he said, evasively, "I scarcely understand yet what it is you purpose."

"Patre, in a few days the *Sea Snake* must put in at a place on the coast of the mainland known to the captain, to take in water for the long voyage. Thence I can make my way back to my own country and my own people, and give them the message that burns on my heart and on my lip—the message of love from their King and mine."

"And travel first many hundred leagues through unknown lands, filled with barbarous tribes? José! José! you will never reach Peru alive."

"Haply yes; haply no. Alike in either case it is well with me."

"And then," Fray Fernando continued with anxious haste, "even suppose you do, there are the priests and friars. You will be hunted down as a heretic."

José smiled, and pointed to the waves beneath them. "The white men know as little what we talk and think among ourselves as we know the thoughts of God's innocent creatures down yonder," he said. "Once with my people, I am safe. But for *you*, patre—" His voice faltered, died away.

After a long pause he resumed, stretching out his right hand, —"Yet, if you are willing to send me forth on this service, and bid me God-speed,—take this hand of mine in yours." There was a struggle in Fray Fernando's heart. Not long if measured by time,—not five minutes' work, perhaps. Yet he was years older when it ended. He took the thin brown hand in his and pressed it. "God's will be done in thee and me," he said firmly.

"Amen," José murmured, and turned to go. But turning back, he added, the trembling of his voice kept under by an iron will, "Patre, I think that on the happy shores of the good land beyond the sea, God will make His promise true to you, who have left all for His sake—' an hundredfold now in this time, houses, and brethren, and sisters, and mothers, and children, and lands.'"

Far away on the other side of the world, in a region José never knew, stands a wild mountain famed in song. Near its summit is a lonely rock, consecrated by a strange legend. It is said that he who dares to sleep upon it will be found at daybreak with life extinct;—with reason fled forever;—or else endowed with the matchless gift of song, heir to the poet's immortal crown. There are lonely places of conflict to which souls are sometimes led, not unlike the rock of Cader Idris. Sore is the peril of madness—of despair, which means death; but if God answers His servant from the secret place of thunder, and with His own right hand upholds and delivers him, he will come down from that mountain with face transfigured, and lips baptized with living fire. It is to such God gives His messages. And those messages they must needs deliver, or die.

Days and nights glided by, noiselessly and all too swiftly,—until at last there came a day unlike any before or after. A day "much to be remembered," marked evermore in Fray Fernando's calendar, though not with white.

All through its sultry hours the sun blazed down upon the grimy hull of the *Sea Snake,* lying moored in a quiet bay. Dense woods of lofty smooth-stemmed palms with fan-like feathery crowns, and luxuriant thick-leaved ceibas, met the pebbly beach, and fringed the bay on either side; while the one bold headland of granite that formed its southern extremity stood out into the sea, bare and bleak, save for a solitary cluster of graceful cocoa-palms that crowned its summit. Already it is late in the afternoon. The last water-cask has been rolled on board; the last loiterer has come back from the woods with his spoil of cocoa-nuts and bananas. The wind is favorable; the sails are set; soon the shores of the New World will glimmer and fade away beneath the eyes that watch them from the deck of the *Sea Snake.* If it were only on this fair earth that watching loving eyes must look their last!

Everyone on board, from the captain to the cabin-boy, has wrung the brown hand of José, and prayed God to speed him on his way. And more than one manly eye has glistened through unaccustomed tears at his earnest, simple words of grateful farewell. Walter Gray he has embraced, with a fervent "God be with thee, true friend."

And now, as he stands for the last time on the deck of the English ship, all see him—but he sees only one.

Yet once more he turns to Fray Fernando, kneels at his feet —"My father, bless thy son."

Fray Fernando raises him, folds him in his arms—"God's best blessings rest on thee, now and ever— my son—my son!" Heart beats against heart, lip burns against lip, in one long passionate embrace. But the end must be. "We shall meet —yet," Fray Fernando murmurs.

"When they come from the East and from the West to the feast of the great King," José answered. Then the white-robed figure descended the ship's side, entered the little boat, and was rowed on shore. There were others besides Fray Fernando who could not see for tears how it disappeared into the forest. But by-and-by, as the ship sailed leisurely along under the headland, José Viracocha was seen once more. Beneath the tall graceful palms, the feathery fringes of their great leaves quivering in the evening breeze, and the crimson-tinted clouds of sunset glowing over them, he stood, a statue of bronze, his dark hair floating loose as he waved his scarlet cap in parting salutation.

"Child of the Sun—Child of Light! God guard and keep thee, until one day He set us both in His light together!" Fray Fernando prayed weeping.

But the sun set; the ship sailed on; the cocoa-palms, the rocky headland, the forest-clad shore faded into distance, and were seen no more. And with them passed away the Foam of the Sea. Never more, except in dreams, did those dark wistful eyes look into Fray Fernando's, or that beloved voice breathe any song or legend from the "lengua del Inca" into his listening ear. Never more on earth.

Old England Again

"*Waft, waft, ye winds, His story;*
And you, ye waters, roll,
Till, like a sea of glory,
It spreads from pole to pole;
Till o'er our ransomed nature
The Lamb for sinners slain,
Redeemer, King, Creator,
In bliss returns to reign."

~ HEBER

ONCE MORE WE REVISIT THE old manor-house in Kent. It is the evening hour. The great hall no longer looks gloomy and cheerless, for a noble wood-fire blazes and crackles on the hearth, lamps are lighted, and servants are passing to and fro, placing bread and meat and ale upon a board spread with snowy drapery. And soon the family take their seats around it. A tall fair-haired man presides, wearing a cassock and Geneva bands—the Reverend Walter Gray, known far and near as a faithful shepherd of souls and true servant of his divine Master. Opposite sits his pretty, useful, loving wife, Dame Lilias—after the fashion of those times still often called Dame Lilias Noble. There are two fair children, glowing with health and happiness, and just now clinging lovingly to a gray-haired lady, whose thoughtful chastened face wears that look, rarely seen, but unmistakable, of one who has passed through suffering into peace,—who has trod the great water-floods upheld by a Savior's hand, and ever afterward retains the memory of that touch. Lastly, there sits beside Walter Gray a man whom certainly "no one could have passed without remark." His dress is plain, and might be taken for that of an English merchant or yeoman; but southern suns have browned his cheek and kindled the fire that burns in his dark eye. His frame is worn; health has never quite returned since that long agony in the hold of the Spanish ship, yet enough is left to him for much labor in the cause dearest to his heart. Here he is only an honored guest; his home lies far away, amidst the din and smoke of that great city whither come the exiles from foreign lands to whose wants of soul and body he delights to minister.

On this occasion Fray Fernando has come down to Kent to be present at the baptism of Walter's third and youngest child, for whom he has promised to answer at the font.

One absorbing topic fills all hearts tonight, and would have filled all mouths, but for tender consideration for the feelings of the Spanish guest. It was the year 1588—the glorious year of "England's Salamis." Scarcely has one moon run her course since "the great Armada, boastfully called Invincible,' was, by thirty of Her Majesty's ships of war and a few of our own merchants, beaten and jostled together, even from the Lizard in Cornwall—first to Portland, from Portland to Calais, and from Calais driven with squibs from their anchors, were chased out of sight of England, round about Scotland and Ireland."[1]

Even now, as then, England has good reason to give thanks for the result of that conflict. And even now, as then, England ascribes the glory, not to her gallant navy or her stout merchantmen, not to the brave hearts and hands of her dauntless sons, but to Him, and Him alone, who was unto her "a strong tower from

---

1.   Sir Walter Raleigh

the face of her enemies," and who "blew with His wind, and they were scattered."

Just then the great nation's heart was thrilling with the joy of deliverance from a near and terrible danger. There were many private as well as public causes of rejoicing. The gentle heart of Lilias was very glad, since her three brave brothers, Harry, George, and James, were safe and well, and honored for signal gallantry in the hour of danger. Nor was Fray Fernando without his interest in the great event, though he did not allude to it until, the pleasant social meal and the family worship that succeeded it being over, all had retired to their places of rest, except himself and Walter Gray.

As they sat together by the fire, Walter addressed his friend in Spanish. "We are determined to keep possession of you this time," he said; "I hope you are prepared."

Fray Fernando shook his head, and answered in the same language. "But for your letter, and the pressing message sent me through your good uncle, I should not have left London at all. Those crowds of miserable soldiers and seamen, my poor unhappy countrymen, who are now in the city, waiting for the means of transport beyond the seas, need all, and more than all, that one man can do for them."

"You must own, at all events," said Walter, "that our gracious Queen is behaving with a large-hearted generosity that beseems her well, in sending these her enemies, who came to destroy her and her people, freely to their homes again."

"True," said Fray Fernando. "And your uncle and others contribute in a noble and Christian spirit to the relief and comfort of the prisoners; thus returning good for evil. Nor am I without hope that some of these poor captives may take home with them, instead of the English spoils they thought to gain, a treasure of which they never dreamed,—even the light of the knowledge of the glory of God in the face of Jesus Christ. God grant it! He only knows how my heart yearns over those my brethren according to the flesh."

"I have some thoughts," Walter answered, "of going back with you, and helping for a season in your good work; that is, if I can provide for my duties here." And then he talked a little of his own parish with its cares and interests, of Lilias, and of the children.

"You have not yet told me," Fray Fernando said, "what name you have chosen for my godson."

"We are all agreed," Walter replied with a smile, "in giving him the English form of a dear friend's honored name—Ferdinand."

"Nay, my friend, not so," returned Fray Fernando. "Do not choose *that* name."

"And why not, my friend and father?"

"For many reasons. In the first place, it is

no name of mine. My true baptismal name, unused for half a lifetime, would be strange to your ears, and indeed to my own now. But if, indeed, you list to please the wayward fancy of a lonely man, then call your boy for me by the name of the patriarch's best loved son—the separate from his brethren, upon whom the blessing came—' Joseph is a fruitful bough, a fruitful bough by a well, whose branches run over the wall. The archers have sorely grieved him, and shot at him, and hated him: but his bow abode in strength, and the arms of his hands were made strong by the hands of the mighty God of Jacob.'"

"So be it then, with all my heart," said Walter Gray; "and God add his blessing to the child. It is a name that I too have cause to re-member with grateful love." After a pause, he asked rather suddenly, "Father, do you ever re-visit in dreams that far-distant land where you and I first saw each other's faces?"

"Indeed, Walter," Fray Fernando answered, with a smile half bright, half sorrowful," I dream of little else. Night after night I seem to gaze upon the snowy line of the Andes as we used to see them from Callao, or the grand peaks of crystal that pierce the sky of Cerro Blanco; or perchance I look down from the height on the lovely vale of Nasca winding far beneath. Sometimes I wander through those marvelous tropical forests, pushing my way amongst the thick shrubs and the tangled lianas, and gathering great white and purple flowers—dream-flowers, yet not more wonderful than those I have actually seen and touched. Anon we are floating over crystal seas, with the mild light of the Southern Cross shining in the far heavens above us. All is so real, so present, that I cannot choose but take it for a pledge that these eyes shall yet behold again that new, familiar world beyond the western wave. Yes, Walter, when the King comes, and this beautiful ruined earth is cleansed and renovated, and made fit for His throne and habitation, I dare to cherish a hope that my foot shall press those shores once more—that I shall walk there with—with—" But here his voice failed,—died away into that silence which is more eloquent than many words, and often like a fragrant balm preserves and consecrates our dearest names.

After a pause of sympathy, Walter resumed—"There is much for the King to do when He comes."

"There is much for us to do while we wait and watch for His coming," Fray Fernando answered with cheerful earnestness. "We have to hasten that coming by our holy conversation and godliness, our prayers and our efforts to spread abroad the knowledge of His name. And amidst all the sin and all the sorrow that we see around us, we have to keep fast hold of our faith in Him, and to rejoice in sure and steadfast hope of that blessed day when the kingdoms of this world shall have become the kingdoms of our Lord, and of His Christ, and He shall reign forever and ever. And the earth shall be filled with the knowledge of the glory of the Lord, as the waters cover the sea.'"

"Amen!" said Walter Gray.

"THY KINGDOM COME."